One Life to Lose

The Douglas Files:

Book Seven

Nathan Lee Birr

Published by BEACON BOOKS, LLC

Cover Image Copyright ©
MBPROJEKT_Maciej_Bledowski/iStock/Thinkstock

THE HOLY BIBLE, NEW INTERNATIONAL VERSION®, NIV®
Copyright © 1973, 1978, 1984, 2011 by Biblica, Inc.®
Used by permission. All rights reserved worldwide.

ISBN: 978-1-7321373-0-1 (hc)
ISBN: 978-0-9981813-9-4 (sc)

www.nathanbirr.com

Also by Nathan Birr

Author's Note

MY GRANDFATHER SERVED in the United States Army during World War II. I can fondly remember listening with childish amazement to his "war stories," looking at black-and-white photographs of Salzburg and Vienna, and handling mementos like his gun and a pocket Bible with a metal cover designed to protect the heart from a bullet. Sadly, the memories have faded over time until they are mere snapshots, and I lament that Grandpa is no longer around to recount his experiences anew. I lament even more that he simply is no longer around.

Grandpa's military service was rather pedestrian. He didn't ascend through the ranks to Colonel or General. He didn't perform extraordinary feats that made his a household name or that warranted the attention of a Hollywood script. His heroism was that of countless other men and women over the centuries who fought for freedom without fame or fanfare. In some ways, that makes them even more heroic than those whose names fill our history books. Before he was the patriarch of our family, an elder and Sunday school teacher in his church, a respected member of the community—and my namesake—Lee Birr was just another farm boy who helped save the world.

Over the years, I've come to more greatly appreciate—to the extent a lifelong civilian can—the bravery and sacrifice displayed by our service members. My gratitude runs deep for the Massachusetts Minutemen and the brothers taking up arms on opposite sides of our Civil War for what they believed was right, and for the thousands who endured the jungles of Vietnam and the modern-day gladiators who combat terror in the name of freedom—it runs deeper than words can say. And yet, words are what I know. So I humbly dedicate this story to those men and women whose blood, sweat, and tears have purchased and protected the freedom in this great country to write and express an opinion or a novel and the opportunity to chase this dream of mine.

Because of my grandpa and his war stories, because of what was at stake in World War II, and because there are so precious few of them remaining, the men and women of the so aptly named Greatest Generation hold a special place in my heart. Their uncommon valor, dutiful service, and staggering sacrifice may be unfamiliar to many in my generation, but we are still enjoying the fruits of their labor. To them, and to any veterans who may be reading this, I say, please accept a heartfelt thanks and know that your service will never be forgotten.

In loving memory of
Staff Sgt. Lee Wilbur Birr,
63rd Signal Operations Battalion,
United States Fifth Army . . .

A devoted husband, father,
grandfather, patriot,
and soldier of the cross.

Chapter One

Wednesday, March 20, 2013
4:57 p.m.

"THERE'S NO EASY way to say this, Maggie. We're firing you."

At first, Maggie didn't react. When her editor Walter had asked her to stop by his office before she headed out for the day, she'd expected a fifteen-minute chat mostly about nothing. That was sort of typical for meetings with Walter—he liked to think out loud. Sometimes he commented in response to a past article or suggested a direction for her next. More often than not, he talked for a while without saying much and just delayed Maggie from getting any real work done. (He was particularly chatty on sunny afternoons when she just wanted to get out of the office.) There had been nothing to suggest that this bombshell was coming, not even when he had wandered around his desk to lean on the front of it and advised she have a seat. That was Walter's typical style.

"I'm sorry," he said. "I liked you, Maggie. I really did."

Liked? Past tense?

Maggie forced herself to take a deep breath as she sat back. Half a dozen questions fought to get out first, and she only managed to utter, "I don't understand."

"I'm afraid the decision's been made. It's out of my hands," he said with a shrug.

"Why?"

"Your columns, Maggie. They seem to have an . . . agenda."

"An agenda?"

Walter nodded. He was in his early sixties, with wispy gray hair that grew wispier as each day went on. He liked to wear cardigans, even on warmish spring days like today, and argyle socks. Walter's face was a blank canvas, expressionless, his eyes sleepy. He looked like a grandpa who should fall asleep in a living room chair during family gatherings, not the guy dropping the ax on Maggie's career.

"There's a slant to what you've been writing lately, Maggie. Management disapproves."

"It's a column," Maggie said. "It's supposed to be an opinion."

Walter only shrugged.

"So what's been wrong?"

"There's been a religious tenor to what you've written since you returned from Israel. I'm not sure what happened over there, but your writing has changed. Frankly, I think it has zip to it, but it also has . . ."

"An agenda?"

He nodded again.

"What happened to freedom of speech? What happened to columnists being hard-hitting and on edge? For crying out loud, Walter, we have a religion section!"

"I know that, Maggie. But your columns lack a certain . . . objectivity. They seem rather close-minded."

"So it's not a problem that I have an opinion, it's that I have *this* opinion?"

Walter said nothing.

"Then let readers argue with me like they do with everybody else. Ask me to print a retraction—which I won't do. Why fire me? Without warning?"

"According to P.J., you had a warning."

Maggie frowned. "What warn—You mean when he suggested I tone down my rhetoric?"

Walter nodded.

"One off the cuff remark?"

"He is the Vice President of the paper."

"And I don't use rhetoric anyhow. You know that, Walter. I thought he was just blowing steam like P.J. does. Last week he laid into Emily over a split infinitive. Emily, who's never uttered a grammatically incorrect sentence."

Walter again said nothing.

"What happened to chain of command anyhow? P.J. mentioned it in passing, literally walking by me in the hallway. If it was a legitimate directive, I thought it would come through you."

Walter only shrugged.

Maggie stood. "What's going on, Walter? This isn't about my columns."

"I'm afraid it is, Maggie. And I'm afraid it's final. I'm sorry."

She turned and stared out Walter's expansive window. The Los Angeles skyline was marred by streaks of rain, leaving the sky gray and foreboding. How apropos.

"You've been here almost seven years, Maggie. I got you a nice severance package. And I'll be happy to write a letter of recommendation to anyone you choose."

She wanted to lash out, but she knew this wasn't Walter's decision. Still, she almost choked muttering, "Thank you."

Walter nodded as if she'd made a reasonable decision and they could all be friends now.

"Anything else?" she asked.

"No. I'll let you keep your credentials for a day or two so you can come clean out your desk at your leisure. Just turn them in to me by the end of the week."

Maggie reached into her pocket and withdrew her badge that gave her access to the building, along with other benefits. She tossed it on the table. "No need. So long, Walter."

She took a small measure of satisfaction in seeing a somewhat shocked expression on Walter's normally stoic face as she walked out of the office, resisting the urge to slam his door behind her. She stood for a moment outside the door, surveying the bullpen where she worked. *Had* worked. First writing space-filling copy, then as an investigative reporter before being promoted to a columnist just a few months ago. Her big break had come when an exposé had uncovered a corrupt oil deal in Mexico that was tied to the assassination of several U.S. and Mexican politicians. And now, canned for being too spiritual in her columns?

Maggie returned to her desk and quickly stuffed her laptop, a few notebooks, a couple of knickknacks from her desk, and anything else she could conceivably argue was hers into her backpack. She whipped on her leather jacket and, hoisting the backpack onto her shoulders, headed for the exit.

Too spiritual? She had infused her columns with a different perspective since returning from Israel, but it wasn't as if she was laying out the gospel message or attacking homosexuality or something "heinous" like that. She had merely suggested a few things, implied a few more. And it was a column. What columnist didn't interject his or her personal opinion into their work? What kind of columnist would she be if she didn't?

"Hey, Mags, wait up!"

Had she not recognized the voice, she wouldn't have stopped. She turned with a huff as Jake walked over. The *Los Angeles Times'* poli-sci expert was not the straight-laced, tie-wearing, future congressman type Maggie had come to expect in such a position. He was laid back, a little scruffy, with hair more befitting a One Direction member than a political wonk. They had built something of a friendship over the last six months—something enough that Maggie stopped and waited for him. He wore his typical crooked smile, the one that usually preceded a wisecrack or amusing story that made the work environment a little less stressful. Normally. Today it wasn't working its magic.

"What's up?" she asked.

"I'm headed out myself," he said, grabbing a rain jacket.

"I'm not much for conversation today, Jake."

He frowned. "What's wrong?"

"I'm out on the street."

"What?"

"They canned me," Maggie said, turning toward the steps.

Jake hurried to catch up to her. She didn't slow, and he finally had to grab her arm on the landing. "They fired you?"

"Yep. My columns apparently have their dander up, being pervaded by my new Christianity."

"What? Your columns have been great. Very fair."

"Tell it to P.J."

"He's the one who fired you?"

"According to Walter."

"Sue."

"I don't have a lawyer."

"Get one. I'll give you my lawyer's name. She's a real—"

"Forget it, Jake. They'll bury me. I'm out."

She started down the steps again, and Jake waited a moment before calling after her. "Hey, Maggie."

"Yeah?"

"Lunch sometime?"

"Sure, Jake. Nice knowing you."

Maggie continued down to the parking garage where her Yamaha FJR1300 was parked. Every time she saw the black and silver body of the motorcycle, something inside her sparked. Except for today. Today all she could think about was the rain that would mar her ride.

She zipped her jacket and tightened the straps of her backpack before pounding a black helmet over her wavy chestnut hair. It was getting long again, due for a cut. She'd been putting it off for a few weeks, what with her hectic work schedule. So much for that.

Never the gentlest of drivers, Maggie tore out of the garage and onto the rain-slicked L.A. streets. She'd been riding for years and knew how to handle the motorcycle in all elements. As she weaved in and out of downtown rush hour traffic, Maggie contemplated her firing.

Even in a liberal-driven, overly tolerant, postmodern world—and even in California—she expected to be able to opine on matters of a religious nature—much less secular matters with a slight spiritual bent—without getting fired. There had to be more to it, but what? Had something she said jabbed at someone in particular? P.J. or a family member or some other bigwig at the *Times*?

Or was this bigger? Maggie's Mexico exposé had ruined the career of a man named Leonardo Vasquez. Could he be behind this all as some form of retribution? Or had someone from her family back east decided to retaliate for her part in revealing their criminal operations?

Maybe it's time to stop exposing people, Maggie.

She refused to believe that. She had only ever done her job. Now she felt a greater calling to speak the truth, to expose corruption, to use her platform to make some kind of difference. Only she didn't have a platform any longer. Maggie had started reading through the book of John and had just recently come across the verse where Jesus said He had come so that His sheep may have life to the full. She had taken that more as a promise than a threat, but now she was second-guessing that assumption.

From somewhere inside, a Voice told her to cool it. It was a Voice she was still learning to recognize, one that hadn't been there most of her life. It reminded her she hadn't come to Christ to make this life better. Then another verse from John flashed through her head: ...*in this world you will have trouble. But take heart! I have overcome the world.*

Maggie was still somewhat new to the idea of praying. She didn't have the proper, Sunday school-taught technique. But straightforward honesty had always been her policy, and she figured God must appreciate straightforwardness, and He certainly appreciated honesty.

God, I don't understand. I thought I was doing the right thing. And this was not the plan. She paused while traffic demanded more attention. *What am I supposed to do now? I'd sure appreciate some help.*

From her somewhat limited understanding of the Bible, Maggie thought a mystical peace was supposed to wash over her. It didn't. Instead, the rain intensified. Life to the full.

Maggie lived in an apartment in Hancock Park, in a sprawling, multi-building complex known as Park La Brea. Her unit offered views of the mountains north of L.A. as well as the downtown skyline—usually very soothing after a long day's work.

After stowing her motorcycle in the underground garage, Maggie stopped to grab her mail before taking the elevator to the third floor. She was joined by a middle-aged couple who gave her a somewhat condescending look. Then again, they were dry, and she looked like a drowned rat.

Middle-aged. Funny how she made that distinction. She was now—as of yesterday—twenty-nine. Not far from middle age, and suddenly without a career plan or any direction. How had this happened in the span of a late afternoon?

Maggie let herself in and tossed the mail on the counter without looking at it. She dropped her backpack in the living room and hung her dripping jacket up in the entryway. Her clothes were soaked, so she quickly changed into sweats and a New York Rangers tee, toweling off her hair and putting it in a out-of-the-way ponytail. She took a few ibuprofen for the headache that was sure to come and headed for the living room. She watched the rain fall on downtown. This particular thundershower had moved past her apartment, and she spotted a rainbow to the northeast. It did not fill her with warm fuzzies.

Maggie's apartment was nice, but it was small, and she knew she couldn't spend the whole night ruminating or she'd end up bouncing off the walls. So she found her cell phone in her backpack and dialed Jackson. If anyone could help, it would be him. He was the one who had never shied away from telling her she needed Jesus. He hadn't badgered her or hit her over the head, but he hadn't backed down or compromised. If not for him, she doubted she would be where she was now. Maybe he would know what to say. If nothing else, just hearing his voice would help.

For the better part of two years, Maggie and Jackson had enjoyed a casual, non-relationship relationship. They hung out, went on what bordered as dates, but never made any declarations or commitments. Friends with benefits, as they said, only Jackson's Christian views had meant none of *those* benefits. Maggie had dated other guys during that span, but nothing serious had ever developed. Almost as if she was waiting until things with Jackson went to the next level. After Israel, they had both agreed to maintain the status quo for a while. Maybe that while was over. She needed someone.

Jackson's voicemail picked up after the standard four rings.

"Hey, Jack, it's Maggie. I need somebody to talk to. Give me a call when you get this. Thanks."

Maggie tossed her phone on the coffee table in frustration. Then, with no other recourse, she went for the rocky road in the freezer and flipped on the TV.

*   *   *

6:11 p.m.

THE RAIN had returned, and Maggie had found nothing on TV worth watching. So after downing a quarter of a pint of rocky road ice cream, she decided to make some real dinner. She looked through the freezer and refrigerator twice and saw nothing that interested her. She thought about ordering a pizza but figured she'd better use some discretion now that she had no steady income.

A Denny's commercial came on her muted TV, showing an array of breakfast meals. For whatever reason, waffles especially appealed to her, and she decided to make some. She spent the next ten minutes mixing batter while her waffle iron heated up. Then, while the first batch was cooking, she opened her mail.

There was a bill for her cable, suddenly an exorbitant expense, and a promotion for the upcoming spring election. She wasn't even sure what position was up for election. And didn't care. Let Jake worry about it. There was a birthday postcard from Yamaha and a pre-approval for a credit card. Lastly, there was a plain envelope from her apartment complex, probably her monthly statement/invoice. She set the bill on the coffee table, pitched the promo, postcard, and pre-approval, and sat at one of the stools facing her galley kitchen and tore open the remaining envelope.

It contained a single sheet of paper, folded in thirds. Maggie opened it, skipped the preliminaries, and read the first paragraph.

This notice is to inform you that your lease will not be renewed. Please find alternate living arrangements by April 30 of the current year. If you vacate your apartment prior to the end of your lease, a prorated reimbursement will be mailed to you. If you have any questions, please contact . . .

Maggie quit reading and dropped the letter in disgust. She was being evicted? She picked the letter back up and searched it for any rationale behind the decision. But there was none. Just a cold, brief notice.

She dropped her head onto the counter. First her job, now her apartment. Was someone out to get her? Leonardo Vasquez again jumped into her head. He had the power to make this happen. But why now? And if he wanted revenge, why not . . . kill her?

Maggie raised her head. Not only did she have to find a new job, now she needed a new apartment. She liked this place. It had the view, had personality, had memories. It was her. She didn't even know where to start. Job then apartment? Apartment then job? Stay in L.A.? If not, where else? And the end of April wasn't far away. She sighed.

And remembered her waffle iron. She turned to see batter dripping down the sides and onto the counter while steam billowed out the edges. Her patience ran out, and like her waffle maker, she boiled over. Her rage came out in a guttural scream as she scrunched the letter into a wad and flung it against the wall. It fell to the floor noiselessly, but the lack of a satisfying thud was made up for by the pain from nearly throwing out her shoulder.

Chapter Two

6:27 p.m.

AS FAR AS Wednesdays went, it had been a pretty slow day in the ER. But it was still early. The really crazy stuff—and in her six and counting years at UCLA Medical Center, Santa Monica, Samantha MacRaney had seen plenty of crazy—didn't usually happen until well after dark. Even so, as she exited the restroom and headed for the nurses' break room and her dinner of leftover chicken Caesar salad, she couldn't help but think maybe this would be an easy shift. After almost a week of twelve on, twelve off shifts, easy would be a welcome respite.

Sam smiled and said a soft hello to a fellow nurse who exited the break room as Sam entered. She turned to the left, toward the refrigerator, and stopped cold.

A rather well-dressed man—despite his rugged appearance—stood from an end chair in the corner. He wore yellowish-brown khakis, an untucked plaid shirt, and a navy sports jacket that, remarkably, matched the shirt. His hair was typically disheveled, and his beard was in need of a trim. Even so, it couldn't hide a smile tugging at the corner of his mouth or dim the twinkle in his blue eyes. At the same time, they also looked tired, and his shoulders seemed to bear more than the weight of an overnight bag that sat on the floor beside his chair.

"Steve," Sam said, sure the shock of seeing her brother was evident on her face. Perhaps it explained the grin and twinkle. She shook away her confusion. "What are you doing here?" she asked, walking over and giving him a tight squeeze.

"I came to see you, Baby Girl," he said as he embraced her back. Older than her by two years, Steve had somehow discovered that for about a week after her birth, their parents had been unable to decide on a name for Sam, and had referred to her as "Baby Girl." It had been his term—mostly of endearment—for her ever since.

She pulled back. "How'd you get in here?"

"I told somebody at the desk I was here to see you, and they said you were about to go on break. You look good."

"I look stressed, Steve," she said, tucking a strand of blond hair behind her ear. No matter how tight the ponytail, it never held for an entire shift. "Seriously, why are you here? Why now?"

"I'm actually on my way to Phoenix. Tactical technique seminar."

"You mean throwing each other around on mats for a weekend?"

"Something like that."

Sam shook her head. "L.A. isn't on the way from Frisco to Phoenix."

He sighed.

"What aren't you telling me, Steve?"

He nodded at the chair adjacent to his. "Have a seat."

Sam frowned. "Now you're scaring me."

"Sorry, I didn't mean to. I wouldn't have come to work, but it's the only time I have."

"What's going on Steve?"

He took a deep breath. They were both sitting by now, and Sam leaned forward. Steve did not get nervous—not about tests in school or a new job, not about asking girls out on a date, not about the frequent times he got into nominal trouble with their parents. So the fact that he was hesitant told her something was wrong.

"Mom has cancer."

"What?"

"Breast cancer," he said. "Very early stages, very treatable. Sounds like no chemo, no radiation, no mastectomy."

He said something more, but Sam didn't hear it. She fell back into the chair, letting it envelop her, wishing it could do more than just support her body.

She looked at Steve. "How long has she known?"

"Since Monday."

Sam shook her head. "Why didn't she call? I didn't even know—"

"I just found out Monday too. She said she didn't want to alarm us with possibilities until she knew something. She was going to call you, but

I suggested I alter my travel plans a little and tell you in person. I thought it'd be better to hear it from me than over the phone."

Sam took deep breaths, already reassuring herself with statistics and numbers and percentages. Trying to reassure herself, more like. Statistics and numbers and percentages didn't work when it was your own mother.

Steve put a hand on her arm, and she reached and clasped it with both of hers, looking at him somberly, trying not to cry.

"They said they caught it very early. Her prognosis is outstanding, and those are the doctor's own words, and you know doctors, Sam, they never make promises."

"I just can't believe it," she said.

"I know," he said, placing his other hand over hers and squeezing. They felt so much like their dad's hands, and at that moment Sam realized how much Steve was becoming like him. Had been for quite a while, actually, but this moment seemed to drive it home.

He pulled her close and kissed her forehead, then drew her into another hug as they both sat on the edge of their chairs.

"How long you work tonight?" he asked.

"Midnight," she said into his shoulder. She lifted her head. "How'd you know I worked, even?"

"Stopped by your place first. I actually don't fly to Phoenix until tomorrow. I was hoping to crash on your couch."

"Yeah, of course. Steve, why didn't you call ahead?"

"You'd have been suspicious."

She sighed. "I suppose."

"Midnight mean midnight or whenever the blood stops flowing?"

"It all depends. Did you really fly down a day early just to tell me this?"

"Not just to tell you. I also wanted to see you."

"I wish I'd have known. I could have swapped shifts with somebody."

"Don't worry about it. Give me your key, and I'll go catch a nap. Then call when you're headed out, I'll order a pizza, and we'll catch up and commiserate and yada, yada, yada."

Sam looked at her brother. She wasn't sure if he was really at peace with the news, putting on a brave face for her, or covering his true emotions with nonchalance. Ten years ago, covering for sure. More mature Steve, she guessed one of the first two.

"There's a spare in a small black box in the flower pot left of the door."

"*In* the flower pot," he said, snapping his finger. "I looked under."

"That's why it's in."

"Smart girl."

"I learned from the best."

They stood and hugged again. Although it had thrown her, Sam was glad Steve was there—glad she had him to hold. She was even more thankful that he lived ten minutes from their parents' house, close enough that they had somebody to hold.

He kissed her head again. "Don't worry, Baby Girl. Mom will be fine."

She nodded without conviction.

"Just work on patching up the shooting vics and meth addicts and on getting off on time."

She playfully slapped his arm. "Get out of here. I have to eat. Besides, I'm not the only nurse due for a break, and the last thing I need is my brother hitting on my coworkers."

"And she finally deduces my true motivation for being here."

Sam smiled.

"Call me when you're headed home."

"I will. I'm glad you're here, Steve."

He winked as he turned to leave. Sam watched him go, then set about prepping her dinner. As she did, she kicked herself for worrying and trying to comfort herself with the odds of her mom's survival instead of first taking her cares and concerns to her Heavenly Father. She did so quickly as she tossed the dressing with her salad, and made plans to do so in much more detail later when she had a chance to focus.

She flipped through a magazine as she ate, trying not to think about her mom and cancer and the numerous sad stories she'd heard over the years and as a nurse. She wanted desperately to call her—and would, but when she could break down and cry and not have to be at her occupational best minutes later. She had a little vacation time coming—

maybe she'd squeeze in a quick visit too. She hadn't seen her folks since Christmas—and mid-summer before that. Steve's news was another reminder that time was precious and limited, and she needed to make the most of it.

Finished eating, she quickly cleaned up and prayed for strength and focus. She only had five hours—or so—left, she reminded herself as she checked her appearance in a mirror. She ended up redoing her ponytail entirely, dabbing her eyes and blowing her nose with a tissue when she was done. Then, as best as possible under the circumstances, she deemed herself ready to resume working.

Fortunately, so to speak, the ER quickly became chaotic. For the next several hours, Sam didn't have time for more than a passing, almost subconscious, thought about her own family's health issues.

*   *   *

7:38 p.m.

MAGGIE EVENTUALLY calmed down. Sort of. But not until after she had thrown the waffle iron, the rest of her batter, and the bowl containing the batter into the garbage can. She poured herself a bowl of Grape Nuts and watched a rerun of *Cheers* on one of the local channels. Everybody there solved their problems by heading down to the local bar. Maggie's conversion had not turned her into a teetotaler—not yet, at least—but she also didn't feel like alcohol was the answer.

She tried praying but didn't know what to say. She tried reading her Bible but didn't find the inspiration or encouragement she was hoping for. She tried watching more TV, but the half-hour resolutions to all of life's problems annoyed her. She tried Jackson again, but he still wasn't answering. Sitting on her small balcony facing north, Maggie lowered her phone with a sigh.

The night was warm, and the rain had quit. There were still a few flashes of lightning east over the San Gabriel Mountains, but the radar on her phone indicated western Los Angeles County was in the clear. After staring at the darkness for a while, Maggie decided to get on her bike and ride. Sitting in her apartment wasn't doing her any good, and riding cleared her mind. Besides, she didn't have a self-imposed curfew; she had no place to go in the morning, thank you, P.J.!

She changed into a dry pair of jeans but left on the Rangers tee. Her jacket was dry, and five minutes later, she was cruising. She thought about heading into the hills, but since it was dark, decided against it. Instead, she got on I-10 and headed toward downtown.

Her mind had been running all night, trying to answer questions of what, why, and what now. It had left her with a lot of anger and frustration that turned into more anger. Maggie found speed to be an outlet, and as she turned south on I-110, she opened the throttle. Traffic was light, and she burned some serious rubber. It was stupid, but she didn't care. Something about pushing the speedometer made her feel good, in a teenage boy sort of way. Until she saw flashing lights behind her.

Oh, you've got to be kidding me.

She guided the motorcycle across two lanes to the shoulder of the road and coasted to a stop. She popped off her helmet, resisting the urge to fling it against the concrete guardrail. Instead, she hung it over the handlebar as she killed the motor. As the patrol car stopped behind her, its floodlight blinding her, Maggie dropped her head back.

God, please. I do not need any more today.

"Evening."

Maggie turned to see a young, fairly good-looking patrolman and decided to try something she'd never done before. She flirted shamelessly in an effort to get off, or at least get reduced to a warning. It didn't work. Apparently going 86 wasn't something a girl could flirt her way out of.

Soon to be poorer, Maggie continued at a more reasonable pace. She took the 105 west toward LAX, then turned north on the 405. The joy in riding was gone, and all she wanted to do was go to bed and forget that March 20 had ever happened.

For whatever reason, she took the wrong ramp and instead of going east on I-10, went west. Maggie had never been one to use a lot of foul language, but she had to bite her tongue to keep from cursing into her helmet. Through gritted teeth, she mumbled a prayer that was as much a groan of desperation as anything.

I-10 led into Santa Monica, and Maggie thought about buzzing up to Jackson's house in Pacific Palisades to see if he happened to be home. It wasn't beyond the realm of possibility that he was so engrossed in his virtual Los Angeles Rams that he was ignoring his phone. But she liked to think that he would have picked up one of her calls. Then again, she would have liked to think he'd have remembered her birthday too, but it had come and gone without a word from him. She opted for the beach instead. Maybe a walk along the pounding surf would calm her down. It wasn't like she'd be able to sleep anyhow.

Maggie parked north of the Santa Monica Pier and left the noise and lights behind her. A cool breeze blew in off the Pacific, and Maggie took her hair out of her ponytail and let it blow.

She was still new at this whole Christian thing, still sorting stuff out and learning the ropes. For example, doing something dumb and then asking God to spare you the consequences didn't work. Much of what she knew, she'd learned from Jackson. He'd lost his parents and brother in an explosion that had devastated him. For a while, he'd been Mike Tyson groping around for his mouth guard while the referee counted to ten. But he had survived. He was still devastated, but he was coping. And he cited a lifetime of biblical instruction from his parents as the reason. He'd been taught, and thus resided in, the fact that God was good, even when all evidence pointed to the contrary. But Maggie didn't have a lifetime of faith in reserve. She'd been a Christian for a month.

I guess this is where the rubber meets the road, huh? After all, having faith is an action, right? If this is going to work, I'm going to have to trust You. Jackson tells me that You're worthy of nothing but reverence and respect even when the whole world's going to . . . uh . . . You know. And I don't even know where in the Bible he gets that. But I guess I'll have to take his word for it.

She wandered for a while, past an old man with a dog. The beach was empty, and she trudged toward the ocean, stopping just before her shoes would have gotten wet. As beautiful as it was during the day, the ocean was even more impressive at night, dark and powerful. Each wave was a thunderous but muffled boom.

So how are You good, God? How in all the crap—Is crap one of those words I shouldn't say now too? Is it different in prayer? Do You really care about little things like words? Or big things like words I won't be writing any more? Or is that a little thing too, given AIDS, and North Korea and Iran, and all the . . . crap in the world?

She watched the whitecaps appear out of the blackness and pound the sand for a few minutes.

I guess . . . and I'm sorry if this is too forward, but if this is going to work, I think I'm going to need You to show me some of this stuff. I don't have a lifelong relationship to fall back on. All I have is now. So . . . help me out?

Chapter Three

8:48 p.m.

MAGGIE WATCHED THE waves a while longer before turning back toward her bike. If nothing else, the sea air had seemed to clear her head. Instead of getting back on the freeway, she rode through town. She didn't know why. And she didn't know why she turned onto 10th Street. It was almost as if she was on autopilot.

But there she was, at the small church she'd been going to for a few weeks. It was Jackson's church, and having no druthers or reason for selecting any particular church, she had gone with him. She wasn't sold yet, but then again, she wasn't sure what the selling points of a good church should be. But at any rate, here she was, idling at the curb.

There were a few cars in the lot, and Maggie killed the engine.

What exactly are you doing, Maggie?

She hung her helmet over the handlebars and started toward the front door. She didn't see any lights. Maybe the cars were part of a carpool or something. She walked through the lot and around to the side door. It was unlocked.

This is crazy. Go home and take a Unisom.

She entered a dark hallway, lit only by an exit sign above and two dim, recessed lights at intervals in the hallway. On the left were the church offices. Straight ahead, the main entrance and foyer with access to the sanctuary. Ahead and to her right was a hallway leading to classrooms. Maggie took a few steps, her heart pounding. She didn't get nervous. What in the world was going on? Why wasn't she on her way home?

There were lights down the Education Wing, as they called it, and it dawned on Maggie that it was Wednesday. Probably a prayer group or

Bible study. Hadn't Christians long ago decided on Wednesday as their midweek gathering night?

What are you going to do, Maggie, barge into some Bible study? It's almost nine o'clock anyhow; they have to be about done.

This was nuts, and Maggie turned to leave. She stopped when she realized a light was coming from the foyer. She had no idea why she had driven to the church, why she had stopped outside it, or why she was walking toward the light now. Was this what being a Christian was about—doing random, strange, totally out of character things for reasons you couldn't understand? Somehow, she didn't think so. It didn't seem to be for Jackson. Then again, following an all-powerful God would occasionally lead to something other than the normal, wouldn't it?

But how did following God have anything to do with her being at the church tonight?

"Can I help you?"

Maggie turned to see a man standing in the open doorway of an office. The light was mostly behind him, so she saw as much silhouette as anything, but she thought she recognized him as Pastor Rick, the senior pastor.

"Um . . . no," she said. "I mean . . ."

"Are you looking for someone?"

Maggie sighed. "I don't even know what I'm doing here."

"Would you like to talk about it?"

"I don't want to take up your time."

"It's what my time is for," he said. Maggie recognized his voice from behind the pulpit. It was definitely Pastor Rick. His voice had stuck with her since the first sermon of his she'd heard. It was so simple and plain that she had expected to fall asleep before he got to his second bullet point, but it also carried with it a certain cadence and authority . . . Maybe it was sincerity.

Maggie shrugged but found herself walking toward him. Pastor Rick stepped out of the doorway so she could enter his office. "I'm Rick," he said.

"Maggie."

"Please, have a seat."

Maggie sat down in one of three chairs in front of his desk and studied the office. A window looked out on the front lawn and the street. On the opposite side of the room, a door joined Pastor Rick's office to the associate pastor's office. Behind his desk, a floor-to-ceiling bookshelf was full. A short couch, chair, and coffee table occupied the corner. On his desk were several photos, one of which showed a much younger Pastor Rick, presumably his wife, and two little children. A nice-looking family.

Instead of sitting behind his desk, Pastor Rick took a chair next to her. "So, Maggie, you've been coming here the last few weeks, haven't you?"

Her surprise must have shown on her face, for Pastor Rick smiled. "I'm very good with faces. Names, not so much. I'll be calling you Mandy or Peggy or something before long."

His smile was infectious. He had a calming demeanor, very good for being a pastor, she supposed. And yet, he didn't seem like a lightweight. There was something about him, a realness, that struck Maggie almost immediately.

"I've only been a Christian a few weeks," Maggie said. "I was in Israel, on this expedition to find crusader treasure, if you'll believe it. I was there as a reporter to chronicle the search."

She had no idea why she had suddenly launched into her life story, but Pastor Rick prodded her on. "Sounds exciting," he said.

"Oh, it was. I was kidnapped with two other women, and we were tied up in a cellar somewhere in the West Bank. There I was, facing imminent death, and suddenly everything I'd heard about God started to make sense. No atheists in foxholes, they say. But it was more than just that . . . It was suddenly relevant. My friend Jackson has witnessed to me—That is the term, isn't it?"

Pastor Rick nodded.

"Anyhow, I knew all the ins and outs. So I prayed and asked Christ to save me because, frankly, I didn't think I had long in this world."

"What happened?"

"The rest of our team found us, rescued us, brought us home. It all happened in a whirlwind."

Pastor Rick nodded again. "So if I may ask, what is it that has brought you here tonight?"

"I don't know," Maggie said. "I was just out for a ride, and I found myself here."

The pastor smiled. "You said you've only been a Christian a short time, Maggie, so I doubt you've had the pleasure of debating predestination and free will with an old elder for hours some Friday evening." He grinned a little wider to show his sarcasm. "I tend to shy away from either end of the spectrum—God controls everything, and we are nothing but puppets on a string or that He sits back with indifference, never influencing us one way or the other. But I do believe He prompts our decisions from time to time. Especially when you are one of His children, Maggie. What I'm trying to say is, I think it's possible that God was the one directing you—maybe even subconsciously—to make this or that turn and to come in here this evening."

"Why?"

"That I don't know. But I gather you might."

He said it tenderly, and she looked down, fidgeting with her hands.

Go on, you've come this far.

With a sigh, she began to recount the events of her day: getting fired, the eviction notice, the speeding ticket. She left out the waffle iron mess; some things should stay private. She was up to her walk on the beach and her subsequent prayers when she sensed footsteps in the foyer.

"Hey, Dad, Mrs. Bahr's in the library. She wants to—"

Maggie turned over her shoulder and saw a tall, pretty good-looking guy. The striking feature was a relaxedness that played out over his entire face, even when he realized he was interrupting and his blue eyes widened. "Sorry. I didn't know you were in a meeting."

"No, it's fine," Maggie said. "I should be going anyhow."

"Don't leave on my account," the guy said. "I'll see if Mrs. Bahr can make an appointment later in the week."

"No, please," she said, turning back to Pastor Rick. "I just needed to unload on somebody. Please, go talk to her. I'll be fine."

"Are you sure?" he asked.

"I'm sure." She stood and offered him a hand. "Thank you."

"You're very welcome. I doubt I'll be long with Mrs. Bahr. If you'd like to hang around, I'd be happy to talk with you more when I get back."

"Thanks, but I'll be fine."

Pastor Rick nodded as he skirted the chairs. "Oh, Maggie, this is my son Russell. Russ, Maggie."

"Yeah, I've seen you here," he said, offering a hand. It was strong but soft at the same time, and his handshake was firm. "It's nice to meet you."

"Nice to meet you too."

"Excuse me," Pastor Rick said, squeezing past his son and out into the dark foyer. Maggie started to follow but stopped when Russell nodded at her shirt, showing under her half-open jacket.

"New York Rangers?"

Maggie smiled. "Yeah."

"You from New York?"

"Originally."

"What brings you to the Left Coast?"

"It's a long story."

"Work? Boyfriend? Warmth?"

He grinned while he spoke, almost a smirk. But a smirk conveyed arrogance, and Russell didn't strike her as arrogant. He easily could have been. He was handsome, with short but ruffled brown hair, a five o'clock shadow that was actually more like five o'clock on day two, and a sharp nose. He wore a blue and green plaid shirt with the sleeves rolled to the elbows, dark khakis, and gray and white Vans. A loose, earthy necklace added to his vibe, as did a couple silicone gel bracelets. He was good-looking, but by SoCal standards, nothing special. Yet there was something else about him that Maggie couldn't quite put a finger on, something that made his questions unobtrusive. He wasn't pestering her, and he wasn't hitting on her. He was just a guy having a friendly conversation.

So she conversed. "School first, actually." It wasn't entirely untruthful, she figured, and Christians weren't supposed to be untruthful, especially to a pastor's son.

"Which school?"

"Long Beach State."

"What class?"

"Oh-six."

He nodded. "I had a buddy graduate in '05." He leaned against the doorpost. "Why LBSU?"

Maggie shrugged. "I was looking to get away, and this was away," she said, marveling at how much she was disclosing to a stranger. Again. "They had a good journalism program, and the guidance counselor was cute."

"Yeah, my guidance counselor at Northern Arizona was a looker too," he said, the grin a little lopsided. "So, are you a journalist then?"

"I was," Maggie said. "Until today."

For the first time, Russell's smile waned. "What happened?"

And for the second time that night, Maggie found herself recounting the events of her day. Russell listened much the way Pastor Rick had. Like his father's, Russell's eyes conveyed warmth and compassion even though he didn't say a word until Maggie explained how she had shown up at church. By the time she was finished, Russell was nodding.

"I've been there."

"Canned, evicted, and cited for breaking the law in the same day?"

"No, not exactly," he said with a smile. "I got saved when I was a little kid, but when I was about twelve or thirteen, I started to be something of a rebel."

"Really?"

He nodded. "Hard to believe now, right, looking at the well-behaved specimen in front of you? But yeah, I was turning into a little punk. When I was sixteen, I got into a fight at school. Busted the other kid's nose, needed some stitches myself." He looked over his shoulder, back into the hallway. "My dad's a pretty mild-mannered guy, but that was as angry as I've ever seen him. Anyhow, that night we had a good long talk, and I realized I had to make some changes in my life. I don't want to throw around the typical Christian clichés, but I 'rededicated' myself that night to following God."

He leaned forward slightly, straightening up against the doorpost. "Within the next two weeks, I was in a car accident that totaled my Escort—not to mention raised my insurance about two hundred bucks— the dog we'd owned since I was four died, and my girlfriend dumped me."

He tipped his head to the side. "Well, technically, I wasn't allowed to date until I was eighteen so she was more like a girl friend, but she dumped me anyhow."

"And look at you now."

"I know, right? She's so missing out," he said with a big grin. "But my point is, you—like I had then—had just switched sides."

"So the devil's out to get me, is that what you're saying?"

Russell shrugged. "Not necessarily. I don't mean to imply that there's a demon behind every bush, luring dog's into the street or whispering to your boss to fire you. But the devil's lost you. And there's nothing he can do about that. The Bible says you're secure in the Father's hands. So the devil tries to make your life miserable. That can take a number of forms: temptation, discouragement, sometimes rotten circumstances."

"So this is what I've got to look forward to?"

"It's not all bad," Russell answered. "God never allows you to go through more than you can bear. But sometimes He lets you be tested for a while."

Maggie shook her head. "I'm new to all of this. Why would God test me? Doesn't He know everything?"

Russell nodded. "But you and I don't. Sometimes He allows us to be tested to make a point to us."

"Sounds like there's a lot more to this than I thought."

"Trust me, Maggie, you'll be saying that twenty years from now. But you'll also be glad you switched sides. The Christian life is hard, I won't lie. But it's also rewarding."

"Yeah? How so?"

"For example, moments like this."

Maggie raised an eyebrow.

"A chance to share with someone else who's struggling. Sometimes you can impart wisdom from a past experience. Sometimes you can give guidance from something you've learned from Scripture. Sometimes you just offer a listening ear and a promise to pray. Whatever the case, you're there, part of a family, in it together."

Maggie studied Russell for a second. "That is either the worst pickup line I've ever heard . . . or moderately encouraging."

"Oh trust me, my pickup lines are far worse."

Maggie couldn't help smiling. "I should get going. Thanks for the listening ear."

"You're welcome. Anytime."

"Thank your dad for me too, will you?"

"Of course." He nodded as she turned for the door. "I'm headed out too. I'll walk you out."

"So what brings you to church on a Wednesday night?" Maggie asked.

"I meet with some guys every week. More often than not, it's here."

"Bible study?"

Russell tipped his head back and forth. "More of a mutual mentoring type of deal. A support group."

"Oh."

He got the door for her.

"Thanks."

Russell scanned the parking lot. "Which car is yours?"

"That one," Maggie said, pointing to her bike.

"You ride?"

"Uh-huh."

"Somehow that doesn't surprise me."

"No?"

"Leather jacket, hockey fan, you've got a little bit of an attitude."

"I do?"

"In a good way. Call it spirit."

Maggie nodded and grinned. "Nice save."

"Yeah, well, I'll get out while I'm behind. It was nice talking to you, Maggie."

"Same here."

"I'll pray that God gives you guidance about what to do next. And strength to endure whatever the devil throws at you."

"I'd appreciate that."

Russell nodded. "Take care, Maggie. Maybe I'll see you Sunday."

She nodded too. "Yeah."

They turned their separate ways, Maggie trying to piece together what had taken place over the last half hour. Had God really orchestrated her route, bringing her to the church to talk to Pastor Rick and Russell? As she put on her helmet, she took a look back at the parking lot, where headlights on a Chevy Avalanche had just lit up. After talking with Russell, she did feel a little better about her circumstances. Maybe God had led her there after all.

But if so, why did she still feel all chaotic inside?

Chapter Four

SAM WAS SOMETHING of a creature of habit—at least as much as possible for someone whose work schedule was inconsistent from week to week and day to day. So despite the pleasure of having her brother take her out for breakfast, Sam's Thursday was off to a tumultuous start.

Three car accidents, two stabbings, a gang-related shooting that injured three, several drug overdoses, a handful of viral infections, and a power tool injury that had turned even Sam's hardened stomach had kept the ER hopping Wednesday night, and had kept her from getting out until close to one. Steve had still insisted on ordering pizza, and they'd stayed up until almost three eating, catching each other up on recent events, and reliving memories of years gone by. Sam's heart had been light as she'd finally fallen asleep, but she'd awakened groggily less than six hours later, and with an ever-present reminder of why Steve had come in the first place.

Steve's flight left LAX at noon, so he'd woken her with a flying pillow to the face—as if he was twelve and she was ten all over again—and hurried her through her morning routine so they could get to breakfast. She'd skipped her Bible reading and prayed absent-mindedly while showering and quickly dressing. Breakfast had been good but rushed, and then Steve had practically slapped a kiss on her cheek before darting out to his waiting cab, promising to keep in better touch than usual.

And then Sam was alone in the booth at IHOP, overwhelmed by a sudden emptiness. Some of it was missing her brother, whom she wished she could spend more time with, despite his collegial attitude and teasing.

Much of the feeling was attributed to the news of her mom's breast cancer diagnosis and the numerous questions and possibilities it raised. Sam had been a practicing Christian most of her life and had seen firsthand how God had sustained her and her family through difficult times. Even so, this rocked her, and she wasn't sure she was strong enough to withstand the potential waves it might cause.

But something else was also gnawing at Sam, something she couldn't quite place. Steve had paid the bill, so she left the restaurant and returned to her car, trying to figure out what it was that was causing her stress. This wasn't like her. Worry and anxiety weren't part of her daily life. Nor was a feeling that something was missing. So what was it?

Instead of driving off, Sam mulled for several minutes, then dug out her phone and called her mom. They cried and laughed for half an hour, and Sam finally ended the call feeling the same as she had after talking with Steve—better and yet not better. As she drove back to her apartment, she thought some more, doing her best to analyze her feelings to see what it was that was giving her pause. She was good at feeling, at emoting, at empathizing. She was not so good at analyzing, and came up with nothing.

Cast all your anxiety on him because he cares for you.

The Bible verse came back to her as she climbed the steps to her second-floor apartment. She put down her purse and keys and crashed into the loveseat. She pulled her feet up and hugged her knees to her chest, and spent some time doing just that—casting her anxiety on Jesus.

I don't know where this may lead. I can't bear the thought of losing her. I don't know what this restlessness is within me. But You know all, and I know You have me in Your hand. Let that be enough . . .

It didn't seem to work. Sam knew that faith was not some bing-bang-boom ta-da experience where everything suddenly and magically got solved. But usually, when she rested herself in God's hands, she felt the burdens of life fall off. So what was different this time?

Glancing at the clock, Sam hit upon an idea. She'd been through a few rough patches like this before, where casting her anxieties or cares on Christ hadn't seemed to work. She'd come to find out it was not Him letting her down; it was her aim in casting. Prayer, Scripture reading, and talks with fellow "casters" had seemed to reorient her. Short of her family, there was one person who Sam felt could relate. He'd never say so—he felt like he was woefully inept at trusting and walking with God. Yet Sam had seen in him a resolve and resiliency that could only be a product of faith. Numerous times, she'd been there for him. Now she hoped Jackson would be able to help her.

She had an afternoon "coffee" date at two and worked again at six, so she calculated she had just enough time to run to Pacific Palisades now. She'd dressed hastily that morning, just throwing on the first thing she found and sticking her hair up behind her head. She changed into a lavender top and a nicer pair of jeans and took the time to style her hair. It fell almost to the middle of her back, and lately she had considered hacking it to her shoulders. But didn't Scripture say, *"if a woman has long hair, it is her glory?"* Besides, it had been her look forever.

Her hair didn't want to cooperate, and she found herself fussing over every curl.

Is this because you're going to see him?

Of course not. It's because I'm sick of looking haggard and bedraggled.

Right, and the kiss had nothing to do with it.

The kiss. Christmas Eve. After a group dinner, she and Jackson had gone for a walk on the beach. It had been cool and drizzly, and they had taken shelter under a secluded gazebo. The moment had gotten to them, and they had shared a quick kiss, followed by a longer one.

"Ugh," Sam said, setting down her curling iron with as much force as her gentle demeanor allowed. She studied herself in the mirror.

It looks fine. I look fine.

Who cares anyhow? Since when do you primp for Jackson? Get a hold of yourself.

Sam unplugged the curling iron and called it good. It must have been the stress of so much work, her mom, and the hectic morning. She was not usually a mental basket case like this. Especially regarding Jackson. They had talked about the kiss, agreeing it probably wasn't wise. Neither of them was ready to take their friendship to the next level, and neither of them wanted to start getting physical outside of a committed relationship.

So why does the thought of seeing him suddenly have you acting like a schoolgirl?

Are you sure it's his "help" you want?

Or is it something else making you nervous?

Sam shook her head and thought about changing plans. Maybe what she really needed was more sleep. The last thing she wanted was to see Jackson while she was vulnerable and with an assortment of feelings swirling around inside her. It wasn't that she didn't trust him. It was more that she didn't trust herself. And that was really scary.

Sam tried to put it all behind her and concentrate on the beautiful day. After a night of rain and storms, the sun was out in full force, warm and bright and cheery. But as she zipped north in her cute little Ford Focus, the butterflies in her stomach resumed fluttering.

Okay, so you're a little anxious to see him. Just because you both agreed not to kiss anymore doesn't mean you can't have some feelings for him.

So do I have feelings for him?

Of course you do.

I mean real feelings? Or is this just an overreaction to everything that's going on? Or to his getting shot?

New Year's Eve, a week after their kiss, Jackson had been shot by the stalker of an actress he had worked for. It hadn't been serious, at least as far as bullet wounds went, but it had still shaken Sam—more than it had shaken him. Jackson's life as a private investigator brought more danger than she was comfortable with. In the last year alone he'd rescued an undercover police detective from gangsters, gotten into a firefight with a rogue military group at an abandoned military base in the Nevada desert, duped various governments out of an old Bible allegedly containing CIA secrets, and chased a crusader treasure across Europe and into the Middle East. In addition to getting shot. Whether her feelings were romantic or just platonic, Sam was concerned for Jackson's long-term safety.

So maybe that's it? Maybe I just need to check up on him?

But you've been concerned about him for months. So why all the butterflies now?

Sam sighed away her analysis and focused on the drive.

Jackson lived in a Pacific Palisades neighborhood that was way out of the league of a young private eye. He'd found a house whose previous owners had been drug dealers or drug makers or something. They'd been foreclosed on, and he'd gotten an old house for a song and had taken his time fixing it up. He was rewarded by having a nice place in a great location, with spectacular views out toward the Pacific. Sam had spent many a warm summer evening on his deck, enjoying his grilling and views of the sunset. As she turned onto his street, she couldn't help but wonder why neither of them had ever pursued a serious relationship. They were both clearly interested in each other. Was there someone else? Was he afraid of commitment? And what was her excuse?

And why was this, with all else that was going on, suddenly on the forefront of her brain?

Jackson's 1976 Granada was not in the driveway, so Sam parked there. She took a deep breath, flicking her eyes up to the rearview mirror. Her shoulders sagged a little when she realized she'd forgotten any jewelry.

Good grief, Sam, get a grip!

She got out and walked to the front door. She rang the doorbell and waited, hands in her pockets. There was no answer. He could be in the bathroom, or deep in the UCLA red zone, she thought with a smile. She gave it a minute, then rang the bell again.

"I haven't seen him lately."

Sam turned to the left. Jackson's somewhat boisterous neighbor Connie had backed out of her garage, paused in the middle of the driveway, and rolled down the passenger window to holler at Sam.

"I think it's been since Monday night."

Sam wandered off Jackson's step and across the yard. She peeked in his window. The blinds were drawn but open. She couldn't see much.

"He didn't happen to say where he was going?" she asked.

Connie parked the vehicle and got out.

"I'm sorry," Sam said. "I didn't mean to stop you."

Connie waved her hand, causing bangles on her wrist to clang together. She was dressed in a zebra print blouse and gaudy pink pants. The pants matched the lipstick and nearly the hair. It was bright red, dyed beyond any natural hue. In her mid-forties, Connie was divorced three times. She was opinionated, nosy, and superstitious to a fault. But she was also very friendly, compassionate, and a great cook. Sam had sampled her culinary creations more than once.

"It's Samantha, right?"

Sam nodded.

Connie shook her head. "Honey, I've told Jackson half a dozen times he needs to stop fooling around with all these different women and settle down." She leaned over the hood. "Personally, you're my favorite."

Sam was taken aback and couldn't help but ask. "All these women? Fooling around?"

"Oh, you know. One day he's saving one from a tribe of natives in Mexico and then he's rescuing another from a cult in Nevada. He's got them over here all the time, clients needing this and that. I keep telling him he needs to find a respectable job. You know how rumors start."

"I do," Sam said, feeling a little better at Connie's explanation. A little. "He, uh, didn't say where he was going?"

"What? Oh, no," she said with another wave. "Probably another case."

"Do you know if he had one?"

"Hmm? No, I don't think so. He said things were slow, but that was almost a week ago. He was mowing the lawn and complaining about his career path or something. You know Jackson, he complains a little."

"Well, if you see him, would you have him call me?" Sam asked.

"Of course, dear."

Sam thanked her and returned to Jackson's property. She waited until Connie had driven off before ringing Jackson's bell one more time. He didn't answer, and as Sam returned to her car, Connie's words replayed in her head.

Not the part about Jackson fooling around. She wasn't afraid that he was acting inappropriately, and if he did have lots of women over like he did Sam, he had every right to do so. They didn't have an exclusivity clause. She'd gone on a few dates herself. She didn't even feel jealous. Much.

No, what worried her was the part about another case. Jackson was usually pretty good at keeping those close to him informed when he was going to be out of touch for a while. And the fact that neither Sam nor Connie had heard anything caused Sam's normally calm heart to race just a little bit more.

*   *   *

3:44 p.m.

THE PREVIOUS July, Jackson had come upon Stephanie Kane while she was being physically assaulted by her husband, Brady. Jackson had intervened, and the long story short was that he had forced Brady to get therapy for a violent temper while providing Stephanie a safe place to stay. Initially, that had been with Connie. Then, for the better part of five months, with Sam.

They had bonded deeply during that time as Sam led Stephanie to Christ, counseled her through her myriad feelings for Brady, and encouraged her during a pregnancy discovered just after Jackson had rescued her. Now Brady and Stephanie were back together, and by all accounts, things were going well. Sam had maintained a close relationship with Stephanie, who was due any day, including weekly get-togethers for smoothies, tea, ice cream, or whatever.

This "coffee date" had helped calm Sam's unusually anxious heart until she checked her phone after dropping Stephanie back at her apartment. She had called Jackson on her way to Stephanie's, and he hadn't answered, nor returned her call in the interim.

You're turning into a stalker, Sam, she thought as she dialed again. As it had the previous time, it went straight to voicemail.

"This is Jackson Douglas. Leave me a message, and I'll get back to you when I can. Thanks."

"Where are you, Jackson?" Sam mumbled under her breath. She checked her watch, concluded she had time, and set her aim for Marina del Rey.

There were two people Jackson confided in more than any other— two who would know if he had gone somewhere or was involved in something. The first was Leroy Douglas, Jackson's grandpa. Since the death of his wife over fifteen years ago, Leroy had lived on a houseboat named after her. He kept it parked in Marina del Rey, enabling him to enjoy not only the beautiful scenery and climate but also plenty of fishing. Along with studying the Scriptures (Leroy had been a preacher for fifty years), it was his favorite pastime.

"Anybody home?" Sam called after parking and walking to the end of the dock. She thought she heard a groan, then aged, tan arms appeared on the railing. At seventy-six, Leroy Douglas looked and acted younger than he was. He had clearly passed on his casual nature to Jackson—Leroy wore jeans and a plain gray T-shirt. His hair was still mostly brown, but today it was hidden under a faded Los Angeles Dodgers baseball cap. Dark eyes peered out from under it to see who had called out. They settled on Sam but didn't immediately spark with familiarity.

"It's Sam," she said. "Jackson's friend."

"I recognize you," he said with a wave. "Come on up."

"Where do I get on?"

"Around back," he said. "Just watch your step."

Sam stepped through a swinging gate onto a back porch, then climbed a spiral staircase to the deck. Aside from a rarely used helm at the front and a picnic table under a canvas canopy in the middle, the second level of the houseboat was wide open. Leroy sat in an old-fashioned metal and vinyl lawn chair, a fishing pole resting between his knees and against the deck railing.

"How are you doing, Leroy?" Sam asked.

"Oh, can't complain. How about yourself?"

"Tired," Sam said in summary.

Leroy nodded at a second lawn chair off to the side. "Have a seat."

"Thank you."

"You want something to drink?"

"No, thanks," she said as she sat down. "You catch much here?" she asked, looking down into the channel.

"I have. Not today. But I'm too lazy to take her into some real water."

"I doubt that," she replied with a grin.

"So what brings you to my humble abode?"

34

"I was just wondering if you've seen or talked to Jackson lately."

Leroy removed his hat and scratched the side of his head. "Couple 'a days ago, I think. They kind of run together when you're my age." He set his hat back on his head. "Why do you ask? Something wrong?"

Sam shook her head. "No. I just haven't spoken to him in a while and I . . . It's a long story. Anyhow, he hasn't returned my calls and wasn't at home, and his neighbor hasn't seen him in a few days either. I thought maybe he was on a case or something."

"Not that I know of. He did take on this little case for a friend of mine Sunday. Not really a case even, by his standards."

"Do you know what it was?"

"My friend rotates around some of the nursing homes and assisted living places around the county, just talking, making connections, witnessing some. Anyhow, he ran into a woman named Phoebe whose grandson had called, asking for a lot of money. Or I should say, someone claiming to be her grandson had called. She was suspicious and said something to my friend. He promised to check it out, mentioned something to me, and I told him to give Jack a call. He's been slow since he got back from chasing treasure, and I figured it'd be good for him to help out a fellow old codger. More his line of work than my friend's anyhow."

"What'd he find?"

"Don't know. I haven't talked to him since Sunday. No, might have been Monday."

Sam looked down.

"Don't worry about Jackson," Leroy said. "He's tougher than old hayin' strings."

"Than what?"

Leroy grinned. "Never mind. I'm sure he's fine."

Sam nodded, but it lacked conviction.

"So tell me about your life, Sam. You still working in the ER?"

"I am," she said, and then proceeded to dump everything that was going on—except her uncertainty regarding her feelings for Jackson—on Leroy. The former preacher listened attentively, saying nothing while Sam poured out her soul. "And this isn't like me," she concluded. "This restlessness, this uneasiness . . . I can't explain it."

Leroy nodded slowly. He'd long since ignored his fishing pole, and his focus was solely on her. "You know, when Jackson tells me what's on his mind, he expects me to fix it all with a pithy line of homespun wisdom."

"From what I hear, you usually do. Not to put pressure on you."

"I say that because sometimes there aren't easy answers. Could be this is something you're going to have to wrestle with and sort through and figure out. Or it could just be a temporary reaction to having a lot of emotional issues on your plate—your mom, Stephanie, not to mention working in the ER and seeing all that. Jackson."

Sam frowned. "Jackson?"

Leroy smiled. "He'd throw me overboard if he knew I was saying something, but it's obvious there's something between the two of you. What that is . . ." He shrugged. "But there are other women in Jackson's life—not girlfriends, mind you. Don't get the wrong idea. Boy, he'd really clobber me if he heard me say all this. Point is, Samantha, you're the only one who's come here looking for him." He tipped his head to the side. "That tells me something."

Sam sighed.

"Try not to worry about it too much," Leroy said. "If God's tugging on you in some way, He'll make sure to let you know what He's doing. And if it's just emotion and stress, well, it won't do any good to worry about it."

"No, I suppose not." She took a deep breath and prepared to stand. "Thanks for the talk, Leroy."

"Anytime. If I hear from Jackson, I'll be sure to tell him to call you."

"Thanks." She stood and wished him good luck with the fishing.

"I could use it."

Sam turned to leave. "Say, Leroy?"

"Yeah?"

"You said the woman Jackson worked for was named Phoebe?"

He nodded. "That's right. You planning on doing some investigating?"

"I don't know. Maybe."

"She's at Peaceful Shores Assisted Living in Malibu. Sounds nice and swanky."

"Thanks, Leroy."

"Good to see you, Sam. Take care. And don't worry."

She nodded and smiled as she headed for the steps. As far as things went with her mom and the restlessness she was feeling, Leroy's talk had helped. But when it came to Jackson, she found herself even more uncertain. What about talking with a woman at a retirement home could possibly have led to him not answering his phone or returning home? Surely he hadn't run into any real trouble there, had he?

More than that, what did Sam make of Leroy's statement about there being something between her and Jackson? Had Jackson said something? Had Sam given something away? And why was it so obvious to Leroy when she couldn't even figure out what was going on herself?

As she drove home and began to prepare herself for another twelve-hour shift in the ER, Sam almost welcomed the chaos that was sure to ensue. It beat trying to figure out what was going on inside her.

Chapter Five

MAGGIE WAS ABOUT to lose her mind. She'd spent the entire day in her apartment for the first time since she'd gotten the flu about a year ago. She'd slept most of that day away. She had been painfully conscious for this one.

After breakfast (cereal, although she had thought better of it and rescued the waffle iron from the garbage), she had done a little online apartment browsing. It was hard because she had no idea where she would end up working. Or what she would even be doing. Commutes were terrible in L.A., and she didn't want to make it any worse. But maybe she had it backward. Maybe she should figure out where she wanted to live—by the ocean, closer to the desert and motorcycle paths, in a different state?—and look for a job there. Her search didn't get very far.

She also fine-tuned her résumé, although the way technology had evolved in recent years, maybe résumés were passé. Maybe now it was all done via LinkedIn and Twitter. Or were they passé too? It wasn't likely to matter because Maggie had no idea where to think about applying. Some small community weekly? Another major paper like the *Times*? McDonald's? Maggie was okay financially for a little while, but sooner than later she would need a steady source of income.

Which brought her back to apartment hunting. She didn't want to find the dream place without the job to afford it. It was a vicious circle, and she gave up before lunch.

The afternoon had really lagged. She thought a few times about cruising around on her motorcycle, but that had ended in a rather expensive ticket the night before. It had also led her to church, where she'd confided in Pastor Rick and Russell. He was praying for her—they both were, probably—but it hadn't helped yet. And she was still confused about how that all worked.

Jackson still wasn't answering his phone, and she had left him two more messages. The first had been after her third call to him of the day and at the most frustrating point of her afternoon, shortly after her neighbor had complained about Maggie's saxophone playing. She wasn't Kenny G, but it wasn't like she was the stereotypical kid tormenting his parents and siblings with flat notes and screeches either. She had called back an hour later to apologize to Jackson for being snippy, and also hoping he'd happen to answer. He hadn't. She couldn't remember a time when he'd been away from his phone for twenty-four straight hours, and it somewhat concerned her. Mostly, it just annoyed her. She needed someone to talk to.

The Rangers came on in the late afternoon on one of Maggie's soon-to-be-canceled cable packages, and they provided her a respite from the rest of life's problems. But it wasn't their day either, and they fell to the Flyers 4-1. Grumpy, hungry, bored, and getting angry, Maggie sat on her couch as darkness fell over Los Angeles and her apartment. The TV was still on, muted, on a rerun of *House*. Her saxophone leaned against a living room chair, and she had half a mind to blow her brains out on it. And her Bible sat on the coffee table. She'd flipped through it a few times that day, hoping to find something to guide her. But nothing had struck her particularly poignantly.

God, can You please—

Maggie's cell phone rang. She raised her head, sat up straight, then stood as it rang again. It was on the counter, and she scooped it up and checked the number in one motion. It wasn't Jackson. It wasn't even familiar. One of her utilities about to be cut off because of a missed payment? Maybe her motorcycle was being repossessed?

With a sigh, she answered the call. "Hello?"

"Maggie? It's Russell James."

"Hey," she said, her voice rising an octave halfway through the word as realization hit. "How did you get my number?"

"You filled out a connection card a couple of Sundays ago, and I abused my position as a pastor's kid to look it up."

"Is that so?" Maggie asked, the challenge in her voice friendly. She had paced to the window and saw in the reflection that she was smiling. But why?

"It is," Russell said. "After last night, I wanted to check in and see how you were doing."

"Really?"

"Well, it's not every Wednesday night a woman on a motorcycle rides up to church after having the worst day of her life."

"Thanks for reminding me."

"Sorry. But seriously, yeah, I just wanted to check and see if you were doing okay."

"That is very kind of you."

"Today any better?"

"Um, not really," Maggie said, the smile fading from her face. "I did some job and apartment hunting, got nowhere, and then sat around bored all afternoon. I don't know what to do with myself when I'm not working. And the Rangers lost."

"Sorry to hear about that."

"Are pastor's kids allowed to be smart alecks?"

"On occasion. Anyhow, if you need somebody to talk to, I'm here."

Maggie said nothing, thinking, looking at her reflection in the window. She couldn't believe she had poured herself out to a stranger for the second day in a row. But Russell didn't feel like a stranger. In fact, he was quite disarming.

"Maggie, you there?"

"Yeah. Yeah, I'm just . . . I'm trying to figure—"

"Figure out if I'm running game on you?"

"Yeah."

"I give you my word, Maggie, I don't work that fast. I don't work much at all, actually. I'm calling as a friend."

"Okay."

"And it's just a friend asking if you'd like to grab coffee, chat, just get out of the apartment. You can say no, and I won't be hurt. I'm just trying to help, and I have to admit I don't always know how."

"No," Maggie said.

"Fair enough. If—"

"I mean, no, you do know how. I would love to get out. I haven't eaten yet, so could we find a place that has more than coffee?"

"You pick," he said.

"Where do you live?"

"In the parsonage by the church," Russell said. "I'm above the garage, very Millennial."

"What about The Pizza Stone, on Westwood?" Maggie asked. "It's about halfway between us."

"I know it. Say eight?"

"Sure."

"I'll see you then, Maggie."

"Okay. Bye."

Maggie slowly lowered the phone, feeling butterflies in her stomach. She wasn't sure why they were there, since Russell wasn't anticipating this to be a date and she wasn't either. Then again, when two people got together to have dinner, what else could you call it?

It took her five minutes to change into something a little more presentable than sweatpants and an old T-shirt. Since this wasn't a date, she had no problem tying her hair back in a ponytail, especially since she would be cramming a motorcycle helmet on top of it. At twenty till, she left her apartment for the first time that day and headed down to the garage.

All the way to The Pizza Stone, her mind kept running, wondering why Russell really wanted to meet with her. She believed him that he wasn't coming on to her, but at the same time, his concern over her seemed a little over the top for having just met the day before. Could he have another angle? Was he one of Jackson's pals, setting her up for some reason? Was he playing the friend card to get to her? Or was he really just that sincerely interested in her wellbeing?

The Pizza Stone was an L.A. original, serving every imaginable type of pizza in just about every imaginable size, including by the slice. In addition to the best pizza around, it also had a laid-back, casual atmosphere—a vibe, really. By eight o'clock on a Thursday, the vibe was dying a little, but there were still plenty of people in tables in the middle of the restaurant or at booths around the edges.

There was no hostess at The Pizza Stone, so Maggie scanned the room, looking for Russell. She spotted him in a booth in the back corner at the same time he spotted her. She had to go down a few steps into the main seating area, then back up steps to the ring of booths. She slid in opposite Russell, then shrugged off her jacket.

"I like your shirt."

She looked down at the blue and white plaid shirt she was wearing, then up at him. His eyes gave nothing away as he extended a menu to her. Was it possible he was just being nice, just being real? She'd been in L.A. too long, she realized, and had come to be suspicious of authenticity.

"Thank you," she said as she took the menu. She scanned it for a moment, then lowered it.

"Yeah?" he asked.

"Thanks for meeting me. You were right. I needed to get out, talk to somebody."

"I've been where you are, so to speak. Not sure what to do, where to go, how to spend the next five minutes, much less next five days."

"Does it get better?"

Russell shrugged. "Depends."

"On?"

"If I knew that, I'd do whatever it depended on so as not to get into a dependent situation in the first place."

"And I thought I was a wordsmith."

He grinned. "But it's like I told you, God won't let you have more than you can handle."

"I guess that's something."

"So what looks good?"

"Are you actually hungry or just here for moral support?"

"I always have room for pizza."

"They have a great seafood pizza."

"Seafood?"

"Shrimp, scallops, crab."

"On pizza?"

Maggie nodded.

"I'll try almost anything once. Why not?"

They haggled over crust, then size, and whether they wanted a side. They settled on just pizza, and after they had ordered, Russell sat back. He was dressed in layers...a couple of shirts, a blue polo over a brown tee. Same necklace and bracelets as the night before. Maggie couldn't help thinking how he just looked incredibly comfortable.

"So what should we talk about?"

Maggie shrugged. "You called me."

"I did, I did. Your bio or mine?"

"Mine is somewhere in the in-between stages. How about yours?"

"Fair enough. I told you about my childhood, straying, coming back. And I think I mentioned I went to Northern Arizona . . . uh, the school not the region."

"Why NAU?"

"At the time, Dad was pastoring in Flagstaff. My brother was in the Marines, so I thought it would be better for Mom and Dad if I was around."

"What'd you major in?"

"Uncertainty. I only went for a year. College wasn't for me."

"So what'd you do? Europe? Missions trip?"

"Both, actually. And Nepal."

"Nepal?"

"I spent about three years traveling the world, going on various junkets."

"Finding yourself?"

"In a manner of speaking. More trying to figure out what God had for me. Missionary? Missionary nurse? Missionary pilot? Missionary support staff? Not a missionary at all? Living overseas? Living at home?"

"So how'd you end up in Santa Monica?"

"Dad took a job here. I still had nowhere to go, and at the time, the church was too small to afford any more pastoral staff but big enough that they had more work than Dad could handle. So I moved in with Mom and Dad to help out. I did odd jobs and temp work where I could to make ends meet. I'm still doing it sort of."

"The odd jobs?"

Russell nodded. "I still work at church some, but also with a lot of other organizations around the area. I do odds and ends, sometimes for pay, sometimes not. I told you I live at home, above the garage. We renovated it so it's my own place, but I still share some of the utilities and fees with Mom and Dad. Mooching, I think you call it."

"Sounds like you do plenty of good though."

Russell shrugged. "I'm still waiting, I feel. I mean, I can't just exist like this forever. But until God shows me what He has for me, at least I'm doing something."

"That's admirable."

He shrugged again.

"So is this work?" Maggie asked. She smiled. "Not a loaded question, by the way."

Russell returned the smile. "I'm not getting paid for it if that's what you mean, but I guess you could say in a way that it is. I like people. I like helping if I can. That's just the thing—most of what I do I don't really consider work."

Maggie nodded and sat back as the waiter brought out their sodas. He announced their pizza would be up in a few minutes.

"At least your life must not be dull," Maggie said.

"No, it's not. Yours? I mean, life before yesterday?"

"No. Not at all. I loved what I did. I felt it was what I was made for. Especially . . ." She fingered her straw. "Especially since coming back from Israel. I felt I had a higher purpose now. And now it's gone."

"No, not necessarily," Russell said. "Have you read about Joseph?"

"Coat of many colors, sold by his brothers?"

"Yeah. He went from being his father's favorite son to being sold as a slave to being treated well by his master to being accused of rape and thrown in prison to being the second in command in Egypt after only Pharaoh himself. A real roller coaster."

"Does it always work that way?"

"No. God doesn't seem to use cookie cutters. But we're told He never changes. And I like to think we have a lot of the Old Testament narrative for more than entertainment."

"Meaning?"

"Meaning, there are still principles, particularly about the nature of God, that apply to our circumstances today."

Maggie nodded. She took another drink.

"Tell me about Israel. You said the other night you went there to report on the search for crusader treasure?"

"You talked to your dad about me."

"I did."

"What happened to clergy confidentiality?"

"Don't be mad at him. I pried it out of him since I was planning on giving you a call."

"I'm not mad."

"Good."

Maggie stopped playing with her straw and pushed her glass away. She leaned her elbows on the table. "I was hired by a man named Joel Robinson. He wanted me to chronicle his team's search for a crusader-era treasure. I ran the idea past Walter, my editor. He okayed the trip, not knowing what I might find or end up writing, but confident since my junket to Mexico had panned out."

"Mexico?"

"I didn't tell you about that?"

Russell shook his head.

"Well, that's the next story, then. Anyhow, I went sort of as a freelancer, but with the *Times* having first dibs on whatever I found. When I got back, I gave Walter my story. He said it was great, but they couldn't publish it."

"Why not?"

"Too much personal account, not enough fact. Plus it made some pretty heavy accusations against a Frenchman who double-crossed us. The bigwigs at the *Times* were afraid of getting sued for libel and slander and who knows what else, so they quashed it."

"So you still have the story?"

She nodded.

"I mean, the rights to it?"

She nodded again.

"So what are you going to do with it?"

"I have no idea. At the *Times*, I had some contacts I could have gone through. Now . . ."

"Hmm."

"Yeah."

Their pizza arrived, and Russell said a quick prayer over the food. That one was still new for Maggie. She saw a lot of people pray before meals and thought it seemed like little more than a habit. But Russell, while simply thanking God for a meal and the finances to be able to eat, seemed quite sincere. Then again, everything about him did.

"What do you think?" she asked after they had each taken a slice and Russell had sampled his.

"Interesting. But not bad."

"I told you."

"You did." He took another bite, swallowed. "So, do I have to wait for you to find a publisher, or can I get the inside scoop now?"

Maggie grinned and launched into a detailed account of the trip to Israel, which had started as a trip to New York, then France, then Greece, and then the Middle East. They each downed two slices of seafood pizza while she told him the ins and outs of the search for crusader treasure. He had plenty of questions, and as had been the case while on the trip, Maggie didn't have a lot of answers. But he was fascinated.

Over a third slice, she told him about Mexico, her big break. It had lasted all of four months.

"But now your name is out there," he said, brushing crumbs from his crust onto his plate. "People know you. They'll be clamoring for your columns at the *Times*. If you land somewhere else, they'll know you."

"Yeah. If."

"I know," he said. "'If ifs and buts were candy and nuts, we'd all have a merry Christmas.'"

"What?"

He grinned as he reached for another slice. "Something my brother used to say."

"I'd always heard, 'if frogs had wings, they wouldn't have to drag their butts when they jumped.'"

Russell paused a moment. "No, I guess they wouldn't."

He took a bite, and a glob of sauce fell onto his wrist and one of the colored bracelets he wore. As he reached for a napkin, Maggie asked, "So what are those for?"

"These?" He grabbed the blue one. "This one's for a teenage boy from our church, hit by a hit-and-run driver last fall. On the way to a high school football game. The white one symbolizes purity, my commitment to remain a virgin until marriage."

Maggie swallowed, suddenly aware of past indiscretions. Jackson knew. Didn't approve, argued with her about it, but didn't seem to judge her. She wondered if Russell, the pastor's son, the guy whose life was wrapped up in ministry, would be the same.

"And the black one is a reminder of what I am without Christ. Sinful, rotten, black."

"Sort of a Johnny Cash 'man in black' sort of a deal?"

"Something like that."

"What about the purple one?"

"I'm a basketball fan. Born in Sacramento, moved to Arizona, now I live in L.A."

"Kings, Suns, and Lakers."

"All purple. Very good."

"That's deep."

"Yeah, well."

Maggie's lack of solid meals and lack of activity all day had caught up with her, and she reached for a fourth slice of pizza. She found herself comfortable around Russell. Some of it had to do with just needing someone to talk to. Some of it had to do with his assurance that he wasn't on the prowl. But most of it had to do with him. He was relaxed, easy-going. He made it easy to be the same.

They talked until almost ten o'clock, sharing more about their childhoods, spiritual journeys, future dreams. By the time Russell walked her to her motorcycle, Maggie felt as if she had known him for years instead of twenty-four hours.

"Thanks again," she said, reaching for her helmet.

"You're welcome. I'll be praying, Maggie. If you need to talk again, let me know."

"I'll do that."

He tipped his head, one eye closed. "There something else on your mind?"

"No. Well, sort of."

"You want to share?"

Maggie sighed. "I've told you about Jackson, about . . . how he was instrumental in me coming to Christ."

Russell nodded.

"After everything happened yesterday, I tried to get a hold of him. I needed somebody to talk to. He's not answering. And he still hasn't returned any calls."

A frown intruded upon Russell's normally positive face. "That unusual?"

"Jackson's a private investigator, so he has an odd schedule. But the fact that he isn't returning calls is a little disconcerting."

"Have you talked to any of his friends, checked hangouts?"

"No, not yet. I'm trying to convince myself I'm just panicking. But I can't shake the feeling that something's wrong."

Russell nodded. "I get that feeling a lot. It's usually wrong. I think it's the devil trying to mess with us."

Maggie nodded.

"But I'm not trying to minimalize your fears, either. I'll ask around."

"Ask around?"

"I have a lot of contacts who themselves have a lot of contacts."

She studied his eyes, but they didn't give away anything. Neither did he.

"In the meantime, Maggie, try not to worry."

"Yeah."

"I'll see you around?"

"Yeah," she said with more conviction. "Thanks again."

"Anytime."

She put on her helmet as he walked toward his Chevy Avalanche. How did a guy who traveled the world and then worked odd jobs afford what, by all appearances, was a new truck?

Maggie shrugged it off as she revved her bike, checked traffic, and whipped out into the street. As she rode home, all of her circumstances still swirled around her. But for the first time since leaving Walter's office the day before, she felt some of the weight off her shoulders. She remembered the prayer she had started as Russell called. She had been asking for help.

And just maybe God had answered her.

Chapter Six

NO LESS THAN seven African warlords stood in Agent Black's path. Armed with nothing but a knock-off Russian automatic weapon with a near-empty magazine and his throwaway gun—a nine mil with only nine rounds remaining—the odds were against him. But Agent Black wore a trademark sneer, unafraid, undaunted. Two bullets had already grazed him. A grenade had exploded just as he had dived for cover. Agent Black was undeterred.

With the automatic in hand, he sprinted right, firing three shots to his left before taking shelter behind an empty shipping container. Two of his targets fell. He checked his mag. Four bullets remaining. He spun around the container and fired two shots, then raced to the other end, and emptied the gun. Two more men fell.

Agent Black quickly unholstered his throwaway, racked the slide, and made a mad dash for the cover of a tree fifty feet right of the container. Bullets spat at his feet and sailed over his head. Agent Black somersaulted, popping from his roll to a standstill behind the tree. In seconds, he spun to either side, firing three shots from each. Two more warlords died.

Three bullets left. Agent Black waited. Almost a minute passed before the last warlord darted behind another tree. They took turns exchanging fire, and Agent Black's final bullet found its mark, plugging into the warlord's forehead. As he stepped from behind the tree, Agent Black blew over the top of his gun, then chucked the now useless weapon into the sand.

He made a 360-degree turn, surveying the carnage. In addition to the seven warlords who had united against him, Agent Black had taken down more than a hundred of their underlings. Not a bad day's work. Now, this small African nation could finally have peace.

A slug tore through Agent Black's shoulder, spinning him around. The damage was significant, but he was able to twist to the side and avoid a second, then a third shot, taking refuge behind a large boulder. After a quick check on his health, Agent Black peeked over the rock. One of the fallen warlords had risen and emptied his final three rounds. Now he stalked toward the boulder.

Despite the wound, Agent Black sneered again. He stood, shook his shoulder once, then charged. It was not a fair fight. With a few quick mixed martial arts moves, Agent Black broke several bones in the warlord's arms and legs, then snapped his neck. The warlord fell with a dry and dusty thud.

"Congratulations, Agent Black," a garbled voice said through the communication device in his ear. "The chopper is waiting for you at the rendezvous point."

"Copy that," Agent Black said, turning and leaving the bloodshed behind him. Another mission was completed.

Kyle Joshua Polinski—"Mouse" to his friends—pushed back from his desk, dropping his controller with a thud. He swiped a bottle of Mountain Dew off the desk and took a swig. This was not his best work. Three hits, including the major wound to the shoulder? He was better than that, although the game could be blamed for the last hit. He'd had no control over Agent Black when the fallen warlord had taken his first shot.

Mouse followed up the Dew with a handful of Cheetos, wiping his hands on his pants before reaching for his controller again. Agent Black had more work to do.

The front door opened, and Mouse could hear his sister Pam's bangles clanking as she entered the house. Soon the mixture of a dozen perfumes would waft down the hall to his room. She worked the cosmetics department at Kohl's and always brought the fumes home with her.

Most nights she merely hollered down the hall that she was home, then hollered again when dinner was ready. Hamburger Helper or something microwaved. Take-out if Mouse was lucky. Dinner always brought the usual complaints about his video gaming and questions about why he didn't work more. He'd learned over time to just let her rant; answering only prolonged the discussion and made things worse.

The clanging and the odor grew louder and stronger and, as Agent Black was getting dropped into his next third-world scenario, Pam peeked her head into Mouse's room.

Whereas he was thin and a little wiry, Pam was . . . well, not wiry. She wasn't fat, but whatever diet she was currently on wasn't any better than the last dozen. She had a fake tan and fake blond coloring in her otherwise brown hair. She dressed as if she weighed twenty-five pounds less than she did, today in a tight-floral blouse and black pants. And for some unusual reason, she was smiling.

"I'm getting married."

Mouse froze.

"Did you hear me?"

"M-married?"

"Y-yes," she mocked.

"To . . . to Clark?"

Pam made a face. Apparently, that was a stupid question. "No. His name is Gary. He runs a ranch in San Jacinto."

Mouse opened his mouth, but no words came out.

"We haven't set a date yet, but it will be soon. You should probably come."

Still nothing.

"Did you make dinner?"

"N-no. I just ate some—"

Pam cut him off with a huge sigh, then was gone. Mouse sat in a stupor for at least five minutes before the panic set in. He and Pam had shared their half of an old duplex in Culver City for over four years and had lived together since their mom died almost ten years ago. Now she would definitely move in with Gary. So where would Mouse live? He couldn't afford rent by himself. He'd have to get another job, which he wasn't qualified for, and the job market was terrible. And what a life— working all his waking hours just to pay rent. The only thing that would be worse was living with Pam and her husband. He'd end up mucking stalls on a ranch. He needed help.

Mouse rolled his chair over to the door and kicked it closed. Then he grabbed his phone and called Jackson. Not that he could do anything about it, but sometimes a guy needed a friend.

"This is Jackson Douglas. Leave me a message, and I'll get back to you when I can. Thanks."

"Jack, Mouse. I've got trouble, man. Pam just rolled in and tells me she's marrying some rancher named Gary. I think she's flipped. Last I know, she and Clark were back on. I don't know what I'm going to do. A rancher? Can you see Pam roping steers with this guy? This is a disaster, man. Call me."

Mouse dropped his phone and panicked for a few minutes. Then he realized his only rational strategy was to immerse himself in the world of Agent Black until Jackson or somebody gave him a clue on how to cope.

*   *   *

Friday, March 22
9:55 a.m.

HUMMING, THEN singing a little under his breath, then humming some more, Reggie Cameron tinkered under the sink in the women's bathroom of the restaurant he owned. Standing at his feet was Suzanne, the hostess. Her function was twofold. She made sure no customers would wander in and discover a six-foot-three, two hundred forty-five pound man lying under the sink, and she urged him to hurry up.

"I don't understand why you don't call a plumber anyhow," she said.

"I thought you wanted this done quick," Reggie said.

"I do."

"I'm here. And almost done." He resumed humming.

"We'll be getting the lunch crowd in an hour. We can't afford for this sink to be clogged."

Reggie sang a little, hummed some more.

"What is that?"

"Bob Marley." He felt behind him for the wrench and tightened the PVC fitting.

"Bob who?"

Reggie scooted forward far enough to make eye contact with Suzanne. She was in her twenties, whiter than snow, and not all there. But she was good at her job and had a pretty face. Suzanne hadn't been hired because of her looks, but as the first face customers saw when they arrived, her looks didn't hurt.

"Marley," Reggie said, slowly getting up. "He's sort of famous," he added with a groan. Reggie had played football in college and for a summer with the Chargers before getting cut. That had been years ago—a lifetime ago—but his body still punished him for the violence to which he'd subjected it over his career. Especially when he reached into cramped locations to unclog sinks.

He wiped his hand on a rag, then tossed it over the rim of his bucket. Still humming, he turned on the water full blast, letting it run for almost a minute before turning it off. No pooling, no clogs.

"What a relief," Suzanne said. "I just hope it lasts."

Still humming, Reggie picked up his bucket and tools and left the women's restroom.

"What song is that?" Suzanne asked, following him.

He was saved from telling her it was the somewhat fitting "No Woman, No Cry" by the ringing of his cell phone. He excused himself and pulled the phone from the pocket of his blue jeans. Owning a restaurant was not going to dictate his style of dress.

"Cameron."

"Reggie, it is Pan. I have a question for you."

"Shoot."

"The new Bacon Me Crazy Burger. Are you sure you want three strips of bacon both on top and beneath the hamburger?"

"Yes. Bacon on top, bacon underneath, bacon stuffed inside the patty, and bacon baked onto the bun. Bacon everywhere, Pan."

"You are sure?"

"Positive. We've done the sampling on this, man."

"All right. Thank you."

Reggie closed his phone with a sigh. Pan was a great chef, but he asked too many questions. Just cook, man, just cook. Reggie rubbed his massive head and turned back toward his office. There were some bills that needed paying and a couple of contracts to review and renew. This was the part of ownership Reggie hated—that and the questions.

He had debuted Cameron's six and a half years ago, with additional restaurants opening in Newport Beach and Mission Beach since. Reggie had no interest in turning his restaurant into a chain, and frankly, was wondering if he should take it in a different direction. The current format split the restaurant in two, with a casual, open to the beach dining area below and a more refined dining room on top. There was something for everyone at Cameron's, but Reggie wondered how long it could last without having something unique and special—something only Cameron's did or something Cameron's did better than everyone else. But those were worries for another day.

Reggie was ten minutes into his paperwork when his cell rang again. Suzanne. He resisted the urge to hum.

"We have a high school who wants to host their after-graduation party upstairs," she said.

"Okay."

"They have two hundred people."

"No."

"They were really quite persistent."

"If the weather's good, we can fit them downstairs, but we can't offer them privacy."

"They really want the upstairs."

Reggie sighed. "Fire code limits us to 156."

"I told them that."

"And?"

"They asked if we could make an exception."

"If they want to pay the fine. Answer's no, Suz. Blame the fire department."

"Okay," she said shrilly, as if he was making a grand mistake.

Reggie shook his head as he lowered his phone. Some days the business drove him nuts.

He spent another half hour on paperwork before taking a break. It was a beautiful spring day, so he slipped out the side door and took a short walk down the beach. That was the other draw to Cameron's—its doors were less than a hundred yards from the Pacific.

Reggie walked with hands in his pockets for a few minutes, then drew out his cell phone. Jackson didn't answer his call, and Reggie left him a message.

"Hey, J, me again. Just checkin' if you want to kick it later, man, maybe watch some Madness together. And we've got a new Bacon Me Crazy Burger. Right up your alley, man. Give me a call."

He clapped the phone shut. Jackson hadn't answered Wednesday, nor returned Reggie's call. That was unusual. Even when he was away on a case, Jackson usually kept in contact.

Turning back toward the restaurant, Reggie made another call.

"Hello?"

"Hey, Leroy. It's Reggie."

"How's the restaurant business?"

"It's been better, man. How are you doin'?"

"I'm managing. You looking for Jackson?"

Reggie grinned. "Yeah, man."

"I figured. Only reason anybody calls me. I haven't seen him since beginning of the week."

"You heard from him?"

"Nope. You?"

"No."

"Hmm," Leroy said. "Now you got me starting to wonder. One of his girlfriends stopped over the other day all anxious about his not being home. Now you. Maybe I should be worried too."

"I doubt it, Leroy. He's probably just in a video game-induced daze at Mouse's house."

"Who?"

"The hacker."

"Hacker?"

"The skinny kid who's a whiz on a computer. Anyhow, I'll check it out, man. Don't worry."

"All right. Let me know what you find out."

"Will do, Leroy. Take care."

"You too, Reggie."

Reggie again closed his phone as he reentered his office. Leroy and one of Jackson's girlfriends—Maggie or Sam?—were both concerned.

And given that, so was Reggie. He decided paperwork could wait and called Suzanne to let her know he was stepping out for a short time.

"Actually, there's someone here to see you."

Reggie frowned. He didn't have any appointments. "Who is it?" he asked.

"Her name is Olivia Williams. She said it's about a friend of yours, Jackson Douglas."

"What about him?" Reggie asked.

"She didn't say. Should I send her to your office?"

"No, I'm on my way up."

As he ended the call, Reggie's concern for his best friend was matched by a feeling in his gut that Olivia Williams didn't come bearing good news.

*   *   *

9:56 a.m.

MAGGIE HADN'T been able to fall asleep Thursday night, and with nothing to get up for on Friday, she slept till almost ten. She couldn't remember the last time—aside from jet lag, that was—she had slept so late. And she wished she hadn't.

She woke incredibly confused. Driving home from The Pizza Stone the night before, she had felt as if a weight had been lifted from her shoulders. But when she faced a second weekday with no job, an apartment she needed to vacate, and total uncertainty about what the rest of her life entailed, she realized the weights were still there. Russell had just provided her with a cortisone shot so she didn't feel the pain.

And Russell was the source of her greatest confusion. Last night had not been a date. In fact, it had specifically been declared not to be one. And yet, it felt like one. He'd paid for dinner; she'd let him. They'd talked, shared life stories, opened up to each other. Worse yet, Maggie realized she wouldn't have minded at all if it had been a date.

So why did that scare her? Was it because she felt some obligation to Jackson? Was it because she didn't like the idea of falling for somebody so quickly? Maggie had been fine going on dates without much thought and had even opened up physically rather quickly at times. But this was different. This felt like . . . chemistry.

She hated that word. She wasn't a hopeless romantic, didn't buy into the notion of love at first sight or soulmates or whatever. She preferred a casual relationship, no commitment, no expectations, no rush. And she didn't get nervous around guys, didn't start acting girly. So what exactly was it she was feeling? And why?

Maggie hashed through it all while she showered and dressed, and concluded she needed to talk to Jackson. He was her rock, the one who had led her to her new faith and had as many answers as anyone. And while it had always been casual, while there never had been any expectations, she did have something of a long-term relationship with him. It was so *Boy Meets World*, but she had to see him—somehow, it would make whatever was going on with Russell clearer.

So for that matter, would some fresh air. It was a glorious day, and Maggie began to think she was just in a fog. Her job, her apartment, sorting out her new faith, Jackson not being there for any of it, now a friend with whom—yes, she had to admit it—there was some chemistry. Maybe she should just get away for a few days.

Instead, after a somewhat leisurely breakfast of eggs, toast, and yogurt on the patio, she guided her motorcycle toward Pacific Palisades. Jackson had not answered his phone again that morning and had not returned any of her calls. Something was up, and before she got worried, she was going to make sure he wasn't holed up in front of his Xbox or obsessing over a busted NCAA tournament bracket or something stupid and neglecting his phone's dead battery.

The drive again allowed her to clear her head, and by the time she arrived at Jackson's house, she was starting to feel like her old self. That is until she got off her bike and walked up to the front door. What if he was there? What would she say to him? She was behaving like a TV junior-higher. Maybe she should just kiss him and see if sparks flew.

He didn't answer.

Maggie leaned over to peek in the window. The house was empty.

She jammed her hands into her pockets for a moment, thinking. Then she tried the front door and the garage door. Both locked. Sure that a nosy neighbor was about to call 9-1-1, she walked around the side of the house to the deck. It had been a while since she and Jackson had enjoyed a steak on a warm, breezy evening, and she missed it. One or the other of them had just been too busy. And now . . .

She rapped on the sliding glass doors leading to his dining room. She didn't expect an answer and didn't get one, so she put her face to the glass, shielding her eyes from the sun. The house looked pretty standard. No tipped over table and blood spatter, no food on the table or kitchen counter to suggest Jackson was just upstairs or in the bathroom. So where the heck was he?

"He isn't home."

Maggie stepped back and turned to her right, to the neighbor's deck. Connie, if she remembered from Jackson's rants. She stepped down off her deck, clad in brown capris and a flamboyant red and white striped shirt. She looked like a pirate first mate, right down to a slight limp and the drink in her right hand. Although Maggie doubted many pirates had used umbrellas in their rum.

"Haven't seen him since Monday," Connie continued, ambling across the lawn. Maggie saw no obvious signs, such as a cast or a brace, for the reason she favored her right leg. Maybe it was the extra weight and advancing years wearing on her knees?

Maggie left Jackson's deck and met Connie halfway. "Do you know where he is?"

Connie shook her head. "No. He doesn't exactly clear his travel schedule with me." She muttered something in another language, Italian it sounded like. "I wish he would. I don't get paid to be his secretary." She took a drink, then looked up. "Don't mind, I didn't mean you. It just seems every day there's another woman looking for Jackson. If he's going away, he should either tell them or me."

"Another woman?" Maggie asked, telling herself it was curiosity and not jealousy.

"Mm-hmm. Blond, pretty. She was worried about him . . . yesterday, I think it was. Apparently, he hasn't told anybody where he is."

"He didn't say anything about working a case?"

"No. In fact, he said things were slow. I don't know. He goes and on and on and I tend to let him ramble," she said, taking another drink. Maggie hid a smirk. Jackson said the same thing about Connie.

"Well, if you do see him, would you mind mentioning that Maggie's looking for him?"

"No, I don't mind. Maggie. You're the one he went to Paris with."

"Marseille, actually."

"France is France, dear." Connie winked her eyebrows. "I guess you rate pretty high."

"Rate?"

"I don't think he takes just anyone to France. Kind of buttoned down, actually."

"It wasn't a getaway," Maggie said. "We were on a case."

Connie touched her nose. "Whatever you say, dear. Say, you want a drink? Rude of me not to offer."

Maggie did want a drink, but she declined. She still wasn't sure where the occasional alcoholic drink fit into being a Christian, but she knew Jackson never touched the stuff. Until she figured out the what's and why's, she was at least avoiding rum before noon.

"Well, I'll have Jackson call you if I see him," Connie said.

"Thank you."

Maggie stood in place while Connie returned to her deck and a lawn chair. Maggie stared at the distant ocean for a minute, contemplating Connie's remarks. Who was Jackson's other woman, the pretty blonde? The same pretty blonde from church who'd been tending to him after he was shot? Maggie wasn't sure if she was more upset because she was jealous or because the blonde concerned about Jackson represented another reason Maggie should be too.

With a sigh, she turned around and trudged around the house. There was nothing more she could do here, which meant there was nothing more she could do. She was about to straddle her bike when a rumble drew her attention down the street. A black Hummer H3 charged down the road, slowed slightly, then careened into Jackson's driveway.

Chapter Seven

10:40 a.m.

THE WOMAN WAITING for Reggie at the front desk was tall and built like an athlete. Her skin was the color of cocoa, and bouncing curly hair made her appear even more than the six feet at which Reggie placed her. She wore knee-high, high-heeled boots over black pants and a loose, elbow-length pullover with wide red, white, and black diagonal stripes. Mascara darkened her eyes, and sparkling lip gloss drew attention to a smile that exuded something between enthusiasm and spunk. If Reggie could be so bold as to make such a judgment based on an initial once over.

"You must be Reggie," she said, stepping forward and extending a hand. A locket that was almost a medallion bounced at the end of a silver chain, hanging halfway between her neck and waist. "Olivia Williams. Thanks for taking time to see me."

She spoke with a mild, Caribbean accent. Hers was the voice that should be welcoming him to a resort hotel or enticing him to book a Bahamas cruise.

"My pleasure," he said, shaking her hand back. "It's nice to meet you, Olivia."

"I appreciate you are a busy man, so I won't take up much of your time. But is there somewhere we could speak?"

"This way," Reggie said, extending a hand to gesture down the stairs. Olivia's smile widened briefly as she strode by him, leaving a whiff of synthetic perfume in Reggie's nose as he followed her down the stairs. Instead of directing her to his office—which was currently a mess—he guided her into the downstairs dining room. The breakfast crowd was mostly gone, and it was too early for lunch, so only a few patrons speckled the twenty tables and booths. A few more sat at the U-shaped bar. On either side of it, massive sliding glass panels looked out at the beach, where a few more tables sat in the sand.

Reggie showed Olivia to a booth on the right side of the room, away from any other patrons. "Can I get you something to eat, drink?" he asked as she slid into the booth.

"No, thanks."

He nodded and sat down opposite her. "You told Suzanne this had something to do with Jackson?"

"I did," Olivia answered. She reached into a pocket and withdrew a small wallet, which she opened and set on the table between them. Reggie studied the credentials inside it as she spoke. "I work for the German BfV—the *Bundesamt für Verfassungsschutz*. That translates to the Federal Office for the Protection of the Constitution."

"Thanks. My German's a little rough."

"So is mine. I'm originally from Trinidad and Tobago, and although I'm a German citizen, I spend as much of my time abroad—mostly in the U.S.—as in Germany."

Reggie frowned. "Isn't the BfV a domestic agency?"

Olivia wrinkled her brow. "You know of it?"

"Just by what you said, Protection of the Constitution."

She nodded. "You're right, it is. But in this day and age, the line between foreign operations and domestic ones is blurred. I often liaise with the BND—our foreign intelligence agency—as well as agencies in the U.S., Canada, and throughout the Americas. And that's what brings me here today."

Olivia spoke fluidly and easily, not like a federal agent but like a woman having drinks with someone. Odd, Reggie thought, that his mind came up with such a comparison.

He slid the credentials back to Oliva, and she pocketed them. "About five years ago," she said, "we began tracking an ultra-right-wing group operating out of Munich: *Wolfskinder*."

"Wolf children?" Reggie asked.

She nodded. "They see themselves as disciples of Adolf Hitler— Adolf meaning, essentially, noble wolf."

"Neo-Nazis," Reggie said.

"Correct. You can understand why such a group would be on our radar."

He nodded.

"At first, they were little more than a public nuisance, hassling people, staging some demonstrations, spouting hate speech. They were issued a few citations but avoided any real trouble until 2010, when fringe elements of the group were linked to a series of car bombs in and around Munich. At that point, our focus intensified."

As she spoke, Reggie couldn't help noticing little things about Olivia—her narrow brown eyes, silky skin, and the way curls of her hair fell in a sort of controlled chaos. Reggie's wife had divorced him seven years ago, and the experience had soured him on women. Not that he didn't still notice them or find them attractive—such observations were always just theoretical instead of practical. But somehow, and he couldn't figure out why, his observations of Olivia seemed like an exception.

"We implanted a mole inside *Wolfskinder*," she continued, "which led to the discovery that the organization was much larger than we had realized, with cells throughout Germany and Europe. We also discovered they had plans to launch a series of attacks on prominent members of the Jewish community around the world."

"What, trying to reimplement the Third Reich or something?"

"Their goals were never so grandiose, at least not that we could detect. From the intel we gathered, it was clear that *Wolfskinder* understood their limitations, and their objectives fell within that scope."

"What kind of objectives?" Reggie said, curiously drawn into Olivia's story even if he didn't see the relevance to Jackson or her visiting him.

"An ethnic cleansing, of sorts. Their intent was to kill people of Jewish heritage around the world. Using guerrilla and terrorist tactics, they would inflict as many casualties as possible and also instill fear in other Jewish people that they might be next, given the apparent randomness and widespread nature of the attacks."

"To what end?"

"Sadly, decimating the Jewish race. They know they lost the war, and unlike so many similar groups over the years, *Wolfskinder* doesn't seem to have this overarching belief that they can somehow reignite a massive, global undertaking. They're terrorists, plain and simple, and they want to inflict as much death and terror as possible."

Reggie nodded. Then he shook his head. "That's all very interesting, but you did say there was a connection to Jackson."

"I did, and if you'll bear with me a few more minutes, I promise I'll get there."

He nodded.

Olivia continued. "As I mentioned, we had a mole in *Wolfskinder* for quite some time, but we had to pull her out recently. We feared her life was in danger, and she appeared to have uncovered as much as possible. They have done a remarkable job at keeping their activities covert, moving their bases of operation, keeping their information in silos, such that the German government hasn't been able to do more than nip at their edges. Furthermore, they've spread like a virus, similar to the way al-Qaeda has spun a web into dozens of countries on multiple continents under various names and faces."

"You're telling me this neo-Nazi group is like al-Qaeda?"

"Not in scale, but similar in design. The point is, we can't just raid a compound and be done with them. What we have done, however, is turn our attention to studying their methods and trying to uncover patterns—patterns that will show us how and why they think, which we hope will enable us to curtail their damage until we're able to find a way to infiltrate them once and for all. We don't want to go in less than fully organized, fail to apprehend them, and have them scatter and go even deeper underground. But at the same time, we don't want to let them operate and inflict any more casualties."

Reggie nodded, feeling like she was losing him. Not that he couldn't track with what she was saying, but he had no idea how this Caribbean-born German intelligence agent could possibly have any interest in Jackson—unless he'd accidentally ticked off some neo-Nazis while working a case or something.

"I told you I liaise with a lot of foreign agencies," Olivia said. "Primarily, of late, my role has been to share our intelligence *quid pro quo* with various other countries in an effort to stem *Wolfskinder's* movements.

Knowledge is power, and the more we have, the better we can protect innocent lives."

Reggie leaned forward. "I hate to be brusque, Olivia, but how is this tied to Jackson?"

She leaned forward on her elbows, rubbing her upper arms as if she was cold. In the process, she raised her sleeves a few inches, revealing a Band-Aid on the right arm, just above the elbow, and the bottom half of a tattoo on the left bicep. Reggie only got a brief glimpse of it, but it appeared to be a human face—a young human, if he was reading the ink properly. Reggie had several tattoos himself, remnants from a past life. Each of them had had meaning at the time, albeit not the deepest of meanings sometimes. He wondered what Olivia's tattoo signified. Something about it bugged him. He only saw the bottom half of the face, but it had looked familiar, and as concerned as he was about Jackson, he couldn't help but be distracted by trying to place that half a face.

"Are you aware of Jackson's ethnicity?" Olivia asked.

"Other than it's different than mine," Reggie said with a grin, "not really."

She nodded. "Jackson's mother, Hannah, was seventy-five-percent Jewish. Her father, Jackson's grandfather, Reuben Goldman, could trace his lineage back to the tribe of Benjamin."

Reggie leaned forward, suddenly disinterested in Olivia's tattoos. "Are you telling me you think Jackson is a target of these people?"

"We think it's possible," Olivia said. "We also think it's more than possible—it's highly likely—that the explosion that killed Jackson's parents and brother twenty-two months ago was not an accident."

Reggie sat back. "What?"

"The evidence is circumstantial, entirely, but it is strong, suggesting that *Wolfskinder* was behind the bombing at the restaurant in San Diego."

"Bombing." Reggie shook his head. "They never found a bomb."

"No, they didn't. My understanding is that the bomb blast was so intense . . ."

Reggie sighed and rubbed a hand over his head and face. He shook his head again. "Why? Why Jackson's family? Why him?"

"Remember *Wolfskinder's* goal, to kill people of Jewish heritage and terrify others. Hannah Douglas had no particular claim to fame, but her husband was a career Navy man, a member of Naval Intelligence—what they might call a high-value target. Jackson's brother was a member of LAPD, and his fiancée, who I understand was originally expected to be at the restaurant, is an up-and-coming attorney at one of Southern California's most prestigious firms. The collateral damage would have been—was—huge and incited a lot of terror."

Reggie sat back, trying to process Olivia's story. He couldn't believe it, and yet . . . it did make a strange sort of sense. The explosion had been ruled an accident, but Reggie knew that hadn't always sat well with Jackson. In truth, it had seemed a little dubious to him as well, but there hadn't been any evidence leading elsewhere. Until now.

"If their goal is to incite terror, how come they didn't claim responsibility?" he asked. "Islamic terrorists can't wait to tell the world when they strike. How does it incite terror if it's thought to be an accident?"

"That wasn't supposed to be the only attack," Olivia answered. "We've uncovered evidence of three more planned assassinations that were to occur at roughly the same time that weekend. One hired perpetrator apparently chickened out, one was foiled by a police raid, and the other we're not sure about, frankly. But the intent was to have four attacks carried out simultaneously, two here in California, one in Las Vegas, and one in Glendale, Arizona. All involving Jewish people who were prominent in the community, people who had military connections, and involving significant collateral damage."

Reggie exhaled again. "So you think since only one of four attacks went off, they decided not to claim responsibility and let it look like an accident?"

"That, or they never intended to claim responsibility. *Wolfskinder* has always tried to operate under the radar, and a 'good'—if you'll excuse the term—terrorist organization lets people foment their own terror. Think about it. If four attacks go off at the same time, all involving military personnel with Jewish ties, the talking heads at Fox and CNN—not to mention the average person on the street—will be able to link them together. It would be easy to recognize someone is targeting a certain segment of the population. What's more terrifying, knowing who they are and how they operate or being in the dark?"

This time, Reggie rubbed both hands over his face. He took a deep breath. "Okay, so why Jackson, why now? Trying to clean up a loose end?"

"In the last two years, Jackson's become something of a celebrity, at least in his line of work. Taking down the leader of the Grays gang, uncovering what was going on in Nevada and the corruption stretching from the CIA to a U.S. senator, his recent adventures in Europe and the Middle East. If I can speak candidly, Mr. Cameron, he's made himself something of a high-value target. And he is nearly one-half Jewish."

"He finds out they're responsible for his family's death, they'll be the ones with bullseyes on their backs."

"Our intel is iffy at best regarding Jackson being a target. It's a possibility, so I want to talk with him, to warn him, and to see if he's observed anything that matches or contradicts our intelligence by way of telling us if he is in danger or not. I also want to tell him what we know about the explosion and see if he knows any details that can help us catch the people responsible."

Reggie sighed, picturing Jackson hearing that news. He'd been touch-and-go much of the last two years, and Reggie wasn't sure how his friend would handle this revelation.

"That's why I came to you," Olivia said. "I haven't been able to get in touch with Jackson. I've called him several times and left unreturned messages, and I stopped by his house the other day and again this morning. From the intel I've gathered, you're the best friend he has. If anyone knows where he is, I thought it'd be you. Plus, given the nature of the news I have to tell him, I thought it might help having a friend present."

"I appreciate that," Reggie said. "And so will he. Truth is, I haven't heard from him in a couple of days either. I was actually just headed to his place now."

Olivia nodded. She reached into a pocket and withdrew a business card. "This has my office extension and e-mail, and my cell. If you find him, would you let me know right away? It's just as possible that he's not in any danger, but I'd feel better if we talk to him as quickly as possible."

"Of course. You'll do the same?"

"I will," she said with a warm smile.

Reggie extended a hand. "Thanks for your time, Olivia. I'm sure you didn't have to be this open and forthcoming."

"I should be thanking you. I get paid to be thorough."

They stood, and Reggie walked her up to the front entrance. For just a second as she waved goodbye, he felt something akin to a stirring in his gut, like something he hadn't felt in a very long time.

He squashed it and turned his focus to finding Jackson.

It took fifteen minutes to drive up the coast and slightly inland to Jackson's house in the Palisades. Maggie was standing at the curb beside her motorcycle as Reggie swept into the driveway, but there was no sign of Jackson. Reggie stomped on the brakes and was out of his Hummer before the turn of his key had killed the ignition.

"I take it you're here for the same reason I am," he said as Maggie returned her helmet to the handlebars of her motorcycle and started toward him.

"Then I take it you don't know where Jackson is either," she replied.

Reggie shook his head. "I haven't been able to get a hold of him for a few days, and Leroy said the two of you hadn't heard from him since early this week."

"Leroy?"

"Jackson's grandpa."

"Right." Maggie shook her head. "I didn't talk to Leroy."

"Well, then there's four of us looking for him. Popular man."

"I just talked to his neighbor," Maggie said, nodding over her shoulder. "She hasn't seen him since Monday. And I walked around the house but didn't see any signs that he's in there."

Reggie held up his keys. "Let's check it out."

"You have a key?"

"I thought somebody should have emergency access."

"Emergency, huh?"

"So to speak. Come on."

Reggie opened the front door and held it for Maggie. She stopped in the living room as he took a step toward the stairs. "J, you here, man?"

There was no answer.

"Wait here, all right?" Reggie said.

Maggie nodded.

"And just to be safe, don't touch nothing."

She nodded again.

Reggie took two minutes to peek into the garage—no Granada—and to check upstairs to make sure Jackson wasn't there and that nobody else was either. He was starting to get a bad feeling about things and felt caution was necessary.

"House is empty," he said as he lumbered back down the steps. "Here." He reached into his pocket and pulled out a set of latex gloves.

"You come prepared," Maggie said.

"I hope it's just a precaution, but if it turns out something happened to him, I don't want our prints confusing things." He snapped a pair of gloves onto his hands.

"So what are we looking for?"

"Anything," Reggie said. "I'll take the kitchen."

He swept his gaze through the living room as he walked to the dining room and kitchen. Nothing jumped out at him as being out of place. There were a few dishes by the sink—not uncommon. The refrigerator was stocked, the milk and a carton of orange juice still good. No papers lying around, no obvious clues to be found. The sliding glass doors were locked with no evidence that they had been forced. Checking the windows too, Reggie returned to the living room.

"Find anything?" he asked.

Maggie shook her head.

"When was the last time you talked to him?" Reggie asked.

"I saw him at church on Sunday."

"He didn't give any clue about where he might be going?"

"No. We didn't talk much. You?"

"Last weekend. He didn't say anything to me either."

"The house looks clean," Maggie said.

"That's a concern in and of itself."

"But his car was gone, right? That must mean he left on his own."

"Yeah, but didn't tell nobody. So why?"

"You think he's on another one of his . . . adventures?"

Reggie hesitated, wondering if he should tell Maggie what he'd learned from Olivia. He didn't see how it could help. It would only make her worry more, something neither of them needed. "I don't know," he said. "But I don't like it. You think after everything he's been through, J'd know not to go off the grid. Let's check upstairs."

Jackson had remodeled the upstairs of the house, turning two rooms into one big bedroom/office. He had a huge walk-in closet and a separate bathroom, and they split the two. The bed was made, as well as any man could make a bed, and there were no notes on his desk or anything to suggest a case he might be working on.

"Nothing's missing from the bathroom," Maggie reported as Reggie sat behind Jackson's desk, going through various drawers.

"I saw some clothes missing," he said. "Or didn't see, I guess."

"So he packed."

"Or threw them out. Or they're in the laundry, but I ain't digging through his dirty clothes. Not unless I see blood splattered on something."

"Still a dead end, then," Maggie said.

Reggie kicked a drawer shut. "You saw him Sunday?"

She nodded.

"And haven't talked to him since?"

"I've been leaving him messages for two days. He missed my birthday."

"Missed mine last year too."

"I kinda thought . . ."

He looked at her.

"I expected him to remember."

Reggie nodded. "Yeah, I would too." He sighed. "I'll check in with some other people, see if any of them know where he might have gone."

"You'll let me know if you hear anything?"

Reggie nodded.

They headed back downstairs and outside. "Are you worried?" Maggie asked as she got on her bike.

Reggie shook his head. "Nah. J's got a little John Wayne complex sometimes, but he's not stupid. I'm sure he's fine."

Maggie nodded, thanked Reggie, and got on her bike and rode away. Reggie watched her leave, hoping he'd convinced her more than he had convinced himself. He took out his phone, and as he got into his Hummer, he searched his contacts list for Sam's number. If Maggie hadn't been the one to talk to Leroy, it must have been Sam. Unless Jackson had a third "girlfriend." As he backed out of the driveway, he hoped Sam could shed some light on things.

Chapter Eight

11:50 a.m.

SAM DID NOT wake up to the warm sun streaming through the blinds. She awoke with the sheets twisted around her, a pillow half on top of her head, and a loud ringing in her ear. It took her a moment to figure out that she was awake and not dreaming and to identify the ringing. Her cell phone.

She rolled over and tried to get up, but she was twisted up in the sheets even worse. How had that happened? She slept peacefully, not tossing, turning, and thrashing. She flashed back to her dream—her and Jackson in a dark, abandoned hospital, dodging unseen pursuers. She didn't have nightmares, either. What was going on? Was this all because she was concerned about Jackson and her feelings for him? Was it related to the news that her mom had cancer? Was it the stress of a very hectic, twelve-hour shift in the ER? All of the above?

The phone was still ringing, and Sam had to resort to the verge of violence to get herself untangled and out of bed. Her phone was on the dresser, and she scooped it up somewhere between the fourth and fifth ring. "This is Sam."

"Sam. Reggie Cameron."

It took her a moment, still being in the morning fog. She was still sorting dream from reality, and images of a four-to-four shift at the hospital were coming back to her. It explained why she had slept until almost noon.

Reggie. The restaurant owner. Jackson's best friend. Good news or bad?

"Hi, Reggie."

"Hey. You happen to be looking for Jackson?"

She sat back on the edge of her bed. "Yeah."

"You visit his grandpa?"

"Yeah."

"Yeah, he mentioned Jackson's girlfriend stopping by."

"Girlfriend?"

"Leroy's words."

"Oh."

"I take it you haven't heard from J?"

"Um, no. Not since Sunday. No, that was the Sunday before. So it's been almost two weeks." She sighed. "I stopped by his place yesterday, and he wasn't there, and he hasn't returned any of my calls."

"Yeah, that seems to be a common refrain."

"Reggie, should I be worried?"

"No," he said, but after a short pause. "I'm just trying to put together a timeline to see when anybody last saw him."

"I talked to his neighbor, Connie, and she said she hadn't seen him since Monday."

"Same as Leroy. She say anything else?"

"No, I don't think so," Sam said, trying to remember. Thinking seemed to exacerbate a forming headache. "When I talked to Leroy, he said something about Jackson taking on a case at an assisted living home in Malibu. He didn't think it was anything, but I was going to swing by there today and ask around."

"You want somebody to go with you?"

She thought about it for a moment. "No. I'm sure it's nothing, and you've got things to do."

"All right. You hear anything, you let me know."

"I will."

"Don't worry, Sam. I'm sure he's all right."

"That's what Leroy said too."

"Smart man. Take care."

"You too."

Sam lowered the phone. Everyone said not to worry about Jackson, that he could take care of himself. But everyone, including Sam, seemed to be worrying about him. Remembering how she started every day, she got up to head into the living room to pray and read her Bible.

Then she would head to Malibu.

*   *   *

11:55 a.m.

MOUSE WOKE up to a pair of very irritating noises. One was the ringing of his phone. The other was shouting from Pam. Hearing her voice reminded him that she was getting married. To Gary, a cattle rancher from San Somewhere. He'd hoped that a night's sleep would make it all disappear. It hadn't.

"Kyle! Answer the stupid phone!"

Mouse rolled out of bed, landing on his knees on the floor. He reached for the phone by his bed and pushed it to his ear as he leaned his other ear against the bed. "Yeah?"

"Mouse. It's Reggie."

"Who?"

"Reggie Cameron. Jackson's friend."

Mouse blinked. "Yeah. What's up?"

"Jackson happen to be with you?"

"No. I don't think so. No."

"No or you don't think so?"

"No, man. I haven't seen him. I need to see him."

"When was the last time you talked to him?"

Mouse swallowed. It was hard. "Where, uh . . . I mean, when . . . what day is it?"

"Friday, man."

"Last weekend. We played some Xbox last Friday or Saturday night."

"He say anything about where he might be goin'?"

"No. I don't think so."

"You all right, man?"

Mouse hesitated. He and Reggie, while both pals with Jackson, weren't exactly best buds. Mostly because Reggie intimidated him. The guy was a former linebacker or something, a real dude. And Mouse hacked and video gamed. Skills were skills though. At any rate, Mouse wasn't keen on opening up to the big man.

"Yeah, I'm fine," he said. "Just let Jackson know I need to talk to him."

"You and the whole world, man. I'll let him know. Call me if you hear something."

"Yeah, sure."

Mouse dropped his phone.

"Who was that?" Pam asked, suddenly appearing in his doorway.

"Nobody."

She shook her head in disgust. "We're having dinner with Gary tonight."

"We who?"

"You and me."

"What?"

"You should meet him. Seven o'clock. He'll pick us up."

"Wha—"

"Try to have showered and brushed your teeth by then. And wear something respectable."

She turned without waiting for an answer. Mouse sat and stared at the floor. He wanted to cry. But he had learned long ago the hard way that crying wasn't the answer. So he did what he always did. He trudged into the kitchen, grabbed a can of Mountain Dew, and returned to his room to see how many baddies Agent Black could take down this time.

*   *   *

1:34 p.m.

AFTER HER morning-turned-afternoon devotions, Sam had showered and dressed, all the while praying for wisdom. She was scheduled to work a six p.m. to six a.m. shift at the hospital, which she had figured gave her time to run to Malibu and poke around a little. Just to be sure, she had brought her hospital scrubs along so she could change at the hospital if need be.

It was a brilliant, sunny afternoon, and Sam thoroughly enjoyed the drive west along the PCH. On her left, the sun glistened off the pristine blue waters of the Pacific, while the wilderness of the Santa Monica Mountains rose to her right. Sam loved getting away from the hectic, crowded mess of Los Angeles sprawl, and the drive through Malibu—though not devoid of it—always relaxed her.

Today was no different until she turned into the drive for Peaceful Shores Assisted Living Home.

What are you doing here, Sam? You're not a private investigator. You have no clue what to do.

That wasn't true. She had spent any free mental moments on her shift the night before plotting what questions to ask and to whom to ask them. Leroy had mentioned a woman named Phoebe, and Sam thought it was as good a place as possible to start.

She parked and got out. *Lord, please guide me through this. And wherever he is, please protect Jackson.*

The receptionist at the front desk was like looking in a mirror, only her hair was shorter. She smiled politely and asked how she could help Sam.

"I'd like to visit Phoebe if she's up for it."

"Your name?"

"Samantha MacRaney."

The receptionist made a few mouse clicks and looked at her computer monitor. "Are you related to Ms. Henderson?"

"No, I'm not. I'm actually a friend of a friend," Sam said, figuring that really didn't count as a lie. Yet, she felt a twinge of guilt. "Jackson Douglas, I believe he visited her earlier this week. I just had some questions for her about their visit."

The receptionist looked away for a minute. A thin smile formed on her lips, but it was quickly replaced by professionalism. "Yes, I remember Ja—Mr. Douglas. Let me see if Ms. Henderson is available."

"Thank you."

Sam waited for a couple of minutes. The receptionist returned with a smile. "She said she'd be happy to see you. Right this way."

Sam followed her down the hall and into a room with a view of the ocean. A very old woman wrapped up in a shawl sat in a chair by the window. The wrinkles on her face parted and her eyes beamed when she saw Sam enter the room.

"Ms. Phoebe, this is Samantha."

"Hello," Phoebe said in a high-pitched voice.

"Hello, Phoebe. Thank you for seeing me," Sam said with a nod at the departing receptionist.

"I'm happy to have a visitor. I spend most of my days staring out at the ocean."

Sam smiled and made small talk for a few minutes. She couldn't bear to make this a hit-and-run interrogation. The few minutes turned into a quarter of an hour as Phoebe told her about her children and grandchildren. Sam became somewhat confused as to the totals of each and speculated that Phoebe wasn't entirely sure either. Phoebe also asked Sam about her family, her life, her job. By the time Sam was finally able to steer the conversation to Jackson, she felt as if Phoebe was her great aunt or grandmother.

"I understand Jackson visited you earlier this week?" Sam said.

"Was it just this week? It seems like so much longer ago."

"How do you know Jackson?"

"I don't. Or I should say, I didn't. He came recommended from a friend."

"Recommended?"

Phoebe nodded and swallowed a lump. She seemed hesitant, and Sam didn't push. She just smiled.

"I needed help," Phoebe said at last. "I needed him to find my grandson. He's a . . . a private detective, I think you call it. Jackson, that is, not my grandson."

Sam sat up a little straighter. So Jackson had been on a case. A missing person case. That could explain things.

"I guess, I shouldn't say my grandson. I needed him to find someone who wasn't my grandson."

Sam frowned, but only for a moment. "I'm afraid I don't understand."

"I received a call, you see, from my grandson. Only it wasn't my grandson. But I thought he was. He needed money, and I was hesitant to send it to him. Not that I don't have money, mind you, but I've always been rather discreet with it. My late husband Bernard had a very good job and left me quite a sum. Not that I'm not generous with it, mind you, but I didn't want to send it to Trevor if it wasn't really him."

"Trevor's your grandson?"

"Yes. What a nice boy. He just got back from Pakistan."

"Pakistan?"

"Yes," Phoebe said with a smile. "He's in the Marine Corps."

"You must be very proud."

"I sure am."

"Did Jackson find this other person?"

"Which person?"

"The one who wasn't your grandson."

"No. He found Trevor. In Pakistan."

"Jackson went to Pakistan?"

Phoebe furrowed her brow. "I can't say. I don't think so. He was only gone a day."

Sam frowned again. Phoebe was raising more questions than she was answering. Sam didn't have long to ponder them because her phone rang. She excused herself and pulled it out to check the caller. Stephanie Kane.

"Phoebe, will you excuse me? I need to take this call."

"Of course, of course. I'm not going anywhere."

Sam stepped out into the hallway. "This is Sam."

"Sam, it's Stephanie!"

Sam's heart pounded. Was it Brady? Had he done something to her?

"The baby's coming," Stephanie said. "Brady's at work and I can't get a hold of him, and I don't know what to do."

"How far apart are your contractions?" Sam asked.

"About five minutes."

"Okay. I'm in Malibu. I'm coming right now. If they get closer than four minutes, call 9-1-1."

"Okay. Thank you, Sam."

"Of course. Have you called your doctor?"

"No. I'll do that."

"Okay. I'll be there as soon as I can. Just stay calm, keep breathing."

"I will. We're packed and ready. Thank you, Sam."

"You're welcome."

She lowered her phone and returned to break it to Phoebe that she had to leave. The old woman was disappointed but seemed to understand. "Go," she said. "I hope it's a baby girl."

A dozen thoughts swirled through Sam's head as she hurried back to her car. She silenced them by praying for Stephanie. She prayed for a level head (for both of them) and for a healthy baby. As she backed out of her parking spot, Sam did something she never did. She retrieved her cell phone and made a call while driving.

Actually, four of them before she found a nurse who was willing to switch shifts. She swapped her six o'clock to six o'clock for a midnight to noon. That would give her plenty of time to get Stephanie to the hospital, settled, and quite possibly, to get a baby delivered. By then Brady would hopefully be there. If not, Sam could arrange something else.

With that settled, she dropped her phone on the passenger seat and turned all of her attention to driving to Stephanie's house.

Chapter Nine

3:13 p.m.

THE DINNER RUSH at Cameron's started anywhere between four and six, depending on the day. The lunch rush ended sometime between one and two. That left anywhere from two to five hours to get things straightened up and squared away. On bad days, there was no lull at all. Fridays were usually bad days as folks kicked off the weekend throughout the afternoon, keeping the stream of customers coming through the doors steady. Reggie was a hands-on owner, balancing his time between the kitchen and the floor, sometimes cooking, occasionally waiting and serving, but more often just glad-handing. Most Fridays, he didn't take a break from ten a.m. until ten p.m. But this was not most Fridays.

Pulling himself away from more questions from Pan, Reggie holed up in his office to check voicemails. He had none, which meant nobody else had made any progress searching for Jackson either. Or they just hadn't taken the time to call him. He decided to be proactive.

His first call went to Sam, and he was about to give up when she blurted a, "Hello?"

"Sam, it's Reggie. You okay?"

"I'm fine."

"But?"

"I'm driving Stephanie to the hospital right now. She's going into labor."

"Everything all right?"

"Yeah, she's doing great."

"Okay, I'll let you go."

"Reggie?"

"Yeah."

"I went out to the assisted living home and spoke with a woman named Phoebe. She was somewhat confused, but she said she had hired Jackson to find her grandson. His name was Trevor, and he'd just been in Pakistan."

"Pakistan?"

"She said he was in the Marines. I asked if Jackson had gone to Pakistan and she didn't think so. But she was confused several times."

Reggie furrowed his brow. "She say anything else?"

"No, nothing that seemed relevant."

"I'll check it out, Sam. What's the name of this place?"

"Peaceful Shores Assisted Living in Malibu."

"Okay, Sam. Don't worry. Focus on Stephanie."

"Will do. Call me if you find anything."

"I will."

Reggie closed his phone, still frowning. How had Jackson gotten involved with a Marine in Pakistan? Or had he? Before she died, Reggie's grandma had lost her marbles, mixing current events with fifty-year-old history to tell some fantastic tales. Was Phoebe doing the same?

Reggie called Maggie next, but she hadn't heard anything. He didn't tell her about Phoebe. No need getting her worried until he could confirm something. Mouse had known nothing the last time, and unless Reggie needed something hacked, didn't think the kid could offer much in the way of tracking down Jackson. Plus he'd seemed unusually rattled.

That left Olivia, who hadn't returned an earlier call as of yet. Reggie decided not to hassle a foreign operative. She'd said she'd call if she learned anything, so he assumed she hadn't. And, so far, neither had he.

After spending five minutes checking out addresses on his computer, Reggie headed for the hostess desk. A pretty blonde named Katie smiled when she saw him. She had been with Cameron's since the beginning and had a good head on her shoulders. One of these days, she was going to move on to something bigger and better, and Reggie would be forced to replace her. Until then, he maximized having someone as qualified as she was.

"How's it going, Reggie?" she asked.

"All right, K. You?"

"I'm good."

Reggie nodded. "I'm headed out to run a few errands," he said. "You're in charge."

"Okay. You know when you'll be back?"

He shook his head. "If Pan has any questions, just tell him the more bacon, the better."

"You got it."

With another nod, Reggie pushed through the door. He took a deep breath of perfect SoCal beach air. The sun, the sky, the beach—normally they filled Reggie with an upbeat vibe. But today, it couldn't penetrate the overbearing sense that there was something wrong.

Reggie had known this day was coming when Jackson told him he was going to be a private investigator. Jackson had assured him it wasn't like TV, where the P.I.s got into high-speed chases and shootouts every week. A real-life private investigator's life was pretty mundane. Even so, Reggie had feared it was going to catch up with Jackson someday.

And to be honest, this day had come several times. Jackson's thirtieth birthday, where he'd gotten into it with a pair of L.A. gangs. Nevada. Mexico. The stalker who'd shot him on New Year's Eve. And he'd survived them all, at least physically. But it couldn't last forever, could it? One day, he wouldn't be quick enough, wouldn't be lucky enough. And for some reason, Reggie had a feeling this was that day. He wasn't sure why. He didn't believe in sixth senses or clairvoyance or anything like that. But he also couldn't deny the feeling in his gut that usually wasn't there.

Then again, there was also a feeling in his gut that wasn't usually there whenever he thought of Olivia. Maybe Jackson wasn't in trouble, and he wasn't attracted to the Caribbean-German agent—maybe he'd just eaten something bad or was coming down with a virus.

As he tore out of the lot, Reggie cranked the volume on the Bob Marley CD in the player. Bob told him not to worry. Bob told him everything was going to be all right. Bob had spent his days burning tree, so what did Bob know?

Reggie's first stop was off Malibu Colony Drive. Three months after the death of his family, Jackson had been busted for dealing marijuana. He'd been cleared of the dealing charges, a wrong place at the wrong time scenario. But the wrong place had been smoking a joint with some coworkers, an admitted mistake, one born out of extreme grief and pain that wouldn't go away. Jackson had come a long way since, and his one failure had been just that. But the consequences of his actions had included a mandatory monthly meeting with a psychiatrist. Reggie couldn't remember if Jackson usually went on the third or fourth Tuesday of the month, so he wasn't sure if Jackson had just gone or was due. He'd never met Jackson's therapist and was pretty sure he wouldn't get the time of day from him, but it was worth a try.

Furman T. Zachary operated out of an office beneath his house. The building was on a thin strip of land between the Pacific and the Malibu Lagoon, packed between other similar buildings. Half of them had private tennis courts and swimming pools. Zachary's had a perky receptionist named Alaina, who said that Dr. Zachary was with a client and didn't take walk-ins.

"It's something of an emergency," Reggie said. "When his current session is finished, could you ask him if he could spare five minutes with a friend of Jackson Douglas. I'll wait quietly, and if he says no, I'll leave."

Alaina didn't seem to like this, but she nodded. "Fine. You can have a seat."

Reggie sat and waited, observing but not returning half a dozen furtive glances from Alaina. At precisely three-thirty, a woman who looked like a runway model ten years after her career had ended emerged from the office. She spent a moment confirming her next appointment with Alaina before striding out the door without acknowledging Reggie. Also ignoring him, Alaina entered Zachary's office. She returned a minute later.

"You can go in," she said with a conciliatory sigh. Reggie thanked her and entered the office. It was pretty standard, a pair of chairs to the left, a couch to the right, and a glider straight ahead of him in front of windows that looked out at the lagoon and the mountains beyond it. Idyllic.

"Alaina didn't give me your name," a deep voice called from Reggie's right. He turned to see a thin, very tall, oddly dressed man standing behind a desk. He had black hair slicked into a ponytail, a matching goatee, and a hawk-like nose and wide brown eyes that seemed to peer downward at Reggie, even though he and the doctor stood the same height. He wore corduroy pants and what appeared to be a corduroy vest over a short-sleeved dress shirt. In his right hand, he held a pad of paper; in his left, a bottle of Kaopectate. He did not convey the sense of professional austerity Reggie had expected, but then again, this was California.

"Reggie Cameron," he said, offering a hand.

"Furman Zachary," the doctor said, dropping the notepad and shaking Reggie's hand. "Call me Zach."

"Zach, I appreciate your giving me a few minutes. I'll get right to it. Jackson's mentioned your name to me, has told me a little bit about your sessions. He won't admit it in so many words, but I know you've helped him."

Zachary waved a finger. "No. He's helping himself. I'm just facilitating."

"Fair enough. Anyhow, J's been missing for a few days. None of his friends know where he is or where he might have gone. I know you all have doctor-client privilege and all that, but I'm covering all bases. Is there anything he's told you that might indicate where he could have gone or what he could be up to?"

Zachary slowly licked his lips. Then he set down the Kaopectate. "The last time I saw Jackson was the week after his return from Israel. He briefed me on his adventures, and from what I gathered, he added to his list of enemies."

Reggie nodded.

"Could it be something related to that?"

"Could be anything," Reggie said. He filled Zachary in on a few more details.

"We were scheduled to meet the third Tuesday of the month, but he was overseas last month, and I had a time slot open on the first Tuesday of this month, and we agreed to make the switch permanent. So I haven't spoken to him since and am not scheduled to for another week and a half. But when we did talk, he didn't mention any upcoming cases or trips." The doctor shook his head. "I'm not being coy, Mr. Cameron; there isn't anything I can think of that might help you."

Reggie nodded again. "He say anything about Pakistan ever?"

"Pakistan?" Zachary traced his eyebrow with his index finger. "No, not that I recall. I'm sorry."

"No, I appreciate your time." Reggie handed the doctor a Cameron's business card. "If you should happen to hear from him or think of anything, would you call me at this number?"

Zachary nodded.

"Thank you, Doc," Reggie said, and they shook hands again.

"Oh, Mr. Cameron?"

Reggie stopped at the door.

"Have you called the police?" Zachary asked.

"No, not yet."

"May I ask why not?"

Reggie shrugged. "I guess it hasn't gotten to that yet. Right now, we're all just a little nervous."

Zachary nodded, holding up the business card. "I'll call if I hear from him, but I don't expect to until the second."

"Thanks, Doc."

Reggie thanked Alaina on the way out as well, and as he got into his Hummer, he pondered his words to Dr. Zachary. It hadn't gotten to that yet. They were all just nervous. On the surface, maybe so. But down inside, Reggie was more than a little nervous.

Dr. Zachary had been unable to help, other than to add to the list of people who had no idea where Jackson was. It confirmed that something had happened to him. Jackson wouldn't go dark without letting someone know. Not Reggie, not Leroy, not Mouse, not Maggie nor Sam, not his therapist. Not even a note on his dining room table. Reggie couldn't think of anyone else Jackson would confide in, and as he turned into the parking lot at Peaceful Shores Assisted Living, he hoped someone there could shed light on things.

The receptionist greeted him with a smile, one that seemed sincere in comparison to Alaina's. But when Reggie asked if he could visit with Phoebe, she frowned.

"I'm afraid Ms. Henderson is unavailable at the moment. Can I ask the nature of your visit?"

"She's sort of a friend of a friend."

The frown intensified.

"Is something wrong?" Reggie asked.

"You're the second person who's asked to see Ms. Henderson today, both claiming to be a friend of a friend."

"Was the previous visitor a good-looking blonde, about so high?" he asked, holding up his hand as a measuring rod.

The receptionist nodded.

"We're both looking for a missing friend, Jackson Douglas. It's my understanding he met with Phoebe shortly before disappearing, and I just wanted to see if she knew anything that might be helpful."

"Mr. . . . ?"

"Cameron."

"Mr. Cameron, I'm afraid Ms. Henderson is suffering from the onset of Alzheimer's Disease. I'm not sure she would be terribly helpful. And like I said, she is unavailable right now."

Reggie nodded. "I see."

"However, Jackson did see another resident while he was here."

"Oh?"

"Yes." She looked around. "I probably shouldn't tell you this, but . . . his name was Wilbur Anderson, and he's been missing since Wednesday morning."

"And Jackson visited him before he disappeared?"

"Yes. Tuesday afternoon. I know because Mr. Anderson asked me to ask Jackson if he could spare a minute to talk with him."

"And he did?"

"Yes. He spent the better part of the evening with Mr. Anderson. He even dined here with him."

Reggie rubbed the top of his head. No one else had seen Jackson since Monday, but he'd been here as late as Tuesday afternoon. That was somewhat consoling as it lessened the length of time Jackson had been missing. But it also added some unusual—to say the least—circumstances to his disappearance. And what could this possibly have to do with the neo-Nazi terrorist group Olivia had mentioned?

"Do you have any idea why Mr. Anderson wanted to talk to Jackson?"

The receptionist shook her head. "No. We notified the police Wednesday morning about his disappearance, but they have no leads."

"Do they know Jackson visited with him?"

"I'm not sure."

Reggie nodded. "What else can you tell me about Wilbur Anderson?"

"I'm afraid I'm not allowed to release resident information. I've really said more than I should already."

"I appreciate it very much," Reggie said. He winked. "Our secret. Thank you."

The receptionist nodded, and Reggie headed back outside. He stood for a moment, the warm sun beating down on him. Jackson had visited Wilbur Anderson Tuesday afternoon, and neither of them had been seen since. That couldn't be a coincidence.

But what did it mean?

Chapter Ten

4:14 p.m.

MAGGIE HAD NEARLY gone stir crazy. She'd come home after searching Jackson's house with Reggie and paced until there was a hole in the floor. She knew she should be job hunting or apartment searching, but she couldn't bring herself to do either. Jackson hadn't left her mind all day, and she wasn't sure if that was because he was missing or because Russell was also on her mind. She really needed work, something to throw her energy and her attention into. But she had nothing.

So after an afternoon of puttering around the apartment and feeling the walls closing in, Maggie had decided to go for a ride. After filling up with gas, she'd headed west to the coast, then along the PCH north and west toward Malibu.

The sun had been warm and bright and the view terrific, and Maggie had toyed with the idea of riding all the way up the coast. She'd always wanted to get on her bike someday and just go, no plans, no destination, no clue where the open road would lead. This made a good time. No job to hold her down, no one who would worry when she disappeared. Maybe that's what Jackson had done. Maybe he'd just hit the road, bumming across the back roads in his Granada, the open air rushing in through the windows.

Why not? Maggie had thought. She would just get away. Worry about her apartment and her lack of a job and Jackson and Russell some other time. The further she'd driven, the more she had warmed to the idea. She could buy what she needed along the way, live off her credit card for a little while. And who knew, maybe a weekend getaway would clear her mind.

She stopped at a gas station in Oxnard to stretch and use the bathroom, and while she wandered around looking for something to munch on, she toyed with the idea some more. It was really appealing, but something inside of her told her it wouldn't solve her problems. She still wouldn't have a job. She still wouldn't have a place to live. And she still wouldn't know what to think about Jackson and Russell.

Russell? Why was there anything to think about him at all? He was a friendly guy who'd lent her a listening ear and a few hours of conversation to take her mind off her problems, nothing more. Well, offers to pray too, but she gathered that might be a given with pastors' kids. So why had he been on her mind all day too? Popping her helmet back onto her head, Maggie concluded her emotional and mental faculties were out of whack, a result of stress. Nothing a good ride couldn't fix.

A spontaneous trip to Vancouver was out due to prudence, but that didn't mean Maggie had to go straight home. She got back on her bike and headed east on the 101, along the north side of the Santa Monica Mountains. She crossed The Valley and cut through Newhall Pass to the northern side of the San Gabriels. After topping off the gas tank in Palmdale, she continued east through the desert. Less than thirty miles from downtown L.A., she might as well have been three hundred.

By now, it was late in the afternoon, and the sun cast a long shadow as Maggie cruised along a lone ribbon of highway, flanked by an unending row of telephone poles on her right. The mountains to the south were purple with a few hints of yellow and orange where the sun caught a slope. Everything else was a shade of tan—the sand, scrub, the few buildings scattered along the road, and the haze on the eastern horizon. Maggie was again enticed, this time to speed across the desert to Vegas, daring the cops to catch her.

Instead, she tried to sort her thoughts.

She and Jackson were technically just friends, but it was clear they were more than that. They may not have categorized their relationship as a relationship, may not have followed the typical rules of dating, but there was something there. Why else had Maggie not formed a serious relationship with any other man for the last . . . however long it had been? She couldn't even remember.

So that again raised the question, did Maggie owe Jackson something before she had feelings for another guy? A chance at rebuttal, to win her feelings back? Or did the fact she had feelings indicate that Jackson didn't deserve a rebuttal?

Under her helmet, Maggie shook her head. This was all way too premature. It wasn't as if Russell had asked her out. She wasn't even sure she had feelings for him, besides an initial flutter.

So what was going on inside of her?

God, I don't know why I'm suddenly back in junior high. Can you sort this all out for me? Make it make sense? Get me out of my head?

Maggie accelerated and focused on the scenery around her. It was her favorite time of day, the so-called golden hour, and being out in the open gave her a sense of peace. It always had. Somehow, no matter what was going on around her—or inside of her—getting out under the wild blue skies seemed to take the edge off.

*   *   *

7:00 p.m.

OLIVIA WAS right on time.

She and Reggie had played phone tag throughout the late afternoon before finally reaching each other. The Bacon Me Crazy Burger was proving to be popular, but not so popular that Reggie's qualified staff couldn't handle things without him. So he'd agreed to Olivia's invitation to meet for dinner and compare notes. She'd chosen Elizabeth's, a Santa Monica original known for its old-fashioned, home-cooked meals. Reggie had been there a few times, appraising the competition.

Olivia had changed into a knee-length black dress, a combination between fun and formal, and Reggie felt underdressed until she explained that she had just come from having drinks at the Chestnut Club with a Department of Defense analyst. They had been comparing notes, she said as they settled into a curved booth at Elizabeth's. Dim overhead lighting, flickering candle centerpieces, dark paneling on the walls—this felt like the place Jackson should be hanging out with a client/girlfriend while emulating a '70s or '80s detective, Reggie thought. Jackson brought both a smile to his face and a nervous twinge to his stomach.

"You've got a lot of connections," he said at the mention of the DOD analyst.

"When you've been in the business this long . . ." Olivia said.

He turned a cockeyed glance at her. "You must have started young."

"My family immigrated to Germany when I was twelve," she said. "My father was an investment banker with a prestigious firm in Berlin. I was always a student of history and government, and as we fell in love with Germany, that all blossomed into a desire to serve my new country. I became a citizen the day I turned eighteen, and enrolled at TU Berlin. At twenty-two, I joined the BfV and haven't looked back."

"Still, at the risk of being indelicate or coming across as overly flattering, that still can't be that much experience."

"Quality over quantity," she said.

A waiter stopped by with menus, and they took a few minutes to peruse them and order before getting down to business.

"I spent the first half of my afternoon analyzing data," Olivia said. "There's a reason I didn't become an analyst. Fortunately, I know someone—" She winked at Reggie. "—with your NSA who was able to put me in touch with one of their analysts, and together we crunched the data of all known or suspected *Wolfskinder* attacks in the last two and a half years."

"Looking for patterns."

"Right." She shook her head. "We didn't find much of anything. We've tracked them across Europe and to a small degree into the Americas, and even into Australia and Northern Africa. I analyzed known *WK* attacks separately, suspected *WK* attacks separately, both of them together, just those occurring in the Western Hemisphere, just those in America or involving Americans, just those involving military personnel or families . . ." She sighed. "There just isn't any consistent pattern that would tell us if they are or aren't targeting Jackson. Or why or how."

"Not enough intel and data to form a trend yet?"

"That and they've done a really good job of varying their targets and methods. Israeli citizens, people of Jewish heritage, family members, people who are influential in a variety of ways. They've used bombs, sniper attacks, car 'accidents,' supposed heart attacks. That makes it very hard to sort the data, and also is one of the reasons they've remained so secretive. It's hard to prove a car accident is something more sinister, and even then, it's not always easy to see who's behind it. Especially since we have reason to believe *WK* has started employing non-members to do their dirty work."

Reggie sighed. "So basically, you crapped out?"

"Basically." She reached for the straw in her ice water. "I made a lot of phone calls over the last few hours and had the aforementioned meeting with a contact at the DOD, but it's yet to turn up anything."

"I haven't made much headway either," Reggie said, and recapped his afternoon talks with Dr. Zachary and the receptionist at Peaceful Shores, as well as his visit to Jackson's house.

"You have a key?"

"Yeah."

"And you didn't find anything?"

"No. Place looked like it always does."

"You said his car was gone?"

Reggie nodded.

"Well, that would suggest he left voluntarily, at least. Any idea where he might have gone?"

"None. J's not the type to up and leave town without letting someone know. Me, his grandpa, one of a number of women."

"He play the field?"

"So to speak. It's all casual, almost a game to him."

"You disapprove?"

"I think he's going to get burned if he's not careful."

Salads came, and they dressed them and, in Olivia's case, cast aside the cucumbers.

"What if he's working a case?" she asked.

"Crossed my mind. But he would have let me know if he was going to be gone awhile."

"What if he didn't know? What if it came up suddenly, and he couldn't get to a phone?"

"I suppose it's possible."

She stabbed some greens. "You know anything about this Wilbur Anderson?"

"No. I may have a source on that though," he said, a thought hitting him.

"I'll see if I can run him through some government databases. The name doesn't sound Jewish at all, but who knows what the connection may be."

As they ate their salads, they threw out more theories and conjecture, repeatedly admitting that they just didn't have any way of knowing what was or wasn't true. Over entrées, conversation bounced from various adventures of Jackson's—which Reggie told in part on the off chance they could be relevant, in part to brag on his best friend, and in part to bring a much-needed smile to his face—to Olivia's unclassified experiences as a German intelligence agent and her life growing up in Trinidad and Tobago.

"So it's two islands?" Reggie asked.

Olivia nodded. "And several small satellite islands as well."

"So which are you from, Trinidad or Tobago?"

"Trinidad, like almost everyone. It consists of ninety-percent of the country's landmass."

"I have to admit I know nothing about it except for hearing it mentioned every four years during an Olympic track and field event."

"You're probably thinking of Ato Boldon. He's a four-time Olympic medalist, now a broadcaster with NBC, and our most famous athlete ever. Most famous citizen, likely."

"Our?"

Olivia grinned. "I love Germany and consider myself first and foremost a German. But I will always be a Trini as well."

"You have to have the most unique accent ever, combining those two nationalities."

"Now you're teasing me."

"I'm not. I like it."

She smiled again, and despite the circumstances that had brought them together, Reggie couldn't help but enjoy the smile.

They finished dinner, and Reggie walked Olivia to her car, parked on a side street a few blocks away.

"I have various meetings all day tomorrow," she said. "Like any agency, the BfV is understaffed, so I'm tying up loose ends from a previous investigation, greasing the wheels for an upcoming partnership, and working to track down *Wolfskinder* at the same time. I'll try to keep you posted if I find out anything."

"I'll do the same," he said.

Olivia placed a hand on his arm. "Try not to worry," she said with another smile, one that caused her entire face to radiate. She rubbed his arm for just a second, then lowered her hand and retrieved her keys from her purse. With a quick wave, she was into her car—a Chevy Aveo, likely a rental—and sped off.

For the second time that day, Reggie watched her go with something of a mix of emotions. Chief among them heightened concern for Jackson's safety.

*   *   *

7:34 p.m.

MAGGIE STOPPED in Fontana in search of some serious food. She had miles and miles of city sprawl before she reached home, and while her bike was still good, she needed fuel. She found a Taco Bell and took her order to an outside table where she could watch the back half of the sunset play out. She wolfed down a pair of Volcano Tacos and paused to check her phone for messages.

Russell had called.

Maggie raised her phone to her ear, plugging the other to drown out nearby traffic.

"Hey, Maggie, it's Russell. Wondering if you've heard anything from Jackson. I've talked to a few people who might have a potential lead. Give me a call."

She lowered her phone with a frown. Something in Russell's tone told her it wasn't good news. She took a long pull on her soda, then called him back. He didn't answer, and she left him a voicemail. With a sigh, she resumed eating.

What had Russell said the night before? *"I have a lot of contacts who themselves have a lot of contacts."* What did that mean? And with what sort of lead might those contacts have provided him? Russell was relaxed and easygoing, but there was also the vague hint of mystery about him.

Maggie finished her dinner and, just short of feeling bloated, got back on her bike. Her ride home took her through Ontario, West Covina, and downtown, among other locations. When she finally arrived home some five hours after leaving, she had another voicemail from Russell, responding to her voicemail. He told her to call him after nine.

So Maggie took a shower, washing off the desert and highway's sand and grit. She dressed comfy and crashed on the couch. She caught an episode of *The Dick Van Dyke Show* featuring Jerry Van Dyke as Rob Petri's brother Stacey and decided to watch the end of it. At nine, she picked up her phone to call Russell but was stopped by an incoming call.

Reggie Cameron.

Her heart beating a thump faster, Maggie answered the call. "Hey, Reggie."

"Maggie. Got a favor to ask you."

"Sure."

"I need you to dig up anything you can on a Wilbur Anderson."

"Who's Wilbur Anderson?"

"An old codger who used to live at a retirement home out in Malibu."

"Used to?"

"He disappeared overnight Tuesday after visiting with Jackson."

"Jackson? What was he doing at a retirement home?"

"Not entirely sure. I was hoping you could get me a bio on Anderson. There has to be some tie to J."

Maggie couldn't remember if she'd told Reggie about losing her job, but she didn't think so. He wouldn't have been asking if she had. So she started to object, but he cut her off.

"I wouldn't ask except you have connections at the *Times* that I obviously don't, and this is the first real clue we've got."

She did still have some connections, people who didn't know she wasn't still employed by the *Times*. And surely there were some former coworkers there who owed her a favor. She could at least make some phone calls.

"I'll see what I can do," she answered.

"Thanks, Maggie."

"What was the name of the place?"

"Peaceful Shores Retirement Home or Assisted Living Home or something like that. I don't remember. I'm sure it must have made one of the back pages."

"Yeah."

"All right. I'm just leaving his place now. Gonna take his computer over to Mouse's house and see if he can find anything off it. I feel like a dog hacking J's e-mails, but something ain't right."

Somehow hearing Reggie admit it scared Maggie. He, it seemed, sensed that.

"Hang in there, Maggie. We'll find him."

"Yeah."

She lowered her phone. How did Jackson's visit to a retirement home and a missing senior citizen tie to his disappearance? Was this somehow related to Russell's potential lead? None of it made any sense.

She took a deep breath and redialed Russell. If he didn't answer, she was going to bed.

"This is Russell."

"Hey, it's Maggie."

"Hard woman to reach tonight."

"I was out riding."

"Under the speed limit, I hope."

"Right at."

Russell paused, and Maggie pictured him grinning with his tongue in his cheek. She'd seen it a few times the night before.

"This may sound a little odd," he said, "but how would you like to grab breakfast tomorrow?"

"Breakfast?"

"It's a little late tonight, and I have to work most of the day tomorrow. But I'm free in the morning."

"What's going on?"

"Nothing major. But it might be best if we talk in person."

It was Maggie's turn to pause. "Russell, do you know where Jackson is?"

"No. I just know some people who might be able to shed some light on his disappearance."

"Okay."

"Say nine? You pick the place, and I'll buy."

Something was hinky with this, but Maggie didn't know what else to do. So she suggested a small coffee shop near her apartment that also served a pretty mean breakfast sandwich. Russell agreed to meet her there and told her not to worry before he ended the call.

Maggie slowly lowered her phone. If God was answering her prayer by clearing things up and sorting them out for her, He was certainly taking the roundabout way of doing so.

Chapter Eleven

9:06 p.m.

PAM WAS DRUNK, Mouse was almost sure of it. And Gary, the rancher from Santa Fe, was either stoned or had been dropped on his head at birth. He was sort of normal looking, a little on the lanky side, handsome-ish, with a thick beard that looked like reddish steel wool. The way Pam had kept kissing him all night like he had rescued her from an adrift life raft or something, it was amazing her face wasn't all scratched.

Gary wore flannel but didn't have some hipster haircut. He was friendly and tried to make conversation with Mouse. He didn't make fun of his nickname when Mouse accidentally called himself by it, didn't gripe about his shaggy hair or wrinkled button-down shirt the way Pam had. Mouse actually kind of liked the guy. Except for the fact that he was willing to marry Pam, which told Mouse there was clearly something wrong with him. Denied oxygen too long in the birth canal, or kicked by a horse, or some weird side effect from chewing tobacco. Or maybe they'd met online, and she'd used Jennifer Lawrence as her profile picture, and he was waiting to let her down easy. Whatever it was, Mouse couldn't figure it.

But that paled in comparison to the fact that it was happening. They were getting married. Sooner than later, the way she'd talked when she hadn't been slamming back shots of vermouth. Pam didn't drink, not very often. So the fact that she was drowning her liver told Mouse something. He just wasn't smart enough to figure out what.

Gary drove a big pickup, a Dodge Ram, with a backseat. Mouse sat crammed behind the two of them, smelling hay or straw or cow crap or something, while Pam hugged Gary's shoulder as he drove back to their duplex in Culver City. When he pulled to the curb, Pam turned to him and started sucking face again, and for a few seconds, Mouse thought things were going to get awkward. Then she sat back and giggled.

"Mouse, it was nice to meet you," Gary said, extending a hand over the seat.

"Yeah. Uh, thanks. For dinner, I mean."

"My pleasure."

"You wanna come in?" Pam asked, leering at Gary from inches away.

"I need to get back and take care of some things at the ranch."

"I could come with you," she said, biting on her lip. If Mouse had to watch her make "provocative" faces much longer, he was going to puke.

"You should get some rest," Gary said. He gave her a peck. "I'll call you tomorrow."

"All right," she said, backing up and reaching for the door. It took her a few tries to accomplish the complex procedure of opening it. Mouse slid out as well, then caught Pam's elbow when she waved to Gary. He drove off, and she watched the taillights until they turned the corner.

"Ugh," she said to Mouse. "Could you have been more hulimiating?"

"You mean humiliating?"

"Whatever." She started up the sidewalk, somehow balancing on her high heels. The actual heels must have been reinforced titanium to support her weight. Mouse trudged behind her, trying to comprehend life without her. Not that it wasn't a dream come true in theory, but how would he ever make ends meet? For all her crap, she at least sort of carried him.

Headlights swept across the street as they reached the door, and Mouse looked to see a big, black SUV coasting to the curb.

"Who's that?" Pam asked, fumbling with her keys.

"Hopefully a gang mistaking us for rivals."

"What?"

"Nothing. Just open the door."

"I can't see what I'm doing."

He took the keys from her and unlocked the door as he heard a car door slam. He felt his heart jump when he saw a tall, muscular black guy dressed in black come around the front of the SUV. Then he realized it was Reggie Cameron and recognized the SUV as his Hummer. His relief was short-lived. What was Reggie doing at their house?

"What are you waiting for?" Pam asked.

"Just go pass out somewhere already," Mouse said. He turned and closed the door behind her, trying to play it cool as Reggie approached. "Hey."

"Hey, man. This a bad time?"

"Never a good one," Mouse said. "You find Jackson?"

"Naw," Reggie said, holding up a laptop computer. "Grabbed this from his house, though. Thought maybe you could look it over, see what you can find?"

"Um, yeah, sure. Um . . ." He winced, thinking of Pam. "Wanna come in?"

"That all right?"

"Yeah. Just ignore . . . whatever you might see or hear."

Pam was standing with the refrigerator door open. Mouse didn't know if she was looking for something to settle her stomach or fighting off a hot flash. He led Reggie back to his bedroom, flipped on the light, and closed the door. "Uh, have a seat."

Reggie handed him the laptop and sat on the corner of the bed.

"What are we looking for?"

"I don't know, man. Hack his e-mail, see if he stored any files or anything. You're the whiz, man."

"Right."

Mouse booted the computer and opened a web browser. He quickly scanned the browser history, announcing to Reggie the list of websites Jackson had recently visited.

Reggie crouched down to look at the screen. A lot of ESPN, several sites dedicated to college football recruiting, the Los Angeles Dodgers' homepage, The Weather Channel, a search for Peaceful Shores Assisted Living Home, Domino's, several different mapping websites, LoCal Rent A Car, and a handful of other innocuous sites.

"You see anything suspicious?" Mouse asked.

Reggie shook his head. "Why'd he need to rent a car?"

"His in the shop?"

"I don't think so. Not recently."

Mouse shrugged.

"Can we see where he was looking for directions?"

"If he typed it in," Mouse said. He spent a few minutes clicking through the mapping websites. "No dice."

"What about his Google searches?"

"Yeah, sure," Mouse said. He brought up some more lists of websites, most of which looked innocent.

"These two," Reggie said.

Mouse clicked on the links and brought up two obituaries, one for a man from Salt Lake City, Utah, and the other for a man from Dallas, Texas. Both were old, both had died of heart attacks, and neither had any apparent connection to Jackson.

"What about his e-mail? Can you hack it?"

Mouse raised an eyebrow.

"Wouldn't do it if it wasn't serious, man."

That was sobering. It took Mouse less than three minutes to hack his way into Jackson's e-mail account. There wasn't much there. The obligatory spam, a few trivial e-mails to and from cousins, and a reminder to make his NCAA Tournament Challenge picks.

"Nothing," Mouse said.

"Hold on. Check the junk folder."

Mouse clicked on it, revealing a dozen unwanted e-mails. Reggie jabbed a finger at one in the middle. "There."

"LoCal Rent A Car."

"Open it."

Mouse did, and they both read a confirmation for Jackson's rental for the night of Tuesday the 19th, pick up around nine p.m.

"Why would J rent a car?"

"Beats me."

"His car wasn't in the garage," Reggie said, scratching his head. "Which means . . ."

"He's not alone?"

"Else he wanted someone to think he was gone."

"Why would he want that?"

"I don't know, man."

"A case?"

"Yeah, maybe. His car is conspicuous." Reggie shook his head. "What are you doing now?"

"Looking for anything hidden on his computer. He's locked his case files, but I thought maybe he hid something somewhere else."

"Can't you hack in?"

"Not without the password."

"You can hack the White House but not Jack's My Documents?"

"It's not the same."

Reggie put up his hands. "All Greek to me, man, but I'll take your word for it."

"What about his phone?"

"I didn't see it anywhere." Reggie stroked his jaw. "Every call goes right to voicemail. That means he's on another call or it's turned off, right?"

"Or the battery's dead, SIM card's been removed."

"Yeah. So our only lead is LoCal. You ever rent a car?"

"No."

"They like to know if you're going out of state. Might be a lead." Reggie reached for his phone.

"You calling them now?"

"No. Sam."

"Oh, 'cause I was going to say I might be able to hack in."

"Really?"

Mouse shrugged, and Reggie nodded. "Give it a whirl."

Mouse nodded and fired up his computers. While he worked, Reggie made a phone call, pacing around the room like a caged lion at the zoo. It made Mouse nervous for some reason, and he rocked in place a little faster than usual. And maybe it distracted him too. For whatever reason, he couldn't seem to bypass the rental company's simple firewall. He rocked faster.

"You all right, dude?" Reggie asked.

"I . . . I don't know what's—Dangit!"

"Mouse?"

"I can't penetrate their firewall. I can't even get close." He shoved his keyboard forward in disgust.

"Don't worry about it, man. I'll check it out tomorrow."

"I should be able to get in," Mouse said as he reached out and attacked the keyboard again. "It's not even—Agh!"

"Calm down, man, it's all right," Reggie said, putting a heavy hand on Mouse's shoulder. His instinct was to recoil, but he realized it was a compassionate gesture. "It's all right."

Mouse turned. "How are you going to get anything from them tomorrow?"

Reggie winked. "I have my ways."

Mouse frowned but said nothing.

"I should get going. You all right?"

"Yeah, I'm . . . fine."

"All right. I'll call you if I find anything out, all right?"

"Yeah, sure."

"I'll see myself out. Thanks for your help."

Mouse gave a whatever shrug as Reggie headed out. He waited until he heard the front door close, then soothed himself by wasting some aliens in a video game he had long since mastered. When he took a break an hour later to grab a Mountain Dew from the refrigerator, Pam was slouched on the kitchen floor in front of the sink, still in her dress, barefoot, and snoring.

Maybe Mouse should check if Gary had a single cowgirl sister.

*   *   *

11:30 p.m.

SAM WOKE up Saturday morning and concluded it must have been a dreary overcast day. Why else would it have been so dark? It must have been a late night too, at the hospital, or she wouldn't have slept in her scrubs.

Then it hit her that it was still Friday night. She wasn't sleeping for the night; she was napping. She had to work in thirty minutes. Sam made it a general policy not to complain, but she let a small moan escape her lips as she rose from the bed. She had slept on top of the covers, curled up for warmth, and it left her stiff.

Sam had driven Stephanie to the hospital, checked her in, called Brady, and waited with Stephanie until he arrived. That was about the same time the doctor diagnosed that Stephanie's labor was actually a false alarm. The contractions had stopped, and Stephanie had been discharged several hours after being admitted.

Sam had returned home in time for a late dinner and, feeling the effects of her twelve-on, twelve-off shifts of late, opted for a nap before the midnight to noon shift for which she had traded her original six-to-six shift. She'd hoped it would invigorate her, but now she started to think she'd made a mistake. She felt sluggish and languid, and found the thought of twelve hours in the ER daunting.

Uttering a quick prayer for energy and focus, Sam tidied up in the bathroom, fixing her hair and brushing her teeth. She made sure she had her keys, ID card, Chap Stick, lunch from the refrigerator, and her phone. She didn't have the phone and had to backtrack to her bedroom. As she grabbed it, she quickly checked for messages and saw that Reggie had called. As she left the apartment, she listened to his voicemail, hoping it had good news about Jackson.

"Hey, Sam, it's Reggie. Just checking in. I stopped at Peaceful Shores today and have a possible lead. Call me when you get a chance. I'll be up until midnight."

Sam checked the time. She had a few minutes, with the hospital being just minutes away, and called Reggie as she walked to her car.

"Hey, Sam."

"Hi, Reggie. I'm not calling too late, am I?"

"No. How's Stephanie?"

Sam's sigh was audible. "False alarm. She's at home again."

"She doing okay?"

"She's fine. Just a little embarrassed. And getting impatient."

"I bet. You home now?"

"On the way to work," she said, opening her car door.

"All-nighter?"

"Till noon."

"Snap. Well, something to chew on. You ever heard of a guy named Wilbur Anderson?"

"No, why?" Sam eased her door shut so it wouldn't slam.

"Apparently Jackson spent a few hours with him Tuesday at Peaceful Shores, then he disappeared."

"Jackson?"

"Wilbur."

"Wilbur disappeared?"

"Yeah. And J rented a car Tuesday night."

"Why would he rent a car?"

"I don't know."

Sam sighed. "What does this all mean, Reggie? What is going on?"

"I don't know, Sam. But I intend to find out."

"Thanks for letting me know. I should get going."

"Try not to worry."

They said goodbye, and she lowered her phone. The more they learned about Jackson's disappearance—and she had no idea how Reggie had learned what he had—the more confusing it became. She said a quick prayer for his safety and started the car. If it were a typical night in the ER, she would at least have plenty to keep her mind off Jackson. It was kind of weird, she noted as she drove, that it seemed one crisis—Stephanie going into labor, Jackson missing, her mom's cancer, a hectic career—kept taking her mind off another in a never-ending loop.

The words of the psalmist came back to her. *How long, LORD . . .*

"How long, indeed," Sam muttered. *How long can I keep this up?*

Chapter Twelve

Saturday, March 23
9:03 a.m.

MAGGIE WAS A few minutes late, which was due in part to her inability to decide on what to wear—she'd opted for jeans and a gray Henley—and in part to a traffic accident that made getting out of her apartment complex tricky. She parked on the street in front of Beanie's and entered the small coffee shop. Immediately, Russell caught her eye.

She opted to believe it was because she was looking for him and anxious to find out what he knew about Jackson and not because he cut a striking figure in a red, white, and black checked shirt. He beckoned her to a table by the window where he was sipping coffee, his phone on the table in front of him.

"Morning," he said as Maggie took the chair opposite him.

"Hi."

"How was your ride last night?"

"Good. Long." She explained her journey west to Oxnard, north around the mountains, and back to L.A. on the San Bernardino Freeway.

"Wow."

"Yeah, well, I had a lot on my mind."

A barista stopped by to take Maggie's order—she chose coffee and a fruit plate—and returned in seconds with a cup of coffee. Maggie tested it, added a creamer, and then met Russell's blue eyes, which hadn't left her.

"What'd you find?" she asked.

He nodded. "Maybe nothing. But I talked to a number of people on the street who told me there's rumor of a major drug deal going down this weekend."

Maggie shook her head. "Hold on. People on the street?"

"I work with a lot of people at shelters, clinics, missions. I've developed some contacts, like I said the other day."

"What kind of contacts?"

He shrugged. "Homeless people. Drifters. Some low-level criminals. Guys and gals who run shelters or free clinics or who do outreaches to street people. A little of everything."

"And these people know the word on the street?"

"Sometimes. Sometimes they know people who know. But you'd be surprised what gets around."

Maggie blew into her coffee. "And there's a drug deal going down?"

"That's what I hear. You heard of the Silvaz?"

Maggie paused mid-drink, causing hot coffee to slosh down her throat. She nearly choked, coughing until her eyes watered.

"I take that as a yes," Russell said.

"What about them?"

"For the last year, they've been making a move west, trying to take more territory, predominantly from a gang called the Grays."

Maggie nodded.

"You've heard of them?"

"Yeah."

Russell nodded. "So you know that a year ago, Jackson shot and killed a guy named Tone Sanders, the then leader of the Grays."

"It was a legit shooting," Maggie said. "He saved three lives."

Russell nodded again. "I know. I read all the stories and even got a glance at a police report. I'm not suggesting Jackson did anything inappropriate."

"So what are you suggesting?" Maggie asked.

"Just that he was involved in taking out the Grays' leader, an action that significantly weakened the gang and opened the door for the Silvaz to take over some of their territory. Now, the Silvaz are looking to poach more. LAPD's worried it's going to trigger a gang war, and I'm just wondering if there's any possible connection to that and Jackson's disappearance."

Maggie sat back as the barista brought her fruit. She wasn't hungry.

"I don't know what it could be," she said. "It's not like . . ."

Russell drank some coffee. "Not like what?"

Maggie sighed. "Jackson talked with a guy named Shaq Theobald, the head honcho with the Silvaz. He gave Jackson Sanders' location."

"Why would he do that?"

"Jackson had killed two of Theobald's men while rescuing an undercover cop." She sighed. "Jackson offered to make it up to Theobald by . . . taking out Sanders."

"He took a hit on a gang leader?"

"No. And like I told you, the shooting was clean. Another LAPD cop shot Sanders at the same time. They don't even know which bullet killed him."

Russell sat back, running his fingers through his hair. It still looked salon tousled when he was done. "So Jackson had involvement with both gangs?"

"Yeah."

"And now the Silvaz are eating up the Grays' territory, and Jackson is missing."

"Yeah. But I still don't see how the two might be related."

"They might not be," he said. "But it sure is a coincidence."

Maggie leaned forward. "What kind of deal are we talking?"

"I didn't get specifics. Just that the Silvaz were making a major foray into Grays' territory."

She sat back and looked out the window. "I . . . I just don't see how Jackson would be involved. He's had nothing to do with either gang ever since."

"That you know of."

Maggie cut her eyes to him. "He hasn't."

"Okay." He sighed. "Look, I'm not trying to drag Jackson through the mud."

"You're doing a pretty good job of it."

"I'm sorry." He leaned forward. "Maggie, if you say Jackson is clean, then I believe you. But that doesn't mean he hasn't gotten messed up with them again. Maybe he caught wind of this and did some investigating. Or maybe one or the other gang knew of his involvement with the other and reached out to him. Or maybe it is just a coincidence."

"So what do we do?"

"I've got to work most of the day, but I'll keep asking around. In the meantime, if you know anybody involved with what happened a year ago, give them a call and see if they know anything. If Jackson is investigating this, he had to get his info from somewhere, and I doubt he's on his own."

Maggie nodded.

"Is there anything else I can do to help?"

She smiled. "No. But thank you for the offer."

"So is that all you're going to eat?" Russell asked with a wink. "I am buying."

*   *   *

12:18 p.m.

IT HAD been another insane night in the UCLA Medical Center, Santa Monica. Four car accidents, a couple of bar stabbings, three drug overdoses, more viral infections, burns from a bonfire gone bad, and a husband and wife who'd both suffered heart attacks within the span of an hour. Sam had been ready to drop but found the strength to make it until noon (actually quarter after) when her shift finally came to an end. She had off until Monday night and felt like sleeping most of the weekend away.

Reggie had called around ten, during a brief lull, and asked if she could help him when her shift ended. Tired as she had been, she had known she wouldn't sleep much in the middle of the day, so she had agreed. Now, as she walked to her car, she called Reggie back.

It was warm and sunny, albeit with a sheet of clouds spreading over the coastline. They weren't thick enough to block out the sun's rays; in fact, they almost seemed to magnify it. The air was thick and humid, and Sam's scrubs stuck to her skin as she listened to Reggie's phone ringing. Just as his voicemail kicked in, he answered.

"Hey, Sam. You off?"

"Yeah. What do you need?"

"I told you last night that Jackson rented a car Tuesday, right?"

"Yeah."

"I want to ask around at the rental office, see if they can give us anything."

"And you need me?"

"I'll explain on the way. You home yet?"

"Headed there now."

"You hungry?"

"Starving."

"Then I'll bring lunch, off the menu. What are you in the mood for?"

"That raspberry chicken salad."

Reggie chuckled. "I thought you were starving."

"Heavy on the chicken."

"That's more like it. Oh, and Sam, you got a pair of jeans and a plain blue top? Navy, royal blue, whatever?"

She frowned. "Yeah. Why?"

"Just trust me."

"O . . . kay."

"I'll be there in twenty minutes."

"Okay."

Still frowning, Sam got into her car and drove home. She had just changed into jeans and a blue, three-quarter-sleeve scoop-neck blouse when the doorbell rang. Quickly putting her hair up, Sam went downstairs to admit Reggie.

He held a carryout bag in his right hand and winked when he saw her. "Perfect."

"Perfect for what?"

"I'll tell you while we eat."

They headed upstairs and to the dining room, where Sam got out plates, utensils, and glasses. She offered Reggie some lemonade from a few days back—okay, maybe it was a week—while having water herself. Forgetting to pray, she delved into her salad while he attacked a burger that seemed to have as much bacon as beef.

"So why do you need me to ask around at a car rental office and why do I need to wear blue?"

"So you'll look like a federal agent."

Sam speared a few leaves of lettuce. "What?"

"Blue's the color of cops, so I thought it would work on their subconscious."

"A federal agent?"

"Yeah. Probably not FBI because the Fibbies all wear suits." He shrugged. "We'll see who we run into. Maybe they'll buy we're *NCIS: LA*."

"Isn't that a crime?"

"Technically. It depends how you do it."

Sam frowned.

"All you need to be is the sidekick, Sam. I'll do the talking, but I need—excuse me for saying this—a pretty face along to temper my appearance."

"Do you have a badge?"

Reggie shook his head.

"Then how are you going to convince them you're a federal agent?"

"I'll be undercover."

"I don't know, Reggie."

"I won't force you, Sam. But we need to find J."

"Why? What do you know that you're not telling me?"

"Nothing."

"Reggie?"

"Nothing, Sam. This is our only lead. But my gut tells me something's wrong."

She nodded. "Mine too."

"J's Granada wasn't at the house, and we know he made a reservation for a rental car. So either he left his car there, or he's got a sidekick."

"Who?"

Reggie shrugged. "That's what we need to find out."

"And you think this is the way?"

"Right now, it's all we got."

Sam was not wild about impersonating a federal agent—legal or otherwise. In fact, she was less than not wild about it. She was downright opposed to it. She abided by the rules. But she also trusted Reggie, from what Jackson had always told her about him. The truth was she didn't know him all that well.

"Okay. I'm in."

"Atta girl."

They finished eating, then debated which vehicle to take. Sam thought her Fusion was more of a government car than Reggie's Hummer, but he said bigger would make an impression. And without a badge or ID, they would need to make an impression.

LoCal Rent A Car was located off Santa Monica Boulevard, and Reggie rolled his Hummer into the lot and screeched to a stop a little after one. He had already told Sam to follow his lead and given her brief instructions, so when the Hummer stopped, they both jumped out. Sam followed Reggie as he started walking down the aisle of cars, head turning back and forth. He strode quickly, purposefully, all the way to the back of the lot. Sam followed him, her head on a swivel too. They turned around and returned to the Hummer. Halfway there, they were met by a man in a suit who had come bustling out of the office.

"Can I help you folks?"

"You a manager?" Reggie asked.

"Yes, sir. Michael Webb."

Reggie took and shook the outstretched hand. "Mr. Webb, I'm Special Agent Darryl Rivas with the DHS." He nodded at Sam. "This is my partner, Carol Black. We're working undercover to bring down a drug cartel, and we believe this man is part of it." He pulled out a folded sheet of paper with Jackson's picture on it. "We also believe he rented a vehicle from you on Tuesday night."

"D-DHS?" Webb asked.

"Yes, sir. This cartel has been shipping drugs north through San Diego and the Colorado Desert, and they have recently begun smuggling people as well. Some of whom we have intel to indicate are linked to Islamic terrorist cells. You can understand why bringing down this cartel is a matter of national security."

"Y-yes, s-sir. Yes, I can see that."

"We linked the cartel in Los Angeles to Jackson Douglas," Reggie said, nodding at the photo Webb had taken from him. "We've been tracking him for a week now, attempting to infiltrate his inner circle, but we lost him Tuesday afternoon in Culver City. By working an associate of his, we got a tip that he rented a car from you on Tuesday night. Can you confirm that?"

"If you'll come with me into the office, I can look it up."

"We also believe he may have left his vehicle here. A 1976 Ford Granada."

Webb's eyes widened. "Yes. We do have a Granada here."

"Could we look at it while you check your records? It may contain a clue."

"Of course. Let me get the keys."

Webb left, and Sam turned to Reggie. "That actually worked?"

"We'll see," he said. "He could be checking up on us in there."

"And risk confronting you?"

Reggie grinned, but only for a moment. Webb returned, jangling a set of keys and carrying a tablet. "I have the keys to the Granada," he announced. "This way."

He led them around the back of the building and under a carport. Parked behind a pick-up truck with severe crash damage was Jackson's Granada. Sam tried not to let any expression play out on her face.

Webb opened the vehicle, and Reggie pulled out a pair of latex gloves. He handed them to Sam and told her to check the passenger side while he put on a second pair. Sam had no idea what to look for, but she figured Reggie did, and she'd seen enough TV to know the routine. Feeling a little guilty rifling through Jackson's personal property, she opened the glove compartment.

"L.A. map, lighter, insurance, owner's manual, a pen."

Reggie checked above the driver's side visor, under the seat, in the vents. Sam followed suit, then they both scoured the backseat. Other than a wadded McChicken wrapper and a couple of French fries, there was nothing. With Webb looking on, they also checked the trunk but saw nothing suspicious there either.

"Nothing," Reggie said, his big shoulders slumped.

Webb slid his fingers across his tablet.

"We can confirm that Mr. Douglas reserved a Subcompact at 8:41 p.m. Tuesday the 12th. He picked it up at quarter after nine. A gray Toyota Yaris."

"How long?" Reggie asked.

"Two weeks, sir."

"He say where he was going?"

"No, sir. We ask clients to let us know if they will be traveling out of state, and he said he wouldn't be."

"You remember him?"

"No, sir. It's in the file."

"What else is in there?"

"Driver's license, payment information. He paid in cash, which is a little unusual, but not unheard of."

"Your car have a LoJack or GPS we can track him with?"

"I'm afraid not, sir."

"License plate?"

Webb turned the tablet so Reggie could read the plate number. Sam peeked in too, committing the number to memory.

"Is there anything else you can tell us?"

"I'm afraid not, Special Agent Rivas. Everything seemed aboveboard."

Reggie extended his hand. "Thank you, Mr. Webb." He dug around in his pocket and came out with a business card. "Uh, this isn't mine. Picked it up at lunch. Do you have a pen?" Webb produced one and Reggie jotted down a number. "If Douglas returns the vehicle early, will you call me at this number? Do not attempt to apprehend him. Just conduct your business as usual and give me a call when he leaves."

"Yes, sir."

"Thank you."

Reggie turned to leave, and Sam sent a nod and a smile at Webb before following. When they were enclosed in the Hummer, she asked, "Now what?"

"Now, we're at square one."

"Why would Jackson rent a car if he wasn't going anywhere?"

"Two reasons. Either he was going somewhere but didn't want anyone to know, or he didn't want to be found by somebody who knows what he drives."

"He paid in cash."

"Right. No credit card trail."

Sam sighed. "I don't like this, Reggie."

"Yeah, me neither."

"Maybe we should call the police."

He nodded. "Yeah, I'm starting to think so too."

They returned to her apartment, and Reggie walked Sam to the door.

"How did you come up with all that stuff?" she asked.

"What stuff?"

"Special Agents Rivas and Black and Jackson being a fugitive with a cartel."

"I made it up."

"On the spot?"

"Some of it." He shrugged. "It's what J'd do."

Sam nodded.

"You look beat, Sam. You should get some rest."

"Yeah, I'll try."

"I'll call you if I hear anything."

"Okay, thanks."

He nodded and turned to leave. Sam decided she would try a midday nap after all.

Chapter Thirteen

2:27 p.m.

AFTER DROPPING SAM off, Reggie checked in at work and spent a few minutes on paperwork in his office. Then he mulled everything he knew about Jackson's disappearance, which wasn't much. He thought of Sam's suggestion to call the police and Dr. Zachary asking why he hadn't yet.

It had been four days since anyone had seen Jackson, which suggested something was wrong. But he had also made plans to rent a car, indicating he'd gone somewhere of his own volition. Maybe he was just chilling. Or maybe he was hiding or working undercover. The last thing Reggie wanted to do was draw attention to Jackson if he was trying to avoid it. But he also didn't want to let any more time slip by.

Reggie decided to give Ashley Larson a call. She was a detective with LAPD and had hired Jackson the previous May when an undercover operation with her partner had gone sideways. Jackson had bailed them out, indebting her to him forever. And Jackson had called in the favor a few times, but Reggie hoped Ashley was good for another.

She answered her phone on the second ring. "Detective Larson."

"Detective, Reggie Cameron."

"Reggie Cameron?"

"Jackson Douglas's friend. Big, black, I own a restaurant."

"Right. What can I do for you, Reggie?"

"I'm sorry to bother you on the weekend, but Jackson has disappeared."

"Disappeared?"

"Yeah." Reggie walked her through a few of the finer points, concluding with the knowledge of Jackson's car rental, albeit not how they knew about it or his stint impersonating a DHS agent. "We don't know if he's just kickin' it somewhere on the down low or if something sinister has happened to him. I was hoping you might be able to help."

"He didn't say anything about being on a case or going anywhere work-related?"

"No. Not to me or anybody I've talked to."

Ashley sighed. "We can file a missing person's report, but if he is undercover, we could blow it."

"Can you keep it in-house? If it ain't made public and it's just L.A.'s finest looking for him, maybe we can split the difference."

"We can try."

"I also got a license plate I was hoping you could add to it. Belongs to a rented Toyota Yaris, gray, plate number eight-gulf-bravo-echo-seven-seven-three."

Ashley repeated it back to him. "I'm meeting with someone in a few minutes, but I can file this as soon as I'm done."

"I appreciate it, Detective."

"I'll call you at this number if I hear anything?"

"Thanks."

"Don't mention it."

She disconnected first, and Reggie made Leroy his next call. He updated Jackson's grandpa, who sounded to Reggie like he was trying to sound like he wasn't worried. After talking with him, Reggie called Olivia's cell. She didn't answer, and he thought about leaving a message. Instead, he dropped the phone onto the desk.

He and Olivia hadn't spoken since dinner the night before when she'd said she would be in meetings most of the day. Whenever he'd thought of her today, he felt annoyed. Mostly, it seemed, because he'd thought of her fairly often. He couldn't deny an attraction to her, but that was the last thing he wanted to be thinking about right now, with Jackson in trouble.

Truth be told, it wasn't too high on his priority list if Jackson was sitting on the couch mooching a club sandwich off him without a care in the world. The last time Reggie'd given his heart away, it'd been stomped on. He knew not to let his relationship with Keisha taint every other potential relationship going forward, but the scars were deep. And they weren't all inflicted by her. He didn't know if he was ready for that sort of thing again, so even the initial stirrings of feelings triggered red flags.

But it wasn't just that. Something about Olivia bugged him, but he couldn't place it. Was it just that she, a Caribbean-born German woman, broke his stereotype of an intelligence agent? Was it the way she knew so many details about Jackson's life, her governmental connections aside? How at ease she seemed for a "spy"? How nonchalantly she was dealing with something so significant to Reggie? Was it the fact that a group like *Wolfskinder* had been operating around the world for years and he had no clue?

Or was it that he felt so dangerously close to mixing business with pleasure?

One of Cameron's assistant managers popped in the door to alert him that a cook and two servers had already called in sick for that night, and all her efforts to find replacements were coming up empty. "Looks like we're going to be shorthanded."

"I'll pitch in," Reggie said. "Just give me five to clean up a few things and then we'll figure out how to make this work."

She nodded and ducked back out. Reggie sighed. It was par for the course for a hands-on owner like himself. He wouldn't have it any other way, and as he straightened up a few things on his desk, he was glad for the distraction.

*   *   *

3:13 p.m.

MAGGIE WAITED until late afternoon, when she figured the fewest number of people would be working. At least among the bigwigs. On a Saturday afternoon, nobody who didn't have to be there would be there.

Storm clouds were building on the horizon, but Maggie took her bike anyhow. As she rode, she replayed her conversation with Russell for the tenth time. She couldn't believe that Jackson had somehow gotten involved with either the Grays or the Silvaz—not intentionally. And yet, his disappearance so close to the alleged big drug deal the Silvaz were planning, when combined with Jackson's history with the two gangs, was suspicious. Maggie just didn't know what to make of it all.

She had tried calling Detective Ashley Larson, the woman who had gone undercover as a Valley Girl, hired Jackson, and ultimately gotten him involved with the two gangs to begin with. If anyone might know what was going on, it would be Ashley, Maggie figured. But she didn't answer, and instead of leaving a confusing voicemail, Maggie made a note to call her later.

She didn't have a badge any longer, so she had no access to the *Times* building downtown. But she also knew that the place wasn't exactly Fort Knox. Somebody would be taking a smoke break, getting some air, or not paying attention, and she would be able to use them to get inside.

She parked her bike a block away and walked toward a side entrance. Sure enough, as she approached, she spotted Benny, one of the maintenance men, enjoying a brief cigarette. Benny was in his sixties, at least, and had been working at the *Times* since long before Maggie arrived on the scene. Her laptop under her arm, Maggie strolled up to him, hoping Walter hadn't sent out a memo to all employees that she was no longer employed by the paper.

"Hey, Benny."

He turned. "Oh, afternoon, Maggie." He threw the butt into a receptacle by the door. "Allow me."

He swiped the card attached to his belt in the door and pulled it open.

"Thank you."

"I don't see you in here too often on a Saturday."

"Big story," Maggie said.

"Oh?"

"At least I hope."

He winked. "You ride your bike today?"

"Yeah."

"You'd better hurry. It's going to rain."

Maggie smiled. "I will."

She opened the door into the stairwell with a sigh. Now it was just a matter of laying low.

Maggie had spent the afternoon making calls, asking for information about Wilbur Anderson. All she had been able to come up with was a brief blurb from a police blotter about Wilbur's disappearance from Peaceful Shores Assisted Living Home in Malibu.

Without her network login credentials, Maggie wouldn't be able to login to any of the computers or servers at the *Times*. That left her two options. Find a vacant computer that was already logged in—unlikely—or search the millions of digital pages in the file room. They were all indexed and searchable and didn't require the same level of security as the regular network did since the system was offline.

Pausing at the top of the stairs, Maggie took a deep breath. She still had the fallback story that she was there to pick up some of her personal things. But they were not stored in the file room, so she was hoping to avoid needing to fall back. With another deep breath, she pushed open the door and strode confidently past the restrooms. The hallway opened into the bullpen, surrounded on all four sides by offices.

Her old desk was just to the right, and Maggie was hit with nostalgia. And anger. Maybe Jake was right. Maybe she did have legal grounds to go after her old employer. She filed the notion away for the time being and concentrated on work.

Only half a dozen people were scattered around the bullpen, and none of them paid her any notice. Lights were on in only a handful of offices, and Walter's wasn't one of them. Maggie walked to her desk, set down her laptop, and spent a few minutes rummaging in drawers as if she belonged. Then she picked up her laptop and walked directly across the bullpen to the file room.

Used only for legacy data, the file room contained four computers, in addition to dozens and dozens of filing cabinets. There had been talk of moving everything to the current network, but it would have required a major system upgrade and increased security protocols, and the budget didn't have room as of yet. So for now, Maggie would be able to logon simply by putting an employee ID code into the system. No password was necessary.

She sat down at the computer nearest the door. All were in view if anyone entered the room, and she figured this would give her the best

ONE LIFE TO LOSE

chance of hearing someone approach. She opened her laptop, then entered Jared Stillman's ID code into the file room computer. Jared had shared the desk next to hers for a few years, and they had briefly dated. Jared had moved on to become a pop-culture columnist, and she knew for a fact he worked every Saturday afternoon, so his code wouldn't raise any red flags.

Maggie was undisturbed for the first fifteen minutes, during which time her search of the files revealed basic biographical information on Wilbur Anderson: Born Wilbur Charles Anderson on January 19, 1925, in the small town of What Cheer, Iowa, Wilbur had enlisted in the U.S. Army in 1944, serving two years and seeing action in the European Theater during World War II with the Fifth Army. After the war, Wilbur had returned to Iowa, where he'd married Virginia Campbell in the summer of 1947. They had lived in Davenport, Iowa, where Wilbur had worked as a mechanic until 1962 when they moved to Baltimore to take care of Virginia's ailing sister. When she died in 1965, Wilbur and Virginia had returned to Iowa, this time to Des Moines. Wilbur had again found work as a mechanic and had retired in 1988. Virginia had died two years later, and Wilbur had moved to California in the mid-'90s. He had never remarried, and his life story was pretty quiet after . . . well, after the war, really. There was nothing to tie him to Jackson or to anything even moderately suspicious.

Maggie was caught up in her research and didn't hear the footsteps until a fellow reporter walked into the room. He was familiar, although Maggie didn't know his name. He nodded, perhaps with a slight frown, and walked around behind her to a filing cabinet. Breathing freely again, she continued her research.

There wasn't much else to find but public records related to Wilbur's marriage, driver's license, military service, etcetera. No kids, no criminal record. The only curious thing was his move, after a life lived primarily in the Midwest, to California. But with no family holding him back, trading Iowa for California wasn't so curious after all. At least, not if you asked Jackson.

Maggie momentarily smiled at the thought of Jackson, then remembered that he was why she was here. Saving her notes, she closed her laptop and logged off the file room computer. The familiar guy was still digging through filing cabinets, and when Maggie stepped out into the bullpen, she realized his was one of the desks that had been occupied when she'd come in. Feeling gutsy and determined, she walked over to it and sat down.

The name on the start menu identified him as Randy, and he was logged into the network. Maggie quickly searched the network for anything on Wilbur Anderson, her fingers flying over the keyboard and her eyes skimming info on the screen while also darting from the file room door to the other desks in the bullpen to the offices all around her. She could feel the hair on the back of her neck stand up, and an inner voice told her to get moving.

There was nothing more on Wilbur Anderson, but she stayed a moment longer. Randy was still in the file room, and if there was something to Russell's theory on the Grays and the Silvaz, maybe she could find a clue. She searched recent news stories involving both of them, just scanning headlines. She pieced together only what Russell's street contacts had told him and nothing more.

It was time to get out, and Maggie stood, taking her laptop with her. One more glance toward the file room indicated she was in the clear, and she turned and headed for the stairs.

"Maggie?"

She turned around to see Helen, the head of HR. Tall, plump, always angry, Helen was the last person Maggie had ever wanted to encounter when she had a right to be at the office. Now, she knew Helen knew she shouldn't be there.

But Maggie played it cool. She stopped and turned. "Hi, Helen."

"What are you doing here?"

"Just gathering a few things."

"Does Walter . . . This isn't even your desk."

"I was just leaving."

"You shouldn't have been here."

Maggie looked down at the high heels Helen wore. Her skirt was a size too small, wrapping tightly around her. In a footrace, Maggie liked her chances. So she took a few steps back and turned for the stairs.

"Stop."

Maggie kept walking.

"I'm calling security."

Maggie started running. Behind her, she heard Helen shouting, then her high heels clicking on the marble floor. Maggie rounded the corner and pressed the down button on the elevator. She kicked open the door to the stairs, and the slow-release hinge deliberately swung shut while she darted into the men's room. She pushed the door closed behind her and spun around.

Good, it was empty.

Maggie hurried over to one of the stalls, opened the door, and stood on the toilet seat. She crouched down and waited.

Great work, Maggie.

It might not be all bad. The men's room was the last place they would look, but they probably would look there. So while she was waiting, Maggie opened her laptop, logged onto the office wireless, and loaded her file of notes to a cloud drive. Then she took a deep breath. It had been several minutes. Had Helen really called security? Maggie had had a good start, so maybe all parties had just given up.

Okay, Jack, what would you do right now?

Turn his phone to vibrate, for one thing.

Maggie quickly silenced her phone, then decided to use it to her advantage. She dialed the office and followed the prompts until she was connected to Jared Stillman's extension.

"Stillman."

"Hey, Jared. It's Maggie."

"Maggie. What's going on? I haven't seen you all week?"

"That's because I've been fired."

"Fired? For what?"

"It's a long story, Jared. But I need a favor."

"Okay, shoot."

"Is Helen in today?"

"HR Helen?"

"Yeah."

"Yeah, I think she's here. You need to talk to her?"

"Actually, I need you to get a message to her. I just tried her extension, and she didn't pick up. It's urgent."

"Okay."

"Tell her I'm sorry I missed her, but next time I'm in, I'll be sure to stop and talk to her."

"Maggie, what's going on?"

"Can you just do it for me, Jared? I need to make sure she gets the message ASAP."

"Yeah, sure. Just writing an op-ed that can wait. It's not like we have deadlines or anything."

"I always did appreciate your sarcasm."

"You okay, Maggie?"

"I'm fine. I'll call you once things settle down. It's just been a crazy week."

"Okay. I'll go find Helen."

"Thank you."

She lowered her phone just as the bathroom door opened. Maggie sucked in her breath, hoping whoever had entered wasn't with security. Or didn't have to go number two.

A moment later, she heard him at a urinal. Thirty seconds later, it flushed, and she heard the door close behind the guy. Maggie shook her head. People who didn't wash their hands after using the bathroom should be quarantined.

She waited another ten minutes, hoping that would have given Jared time to track down Helen and pass the message onto her, which in turn would hopefully cause her to give up and call off the search. At any rate, Maggie was sick of waiting. She got down off the toilet and exited the stall. She paused at the bathroom door, heard nothing, and pulled it open. Striding directly to the stairway, she took one glance toward the bullpen. All seemed calm, and no one spotted her.

Maggie paused again at the top of the stairwell. Hearing nothing, she started down, pausing again at each landing. She took a deep breath when she emerged on the ground floor and proceeded to the exit. But not until she had walked back to her bike, loaded her laptop into her backpack, and ridden away did she really breathe easily. Half an hour later when she closed her apartment door behind her, she realized her heart was still pounding. How did Jackson do this for a living?

Maggie took a series of deep breaths to calm herself, then went out onto the balcony. The sky was growing darker, the sun heavily filtered, and Maggie could sense a storm on the wind. She doubted it could rival the one inside her. First her new faith, then the loss of her job and apartment, then Jackson's disappearance and her competing feelings for him and Russell. And now she was Sydney Bristow, playing spy at her old workplace. Maggie was hardly faint of heart, but this was getting to be too much.

So she closed her eyes and prayed, asking for strength, asking for peace. It worked, a little. She at least didn't feel quite as stressed when she was finished.

Taking another deep breath, she went back inside to call Reggie and update him on what she had found.

Chapter Fourteen

5:32 p.m.

SAM SLEPT FITFULLY throughout the afternoon, at first too wound up from impersonating a Department of Homeland Security special agent to drift off and then bothered by concern over Jackson. Finally, when a break to read some Psalms and pray had helped her relax, rolling thunder had continued to wake her. So with a sigh, she gave up.

She got out of bed and walked into the living room. The sky out the window was dark and streaked with rain, but the rain hadn't reached her apartment yet. Maybe this would be a good night to crash at home, watch an old movie, and go to bed early. While she hadn't slept much in the afternoon, Sam had a feeling she would sleep well that night. If the thunder quit, at least, she thought as another boom rattled her window.

She headed into the kitchen to see about dinner, but couldn't concentrate. Her thoughts kept wandering to Jackson, the thunder symbolic of the trouble he was in. Or was he? Maybe things were fine. But why wasn't he answering his phone? Why had he rented a car? Why hadn't he told anyone—Reggie, Leroy, her—what he was up to?

Sam wished there was something she could do, some insight she could provide or some clue she could find. And maybe there was.

She closed the cupboard door. Jackson had to have left a clue of some sort behind. Reggie had explained that he had looked around Jackson's house, and he seemed to have a better mind for this sort of thing than Sam did. But she was a woman and brought a perspective that Reggie wouldn't have. Maybe there was some clue Jackson had left behind—intentionally or unintentionally—that she could pick up.

Another clap of thunder shook the apartment, and it served as a resolution. Sam retrieved her phone and an area phonebook and sat down in the living room. Squinting, she tried to remember Connie's last name. Marco or Marks or something. It was Italian, and she thought there was a "D" in there somewhere.

Come on, Sam, remember.

DiMarco.

Sam flipped through the book until she found the name, then dialed her number. Jackson had given Connie a key a while back, and Sam hoped she still had it and was home.

Connie answered on the third ring. "Hello?"

"Connie? It's Sam MacRaney. Jackson's friend."

"Sam. Of course. How are you, dear?"

"I'm all right."

"Have you heard from Jackson?" Connie asked.

"No, and that's why I'm calling. I'm wondering if I could ask you for a favor."

"Ask away."

"Jackson said once before that you had a key to his house. Do you still have it?"

"I do."

"Would you be able to let me in? I want to look around and see if I can find something to give us a clue where he is."

Connie paused.

"Is something wrong?"

"No. It's just that you . . ."

"Connie?"

"Another of Jackson's friends was here yesterday morning, and I don't think she found anything. But I'm happy to let you in if you think it would help."

"At this point, I think anything's worth a try," Sam said, wondering who "another of Jackson's friends" was. A woman, according to Connie. Sam shooed the thought away. At this point, it didn't matter.

"Well, I'll be here all night if you want to chance a storm."

"Thank you, Connie."

"Of course, dear."

Sam lowered her phone and decided she was not hungry after all. She put her hair in a ponytail, grabbed a jacket and her purse, and headed down to her car. Rain had yet to fall, but the thunder was almost constant, and the air felt charged with electricity. Sam was amazed how dark the sky had gotten, still more than an hour before sunset, and she watched the roiling clouds in fascination. But only for a moment.

Hitting all the lights, Sam made good time and pulled into Jackson's driveway just as giant drops of rain began to fall. She hurried across the lawn and under the roof of Connie's small porch. She rang the bell and was immediately answered by a shrill bark. Fluffy, Connie's Pomeranian. Jackson's arch nemesis.

Connie opened the door while mumbling—half in English, half in Italian—at Fluffy and brushing her aside with her foot. She wore a bold orange and blue floral top and a pair of skinny jeans. Given her size and shape, it was not a flattering look, if it wasn't uncharitable of Sam to think so.

"Here you go," Connie said, handing her small keychain shaped like Florida with a single key attached to the ring. "Have you eaten yet?"

"No."

"You stop by when you're done. I've got *braciole* in the oven."

"Thank you," Sam said. "I doubt I'll be too long."

Fluffy added an exclamation point as Connie shut the door. Sam hurried back across the lawn as the rain started to come down with fervor, and ducked under the soffit over Jackson's front door to keep dry while she unlocked the door.

A flash of lightning lit the living room for a second, and the ensuing thunderclap shook the entire house. "Jackson," Sam called just in case as she closed the door. "It's Sam."

She was answered by silence, aside from the drumming of rain against the windows. She pocketed the key, trying to figure out how to conduct a search. On the old black and white movies, the detective found a dry-cleaning claim slip in a pocket or a movie ticket stub in the trash or something like that. Sam didn't know what to look for and wasn't sure her eyes would recognize something out of place if she did see it. But this was no time to back down.

Sam looked over the living room first, lifting up couch cushions and peering under furniture. She turned on the TV, thinking it would default to the last channel Jackson had been watching. Instead, all she got was a blue screen. Maybe his cable was out from the storm. Or . . . she reached down and pressed the power button on his Xbox, and the TV screen flashed with an Xbox logo. So he'd been gaming and hadn't switched the TV back to TV mode. But he had put away the controller. If he'd left in a hurry or been taken, would he have put it back?

A Clive Cussler novel sat on the coffee table, with no indication as to how far into the book Jackson was. Sam plucked a library receipt from inside the cover, indicating he had also checked out a John Grisham novel. So where was it? She made a note to check for the book when she went upstairs.

She was about to move to the dining room when she spotted Jackson's trashcan beside the couch. She knelt down and looked inside. It was mostly empty. A few scraps of paper, an envelope, and an M&M's wrapper. Nothing messy, so Sam pulled them out and sorted through them. She felt like a snoop, looking at Jackson's bill stubs and a credit card pre-approval. But she kept telling herself it was for a good cause. Besides, she doubted Jackson would care. Or would hesitate to rifle through her garbage if she was missing.

Sam lifted a small bouquet of shriveled flowers with a frown. Had Jackson bought flowers? For himself? For someone else? Were they from someone to him? She set them aside and looked back into the trashcan. She lifted a crinkled piece of paper from the bottom of the can and opened it. Three words were written in the center of the page.

Ivan's here ~Allie

Sam frowned. Neither name rang a bell.

She looked at the slip of paper again. There was a small corporate logo for Glennon Insurance in the bottom corner. Was Allie an employee at Glennon Insurance? A client? Was Jackson working for them? Could that be what had taken him away for the better part of the week? But what did that have to do with Wilbur and Peaceful Shores Assisted Living?

She pocketed the slip and returned the rest of the contents of the trashcan. She moved into the dining room next, finding nothing out of the ordinary. Pretty much nothing at all.

Next, she rummaged through the kitchen. There were a few dishes in the rack by the sink—a couple of bowls, spoons, a plate and a fork, a pizza pan and cutter. No glasses, but the garbage under the sink contained two empty cans of cream soda. Jackson had eaten cereal and frozen pizzas. And a potpie, evidenced by the empty box in the garbage. Sam saw remnants from several other heat-and-eat meals and decided against digging through the rest of the garbage can.

She did, however, open the refrigerator. It wasn't overly full, but it did have all the expected items—milk, eggs, butter, juice, lunchmeats and cheeses, sauces, some hamburger meat. No vegetables. Typical Jackson.

A container in the back caught her attention, and Sam reached for it out of curiosity. It clunked. Cookies or candy left over from Christmas? A block of cheese or a solid piece of meat? Something Jackson had forgotten about and let spoil? She ended the suspense by lifting off the lid, ready to cover her nose with her arm.

It was Jackson's cell phone.

Or rather, parts of it. The battery and the SIM card had been removed and were in the container next to the shell. Why in the world would his cell phone be in the refrigerator? And why taken apart?

Sam's search had made her oblivious to the storm outside, but a deafening boom of thunder reminded her it was ongoing and snapped her away from staring at the phone in the container. She set it on the table and retrieved her own phone from her purse. Checking the time, she called Reggie. As expected, considering it was still the prime dinner rush, he didn't answer.

"Reggie, it's Sam. I'm at Jackson's place, looking around. I thought maybe I could find a clue, as silly as that sounds. Anyhow, I found two things. One is a note on a sheet of paper from Glennon Insurance. It says, 'Ivan's here, Allie.' I don't know any Ivans or Allies. I also found his cell phone, disassembled, in a container in his refrigerator. I have no idea what any of this means but I thought you might. Give me a call when you get this? Thanks."

She took a deep breath and got back to work. She looked over the downstairs bathroom, then Jackson's bedroom and closet. It took awkward to a new level, sorting through Jackson's clothes and personal items. She found nothing to suggest where he was but did find a safe under the bed with no apparent key. She wasn't about to rip his place apart looking for a key, so when a search of obvious locations didn't produce it, she gave up.

Her last stop was the upstairs bathroom, where everything looked normal, at least for a bachelor. About to leave, Sam stopped, her hand just above the light switch. Slowly, she moved forward and knelt down, examining the floor between the vanity and the toilet. A small trashcan between them was slightly askew, and Sam had no intention of digging through it. But the trashcan was not what had caught her attention. Instead, her eyes focused on a small, dark spot almost directly underneath the corner of the vanity top. Upon closer examination, the spot was reddish-brownish, not black, and looked like dried liquid.

Blood.

Sam scanned the room, looking for any other such spots. But it was the only one of its kind. She didn't know what to make of it and tried to calm the fear rising inside of her by offering possible explanations for it. None of them satisfied her. Backing out of the bathroom, she called Reggie again.

"Reggie, it's Sam again," she said when his voicemail kicked in. "I just checked Jackson's bathroom, and I found what looks like blood on the floor, in front of the trashcan. I don't know what it means—I'm trying to reassure myself it's nothing. Anyhow, I wanted you to know. Thanks. Bye."

Sam forced herself to take a few deep breaths, realizing the drop didn't prove anything. She wasn't even positive it was blood, or that it was Jackson's. She prayed again for his safety, and that she and Reggie and the others looking for him would be able to figure out how to help him if he was in trouble. Then, before she broke down at the thought that something beyond their help had happened to him, she headed downstairs.

It was a quarter to seven, and Connie's *braciole* had to be about ready. Sam left everything as she had found it—including putting the phone back in the refrigerator. Outside, the rain was still pouring. So Sam flipped up her hood and, after locking Jackson's door behind her, made a mad dash over to Connie's. She still got soaked, but it was worth it. The *braciole* was just coming out of the oven, and the aroma was intoxicating.

Chapter Fifteen

6:53 p.m.

MOUSE WAS BORED with video games. He couldn't believe it. He never got bored. Maybe with a game in particular, but not with all games. And yet, there he sat, staring at his screen, no interest in any of his assortment of third-person shooter or alien deathmatch or mystical world exploration games.

This had actually happened once before, a few summers ago, when it had been unbearably hot, and Mouse had spent about four straight days chugging Mountain Dew in front of a fan. By the end of day three, he had been bored to tears. He'd hacked into Google's mainframe, just to see if he could do it, and had nearly been identified. He had at least learned his lesson. Sort of.

Pam's voice echoed down the hallway. "Kyle! Phone!"

He'd been in such a stupor that he hadn't even heard it ring.

"Yeah," he said, reaching for his extension. "Yeah?"

"Mouse? It's Maggie."

Maggie? Last time he'd seen Maggie, she'd been dressed to kill for one of Jackson's undercover assignments at a club in San Diego. Thinking of her now, Mouse suddenly had trouble forming thoughts, much less words.

He swallowed. "Uh, yeah. Hi."

"I need a favor, Mouse."

"Okay." It wasn't often hot women asked Mouse for a favor, and he hoped he could deliver.

"Reggie found out that Jackson spent time with a guy named Wilbur Anderson on Tuesday before he disappeared. Wilbur's missing now too."

"Who names their kid Wilbur?"

"Very old people. He's in his upper eighties."

Mouse frowned. "Why was Jackson hanging out with an old geezer?"

"I don't know. I found out he's a World War II vet and some other basic biographical info. But I was hoping you could find out more."

"Uh, like what?"

"See if you can find out what he did in the war, look up his unit, research his army buddies. I have a handful of names."

"Okay. What are you looking for?"

"Anything unusual, suspicious, or that might tie to Jackson."

"Okay."

"You got a pen and paper?"

"Keyboard."

Maggie read through Wilbur's bio, and Mouse typed down the relevant info. Then she gave him half a dozen names.

"These all army buddies?"

"All but Virginia Campbell. She was his wife."

"You think she's involved?"

"She died in 1990, but it might not hurt to check up on her family."

"Okay."

"You have time tonight?"

"Yeah, sure."

"Okay. I'll swing by in about an hour."

"Y-you . . . you're coming here?"

"That okay?"

"Y-yeah. Fine."

"My timing may vary based on the rain. I ride a bike."

"A bike?"

"Thanks, Mouse. I'll see you later."

"Yeah. Later."

He slowly hung up the phone. Maggie was coming to his house? It was a mess. He was a mess. He hadn't showered since . . .

Mouse spent a few minutes debating whether showering, cleaning up his room, or actually doing the research Maggie had requested was most important. He split the difference, spending five minutes tossing junk in his closet and spraying some Axe in the crevices. Then he got to work on the computer.

Any idiot could find out some basic biographical information on the internet, what with the explosion of digitally stored data on the web. But it could be time consuming, and Mouse knew some shortcuts. They were borderline legal, but when all he was doing was gathering information, he didn't worry about blurry lines. Especially when it was for a good cause.

By eight o'clock when the doorbell rang, Mouse had good bios on all of the names Maggie had given him. He grabbed the USB drive containing the data from his computer, sprayed himself again with the body spray, and headed out to the living room. He was just in time to hear the incredulity in Pam's voice.

"*You're* here to see Kyle?"

"That's right," Maggie said.

Pam turned around to holler and saw Mouse standing there, trying to lean casually against the door. He offered a half wave, which probably looked stupid. But Maggie wore a leather jacket over a red V-neck, and she was carrying her motorcycle helmet, and he had all he could do to keep his tongue from sticking to the roof of his mouth.

Pam's jaw actually hung open, but she regained her composure before Mouse did. "Come on in," she said as she turned back to Maggie.

"Thanks."

Mouse finally found a voice. "Uh, this way."

He led her back to his room, wishing he'd taken the time to clean it some more. "It stop raining?" he asked over his shoulder.

"Just in time. You find anything?"

"Yeah." He entered his room and stepped to the side. "Come on in."

Maggie passed him, and he debated closing the door. He always closed it when Jackson came over to give them some privacy from Pam, but he was afraid Maggie would think it inappropriate or something. Then again, this wasn't high school. They were both grownups.

Maggie set her helmet on his bed and removed her jacket. Mouse nearly swooned.

"Which screen?" she asked.

"Uh, this one," Mouse said, pointing to a laptop on the desk. He plugged the USB drive back into it. "Have a seat."

Maggie sat down, and Mouse leaned on the desk beside her. "I didn't find much else on Wilbur Anderson, besides what you had. I didn't have time to hack into any military database to see specifics on his missions in Europe."

Maggie turned her head. "You can do that?"

"In theory."

"What about his buddies?"

"They must have lived better than him," Mouse said. "They're all dead."

"All?"

Mouse nodded. "Page two."

Maggie scrolled down. "Killed in Korea, lung cancer, heart attack, heart . . ." she trailed off. "Two of them died of heart attacks in the last ten days?"

Mouse nodded. "I found that a little odd."

Maggie read the names. "Albert Klein died on the 14th and Ken Waters on the 16th. Dallas and Salt Lake City."

"They were both old," Mouse said. "It could be coincidence."

"Could be. But now Wilbur and Jackson are missing." She looked back at the screen. "What's this about a book?"

"Wilkerson wrote a book about the unit's exploits in Europe. Sold okay."

"*We Saved the World.* I wonder if I could download it."

Mouse shrugged.

"Anything else I should know about?" Maggie asked.

"I don't think so. I checked on the wife's family. They were farmers. Nothing there."

"Nothing that raised a red flag as it pertains to Jackson?"

"No."

Maggie nodded. "Okay. Thanks."

"Sure." He reached for the USB drive and pulled it out. "Here you go."

"Thanks."

She stood and put on her jacket.

"If . . . if you need anything else, let me know," Mouse said.

"I will."

Not sure on protocol, Mouse walked her back to the door.

"Take care," he said with another half wave. Maggie nodded in return and Mouse closed the door behind her.

Pam actually muted the TV. "Who was that?"

"Would you believe it was my girlfriend?"

Pam laughed. "Not if you paid her."

"She's a friend of a friend."

"What'd she want?"

"Nothing."

"Uh-huh."

The phone rang.

"Get it," Pam said.

Mouse didn't answer her but grabbed the phone. "Yeah?"

"Is this Mouse?"

It was a female voice, much higher than Maggie's. She sounded cute.

"Uh, yeah," he answered.

"This is Sam, Jackson's friend."

"Yeah, what's up?"

"Reggie told me you have Jackson's computer, is that right?"

"Yeah, he dropped it off the other day."

"Can you find out if he knows anyone named Ivan or Allie? Maybe Allison."

"I can try."

"One of them might work for Glennon Insurance."

"Glennon Insurance."

"That's right. If you find anything, could you give me or Reggie a call?"

"Sure."

"Thanks, Mouse."

"Yeah, sure."

Mouse hung up the phone and ignored Pam's question. Instead, he headed for his room, wondering if Jackson had any other girlfriends who would call him that night.

*   *   *

8:14 p.m.

AFTER CALLING Mouse, Sam decided to try one more source. She had enjoyed a very tasty and very long dinner with Connie, who had pumped Sam for information she didn't have. But Connie had also served her dessert. *Zeppola*. Delicious. When Reggie hadn't answered again, Sam had tried Mouse, wondering if she should take Jackson's cell phone to him or not. But the fact that it was in such a strange place made Sam wonder if it wasn't there on purpose. Did a refrigerator protect it from being traced or something? Until she talked to Reggie, she decided to leave it where she found it.

But there was someone else who might know something. So Sam thanked Connie profusely and headed for Marina del Rey. The rain had temporarily quit, but lightning occasionally flashed in the western sky to suggest more was on the way.

Jackson often joked that Leroy went to bed with the sun, and Sam had feared he might have turned in already. But when she stepped onto his houseboat and rapped on the door, he answered promptly.

"Sam," Leroy said, smiling and frowning at the same time. "What brings you out here?"

"I have a question for you, about Jackson."

Leroy nodded. "Come on in." She followed him into the living room, and he offered her a seat on the couch. "Can I get you something to drink? Coffee, maybe?"

"No, thanks."

Leroy sat at the opposite end of the couch. "What's on your mind?"

"I went to Jackson's house today to look around. I thought maybe I could find something—a clue of some sort."

"You have a key?"

"No. His neighbor Connie let me in."

Leroy nodded.

"I found a piece of paper in his trashcan with a handwritten note on it. It said, 'Ivan's here,' and was signed by someone named Allie." She looked into Leroy's blue eyes, a shade or two darker than Jackson's. "Do either of those names mean anything to you?"

"Ivan and Allie," Leroy said, tipping his head back.

"It was on a sheet of paper from Glennon Insurance if that means anything. Maybe one of them is a client, or maybe Jackson is?" She shrugged. "I tried calling their automated system, and it let me search by name, and there was no one in their system with the name Ivan or any version of Allie."

Leroy looked at the ceiling. He closed his eyes. "Allie." He opened them and looked at Sam. "I think that was the name of a girl who used to work with Jack. Back in San Diego. I should say it was her alias."

Sam frowned. "Alias?"

"She and Jack worked for an investigative firm, both as assistants. It's what got Jack thinking about the P.I. business. Anyhow, they came across this guy—his name escapes me—who ripped off a bunch of churches or something, and they decided to go after him to get the money back. They ran this con," he said, chuckling as it came back to him, "where they sold him a boat they had chartered. Made him think it was theirs, took him for something like a hundred thousand, and then called the Coast Guard when he sailed it out to sea."

"Oh my goodness. He never told me."

"I think he was always a little bothered by the legality of what they did. Technically, they committed fraud, for a good cause."

"And his partner called herself Allie?"

Leroy nodded. "Real name was Walker."

"Walker?"

"Her last name. I don't know her first. Jack always called her Walker."

"Were they . . . an item?"

"I don't think so," Leroy said with a grin. "But I think he kind of liked her."

Sam processed for a moment. "What about Ivan?"

Leroy shook his head.

"That wasn't the name of the guy they conned, was it?"

"No. I don't remember his name, but it was something hoity-toity sounding."

"Maybe it was a codename they had for him?"

"Could be, I reckon. I don't know."

Sam sat back. "You know anything else about this girl Walker?"

"Afraid not. It's been four or five years now. I'm lucky I remember her name."

"Well, it could be the link we've been looking for. Thank you."

"Glad to help."

Sam stood. "I should get going. It's been a long few days, and I'm bushed."

"Offer you a donut for the road?" Leroy asked, nodding at his counter. "They're from this morning, but they're still donuts."

"I just had *braciole* and *zeppola* with Connie, but thanks."

Leroy walked her to the door, and as she walked back to the car, Sam looked up at the dark sky, smelling the past and coming rain. Maybe, just maybe, she'd found a lead.

*   *   *

9:47 p.m.

WHILE MUTED personalities on ESPN broke down a day of basketball upsets, Reggie flipped through messages on his phone. He'd been busy in the kitchen and on the floor until nine, when things had started to die down. It had been another forty-five minutes before Cameron's staff was caught up and he could disconnect totally and retreat to his office. It was his first chance to check messages, and as he listened to Sam's two, he frowned. Ivan? Allie? A phone broken down and stashed in the fridge? Blood on the bathroom floor? As in, cut himself shaving blood or head bashed in by Nazis blood? Sam's message had been vague, and when he tried recalling her, she didn't pick up.

He sighed, debating whether or not to run out to Jackson's. He decided against it, concluding the blood had to have been minor or Maggie would have spotted it when they'd searched the house. That didn't soothe him much.

Maggie had called as well, giving him info on Wilbur Anderson. None of it provided any indication where or why he had disappeared, or what Jackson's involvement was. The recent deaths of two of his old army buddies were unsettling but didn't necessarily mean anything, especially as it pertained to Jackson. He decided not to bother calling her back, not until he had something concrete at least.

Ashley had not called, which he concluded meant she hadn't found anything. No word from Mouse, Leroy, or Olivia. As he noted that, his phone vibrated, and the display showed what was becoming a familiar number: Olivia's.

"Hey," Reggie said, punching on the phone. "What's up?"

"Hey," she said. "Sorry I haven't gotten back to you sooner. What a day."

"I know the feeling."

"I'm afraid I don't know much. My morning and afternoon were fruitless, and I'm actually in San Diego right now running down a lead on another case. Too many balls in the air." Her sigh transmitted through the phone. "You find anything new?"

"Maybe," Reggie said, and explained about his and Sam's investigation into Jackson's rental car, contacting Ashley, and the note Sam had found in Jackson's trashcan with the names Ivan and Allie. "She also found his phone," he said.

"She found his phone?"

"Yep."

"In the house?"

"Uh-huh."

"Hmm."

"What's that?"

"It's just odd. Who leaves their phone behind? He could have forgotten it, or left in a hurry or . . . under duress."

"It was taken apart," Reggie said. "Battery and SIM card removed."

"He didn't want it traced."

"Yeah."

"Where was it?"

"In the refrigerator."

"What? Why in the refrigerator?"

"Probably because J's seen *Indiana Jones* and thinks all refrigerators are nuclear bomb-proof and that that somehow means a cell can't be tracked when it's inside one or something."

Olivia laughed, and Reggie wasn't sure if it was at Jackson or his description of him.

"So he rents a car, disables his phone . . . He wants to be off the grid."

"It seems that way."

"But why?"

"Don't know," Reggie said with a sigh. "Don't suppose the names Allie or Ivan mean anything to you, huh?"

"Can't say as that they do. Ivan sounds Russian, not German or Jewish. And Allie . . . Sorry, I've got nothing."

"Join the club," Reggie said.

"Are you doing okay?"

He sighed. "Under the circumstances, yeah."

"We're going to find him, Reggie."

"Yeah," he said, lacking conviction.

"Look . . . I'm tied up here tonight and early tomorrow. But I should be back in L.A. by noon, and I'll be able to devote my full attention to finding Jackson. If you can get us into his house, we'll get the phone, and I can run some diagnostics and see if it tells us anything."

"You know how to do that?"

"I'm not an expert, but yeah, I've taken a few forensic technology courses. If I get stumped, I know someone who can help."

Reggie nodded to himself, glad that he had resolution as far as whether or not to go get the phone and take it to Mouse. "All right," he said. "Give me a call when you get back."

"I will. And I still have calls out to some people. Maybe one of them will hear something."

"Yeah," he said with similar conviction as before.

"Hang in there, Reggie."

Her voice was soothing, and Reggie found himself smiling. Even if she couldn't offer any reassurance beyond empty promises, the fact that she was trying meant something.

"I'll call you tomorrow," she said.

"All right, tomorrow."

"Bye, Reggie."

"Bye."

He closed his phone and sat back, rubbing his hands over his face. Then, before the kitchen closed, he went to make himself something to eat. He had a feeling he was going to need his strength before this was all over.

Chapter Sixteen

Sunday, March 24
10:31 a.m.

"MAY THE LORD bless you, and keep you, and make His face to shine upon you. . . . Amen."

Pastor Rick lowered his outstretched hands and offered his congregation a slight nod as he stepped back. A worship team consisting of a keyboardist, a guitarist, and a drummer played a postlude that was quickly drowned out by the din of conversation in the sanctuary.

Sam reached for her Bible and purse and scanned the room for signs of Mouse. She hoped she would recognize him, having only met him a few times. He came with Jackson now and again, but not all that often. Chances were he wasn't even there. But she had called him after leaving Leroy's houseboat the night before, giving him the name Walker and asking him to add it to his search of Jackson's computer for an Ivan or an Allie. She had come to church hoping he would be there with a lead.

Sam didn't spot him in the sanctuary, so she headed for the foyer. There was a second service half an hour later, and it was possible he would attend that service. She greeted a few acquaintances with smiles and picked up a copy of the weekly newsletter that updated worshippers on the events of the coming week. Around her, adults formed conversation circles, teens joined their cliques, and little kids darted back and forth. It was a typical Sunday.

Normally, Sam sought out a few friends or headed for the room where her adult Sunday school met. Today, she hung around in the foyer, looking for Mouse.

A familiar looking woman that Sam couldn't place walked by, giving her the same look that Sam felt was on her own face. Something told her the face was important, that it was tied to Jackson. But she couldn't figure out why.

This was a particularly hectic Sunday, with a table selling pizzas to fund a youth missions trip and sign-ups for a church-wide bake sale, in addition to the usual hubbub of people coming and going. None of them, to Sam's memory, resembled Mouse.

She thought of the woman again. Wavy brown hair, tan skin, dressed in a black top and jeans. She knew she had seen her before, but . . . where? Why couldn't she be better with faces and places? She had half a mind to chase after the woman, but the other half of her mind won out and she continued wandering around the foyer and down a few halls, looking for Mouse.

In the sanctuary, music started, indicating the second service was about to begin. Sam's Sunday school class usually spent the first ten to fifteen minutes shooting the breeze about nothing, so she waited an extra five minutes. When Mouse didn't show, she decided to call him.

Stepping outside, she dialed his number and hoped she hadn't missed him and he was sitting in church with a ringing phone. Or still sleeping. No, scratch that. If he was sleeping all Sunday morning, he deserved to be woken up.

Thunderstorms from the night before had passed, leaving hot sunshine in their wake. Sam squinted against the glare as Mouse's phone rang four times before he answered with a sleepy, "Yeah?"

"Mouse? It's Sam."

"Yeah. Hi."

"Sorry to bother you, but I wanted to see if you found anything about the Walker woman."

"Uh, yeah. I think so. Her name's Tori Walker. There was an old contact in Jackson's e-mail, but no messages to or from her."

"Tori Walker?"

"Yeah. She's got an apartment over in Manhattan Beach."

"What about Ivan or Allie?"

"Nothing," Mouse said. "If we had his phone, maybe."

Sam bit her lip. She hadn't heard back from Reggie yet, after leaving him several messages the night before. She was still hesitant to move Jackson's phone from his refrigerator until she had a chance to talk to Reggie. So she got Tori Walker's phone number and address from Mouse. Then she leaned against the support column of the carport while pondering her next move.

She knew Reggie went to church, so she didn't want to try him until afternoon. She decided to try Tori Walker. Scanning the church newsletter on which she'd written Tori's number, Sam dialed, wondering what to say if she answered.

She didn't have to worry. The call went to voicemail, and Sam disconnected. She was about to head in to join Sunday school when her phone rang. Tori Walker calling her back?

"This is Sam."

"Sam, it's Reggie."

"Hey. What's up?"

"Saw you called a few times last night. Sorry, it was crazy."

"It's okay."

"You found J's phone?"

"Yeah." She explained again about finding it in the refrigerator and recounted finding the note in Jackson's trash.

"I'll swing by this afternoon and get the phone and have it checked out. Might be able to find something there that will give us a clue."

He didn't say how he'd "have it checked out," and Sam didn't ask, lest she be coerced into another felonious role-playing exercise. She did tell him about visiting Leroy and what she had learned about Allie being Tori Walker. "I tried calling her just now, but she didn't answer. I'll try again this afternoon."

"Let me know what you find," Reggie said.

"Okay, you too."

Sam sighed as she lowered her phone. They were making progress, but it was agonizingly slow.

*   *   *

10:52 a.m.

MAGGIE WAS sweating under her jacket as she walked into church. That was the downside of riding a motorcycle—if you wanted to be safe, you couldn't very well go sleeveless. She hung her jacket in a closet off the foyer and headed for the sanctuary. She was a few minutes early on purpose, hoping to bump into Russell so she could ask if he'd heard anything more from his network of street people. At least, she kept telling herself that was the reason she hoped to bump into him. Truth be told, she didn't know anymore.

Maggie had only been coming to church for a few weeks, but already some of the faces were looking familiar. In particular, a blond woman hanging out by the bulletin board. Oh yeah, Jackson's "nurse" after he'd been shot. The same one who'd come around looking for him, according to Connie?

Why are you jealous, Maggie? You and Jackson never promised each other anything.

"Maggie!"

She turned toward the shout and saw Russell waving over and through a crowd. He was dressed in black pants, a dark gray shirt, and a black tie. His sleeves were rolled to the elbow, and she couldn't help but think that he looked incredibly comfortable in his Sunday finest, whereas most guys—one in particular—seemed to hate dressing up.

And she had to admit to herself, hearing him call her name in a crowd brought a smile to her face.

You're pathetic, Maggie.

Russell dodged a few parishioners and met her just outside the door to the sanctuary. "Any word on Jackson?"

"No. We found a possible tie to a guy who disappeared from an assisted living home middle of the week, and we've been checking him out, but we've got nothing so far."

"I checked in with a few people while I was working yesterday," Russell said, "but no leads."

"Did this alleged deal go down?" Maggie asked, lowering her voice. Talking about drug deals in church seemed taboo.

"I don't know."

"Seems to be a common refrain."

He tapped her elbow with his Bible as they entered the sanctuary. "I'm having lunch with a friend of mine who works at the D.A.'s office. She's helped prosecute a number of gang members and might know something. You want to join us?"

Maggie tried to hide a frown, but couldn't. Part of her was jealous—stupid as it was—that Russell was having lunch with another woman. Five minutes ago, she was jealous of Jackson's friend, now jealous of Russell. Did she have some sort of sudden hormonal imbalance?

"Um, I wouldn't be intruding, would I?"

"No. We have to discuss a little business that pertains to some recently evicted friends of mine, but I also wanted to ask her about the Silvaz and Grays and Jackson."

Maggie stepped to the side, out of the way of a family heading for the front. "Yeah, sure."

"I'll find you after the service."

"Okay."

Russell grinned and headed toward the front. Maggie found a seat and tried once again to sort out her feelings. She really was living in her childhood TV shows, falling for two guys at once, but not really falling for either of them since she hadn't technically dated either one. She chalked it up to the gamut of emotions that came with losing her job, her apartment, and Jackson on the same day. Or maybe this was part of the new faith roller coaster Jackson had talked about.

As the worship pastor greeted everyone and called the service to order, Maggie offered yet another quick prayer for clarity. Everyone said that coming to Christ was supposed to make the problems of life make sense. So why did it seem to be the opposite for Maggie?

*   *   *

11:09 a.m.

OLIVIA SOUNDED very chipper when she called to let Reggie know she had just merged onto the 405 in Irvine and would meet him at

Jackson's in an hour. She did not divulge anything she may have learned overnight or in the morning or say some of her sources actually had gotten back to her with anything. For all the contacts she had, she didn't seem to get much intel from them. Then again, what would a bunch of CIA and DOD and NSA liaisons know about Jackson and an old guy from a retirement home?

Reggie killed forty minutes doing a few chores around the house while listening to some gospel rap on his MP3 player. It was as close as he'd get to church this Sunday. Then, a little after a quarter to twelve, he set out for Jackson's house in Pacific Palisades. While he drove, he called Mouse.

"Yeah?"

"Hey, man. You busy today?"

"I have to work, but not till five. Why?"

"If I brought you J's phone, can you pull data off it?" He couldn't put his finger on it exactly, but something about Olivia . . . He couldn't even bring himself to say it. But having Mouse as a backup plan suddenly seemed prudent.

"You found his phone?"

"Sam did," Reggie said.

"Where?"

"His refrigerator."

"Why was it in his refrigerator?"

"Because J's a dork, man. Battery and SIM card had been removed and were sitting beside the phone in a Tupperware in his fridge. I think he was trying to keep it from being tracked or found."

"Well, that would do it, although he wouldn't have to put it in the refrigerator."

"Give him a crash course on spy techniques when you see him, will you?"

"Yeah, sure. What was Sam doing in his refrigerator anyhow?"

"No idea. Look, I've got another line, but if that doesn't pan out, I may call you later, all right?"

"I'll be here."

Reggie closed his phone.

A thought had hit him during their discussion. Maybe Jackson wasn't the dork. Maybe somebody else had hidden his phone, trying to make sure no one else would find it. But why? Did it contain important information? If so, why not destroy it? So anyone searching for him would think he'd gone away on his own and taken his phone? Then why leave it behind at all? Too many questions, not enough answers.

He turned his focus to Olivia and whether or not he trusted her and her forensic technology classes and her ability to run diagnostics on the phone. Maybe it'd be better to entrust that to Mouse, given the way Olivia's resources had availed them so far. Then again, she was the one who'd come to him with intel about Jackson and *Wolfskinder* and a bunch of other things he didn't know. Maybe her sources weren't so bad after all.

Reggie's phone rang as he turned onto Sunset Boulevard. He flicked it open with his thumb. "What's up?"

"Reggie? It's Detective Larson."

"Detective."

"We found Jackson's car."

Chapter Seventeen

11:56 a.m.

"YOU FOUND JACKSON'S car?" Reggie repeated. "The rental?"

"A Toyota Yaris," Ashley answered, "license plate eight-gulf-bravo-echo-seven-seven-three."

Reggie cleared the lump forming in his throat. "Where?"

"Behind a motel in Huntington Beach. Named the Pierless Motel. P-I-E-R, as in the Huntington Beach Municipal Pier on the PCH."

"How'd you find it?"

"Couple of beat cops responding to a disturbing the peace complaint from an apartment behind the hotel recognized the plate from the BOLO I put out."

"Your patrol ask around at the hotel."

"No. Since we didn't file an official missing person report, they just notified me. Like we talked about, if he's undercover or hiding out, that might draw attention to him. And we don't even know if he's at the motel. The car was just parked there."

"Any reason I can't go look around?"

"Not if you abide by the law," she said. "Just be careful."

"I will."

"And Reggie, call me if you find anything."

"I will. Thanks, Detective."

Olivia's Chevy Aveo was parked in Jackson's driveway when Reggie arrived a minute later. He coasted to the curb across the street and reached for his door handle, a host of conflicting thoughts filling his head. He decided to play things close to the vest.

His grandma used to have a saying, "fresh as the morning," used mostly to describe one of her grandchildren who had dressed up nice for an event like Easter Sunday. As he crossed the street and Olivia got out of the car, that phrase popped back into his head. She wore a loose, sleeveless tiered blouse that accentuated her long, smooth, slender arms. Distressed jeans under knee-high boots. Her curly black hair had a little extra bounce, it seemed, and a natural smile lit up her face. The clock on his dash had read 12:01, but he concluded Olivia looked "fresh as the morning" nonetheless. He also concluded, despite his hesitation and his desire to focus on finding Jackson, there was no point in denying the attraction he felt to her.

"Hi," she said, the smile widening.

"Hey," he greeted back. "How was the ride up?"

"Better than expected," she said.

"Made good time."

"I did."

He held up a key, and they walked to the front door. They were almost there when a singsong greeting wafted across the lawn. Reggie turned to see Connie ambling toward them.

"Reggie, is that you?" she asked, squinting under a wide-brimmed visor. She looked as if she had come off the golf course, with a miniskirt (far too mini for her figure) and a sleeveless collared shirt.

With an "I've got this" look at Olivia, Reggie turned her way. "Hi, Connie."

"Have you found Jackson yet?"

"No, ma'am. This is a friend of mine, Olivia."

"It's nice to meet you, dear," Connie said. She cut off a "Nice to meet you too" response by looking up at Reggie and asking, "Where could he be?"

"We don't know. We're going to check out his place again."

"This just isn't like him. I know he went off the map—is that the term?—back in Las Vegas last year, but that was different. We knew where he was, at least. I hope nothing's happened to him."

"I'm sure he's fine," Reggie said, hoping she at least believed it.

She nodded without much conviction. "I'll leave you to it. Call me the second you find him."

"Will do."

She shuffled off, and he opened the door and held it for Olivia.

"You've searched the house already?" she asked.

"Yeah, Friday with Maggie. Then Sam did yesterday."

"Maggie and Sam?"

"'J's girl 'friends.'"

She nodded, wandering through the dining room. "Phone's in the refrigerator, you said?"

"Yeah," he said, following her into the dining room and then into the kitchen. She stopped in front of Jackson's refrigerator as if waiting. Then she opened the door and knelt down.

"Meat and potatoes kind of guy."

"You have no idea."

They began reaching for containers, and it only took them a few tries to find the one containing Jackson's cell phone. They took it out and set it on the kitchen table.

"This is his phone?" Olivia asked, seemingly in disbelief.

"Yeah, why?"

"It's a flip phone."

"So's mine."

"Really?"

"Serves its purpose."

With a nod of assent, Olivia reinserted the SIM card into its slot and replaced the battery. She stood and powered on the phone.

"What exactly can you pull off this?"

"Recent calls or texts, unusual contacts, web searches—if it has that capability," she said with a corner-of-the-mouth smirk. "GPS, maybe." She thumbed through his calls. "Looks like the last call was . . . Monday morning to a Ray Donaldson."

"Made or received?"

"Made. Last received was Sunday night, an 800 number." She continued searching. "Doesn't look like he's made many calls of late."

"Not unless he's on a case."

"Your number, Connie."

"The nice neighbor lady we met."

"Maggie, Sam."

"The girl friends."

"A Jesse MacFarland? A couple unidentified, long-distance numbers." Reggie shook his head.

"That's back to the beginning of the month. Only names that stand out are Donaldson and MacFarland."

"Neither ring a bell. No Tori Walker, huh?"

"No. Who's that?"

He explained about Sam finding the slip of paper in his trashcan. Olivia frowned until he explained that Leroy believed Allie was an alias for a former coworker of Jackson's, Tori Walker.

"It might be something," Olivia said. "I'll run her name through our database, as well as Donaldson and MacFarland. I'll also see if this dinosaur is even GPS enabled," she said, holding up and shaking the phone. "It's been here for a while, but maybe past movement will give us something. Worth a try, at least."

"I'm going to run down to Huntington Beach."

"What's in Huntington Beach?"

"Cops found J's rental car behind a beach motel."

"Reggie," she said, playfully whacking his arm. "Talk about burying the lead."

"I'm not sure it is a lead, yet. J's friend with LAPD put out a BOLO but didn't want the officers to make contact, in case J is working a case undercover. That's why I'm going to go check it out. I don't exactly look like a cop."

"You want a wingman?"

"I do, but you've got another lead to follow. Time's money, right? Best if we split up."

She nodded, albeit reluctantly.

"I know someone who can sub in anyhow. But I'll call you the minute I know something."

"Okay."

"There's one other thing you should see."

"More secrets?"

"So to speak." He nodded toward the stairs, and she took the lead climbing up to the bedroom. He stepped around her and flicked on the light in the bathroom. It took him only a moment to spot the discoloration on the floor, where Sam had said it was, and he stepped back.

"What am I looking at?" Olivia asked.

"By the corner of the cabinet," he said. "Small drop on the floor. Sam found it," he added as Olivia honed in and crouched down. "Thinks it's blood."

She looked up at him. "Hard to say, but it looks kind of like it."

He roamed his eyes across the bathroom, looking for any other signs of blood. A slight discoloration on the bottom corner of the countertop caught his attention. Right above the drop on the floor. Was it blood? Had someone caught themselves on the corner of the counter? Or had something else brownish dripped off the edge?

"Whatever it is," Olivia said, drawing his focus back to her, "it's small. If . . . if something had happened to him here, there'd be more."

"Yeah, that's what I'm thinking."

"That's good news then," she said, standing.

"Yeah."

"Reggie." She reached out a hand and rubbed his shoulder. "It is good news. Everything we've found would suggest that, wherever he is, he's acting on his own."

"It would suggest that," he said. His eyes traced from her hand up her arm to her shoulder. He couldn't help noticing how well toned she was, how smooth her skin was, how . . . bare. It wasn't just a sensual observation. Something about her arm . . .

"We should get going," she said, dropping her hand. "Like I said, I can run some basic diagnostics on his phone—very basic, given the phone. But I know someone I can call who can maybe give me more."

"Okay."

"Call me when you get to Huntington Beach."

"I will."

"Reggie. Is something wrong?"

He shook his head.

She put both hands on his arms, taking a step toward him. "We'll do everything we can to find him."

"Can I ask you something?"

"Of course."

"Have you been here before?"

"What?"

"In J's house?"

Olivia's eyes narrowed. "No. Why would you ask?"

"I don't know. Maybe I'm paranoid, but . . . you kind of seem to know where you're going. You haven't looked around at anything else in the house, just made a beeline for the fridge. And . . . your arm."

"My arm?"

"You had a Band-Aid on it the other day, when we first met."

"So?"

"So, there's blood on the floor here, and blood on the bottom of the countertop, it looks like."

"I got a tetanus shot," she said.

He nodded.

"And I didn't toss the place just now because you said you and two friends already had, and besides, I doubt Jackson left a note telling us where he was going. He took apart his phone and hid it. Clearly, he's not going to leave something just lying around. Our best bet is in here," she said, holding up the phone, "or in Huntington Beach."

Reggie nodded again.

"I know this is a lot—Jackson missing, neo-Nazis, names on phones and in garbage cans. I know you're under a lot of stress. The last thing I want to do is add to it." She reached into her pocket and withdrew a thin wallet. Out of it, she drew a business card. "Here. You can contact the BfV directly. They'll vouch for me and what I'm doing here."

He took the card and met her eyes. "That's not necessary. I'm sorry, Olivia. I just . . . Like I said, paranoid, and stress. I'm sorry."

"Don't worry about it," she said with a smile that seemed genuine and belied any offense she had taken. "I understand." She inched closer. "My number one priority is finding your friend, Reggie. If you believe anything I've told you, believe that."

"I do."

She grinned, then briefly touched his cheek with her hand. "We really should get moving, though."

"Yeah."

They headed back downstairs, to the living room, and out onto the driveway.

"I'll be in touch as soon as I hear anything," she said.

"Me too."

She smiled one last time and turned to get into her car. If Olivia was hurt or questioned Reggie's loyalty, she didn't show it. And he felt a little stupid, having voiced his suspicions out loud. A Band-aid and a drop of blood? And who wouldn't know their way around Jackson's house—it had three rooms.

Only one thing still bothered him as Olivia backed out of the driveway, waved, and drove off. Her reassuring words and disarming smile—they were almost identical to the ones his ex-wife Keisha had so often used to persuade him.

*   *   *

12:57 p.m.

MOUSE LOOKED out his window, taking in the scene along the Pacific Coast Highway. Tall palms lined the sidewalk, which was crowded with beachgoers. Beyond them, Huntington City Beach was packed, as was the pier stretching a third of a mile into the ocean. Typical of Southern California, the people were of every variety and every age. Most of them—at least the women—were hot, and Mouse enjoyed the slow drive. Slow because of traffic turning into or out of the beachside parking lots and pedestrians crossing at every street corner or walkway.

Just after pulling away from a crosswalk, Reggie had to stomp on the brakes of his Hummer. Mouse turned his head to see a pair of surfers nonchalantly jaywalking, their surfboards under their arms. Neither paid any attention to the vehicles waiting for them, and Reggie gave a quick tap on the horn. One jumped. The other just turned his head and made a gesture with his free hand.

As they started moving again, Mouse looked down at the satellite image of the Pierless Motel on his laptop. "Just a few more blocks."

Reggie nodded.

"You think he's there?"

"I dunno."

"What would he be doing in Huntington Beach?"

"Dunno."

"You've been quiet."

Reggie slowly rolled his head to look at Mouse.

"It's okay," Mouse said with a shrug.

"Thing is, I can't think of a good reason for J to be down here, by himself, not telling nobody where he's going." Reggie looked back at Mouse. "That's why I'm quiet. That's one of the reasons I'm quiet."

"There it is," Mouse said, pointing to a two-story neon sign on the left side of the road. "Wow, it's a dive."

Consisting of a single level containing maybe fifteen rooms all facing the ocean, the Pierless Motel had white siding and faded blue trim, doors, and shutters. Weeds grew in place of flowers underneath the windows, one of which was boarded up. Next to the office, which was connected to the rest of the building by a carport, was a fenced in swimming pool. The water was green, with a chaise lounge chair floating on the surface.

"What is he doing here?" Mouse asked.

Reggie just shook his head. Unable to make a left turn across the causeway, he went to the next cross street and made a U-turn. The Hummer barely fit through the carport, which was the only way to get to the parking lot behind the building. Reggie parked in the first available spot, and he and Mouse got out.

"So what do . . . ?"

Reggie started walking, and Mouse followed. They stopped at a charcoal gray car backed into a parking stall against the motel. It had a California plate, 8GBE773.

"This it?" Mouse asked.

Reggie nodded and tried the doors. They were locked.

"Can you pick them?"

"Maybe, but there's too many people around."

Mouse cupped his hands around his eyes and leaned toward the window. "Looks clean."

From the other side of the car, Reggie nodded.

"Now what?"

"Depends on who's manning the desk. Come on."

Mouse followed Reggie through the carport around to the front of the motel. They entered the office where a small TV/VCR unit sat on the counter. A guy in his thirties sat behind the desk, a button-down shirt open over a white ribbed tank top. Half a sandwich sat on a paper plate in front of him. He ignored it and Reggie and Mouse, his eyes on the TV.

Reggie peered at the screen. "Who's winning, man?"

The guy glanced at Reggie for just a second. "Clips."

Reggie nodded. "I need information on a customer."

"Sorry, confidential."

"It's important."

"I'm sure." The guy reached for his sandwich and took a bite, his eyes not leaving the TV.

Reggie grabbed his wallet and pulled out a twenty-dollar bill. He tossed it on the counter, just missing the plate as the guy set his sandwich down. He exchanged the sandwich for the bill and looked up at Reggie.

"His name's Jackson Douglas, drives the Toyota Yaris out back. We think he checked in several days ago."

The guy wiped his mouth with the back of his hand. "You a cop?"

"Think I'd've just spent twenty bucks if I had a badge I could've showed you instead?"

"This Douglas a cop?"

Reggie shook his head. "He here?"

"Might be."

Reggie retrieved another twenty.

"Let me check." The guy spun away from the TV to his computer screen. A minute later, he shook his head. "Don't see the name."

"What about Jack Goldman?"

"Nope."

"About six foot, two hundred, shaggy blond hair, beard."

"Doesn't ring a bell."

Reggie sighed.

"Do you keep a record of license plates?" Mouse asked.

"Yeah. For security."

"Plate number eight-G-B-E-seven-seven-three," Reggie said. He turned to Mouse while the guy checked. "Good call."

"Yeah," the guy said. "Belongs to the guy in 1C."

"Guy have a name?"

"Jim Davis."

"JD," Reggie said.

"When did he check in?" Mouse asked.

"Uh, Wednesday early a.m. Paid for a week in cash." The guy returned to his sandwich.

"So he's still here?" Reggie asked.

The guy shrugged.

Reggie sighed. "Thanks."

He turned, and Mouse again followed him. Out on the sidewalk, he asked, "You think he's here?"

"Something tells me no," Reggie said.

They stopped outside room 1C. The blinds were drawn, revealing nothing. With a look at Mouse, Reggie rapped on the door. He waited thirty seconds, then pounded a little harder. Still nothing.

"Maybe he went for a walk," Mouse said.

"Yeah," Reggie answered, already on his way back toward the office. Mouse followed yet again.

The guy was back to staring at the TV.

"You got a spare key for room 1C?"

"You kidding?"

"No. It's important."

"What are you guys, anyhow? Drug dealers?"

"We look like drug dealers?"

The guy turned from the TV. "Maybe."

Reggie reached for his wallet again. He pulled out two more twenty-dollar bills. "That's eighty bucks total. You can give me the key or I kick down the door."

A hunk of lettuce hung from the guy's lip. "Okay." He turned and reached into a drawer. He handed Reggie a key. "Bring it back."

Reggie nodded and headed back toward the room again. Mouse followed once more. The Pierless Motel used actual keys, and Reggie inserted it into the lock. He pushed open the door and stopped almost immediately.

"What is it?" Mouse asked, stepping around Reggie.

An old guy lay on the farther away of two beds, on top of instead of underneath the covers. He was perfectly still.

"Is he . . . ?"

Reggie nodded. He walked into the room while Mouse remained at the door. The guy had his hands folded across his stomach. He was dressed in cotton pajamas and thick wool socks. A glass of water sat beside the bed.

Reggie stepped back out of the bathroom. "J's not here." He looked down. "But that's his stuff."

"So he was here?"

Reggie nodded.

"Who's the dead guy?"

"My guess," Reggie said. "Wilbur Anderson."

Chapter Eighteen

1:11 p.m.

REGGIE'S FIRST CALL was to 9-1-1. His second was to Ashley. His third went straight to Maggie's voicemail. He didn't have the heart to call Leroy yet. Nor did he know what to tell Olivia. After their talk outside Jackson's bathroom, he did believe her and did chalk up his suspicions to paranoia. But he wasn't one-hundred-percent convinced. Besides, he still didn't know anything more to help them find Jackson.

The police arrived shortly, and Reggie told them everything he knew, straight up. He did not mention Olivia or *Wolfskinder*, as it was above his pay grade and he was starting to doubt the relevancy, given what they had found at the motel. Mouse and the guy from the front desk were also questioned. Both got skittish but apparently didn't draw the suspicion of the authorities. They questioned Reggie for thirty minutes, by which time an ambulance had come to take Wilbur to the morgue.

"Wh-what do we do now?" Mouse asked.

"I don't know, man," Reggie said, rubbing his head, then his face.

"Is Jackson in trouble?"

"Unless he has some good answers."

Mouse sat on the windowsill of the room down from where they had found Wilbur. "Where is he?"

"I don't know. J goes to the assisted living home, hangs out with Wilbur, then they both disappear. Turns out they're hiding out in a motel in Huntington Beach. Now Wilbur's dead and J's missing again." He shook his head. "Makes no sense."

"We know anything about this dead guy?"

The cops had asked the same question, and Reggie had told them exactly what he knew, which wasn't much. Maggie had dug up some basic biographical information, but other than that, their intel was pretty slim. Reggie was sure the cops could find out more, and they probably stood the best chance of finding Jackson too. Reggie just hoped Ashley could mediate so Jackson wouldn't end up in jail for murder.

Reggie's cell phone rang, and he stepped away from the door, where officers and paramedics were still coming and going. "What's up?"

"Reggie? It's Maggie. I got your message. What's going on?"

"We found J's car."

"That's great. Where?"

"A motel in Huntington Beach. He isn't here."

Her sigh was audible. "But his car is?"

"Yeah. That ain't all, Maggie."

"What? What aren't you telling me?"

"We found Wilbur."

"The old guy from the retirement home?"

"Yeah."

"Well, does he know where Jackson is?"

"Wilbur's dead, Maggie. He was laying on a bed in the motel room. Paramedics guess he died sometime overnight."

"He's dead? Why? What killed him?"

"They don't know. Nothing obvious."

"Reggie, what in the world is going on?"

"I don't know, Maggie." Reggie rubbed his head again. "Hey, you ever hear of a girl named Tori Walker?"

"I don't think so. Who is she?"

"Friend of Jackson's. They ran a con on some guy back in the day. We thought maybe it was linked to his disappearance, but nobody can find her."

"I've never heard of her."

"All right. Hey, I got another call. I'll keep you posted."

"Thanks."

Reggie tapped the display to switch calls. "Hey, what's up?"

*   *   *

1:36 p.m.

SAM PARKED in view of Leroy's houseboat and got out of her car. It was as warm of a day as Sam could remember, and on a Sunday afternoon, she would have loved to lounge in the sun with a good book. Instead, she was prepping for her second foray into private investigating in as many days.

She circled the car and stopped as Leroy stepped off the deck of his houseboat. He walked toward her in what could only be described as a fast shuffle. Sam felt a twinge of guilt involving him. But she wasn't going alone, and she didn't want to bother Reggie again. Besides, he'd probably have her impersonate a spy or something.

"Afternoon, Sam."

"Hi, Leroy."

They got into the car and buckled up. "Thanks again for going with me," Sam said.

"If it'll help find Jackson, I'm happy to."

She backed up and turned around. Leroy lived on the west side of Marina del Rey, and to get to Tori Walker's house in Manhattan Beach, Sam needed to circle around the northern side of the harbor before heading south.

"Still not get ahold of her, huh?" Leroy asked.

"No. I called just before I left but she didn't answer."

"That'd be just like Jackson, getting in trouble helping a friend."

"He have a habit of that?"

"I just meant lately," Leroy said. "That woman detective, Stephanie, Hillary, the actress . . ."

"All damsels in distress," Sam said.

"Yeah, well . . ."

Sam turned onto Via Marina. "So what else do you know about Walker?"

"Not a whole lot. Met her once. She seemed nice enough. Pretty girl, but she had a little attitude too."

Sam tried not to get hung up on the nice and pretty parts, remembering Leroy's words the day before that he thought Jackson "kind of liked" Tori. That was years ago, and besides, Jackson and Sam only kind of liked each other anyhow, Christmas Eve kisses aside.

"Do you remember anything more about the con they ran? Or the guy they conned?"

"Afraid not," Leroy said. "I just know it was typical Jackson, flying by the seat of his pants, playing like he had a handful of aces. And it worked out for him. It always does."

"Yeah. Always."

Tori's apartment was a few blocks inland from the ocean, set on a beautiful lot that had more open space than any of those around it. Sam found a space in the parking lot, and she and Leroy got out.

"So how do we play this?" Leroy asked.

"Straight," Sam said. "If she's here."

"If she's not?"

"We'll cross that bridge then."

"Fair enough."

They climbed the stairs to Tori's second-floor apartment, and Sam rang the bell. She waited nearly a minute before knocking on the door. Leroy moved over and peeked in a window. "Might want to take a look at this," he said.

Looking around to make sure no one was watching them, Sam joined Leroy by the window. The blinds were partially open, and by blocking out the sunlight with her hands, Sam was able to see inside. The apartment was a mess, and not just from a lack of good housekeeping.

"Someone's been looking for something," Sam said.

"Else been fighting World War III in there."

Sam peeked through the window again. She saw no signs that anyone was there now, and Leroy agreed. Just to be sure, Sam rang the doorbell one more time. As expected, nobody answered.

"Jackson teach you how to pick a lock?" Leroy asked.

"No. I couldn't anyhow."

He nodded. "So now what?"

Sam sighed. "I don't know. Maybe we should check at the office."

He nodded again, and they went to the apartment office, which turned out to be unit 1. When Sam rang the doorbell, she again got no answer.

"Maybe Jackson and Walker are hiding from whoever did that to her apartment," Leroy said.

"It's a better option than being kidnapped by whoever did it." Sam reached for her phone. "I'm going to call Reggie."

Leroy nodded, and Sam paced away from the door to unit 1 as she waited for Reggie to pick up. She was about to give up when his deep baritone answered.

"Hi, Reggie, it's Sam."

"Hey, Sam. Any word?"

"No. I'm in Manhattan Beach at Tori Walker's apartment with Leroy. There's nobody here, but it looks like somebody tossed her place."

"You got in?"

"Just looked through the window, but it was a mess. A lamp knocked over, couch cushions askew, books and papers everywhere. Something went down."

"Okay. Uh . . . Mouse and I found Wilbur Anderson."

"You did? What'd he say?"

"He was dead, Sam."

She looked up, her eyes drifting across the parking lot. It took her a moment to pull back to the conversation. "He was dead?"

"Yeah. No idea why. The cops and paramedics are here now."

Despite the sun, Sam shivered. "Reggie . . ."

"I don't know. We're about done here, and we'll join you. Maybe we can get the apartment manager to let us in or something."

"I tried. He's not here."

"Okay. Sit tight, Sam. We'll be there as soon as we can."

"I'll try. Thanks, Reggie."

She switched off her phone and reported to Leroy.

He harrumphed. "This is getting stranger and stranger."

"I'm worried, Leroy."

"I know, kiddo. I'm a little worried myself."

Sam's phone rang. It was still in her hand, tightly clasped, and she looked down. It was Stephanie's number. She excused herself to take the call.

"This is Sam."

"Sam! It's Stephanie. I'm going into labor again."

Sam paused for just a second.

"It's for real this time, Sam. My water broke."

"Where are you?"

"Home. And Brady's gone all afternoon with some friends. I don't know what to do."

"I'll be . . ." Sam looked at Leroy. "I'll be there as soon as I can. Steph, if you need to call 9-1-1, do it."

"Okay."

"I'm on my way."

"Baby coming?" Leroy asked.

"Yeah. I can drop you at home."

"I'll wait here," Leroy said.

"What?"

"Go, be with Stephanie. I'll wait for Reggie and Mouse."

"You're sure?"

"Positive. She needs you. Go."

Sam nodded, thanked Leroy, and hurried for her car. Why was it that life always seemed to gang up on you, everything happening at once?

*　　　　　*　　　　　*

2:38 p.m.

MOUSE AND Reggie headed for Manhattan Beach as soon as the cops in Huntington Beach let them go. They would be keeping an eye on the motel in case Jackson returned, so it seemed like wasted manpower for Reggie and Mouse to do so.

They didn't say much on the trip because there wasn't much to say. Somehow, Jackson's disappearance seemed tied to a dead World War II vet and a former coworker named Tori Walker. Mouse hadn't found out much else about her, certainly nothing to tie her to Wilbur or Jackson. He had also tried to dig up anything on the con she and Jackson had run several years ago, but without more details, there wasn't much to search by.

Leroy was waiting in the parking lot of Tori's Manhattan Beach apartment complex. Reggie quickly parked the Hummer, and he and Mouse hurried over to him.

"Where's Sam?" Reggie asked.

"Stephanie went into labor again. She went to be with her."

"What about Brady?"

"He was gone, I guess."

"You tried the office again?"

Leroy shook his head.

"Where is it?"

"Unit 1."

Reggie took the lead, and Mouse fell in behind him and Leroy. Reggie rang and knocked, got no answer, and promptly pulled out his cell phone to dial the manager's number. He grumbled under his breath when no one picked up.

"Okay, let's see this apartment," he said.

Leroy led them up to the second floor, where Mouse and Reggie both peered into the window. Unless this Walker chick had worse housekeeping skills than Pam, something had gone wrong in there.

"What do you know about Walker?" Reggie asked, leaning against her door.

"Not a whole lot," Leroy said. "She and Jackson were coworkers, friends."

"At MTR, right?"

Leroy nodded.

"And they conned some guy out of a hundred grand that he had stolen from a bunch of churches?"

Leroy nodded again. "*Mission: Impossible*-style."

Reggie rubbed his head. "So let's get this straight," he said, looking from Leroy to Mouse. "Five years ago, J and Walker run some vigilante justice on this guy, and now Walker's pad's been tossed, and she's AWOL. And Tuesday, Jackson spends a few hours at a retirement home with a World War II vet, then rents a car, checks into a hotel with the guy, and disappears." He looked at Leroy. "Did Sam tell you about Wilbur?"

"That he's dead? Yeah."

Reggie nodded.

"He was old," Mouse said. "Maybe he just croaked."

Leroy harrumphed under his breath.

"Maybe," Reggie said. "But you know how J hates coincidences."

"Okay, so where does that leave us?" Mouse asked.

"We know he's tied up with Walker because she left him the note. And we know he's tied to Wilbur because the car he rented was at the hotel. So are Walker and Wilbur also tied together, or is J's disappearance only linked to one of them?"

"Maybe neither," Mouse said.

"Great, more possibilities."

Mouse shrugged.

"What'd the police say?" Leroy asked.

"That they want to find J almost as much as we do."

"He a suspect?"

Reggie nodded. "He has to be, until he can clear things up."

"Well if he's already in trouble, then I say we call the cops again. Tell them about Walker, let them look at her place. Maybe they can find something."

"I agree," Mouse said.

Reggie took a deep breath. "This con J and Walker ran . . . they break any laws?"

"Bent a few, if I recall."

"That all comes to light," Reggie said.

"I know. But this isn't just a mystery anymore. A man has died, Reggie. And if we know something that might help the police, we need to turn it over to them."

Reggie nodded. "Just so we understand."

"Yeah, I understand."

Reggie nodded again and reached for his phone.

Chapter Nineteen

4:17 p.m.

MAGGIE RODE IN the front seat of Russell's Chevy Avalanche, her eyes looking out the window and taking in the Santa Monica storefronts and sidewalks lined by palms, with blue sky the backdrop for it all. It was beautiful.

Inside, her stomach churned. Jackson had been missing for going on five days, and every clue that those looking for him found suggested things were worse than they had hoped. One of the people seemingly connected to him and his disappearance—Tori Walker—was also missing. The other—Wilbur Anderson—lay dead in a dive motel in Huntington Beach. Maggie had continued to pray for Jackson's safety, but she didn't feel the peace and tranquility she'd thought Christians were supposed to experience when they prayed. Was she not trusting properly, or was it not always that simple?

Maggie's stomach also churned because of Russell. She was worried about Jackson's safety and at the same time attracted to the man helping her find him. And she couldn't blame herself. After all, he had given up his Sunday afternoon to help her find a guy he didn't even know.

So how did this all end? They found Jackson, and Maggie said, "thanks and nice knowing you," to Russell? Or gave Jackson a glad you're back pat on the back and asked Russell if he'd like to grab something to eat? Or did she just date them both casually? (How low could you get?) That was, of course, assuming Russell even wanted to date her. He'd never said so; in fact, he'd said the opposite. So was Maggie just flattering herself by thinking the attraction she felt wasn't one-way?

"Something on your mind?"

Maggie blinked and realized they had stopped. She slowly turned to face Russell. "What?"

"We're here. You okay?"

She took a deep breath. "No."

He nodded. "We'll find him."

"How do you know that?"

"Because God answers prayer."

"But He says no sometimes, doesn't He?"

Russell nodded.

"So how do you know?"

"Faith."

"Faith," Maggie repeated, thinking. "I'm sorry, I'm still new at this. How can you have faith that God will do something He hasn't promised to do?"

"I'm an optimist. I'm also a realist. I know God doesn't say yes to every request. But I know He can, and I'd rather live in expectation of Him doing so than otherwise."

Maggie nodded.

"Not sure about that?"

"Just thinking it through."

"You'll be thinking it through till you die, Maggie." He tapped her knee. "Come on, let's go."

Reggie and Leroy were waiting for them in the entrance to Cameron's. After introductions, Reggie led them down to his office.

"I thought Mouse was with you," Maggie said as they walked.

"He had to work, so I dropped him off."

"Mouse?" Russell asked.

"Computer nerd," Reggie said. "Mousy sort of a guy."

"So're most people compared to you," Leroy said.

"Touché."

Reggie opened the door to his luxurious office. In addition to a desk and work area, it had a private bath, a couch aimed at a plasma TV, and a table and chairs. Sliding glass doors opened onto the beach, letting in some natural light to the ground-floor office.

"Help yourself to some snacks," Reggie said, gesturing at the table with several plates of appetizers. "Drinks in the fridge," he said. "Grab something and have a seat."

All three guests helped themselves and took seats on the couch and an armchair. Reggie pulled over a chair from the table, set it in front of the TV, and straddled it facing backward. "All right, let's recap what we know."

He then started by stating that the cops at the Pierless Motel in Huntington Beach hadn't divulged much about Wilbur's death, other than that they didn't know anything. They'd asked a lot of questions, far too many of which Reggie and Mouse hadn't had answers for. Jackson was, at best, a person of interest in Wilbur's death, and Reggie had asked Detective Larson to liaise. So far, he hadn't heard anything.

Maggie then summarized what she'd found out about Wilbur's death. She'd called anyone and everyone she could think of—former co-workers, contacts with other news organizations, a friend at KCBS and another with LAPD—who might know something. None of them did. She'd also racked her brain for any mention Jackson had ever made of a woman named Tori Walker. Nothing. She'd Googled the name and found a Tori Walker, P.I., listed on several commercial social media websites. They hadn't provided any further information, and Maggie hadn't been able to find out anything about the con she and Jackson had run five years ago or the person they had targeted.

Mouse's research into Walker had been similarly unproductive, Reggie announced. He and Leroy filled in details about the search—such as it had been—at Walker's apartment, concluding with their decision to call the police. The authorities had asked a lot of questions and, without much to back up the theory, hadn't necessarily bought the connection to Jackson's disappearance. They seemed more interested in why Reggie, Mouse, and Leroy had taken an interest in her place than anything.

Reggie sat back. "Is that it? Anything else we might be missing?"

Maggie and Russell glanced at each other. "Maybe," she said.

"Let's hear it."

Maggie took a deep breath. Russell's lady friend in the D.A.'s office— a reasonably attractive redhead whose relationship with Russell seemed purely professional—hadn't been able to shed much light on things. The drug deal that was supposed to have gone down over the weekend hadn't, or at least it hadn't triggered the repercussions LAPD had feared. She knew nothing about Jackson or any involvement he might have had and had no reason to suspect the Silvaz or Grays were involved in his disappearance. Given recent developments, Maggie was inclined to agree. But she recapped her and Russell's lunch meeting anyhow.

"So you all think this could be gang-related?" Reggie asked.

"Just a thought," Russell said. "I did some research on what happened last year, and I don't mean to suggest that Jackson is messed up with either gang. But they might have messed with him."

"How do Wilbur and Walker tie in?" Reggie asked with a frown.

"We don't know," Maggie said.

"What's the deal with Walker again?" Russell asked. "Maggie said something about a con she and Jackson ran back in the day?"

"That's all we know about her," Leroy said.

"Why do we think she's connected to his disappearance? Besides her apartment being tossed, which we wouldn't have known if we didn't think she was involved in the first place, right?"

Maggie frowned. "Yeah, you never mentioned why you thought she was involved."

"Sam found a note in Jackson's garbage can."

"Who's Sam?" Russell asked.

"A friend of J's. The note said 'Ivan's here' and was signed by Allie."

"I hate to ask . . ."

"Allie was Walker's alias when they ran the con, according to Leroy," Reggie said.

"But you don't remember who they conned?" Russell asked.

"The name escapes my age-riddled brain."

"We've searched Jackson's computer, phone, friends, any records we could find," Reggie said. "Nothing."

Russell sighed.

"Ivan," Maggie said. "From *Magnum, P.I.*"

Leroy frowned.

"*Magnum, P.I.*?" Russell asked.

"'Did You See the Sunrise?'" she said. "It's a classic episode. This old Russian general who tortured Magnum and T.C. in 'Nam comes to

Hawaii, blows up Mac, tries to get T.C. to blow up the Valley of the Temples."

All three men stared at her.

"What?"

"You a closet *Magnum* wonk?" Reggie asked.

"You ever try hanging out with Jackson on a Friday night? It's reliving the glory days of the Rams on his Xbox or '80s TV on DVD."

Reggie grinned. "Yeah, true that."

"Anyhow, everybody kept trying to convince Magnum that Ivan was back, that he was in Hawaii."

"And you think that's what Walker's message is all about?"

Maggie shrugged. "It's a theory. If she used to spend weekends with Jackson."

"And it fits with what we know," Russell said.

"So then we really need to figure out who this Ivan guy is," Leroy said.

"Any chance his name was Ivan?" Russell asked.

Leroy shook his head. "It was something prissy sounding."

Reggie nodded. "Run it for me again, Leroy. What was the scam?"

"This Ivan guy, whatever his name was, ripped off a hundred thousand dollars from a number of churches and charities in San Diego. Jackson and Walker knew about it through MTR and came up with a plan to get the money back. They rented this charter sailboat and sold it to Ivan as if it was their boat. Then they took the cash and sent the Coast Guard after him."

"The Coast Guard?" Russell asked.

"Yeah. They were watching from the beach when the Coast Guard showed up and found Ivan on a boat he didn't own."

"There would be a report of that."

"I reckon."

Reggie stood. "With a name. And I know someone who might be able to get it for us. Actually, two someones. Let me make a few calls."

*   *   *

5:38 p.m.

AFTER PASSING the plate around, Reggie consumed the remaining three mozzarella sticks. They were cold and clumpy, as were the nachos Leroy was finishing. Russell had downed a burger, but no one else had been hungry enough to eat a full meal while they waited for Ashley or Olivia to call back.

A knock on the door snapped the group from a trance. Reggie raised his eyes to see Katie peeking through the cracked doorway. "Olivia Williams here to see you."

He nodded. "Send her in."

Maggie frowned in his direction, but he ignored it as Olivia entered the office. She smiled at him and declined the seat Leroy offered her, instead standing against the wall. Reggie cut off the confusion at the pass. "Olivia, this is Jackson's grandpa, Leroy, and friends Maggie and Russell. Guys, this is Olivia Williams with the German BfV—domestic intelligence."

Maggie's frown was now joined by ones from Russell and Leroy.

"Sorry to drop in unannounced," she said, "but I got your voicemail and thought it best if we spoke in person."

"Why, what's up?"

"I don't mean to be rude, but could we talk in private?"

"Naw, they can hear it. Nobody's closer to Jackson than these people."

"Okay." She stood a little straighter. "What do you know about Wilbur Anderson?"

The smile was gone from her face in an instant, and Reggie kept from stammering by keeping his mouth shut. He narrowed his eyes. "How do you know about Wilbur?"

"Since you didn't tell me, you mean?"

"It's not like that, Olivia."

Well, it was sort of like that. Reggie was having trust issues.

"Maybe we'd better give you two some time," Leroy said.

"It's all right, Leroy," Reggie said.

"I need to use the restroom anyhow."

"I'll join you," Russell said.

Maggie squinted at them. "You ladies go powder your nose. I want to know what's going on here."

Reggie sighed and briefly explained to her how Olivia had approached him. He then related her information about *Wolfskinder* and their possible involvement in Jackson's family's death, as well as their potential pursuit of him now.

"And you didn't tell us anything?" Maggie asked.

"I didn't want to worry you."

"I appreciate that, Reggie, but we're past that stage, I think."

"We didn't have any hard evidence that *Wolfskinder* was involved in his disappearance, and I didn't see how being burdened with that info would help you or Russell with any leads you were chasing. We were in contact, Mags. If anything had changed, I'd have let you know."

"So basically you need-to-knowed me?"

"Yeah."

She stuck her tongue in her cheek. "All right, fair enough."

He turned to Olivia.

"Want to see if you can make it two for two?" she asked with a hint of a smile.

"I didn't call you because I didn't know what to tell you," he said, figuring that was pretty close to the truth. "I had no idea how J and Wilbur could be tied to *Wolfskinder* or this Walker chick or anything else we've found."

"Did you know Wilbur Anderson served in World War II?" Olivia asked.

"We did."

"Know one of the big players in that little conflict?"

"We know he served in Germany at the end of and after the war, yeah," Reggie said with a sigh. "So'd an awful lot of people."

"How many of them are stretched out in a hotel room with Jackson?"

"I take it you found a connection."

"No, not yet. But it sure seems likely. I've got various sources looking up everything there is to know about Wilbur Anderson, but it takes time. And time is of the essence, Reggie."

"I should have called you."

Olivia nodded. "If you don't trust me, say so."

"It's not that."

Her eyes locked onto his.

"It's not that, Olivia."

"Okay." She placed a hand on his arm. "Water under the bridge then."

"Good. So about my call, you know anything about Walker and this sting she and J ran?"

"No. I poked a little, but the U.S. Coast Guard busting joyriders is a little off my sources' radar." She paced back toward the door. "I'm going to chase down a few more leads about Wilbur. Oh, and nothing on Donaldson and MacFarland."

"Who?" Maggie asked.

"Names we found in J's phone."

"I still have some feelers out. I'll call you if I find or hear anything."

"And I will do the same."

She smiled.

"Why didn't you just call, Olivia?"

"I was in the neighborhood, and I wanted to look you in the eye."

He nodded.

"Talk to you later." She winked. "Nice meeting you, Maggie."

"Uh, you too."

Olivia disappeared, and Reggie exhaled. "I guess I'd better go get those two out of the bathroom."

"Hold on," Maggie said, rising. "Who is she?"

"I told you, German Bf—"

"No, I mean to you."

"Nobody."

Maggie raised an eyebrow. Then she touched his arm, mimicking the way Olivia had, and batted her eyelashes. "That woman has a thing for you."

"We're just trying to find J, that's all."

"Uh-huh. And it goes both ways, I think."

"We just met the other day, Maggie. It don't happen that fast."

Her eyes grew distant.

"I'm going to go get them."

She nodded, and Reggie exited the office, wondering if Maggie was right—about Olivia having a thing for him. More than that, was she right about him having a thing for Olivia?

*   *   *

6:17 p.m.

"YOU A basketball fan?" Russell asked several minutes after Reggie had finished explaining who Olivia was and recounting her theory about what had happened to Jackson. A muted NCAA tournament game was on TV.

Reggie shrugged. "Take it or leave it."

"You play any ball in high school or college?"

"Football at Nebraska."

"For real?"

"He was even drafted by the Chargers," Maggie said.

Russell looked to her and back to Reggie. "For real?"

Reggie nodded.

"So how'd you end up a restaurateur?"

"LaDainian Tomlinson had better moves than I did."

"Linebacker?"

"Defensive end."

"Wow. That's cool."

"It was a long time ago," Reggie said, rubbing his head.

"So how'd you meet Jackson?" Russell asked.

"We've got t—"

Reggie's cell phone interrupted him and drew everyone's attention. He flipped it open, pressed a button, and set it on the desk. "Yeah?"

"Reggie, it's Ashley," her voice came through on speaker.

"Yeah?"

"I think I've got a name for you."

"Shoot."

"Chaz Skyler."

"Chaz Skyler?"

"That's it," Leroy said. "I told you it was something prissy."

"Full name is Charles Skyler III," Ashley continued, "and the U.S. Coast Guard apprehended him in 2008 aboard a 38-foot charter sailboat named *The Baby J*. He claimed he'd purchased the boat, but the title proved to be a forgery. He danced out of some hot water with the charter company, and no charges were ever filed."

"So he didn't try to press charges?"

"No record of it if he did. If what you tell me is right, I'm guessing he didn't want to involve the police in his affairs."

"So he just harbored a hundred-thousand-dollar grudge."

"It would seem so," Ashley said. "I checked, and he lives in North Hollywood now and works for a software company. He seems to have moved on and hasn't been in any legal trouble."

"Still, seems a coincidence that J and this Walker girl are both missing."

"It does, and I've passed on what I found out to the detectives working Walker's case and to the ones who are investigating Wilbur Anderson's death. If there's a connection, they'll find it."

"Thanks, Detective."

"There's more, Reggie."

"I'm listening."

"A traffic camera just down from the Pierless Motel showed Jackson leaving on foot, heading north toward the pier."

"When?"

"A little before five last night. Nobody else came or went from his room until you arrived. Not even housekeeping."

"He had a car at the hotel. Why'd he go on foot?"

"We tracked him to a lounge a few blocks away called Scotty's. He met a woman there. They just sent me the photo. I can send it to your phone."

"It's an old-school model. Send it to my e-mail instead," he said. As he gave her his address, he walked to his desk and fired up his laptop.

"I've got another call," she said. "I need to take it. I'll send you the photo right away."

"Thanks, Detective," Reggie said. He closed his phone and logged into his e-mail. In less than a minute, a message had arrived, and he spun the computer so Leroy, Maggie, and Russell could see an attached image.

It showed a woman in a black T-shirt and jeans exiting the building with Jackson. She was white, medium height, good-looking, with short brown—maybe reddish—hair.

"You know her?" Reggie asked, glancing over his shoulder at Maggie. She shook her head.

"Can you blow it up?" Leroy asked. "Isn't that the term?"

Despite the gravity of the situation, Reggie couldn't hide a grin as he enlarged the photo. "You know her, Leroy?"

"Hmm. I reckon so. That's Tori Walker."

Chapter Twenty

7:34 p.m.

CHAZ SKYLER LIVED in a small ranch house on a quiet street in North Hollywood, just off Vineland. Knowing his name and hometown, it had been easy to find his address, and some quick online scouting had given Maggie, Russell, Reggie, and Leroy the lay of the land. After a brief discussion, Maggie and Russell had headed north while Reggie and Leroy had gone south to Huntington Beach, hoping someone at Scotty's could give them something to help them find Jackson.

Russell drove and circled the block, parking on the street adjacent to Skyler's. The sun had just set, but the sky overhead was still light. It had been a beautiful sunset and evening over Los Angeles, the kind of Sunday night Maggie loved to enjoy outdoors, savoring the end of the weekend before the workweek started. How things had changed.

"You got a plan?" Russell asked.

"We ring the bell."

"And what?"

"Improvise."

"This your normal style?"

"My first time, really."

Russell nodded and actually smiled. "Okay. We'll improvise."

They got out and walked around the corner to Skyler's house. Large trees in the front and the back shaded his entire property. There were no lights on in the house, but Maggie rang the bell anyhow.

In the distance, a dog barked. A car backed out of a driveway a few houses down and headed off in the other direction. Otherwise, the neighborhood was quiet.

Maggie rang the bell again, pressing it repeatedly for several seconds.

"You think you can annoy him to the door?"

She shrugged.

Still no one answered.

Maggie turned and began walking.

"Where you going?"

"Around back."

Russell shrugged and followed her. Skyler's house was only a dozen feet from the neighbor's, with shrubs all along the east side of the property. The backyard was small and neat with a large oak in the middle. Sliding glass doors opened onto a patio with a gas grill on one side and a two-person swing on the other.

Maggie rapped on the glass doors with her knuckles.

"Looks like he's gone," Russell said.

Maggie looked left. The neighbor's house was dark, its backyard similarly shaded. A six-foot-high wood fence blocked the view of the west neighbor's house. A lawnmower started a few houses down, its whine echoing through the neighborhood.

"Kind of late to mow," Russell said.

"Yeah. Can I have your shirt?"

"Huh?"

"Your outer shirt," Maggie said, nodding at the plaid button-down Russell wore over a plain tee.

"What are you thinking?"

"Of some non-Christian behavior."

He shook his head. "No."

"We need to find something, Russell."

"Not like this."

"You have a better idea?"

"Yes. We call Reggie and Leroy. Maybe they've found something. Or we can grab some coffees, park down the road, and share life stories and expectations while we wait for him to come home."

"You were right," she said.

"About?"

"Even if he had answered, I didn't know what to say. We wouldn't have gotten anywhere."

"You don't know that."

Maggie's eyes darted around the patio. They settled on Russell's top shirt button. "Is that a no, then, about your shirt?"

"No."

"Okay."

She walked around him and bent down by Skyler's grill.

"What are you doing?"

"Improvising."

"Maggie."

She started to unscrew the propane tank from the supply line.

Russell grabbed her arm and pulled her up. "Maggie, stop."

She jerked her arm free. "I like you, Russell. But I need to find Jackson right now, and if you can't get behind what I have to do, that's fine. I won't make you. But I've got nothing to lose."

"Except three to five for a B&E."

"At least I'll have a place to stay."

"Maggie."

She took half a step closer. "If this was the other way around, and I was missing, I was in trouble . . . a locked door wouldn't stop Jackson. He'd do whatever he had to do—he'd move heaven and earth to save me. He . . . he already did."

"Mexico?"

"And Israel."

Russell nodded. "This is different, Maggie."

"No, it isn't." She bent down and finished unscrewing the propane tank. She twisted it from its base and hefted it over to glass doors, setting it down on the patio. She stopped and looked all around to make sure no one was watching. Everything was still dead in and around Skyler's backyard, and the lawnmower was still humming.

Russell again took her arm. "Maggie, think about this?"

She stood up. "Can I ask you something?"

He nodded.

"That fight you got into in high school, was it with a girl?"

"No."

"So you've never hit a girl?"

"No."

"Well, you're going to have to, to stop me."

"I'm not going to hit you, Maggie."

"Then get out of here. You don't need to be a part of this."

He sighed. "There has to be another way."

"There isn't." She quickly reached for the propane tank, lifted it, and swung it at the glass. It shattered with a way-too-loud, echoing jingle. Shards of glass flew everywhere. Having released the propane tank, Maggie jumped back as it landed on the dining room floor with a thud.

She looked around and saw no signs of neighbors investigating the noise. Maybe the lawnmower had covered it. She didn't waste any time, stepping through and over the broken glass. It crackled under her shoes, and she thought of all the ways she could leave evidence behind. She couldn't worry about it. Jackson wouldn't.

"What are we looking for?" Russell asked, joining her inside.

"I don't know. Anything to suggest he's after Jackson or Walker."

They split up with Russell warning her not to touch anything. She took the dining room, kitchen, and living room while Russell headed for the bedrooms and the bathroom. Without turning on lights that would announce their presence, it was hard to see much, relying on the last vestiges of daylight that filtered through the trees and in the windows.

Maggie worked fast, easy since Skyler didn't keep much clutter. The dining room table was clear, as was the kitchen counter. The refrigerator had a grocery list held in place by a magnet advertising a local mechanic. Neither meant anything. Slipping the back of her hand inside the handle, Maggie opened the refrigerator. There was nothing there to arouse her suspicion.

She moved to the living room, one corner of which had been turned into a home office with a computer desk, open laptop, printer, Bluetooth earpiece, and a notepad full of scribble. Maggie reached for her phone and snapped a picture of the notepad to analyze later. The rest of the living room was devoid of any tells, and she debated trying to access the laptop. What could she use to avoid leaving fingerprints?

"Bedrooms and bathroom are empty," Russell reported.

"Empty?"

"No clues. The guy's a minimalist."

"We need to get on that laptop."

"No way."

"I'll lay something over it, a Kleenex or something, so I don't leave prints."

Headlights caught both of their attention at the same time. They were on the street, but they were slowing down. A blinker came on next.

"Go!" Russell said, not needing to tell Maggie. She turned and made a dash for the dining room, exiting onto the patio as the lights swept across the neighbor's fence, then lit the interior of the house behind them.

Russell on her heels, she headed for the back corner of the property. They cut through the backyard of the house east of Skyler's, shielded from the neighbors on the backside by a hedgerow that ran the length of Skyler's property and the next two.

"Here," Russell said, pointing to a narrow alley between two houses. It was shaded by trees and another row of hedges in the front yard of the easternmost house. Russell glanced right and gave Maggie the go-ahead before they darted toward the sidewalk. They again turned east, away from Skyler's house. Russell reminded her to walk leisurely. He then surprised her by reaching for her hand.

She looked up.

"If no one saw us yet, we're just lovers out for a stroll."

Maggie turned her head. "I don't see anyone out."

"Maybe everyone's watching TV."

"You think anyone saw us?"

"Probably not."

"How long till he sees the broken glass?"

"About now."

"You sure we should stroll?"

"Yeah. We're almost to the corner."

Russell's Avalanche was parked a few houses down on the adjacent street, and he and Maggie reached it without any alarms going off. Very calmly, Russell turned the ignition and pulled away from the curb. Driving at normal speeds, he turned left on Skyler's street, then right on the next street south. He continued zig-zagging for several blocks, finally coming out on a main north-south thoroughfare. Maggie's hands were still shaking.

"Why are you taking this route?"

"Traffic cams," Russell said. "They might look for vehicles exiting the area shortly after the break-in."

She nodded.

"Let's hope the neighbors didn't take notice of an irregular Avalanche parked nearby."

Another nod. Then Maggie froze in horror. "The propane tank."

"Yeah?"

"I touched it. My prints are on it."

"You grabbed under the rim, so you didn't leave much of a print."

She breathed again.

"However, when you unscrewed it from the grill, you might have left one."

Maggie wanted to press pause. Things were spinning out of control. It had sounded and felt so good when she'd given Russell her "Jackson would do it" speech. Now, she wanted to throw up. And she'd thought running from Helen at the *Times* had been nerve-wracking.

"You ever been printed before?" Russell asked.

"No. No, I don't . . . No."

"Then you should be okay. Congrats. You've committed your first felony."

"Are you mad?"

Russell took a while to answer and looked out his window as he did. "No. I understand."

"So is it a sin when you do something wrong for a good reason?"

He turned her way. "There never is a good reason to do something wrong."

"I see. Why are we turning?"

Russell pulled into a McDonald's and parked in the first available spot before answering. "Because my hands are shaking and because we need to talk."

So he was nervous too. Oddly enough, it made Maggie feel better.

Russell cut the ignition.

"Talk about what?"

"What you found in the living room. I saw you take a picture."

"I forgot," Maggie said, reaching for her phone. She called up the picture she'd taken. "He had a bunch of notes on a pad by his laptop."

Russell leaned over to view her screen. "Anything good?"

"These look like . . . a grocery list? He had one on his refrigerator too."

"Maybe he forgets."

"Maybe." Maggie shook her head. "No idea what this is. Stock tips, maybe?"

"Ski hills."

"What?"

"Baldy, Big Bear, and Dodge Ridge are all ski hills in the area."

"He's pricing ski trips?"

"Looks like it."

"That's what the food's for. A ski trip. It's all basic staples you'd need if you were stocking a condo pantry or something. You think that's where he was?"

"It'd give him an alibi." Russell pointed to the bottom of the phone, where Maggie's photo had picked up some scribble on a sticky note. "What's that say?"

Maggie zoomed in. "Tito Gonzalo? And a phone number."

"Name sounds vaguely familiar, but I can't place it."

"This doesn't make sense. He had a laptop, a Bluetooth earpiece. Why is he writing a name down on paper?"

"Maybe he didn't write it there. Although the handwriting matches. Still could have been someone else."

"I suppose."

There was nothing more to glean, so Maggie closed the image file and opened a browser. She searched for the name Tito Gonzalo. After scrolling through several pages, she saw one that stopped her cold. Tito Gonzalo Investigations. She turned the screen to Russell. "He's a P.I."

"Why would Skyler hire a P.I.?"

"I don't know. Why are half of the people in L.A. private eyes? Jackson, Walker, Gonzalo."

Russell shrugged.

"I'll call Reggie. Maybe he knows Gonzalo. Maybe Jackson does. Maybe that's where this all comes together."

"A lot of maybes there," he said starting the vehicle.

"You got any other plan?"

"I can make some calls, ask around. The people I know might know Gonzalo."

"Can you make those calls at this hour on a Sunday?"

Russell exited the parking lot and headed south. "If not, I might be able to talk to some of them in person."

"Okay. Let me call Reggie first." Maggie was about to make the call when her phone rang. "How about that," she said. "It's him." She raised the phone. "Hello?"

Chapter Twenty-One

7:56 p.m.

FOR THE SECOND time that day, Reggie drove past the Huntington Beach Municipal Pier. This time he turned on Main Street and headed inland. One block from the coast and one block from Main, he parked in front of a seedy looking lounge from the '70s. The neon sign over the door was missing a T, but there was no doubt this was Scotty's.

"What exactly do we do now?" Leroy asked. "Jackson didn't give you Grant's badge or something, did he?"

"No, just his *chutzpah.*"

Leroy harrumphed.

"What's that?"

"I didn't know black people said *chutzpah.*"

Reggie grinned. "Come on. I figure we'll try the truth."

"Not a bad option."

They headed inside, and Reggie stopped at the door.

"Dark in here," Leroy said.

"Yeah."

"Can I help you?" a husky voice asked from the right. It took Reggie's eyes a moment to make out a wrinkled woman standing behind a small podium.

"Is there a manager or someone I could talk to?"

"Is there a problem?"

"No. I just have some questions."

"May I ask about what?"

"A couple of customers who were here last night."

The woman shook her head. "I don't think—"

"Please, ma'am, it's very important. If I could speak with the manager."

She wasn't happy, but she nodded. "Just a minute." Pushing away from the podium, she wound through mostly empty tables and around the bar before disappearing through an invisible door. When she returned a minute later, she was followed by a man in a black suit, no tie. Reggie had expected a blue leisure suit, Lamont Sanford style, probably with a beer belly. This dude was svelte and looked like he should be running a place like, well, Cameron's, not Scotty's.

He followed the hostess's gesture and extended a hand to Reggie. "Scott Wiggs, owner and sole proprietor."

Reggie shook and introduced himself, as did Leroy.

"Please, we can speak in my office."

They followed him back, almost choking on smoke. However, when they had passed through a narrow corridor and entered Wiggs' private office, the smoke smell dissipated, and darkness gave way to soft light from a pair of lamps in the two left corners and another on Wiggs' desk. Three chairs were oriented to face the far wall, where a trio of flat screen TVs was recessed into the dark paneling of a bookcase. Sports photographs, panoramas of stadiums and venues, and several small trophies adorned the walls. Reggie admired them for a few moments, then took the seat Wiggs offered him.

"What can I do for you gentlemen?" he asked, sitting down in the third chair instead of behind the desk.

"I assume the police have already been here and asked you about a guy who was here last night."

"They have," Wiggs answered, his eyes darting from Reggie to Leroy. "You cops too?"

"I'm his best friend. This is his grandfather."

"And you're looking for Mr. Douglas too?"

"We are. Not that we don't trust the police, but . . . the more eyes and ears, the better."

"So what can I do for you?"

"We spoke to one of Jackson's friends with LAPD, and she told us that he was here with another woman and they both left on foot."

"Probably saw them on the camera at Mortenson's across the street. Our camera over the front door's been out for about a week now. I can't get a tech guy in here."

"Did anybody here speak to either of them? A waiter or waitress, maybe. The hostess?"

"Doris wasn't working last night, but Missy talked to the cops for a while." Wiggs stood and lifted the phone off the cradle on the desk. "Can you send Missy to my office, please?"

He paced back but didn't sit down. "Can I get you guys something to drink while you wait?"

"No thanks," Reggie said. Leroy shook his head.

Wiggs nodded, then called a, "Come in," when there was a soft knock on the door. A woman entered, dressed all in black, her blond hair pinned up behind her head. "Mr. Cameron, Mr. Douglas, this is Missy Gibbs. She served Mr. Douglas and his companion last night. Missy, these gentlemen would like to ask you a few questions."

"Are you with the police?" she asked, taking the seat Wiggs had been in earlier.

"No. Friend and grandfather."

"I told the police everything I know."

Reggie nodded. "I appreciate that. We just want to know if either Jackson or the woman he was with said anything to indicate where they might have gone next."

"He asked me where he could find a drugstore in the area."

"What did you tell him?"

"Won's Emporium is just a few blocks away. It's a local shop, but they have any nonprescription meds you might need."

"Did he happen to say what he was looking for?"

Missy shook her head. "It sounded like he was going to go to Won's though."

"Where exactly is this drugstore?" Leroy asked.

"Two blocks east, one block south."

"What about the girl?" Reggie asked.

Missy shook her head. "Like I told the police, I assumed they were together. But they said she left separately."

"Anything else you can remember?"

"No. I'm sorry."

"Don't be," Leroy said. "Anything helps us."

"You know how they paid?" Reggie asked. "Together, cash, credit?"

"I don't know."

"They would have paid at the bar," Wiggs said. "We have a register there."

"Any way to check?"

Wiggs grinned. "Sure you're not cops? You're pretty thorough."

"Just anxious to find Jackson."

They thanked Missy, and she returned to work. Wiggs then sat behind his desk and opened a laptop. "We keep backups on a networked server, showing all transactions for the last year, searchable by payment type, date, table, anything. It will just take a minute."

"Appreciate it."

Wiggs nodded. "Okay . . . here we go. Last night, around six. . . They were at table twelve." He tipped his head. "Looks like they paid cash, one ticket. And used a coupon."

"A coupon?"

"Five dollars off. We get a lot from the local hotels."

"Any idea which one?"

"It doesn't say."

"The Pierless?"

Wiggs almost laughed. "No, we don't have a reciprocal deal with them."

Reggie sighed.

"We can ask Lewis, the bartender. He might remember."

"Worth a try."

Wiggs led them back to the bar, where Lewis scratched his head and tried to recall Jackson. Reggie and Leroy took turns describing him, as well as Tori.

"Yeah, I remember her," he said. "She seemed anxious."

"She say anything to you?"

"No, it was her mannerisms. Eyes darting, twitchy, that sort of thing. She just stood back while he paid."

"Do you remember the coupon he gave you?" Wiggs asked. "Five dollars off?"

Lewis scratched his head again. He suddenly snapped his eyes up. "Yeah. The Nines."

"The Nines?" Reggie asked.

"Used to be the Surf 'n Sun," Wiggs said. "On 9th. New ownership renovated it a few years ago."

"You're sure?" Reggie asked.

Lewis nodded. "Yeah, pretty."

Reggie thanked Lewis and Wiggs, then he and Leroy headed outside.

"You figure the drugstore or the hotel's a better choice?" Leroy asked.

"Pick 'em," Reggie said as he reached for his phone. "I'm going to call Maggie. See if they had any luck at Skyler's place."

*   *   *

8:20 p.m.

"HELLO?"

"Maggie, it's Reggie."

"What's up?" she asked.

"We just spoke with the owner of Scotty's."

"Find anything?"

"Maybe. Waitress said Jackson asked where he could find a drugstore and he paid with a coupon from a hotel a few blocks north of here."

"A drugstore?"

"Yeah, we don't know why. What'd you find, anything?"

She paused for a moment.

"Maggie?"

"A possible name. Tito Gonzalo. He's a private eye. You ever heard of him?"

"Gonzalo? No. Leroy, you ever heard of a P.I. named Tito Gonzalo?"

Maggie couldn't hear Leroy's response.

"How'd you find the name?" Reggie asked.

"Long story, but he had Gonzalo's name and number written on a notepad by his computer."

"He let you in?"

"No."

"What are you saying, Maggie?"

"It's what I'm not saying," she said with a glance at Russell. "What can we do?"

"I don't know. We're going to check out the drugstore and then head over to the hotel."

"You think he's at this hotel?"

"Else Walker is."

"I can take one."

Russell looked at her, and she took a quick glance back.

"You're a long ways away, Maggie," Reggie said.

She shrugged. "I can be there in less than an hour."

"Might not be worth the trip. We're going to the drugstore now, then we'll swing by the hotel."

"I'll meet you there," she said. "Russell's going to ask around about Gonzalo."

"You sure?"

"Three of us can canvas more area. Besides, if we find Walker, having a woman might be helpful."

"It's up to you."

"What's the address of this hotel?"

"PCH and 9th in Huntington Beach," Reggie said. "Call me when you get there."

"Will do."

She lowered her phone.

"You're going to Huntington Beach?" Russell asked.

"It makes the most sense," Maggie said. "I can't help you find Gonzalo."

"Not really, no."

"You don't approve?"

"I don't like you going alone."

"You think I'll do something crazy again?"

"I'm worried something will happen to you." He shook his head. "I don't know what happened to Jackson, but it seems like we're in dangerous territory."

"I'll be careful."

"Maybe I should go with you."

"You can do more good trying to track down Gonzalo. Besides, Reggie will probably be there before me. All he has to do is ask around at a drugstore. I doubt they'll remember Jackson coming in." She looked away. "Unless . . ."

"Unless what?"

"Unless he made some unusual purchases. Like if he was hurt or something."

"Didn't Reggie say the cops thought Wilbur's time of death was overnight?"

Maggie nodded.

"And Jackson was seen at this lounge and headed for the drugstore last night, right?"

"Right."

"Probably looking for meds for Wilbur. Maybe his condition was worsening."

"You're probably right."

"We'll find him, Maggie. We're closing in."

"Yeah. I just hope we're in time."

Chapter Twenty-Two

8:33 p.m.

"SO, HOW DO we play this one?" Leroy asked as they parked in the small lot of Won's Emporium. "Truth again?"

"I don't think they'd buy that you and I are cops."

"No, I don't reckon they would."

They got out, and Leroy followed Reggie inside. More than a drugstore, Won's was also a souvenir shop, featuring postcards, mugs and shot glasses, sunscreen, and disposable cameras, in addition to a variety of snacks and novelties. It also had plenty of drugs.

A wiry Asian guy with a bad haircut was manning the sole checkout counter, and the only other patrons were a woman and her young son looking at the freezer full of ice cream treats.

Reggie walked right up to the counter. "Excuse me."

"Can I help you?" the man asked with a thick Oriental accent. His nametag identified him as Liang.

"I hope so. I'm looking for a friend of mine, and I believe he came in here last night."

Liang frowned.

Reggie described Jackson and the time of his visit, but Liang shook his head. "I was not working then. I am sorry."

"Do you have a security camera or something?" Reggie asked.

"We do."

"Is there any chance we could look at the footage? I know it's an odd request, but it's urgent we find him."

Liang took half a step back. "I will call my boss. One moment." He was gone for a minute and returned with a shake of his head. "I am sorry, sir, but we cannot allow it."

Leroy stepped forward. "Please. He's my grandson, and he's been missing for almost a week. Our only lead is that he asked a waitress at Scotty's for a drugstore, and she mentioned your place."

"If we can find out why he came here, maybe find out what he bought, it might give us a clue where to find him," Reggie said.

"My boss . . ."

"Could you please call him again? Let me talk to him. It's very important."

Liang thought for a moment, then gave in. Reggie explained everything to Liang's boss, stressing the urgency while overwhelming the man with politeness. After several minutes, he handed the phone to Liang. He spoke for just a few seconds, then hung up. The woman and her son were ready to check out, and he took care of them. Then he nodded at Reggie and Leroy. "Follow me."

Liang led them to a back room that doubled as a storage closet. "We have two cameras," he said, pointing at a computer screen. "One in the parking lot and one on the front counter and door." He turned on the computer. "When did you say your friend was here?"

"Last night around six, six-thirty maybe."

When the computer booted, Liang typed for a moment and tapped the space key to open a file. "Here we are."

A black and white image filled the screen, showing the counter and the front door, just as Liang had said. He fast-forwarded through several customers until Reggie called for him to stop. He rewound slightly, then paused the screen as Jackson walked through the front door. "Six-ten p.m.," Reggie said. He put a hand on Leroy's shoulder. "He looks good."

"He does."

A bell tinkled, and Liang turned and looked out the door. "Excuse me. I have a customer."

"We'll wait."

Liang nodded and left. He was gone almost ten minutes, during which time Reggie checked his watch several times. Leroy studied the image on the screen, hoping a grainy image of Jackson would give him some clue. It didn't.

Liang returned, and they advanced the video in real-time. Jackson spent maybe five minutes in the store, approached the counter, then stepped away. When he returned to the counter, he had to wait for a heavyset woman buying what appeared to be donuts. Reggie asked Liang to pause the image again as Jackson placed his items on the counter. "Can you see what he's buying?"

"It looks like . . ." Liang leaned forward. "A&W Cream Soda, Combos, and generic pain relievers."

"Hmm," Leroy said.

They watched as Jackson paid cash for the items and headed for the exit.

"Can we see your outside camera too?" Reggie asked.

Liang nodded but was interrupted from queuing the video by another customer. "One moment, please."

They waited as one moment turned to two, and it was another ten minutes before he returned. "I am sorry."

"It's fine. We're thankful for your time."

Liang nodded again and loaded the footage. It took a few minutes to get to the right spot, and they watched as Jackson exited the store. He took a few steps, his eyes looking up and to the right, and stopped as a black SUV stopped in front of him. Both passenger side doors opened, and two men got out.

"Is that . . ." Leroy asked.

"A gun," Reggie said.

A moment later, Jackson dropped the plastic bag containing his purchases. He looked to his right, and as he did, one of the two men grabbed him and herded him into the vehicle. Jackson disappeared inside, followed by the two men. The doors closed, and the SUV raced off.

"No," Leroy breathed.

Reggie looked at him for a moment, then turned his eyes back to the screen. They didn't leave it as he reached for his cell phone. Before he could dial, however, Leroy slumped against the wall of the closet.

*   *   *

9:09 p.m.

FOR THE second time that night, Maggie broke the law. Russell had dropped her off with plans to contact his mysterious sources for any information about Tito Gonzalo. She had gotten on her motorcycle with a promise to be careful and raced off. She got on the 405 and went ten over the speed limit, weaving in and out of traffic, making good time to Orange County.

Eventually, Maggie exited the 405 onto the PCH/Highway 1 east of Long Beach, her old stomping grounds. She arrived in Huntington Beach just after nine o'clock and had no trouble finding The Nines. It was a two-story motel shaped in a U around a central pool area, all of the rooms offering views of the Pacific. The design and structure were old, but everything had been repainted and updated, including the big 9 sign that stood by the street, glowing a soft blue against the night sky.

Maggie parked in the lot beside the building and got off her bike. She settled her helmet on the handlebars and drew her phone to call Reggie. He didn't answer, so she left a voicemail letting him know that she was at The Nines. Then she returned her phone to her pocket and contemplated her options.

She was wearing jeans and a leather jacket over a Henley top. It was the sort of thing lady cops wore when they were going casual, but she didn't have the badge to sell it. She doubted that playing the flirt would get her very far even if the clerk on duty happened to be a younger guy. The straight-up truth wasn't likely to get her past hotel policy. That left her one available recourse: subterfuge.

Her first thought was to try to distract the clerk so she could take a look at the computer showing who was staying at the hotel. But Jackson and Tori, if either of them were there, were likely using aliases, so it was a no-go. How did Jackson make this work? Maybe that's why he always called her for favors.

The office at The Nines had two entrances, one in each of the front corners, leading either to the parking lot or the pool courtyard. Both were massive archways, fitting well in the art deco theme the hotel's renovators had adopted. The office was neat and clean, and the only clerk on duty was an older man with a pleasant face.

"Good evening," he said as she walked in.

"Hi," she said with her most charming smile. "I need some help."

His smile faded slightly with confusion. "What can I do for you?"

"I'm looking for two friends of mine. I think they might be staying here."

"What are their names?"

Maggie leaned on the desk. "That's where it gets difficult. I don't remember."

"You don't remember your friends' names?"

"We just met today, and I'm terrible with names. I think it was Jack and . . . I can't remember. Anyhow, we were both on a sunset dinner cruise out of Long Beach, and we got to talking. The woman left her phone behind," Maggie said pulling out her phone. "I was hoping to return it to her. They had mentioned something about a hotel on 9th Street, I think, and this is the third one I've been to. I really hope they're here."

The clerk had to think for a moment. "I've been here all day. Can you describe them to me? Perhaps I'll recognize them from check-in."

Maggie started with Jackson, her description drawing a blank face from the clerk. But when she described Tori from the picture Detective Larson had sent, his eyes brightened. "Yes, I think I remember her. Talked with sort of clipped speech?"

Maggie nodded.

"And a golden retriever, right?"

"I don't know. They didn't mention anything about a dog."

"I only see a woman registered to the room."

Maggie frowned appropriately. "I thought they were together. Maybe not." She shrugged. "Anyhow, if you let me know the room, I can return it to her."

"I'm afraid I can't give out a guest's room number," he said. "But I can return it to her myself."

Maggie took a moment to compose herself. "All right." She tapped the desk. "Thank you."

It wasn't ideal, but it should get the same result. Maggie left her phone behind and left the office. She hurried across the street, dodging traffic, and took up residence against a palm tree in a small park between the road and the beach. She wasn't sure if the clerk would personally deliver the phone or call Tori's room and have her come to the office. Either way, Maggie should be able to identify what room Tori was in.

Ten minutes later, no one had stirred. The clerk was still in the office, and the only movement in the courtyard or hotel corridors was a family of four returning to their room on foot. Maggie started to question her plan, wishing she hadn't left her phone behind. She was to the point of considering a strategy to get the phone back when the clerk emerged from the office. He turned left down the exterior corridor and Maggie started walking to get a better angle.

She entered a parking lot next to the park and crouched between two vehicles, hoping neither driver chose that moment to leave. The clerk stopped about halfway down the corridor and knocked. Maggie moved a few cars over, trying to get a view of the person who had answered the door, but he or she never came out of the room.

The conversation only lasted a few seconds, then the clerk turned back toward the office. Maggie counted doors twice, making sure she had the right room. When the clerk was back in the office, she stood and casually walked the length of the parking lot. She crossed the PCH at 8th and backtracked a block, entering the courtyard and circling the pool. Less than five minutes after the clerk left, Maggie knocked on the door of room 1H.

At first there was no response, and she raised her hand to knock again. Had someone slipped out while she was looping around? Had she just lost the only lead she had?

Then the door opened, and all Maggie could focus on was the gun aimed at her face.

Chapter Twenty-Three

9:16 p.m.

REGGIE ASKED LIANG to replay the tape, and the young clerk obliged. They watched all the footage again, hoping to see something else they had missed the first time through. Reggie paid close attention to the heavyset woman buying powdered donuts in front of Jackson. He counted the time Jackson was away from the counter, wondering if he'd had any interaction with anyone else. But no one else appeared on camera before or after him.

On the outside camera, Reggie paid special attention to the SUV. Looked like a Suburban or a Yukon. As it pulled away, Liang paused the footage again so Reggie could read a license plate. He memorized it and exited the closet. Leroy was sitting on a stepstool, head between his knees.

"You all right?" Reggie asked, placing a hand on his back.

Leroy raised his head. "I'm fine."

"You sure? You almost fainted in there."

Leroy waved a hand. "I didn't faint. I just . . . I can't believe it's as bad as we feared."

"We don't know what it is yet," Reggie said. "But I did get a license plate. I'm calling Ashley now."

Leroy nodded and took a drink offered to him by Liang as Reggie dialed.

"This is Detective Ashley Larson. I can't take your call right now so please leave your name, number, and a short message. If this is an emergency, please call 9-1-1 right away."

"Detective, Reggie Cameron. We tracked Jackson to a drugstore on 7th—Won's Emporium. Their security cameras show Jackson being forced into a dark SUV, California plate niner-Juliet-alpha-Zulu-six-three-niner. Give me a call when you get this, please. Thanks."

"Not there, huh?" Leroy asked.

"No."

"So what's next?"

"I'm going to call Maggie and Olivia."

Leroy just nodded.

Maggie's phone went to voicemail as well, and Olivia's cell cut out just after Reggie explained what had happened. She called back in a minute. "Sorry about that. You say he was forcibly taken?"

"At gunpoint."

"Did you get a make and model on the SUV, maybe a plate?"

He repeated the info he had just given Ashley's voicemail.

"I'll check it out, see if my sources can find anything before yours."

"I appreciate it, O." He closed the phone and shook his head. "She'll make some calls."

Leroy sighed. "This is enough to make a preacher cuss."

"Is it?" Reggie asked.

"My grandmother used to say that. Granddad was a preacher too."

"He ever cuss?"

"Not to my ears." Leroy stood. "The hotel?"

"No. Maggie said she was going there, so I think we let her cover it. I've got another way to track down that plate."

"How?"

"Mouse. He can hack anything."

"I thought he was working."

"Only till ten," Reggie said, checking his watch. "By the time we get back, he should be off."

"Whatever you say."

Reggie thanked Liang, and he and Leroy hurried out to the Hummer. Jackson had been missing for five days, and now they knew he had been kidnapped over twenty-four hours ago. Despite the positive attitudes he and Leroy tried to maintain for each other, Reggie knew it wasn't looking good.

*   *   *

9:38 p.m.

TO HER surprise, Maggie kept her cool. "Are you Tori Walker?" she asked.

"Who are you?" the woman holding the gun demanded. Her hair was pulled back in a ponytail, and she wore sweats and a tank top, but the scowling face was unmistakable.

"I'm Maggie. I'm a friend of Jackson's."

"Where is he?"

"I don't know. I was hoping you might."

Tori's eyes wavered for the first time, glancing past Maggie. "Come in." She stepped aside to admit Maggie, closing and locking the door behind her. The room had a king bed, an armchair, and a small dining table with two chairs. The bathroom was in the back. A golden retriever sat quietly by the bathroom entrance, its eyes shifting from Tori to Maggie.

Tori uncocked the gun and nodded at the dresser. "That your phone?"

"Yeah."

"What are you doing here?"

Maggie explained how she and several of Jackson's friends had been worried when he didn't answer their calls, how they had found the note in his trash and deduced it had come from Tori, and how Reggie and Leroy had tracked her to The Nines.

"How is Leroy?" Tori asked.

"Good, other than being worried."

Tori set her gun on the table and sat down. She nodded for Maggie to have a chair. "How much do you know?"

"Bits and pieces."

Tori nodded. "I'll catch you up. Five years ago, Douglas and I were both working for MTR Investigative Services in San Diego. We were assistants, doing routine legwork, research, paperwork. One of the associates caught a case investigating a guy named Chaz Skyler. Our client thought he had stolen a promotion from him and was sleeping with his wife. But there was no evidence either allegation was true. But Mace—the associate—did uncover evidence that Skyler was ripping off a number of churches and charities in the area, selling them high-quality electronic equipment—mostly computers—and then delivering cheap junk in their place. He'd scammed over a hundred grand."

Maggie whistled. The dog whimpered but didn't move.

"MTR wasn't willing to go after Skyler without a client to fund them, and there wasn't enough legally obtained evidence to go to the police. But it stuck in my craw—Douglas's too—and we came up with a plan to get the money back."

"You sold him a sailboat, right?"

"We posed as Jimmy and Allie Dawkins, a brother-sister team trying to unload a 38-foot sailboat. Our recon told us he was in the market and looking to buy soon, so we played it up that we were eager to unload. We stalled a little, knowing he wanted to entertain clients on his new boat on Memorial Day. On Friday, we chartered a boat under Skyler's name, using a fake ID, from a place up the coast and took him out for a test drive the Saturday before Memorial Day. He paid by cashier's check that evening."

"How much?"

"One twenty-five."

Maggie whistled again.

"We had fake titles, IDs, everything. Technically, we committed fraud, but figured the ends justified the means. The boat was due back to the charter company on Sunday. Monday, Douglas and I watched from the beach as Skyler sailed the chartered boat out into the Pacific. We called the Coast Guard and anonymously reported that the boat had been stolen. We had the money, and as a bonus, he was in some serious hot water."

"You pulled this all off by yourselves?"

"We had help from a friend of mine, but mostly, it was just me and Douglas."

"Then Skyler showed up and ransacked your apartment?"

"Close. I work with several insurance companies in the Valley, and when I popped in Monday, Skyler was there. Too coincidental. Then Tuesday, I see a Buick Enclave sitting out front of my place, real suspicious like. I had work in Quartzsite for a few days, tying up loose ends and staying off the grid. I hoped everything would blow over. But when I got back Friday night, two guys were waiting for me. I fought my way loose, thanks to some help from Jack here, and got away."

"You named your dog Jack?"

For the first time, Tori's face contained a hint of a grin. It quickly faded. "I tried calling Douglas a couple of times, but must have had an old number. So on the way out of town Tuesday, I stopped and sent him flowers and the note. When I got back to civilization and decent cell service Friday, he'd left a message, and we got in touch. He was working a case down here already but agreed to meet me. I've been laying low ever since while he was doing some work checking up on Skyler. But he missed our scheduled meeting this evening and hasn't answered my calls. So when the manager tells me a friend was returning my cell phone, it piqued my suspicions. When you knocked five minutes later, well . . . Sorry about the gun."

"Don't worry about it," Maggie said. "So the last time you saw Jackson was last night?"

"We had dinner at a place called Scotty's a few blocks from here. We were supposed to meet again tonight, but he never showed."

"You mentioned another case. Any idea what it was?"

"Not too much. He said he was protecting someone from Nazis or something."

"Nazis?"

"He said it kind of offhanded. I don't know what he meant. He said it was complicated."

"Did he mention a guy named Wilbur?"

"Not by name."

Maggie nodded and filled Tori in on what they knew about Wilbur, including the fact that he was dead.

"So where's Jackson?"

Maggie shook her head. "Where were you supposed to meet tonight?"

"Surfside Diner, just a few blocks south."

"What time?"

"Five-thirty. I gave him till six. He's late a lot."

Maggie frowned. "He's never late."

"Well, five years ago he was. Anyhow, when he didn't show after a while, I got spooked and left. I've been here ever since, and I don't know what to do. I'm not the skittish kind, but I'm afraid Skyler means business. The plan was for me to wait until Douglas had a chance to check things out, but it's been several days now."

"You know of a guy named Tito Gonzalo?" Maggie asked.

"No, why?"

"Skyler had his name written on a notepad by his computer. He's a P.I."

"You've been in Skyler's house?"

"Tonight," Maggie said. "He wasn't there."

"You broke in?"

Maggie bit her lip.

"Douglas had a burn phone," Tori said. "I've been calling it all night, but he won't answer. Something must have happened to him. On the way home from Scotty's maybe?"

"I have a friend checking it out," Maggie said.

"What exactly do you do for a living?"

"Until Wednesday, I was a columnist for the *Times*. Now…"

"You seem to have a lot of friends."

"Jack's."

"And you put all this together? To get from the name Allie to finding me here was pretty good detective work."

"It was a team effort."

Tori nodded. "Maybe this friend of yours has a plan. I sure don't."

"He was supposed to meet me here," Maggie said. "Let me give him a call."

*   *   *

9:46 p.m.

SAM WATCHED basketball highlights on TV with complete disinterest. Her mind was a mess, worrying about Jackson, hoping for Stephanie, and praying about both. Being in a hospital—and not for work—had also for some reason made her think about her mom again. Would she end up in a hospital? How much pain would she have to endure? How much heartache could the family go through? Sam knew not to let her mind run wild with worst-case scenarios, but she didn't seem to have the ability to control them. Her mom was too young to die, too young to leave a family behind. She was supposed to be there to share Sam's joy when she finally met Mr. Right, to cry from the front row at her wedding, to sing a grandchild to sleep in her arms. Sam couldn't bear to think of losing her, and tried to console herself with the fact that the cancer had been detected early, and her mom's odds were good. When that didn't work, she tried praying and meditating on Scripture verses that usually brought her comfort. Even those measures seemed inadequate today.

The only thing that distracted Sam from worrying about her mom was the reason she was at the hospital in the first place—Stephanie and her baby. That, and worrying about Jackson. She held her phone in her hands, and several times had thought about calling Reggie for an update. But she expected news at any moment about Stephanie.

Sam looked up as she heard a knock on the door. Brady, dressed in hospital scrubs, stood at the door to the lounge with a smile on his face. "It's a beautiful little girl," he said.

"Ohhh," Sam said, jumping to her feet. "Healthy?"

"Perfectly. You want to see her?"

"Can I?"

"Steph said she hoped you were still here. Come on."

Brady led her down the hall and into Stephanie's birthing room. Stephanie's short blond hair was damp with sweat, and her face looked weary and worn. But her light blue eyes sparkled as she looked down at the bundled child in her arms.

"Sam, meet Mackenzie."

Brady gently lifted the baby from Stephanie's arms and carried her to Sam. It was almost surreal to see the brutish Brady, as she had known him just months ago, now displaying such tenderness as he placed Mackenzie in Sam's arms. Sam cooed in delight.

Mackenzie had her mother's eyes and her father's chubby cheeks. A small tuft of blonde hair broke out on the top of her head. She looked at Sam for just a moment, then closed her eyes. Her arms flailed slightly, little fingers opening, then curling shut. Sam's smile threatened to split her face in two.

"Oh, what a cutey."

"Isn't she?" Stephanie asked.

"How are you doing?"

"I'm exhausted, but I can't stop smiling."

"How about you, Dad?"

Brady shook his head. "I can't believe it's real. After everything . . ." He reached for Stephanie's hand, and she squeezed his hard. Sam looked back at the baby in her arms.

It felt so natural, cradling Mackenzie. For a few moments, Sam's fears and anxieties dissipated. All she could think about was the tiny life that had just entered the world.

Sam held Mackenzie for a few more minutes, then gave Brady and Stephanie some privacy to enjoy their new family of three. They were settled for the night and had everything they needed, so Sam headed for home.

As she walked to her car, her mind again drifted to Jackson. She reached for her phone and called Reggie.

"Hey, Sam."

"Reggie. Any word?"

"Yeah."

She stopped walking. She could hear the trouble in his tone. "What is it?"

"Someone took Jackson."

"Took him? Took him how?"

"They forced him into an SUV as he was leaving a drugstore in Huntington Beach last night. We're trying to track the plate, but that's all we know."

Sam forced herself to breathe.

"How's Stephanie?"

"Um . . . She's . . . she's good. A healthy baby girl. What can I do, Reggie?"

"Right now, nothing. I'm dropping Leroy off, then I'm going to see if Mouse can help me track Jackson down. I also called Ashley and LAPD. We'll find him, Sam."

"Okay. Call me if you hear something."

"I will."

Sam got in her car and closed the door before bursting into tears. She quickly stifled them and grasped the steering wheel.

"Heavenly Father, I've just seen evidence of Your goodness firsthand. Thank You for what You are doing in Brady and Stephanie's lives and for a healthy baby girl. Please show that same mercy to Jackson. Whatever is going on, I know . . . I know he's in Your hands. Please protect him."

*   *   *

10:28 p.m.

MOUSE TOOK the bus most of the way home and walked the rest. Turning onto his street, he saw a black Hummer H3 parked in front of his and Pam's duplex. Reggie.

As Mouse approached, the driver's side door opened and Reggie got out. "Mouse, I need your help."

"What's up?"

"We tracked J to a drugstore in Huntington Beach. Their security footage showed him leaving and being abducted by some guys in a black SUV. I got a plate, but I can't get a hold of Ashley, and LAPD just said they'd look into it. Any chance you can hack into the DMV?"

Mouse shrugged. "I can try."

They hurried inside.

"No Pam?"

"She's with her . . ." He almost said "rancher fiancé" but cut himself off. "Boyfriend." He looked over his shoulder as he flipped on the light in his bedroom. "This bad?"

Reggie nodded solemnly.

"You get a good look at the guys?"

"Not really. Footage wasn't great."

Mouse sat down. "It'll take a few minutes."

Reggie dropped onto the bed, and Mouse got to work. Hacking was pretty straightforward. Track the IP, find an open port, etcetera, etcetera. It wasn't the first time he'd been asked to hack into the DMV database, meaning he should have the necessary protocols to breach their firewall. But for whatever reason, he was denied access.

"What's going on?" Reggie asked.

"I don't know. They must have changed their security."

"You saying you can't get in?"

"I don't know. I'll keep working."

"Maybe there's another option. Can you get me a phone number?"

"Yeah."

"Connie DiMarco."

"Jackson's neighbor?"

"She works for the DMV."

"It'll be closed now."

"She might be able to pull some strings."

Mouse quickly searched for her phone number and read it to Reggie. He dialed, and Mouse turned to listen to his call.

"Connie, it's Reggie Cameron, Jackson's friend. . . . That's actually what I'm calling about. We might have a line, but we need your help. . . . Yeah. I have a license plate number but no way to trace it. . . . Yeah, they took a message. . . . You got any way to login to the DMV database and look up a name? . . . I realize that, but it's an emergency. . . . I do. . . . Thank you, Connie." He read her the plate number, repeated it, then listened for a moment. "Yeah, this number." He lowered the phone. "She's going to log in remotely and get us the name."

"Then what?"

"Depends if I can get a hold of Ashley."

They waited ten minutes, mostly in silence. When Reggie's phone rang, Mouse actually jumped.

"Yeah? . . . Just a sec." He lowered the phone. "You got a pen and paper?"

Mouse scrambled, knocking over a speaker as he reached for a pen, then dug for a pad of paper. "Here."

Reggie took notes from Connie, thanking her profusely. He promised to call her when he knew something and ended the call.

"What'd she say?"

"SUV's registered to a Michael Petrovich in Rolling Hills. Trailhead Court."

"Where you going?" Mouse asked as Reggie stood.

"To talk to Petrovich. You want to come?"

Mouse didn't. Petrovich sounded Russian, probably with the mob.

But he nodded. "Yeah."

"Let's go."

Chapter Twenty-Four

10:33 p.m.

"NO ANSWER AGAIN," Maggie said, lowering her phone. "I don't know why he isn't here. He was just checking out a drugstore before coming here."

"Won's?" Tori asked.

Maggie nodded.

"Douglas was going to stop there on his way back to his hotel."

"He say why?"

"The guy he was protecting had a headache."

Had the headache morphed into something more serious, something that had killed Wilbur because Jackson hadn't made it back with his meds?

"Anyone follow you here?" Tori asked from the window.

"No."

"You were at Skyler's tonight?"

"Yeah."

"There's a black, old-school Camaro parked on the street," she said, peeking through the blinds. "Been there for a while."

"That mean something?"

"Yeah. I lost a black Camaro driving down here Friday night."

"Lost?"

"He was behind me, and I got the feeling he was tailing me. I sped up, he sped up. I took some side streets and lost him."

Maggie shrugged. "Could be a coincidence. Camaro's are a popular sports car."

"This was the old version, distinct. You don't see a lot of them anymore." Tori shook her head. "Not a coincidence."

"I thought it was a Buick tailing you."

"I spotted a Buick outside my apartment, and maybe that was paranoia. But this Camaro was following me, believe me."

"If you say so," Maggie said, raising her phone. "I'm going to try Reggie again."

"Forget it," Tori said. "The last thing we need is him showing up drawing attention to us." She looked around for a moment. "What kind of car you drive?"

"Yamaha FJR1300."

"A motorcycle?"

Maggie nodded. Tori swore.

"It seats two."

"And a dog?"

"Your car out of commission?"

"No, but he knows it. Besides, it's a red '85 Saab. Stands out like Magnum's Ferrari."

"Well, where are we going?" Maggie asked.

"A new hotel. I'm not going home until I can figure out what to do."

"What if I drive your Saab, distract him."

"It's too chancy."

"Yeah, well, I'm kind of into chances nowadays."

"You drive stick?"

"No."

"What is it with people who can't drive stick?" She sighed. "Okay, I'll take my car. I lost him once, I can do it again." She began packing.

"There a back way out of here?" Maggie asked.

"No."

"Want me to cause a distraction?"

"What do you have in mind?"

"No idea. I'm still new at this."

"I'd actually appreciate the company. I can't live on the run all my life, and if Douglas is out of the picture, I'm going to need somebody else to trust. Between us, maybe we can figure out what's going on and get to the bottom of this."

"I'm game if you are."

Maggie's phone rang, and Tori announced that she just had to pack before they could leave.

"Hello?" Maggie said.

"Maggie, it's Russell."

"Hi."

"Any luck?"

"Um, sort of."

"You find Walker?"

"I'm with her now."

"Does she know where Jackson is?"

"No."

"What about Gonzalo? She heard of him?"

"No."

"I talked to a friend of mine at LAPD, and he said this guy's bad news."

"Oh?"

"He's a licensed P.I., but he has a couple of complaints against him and a prior for assault. It sounds like he's the kick in the doors and ask questions later type."

"He happen to drive a black Camaro?"

"Why?"

"Because there's one outside Tori's hotel room right now," Maggie said, glancing at Tori as she flung clothes into a suitcase.

"Where are you?"

"Still in Huntington Beach."

"Good. I'm on the road, headed to you. I can be there in twenty minutes."

"We're actually headed out, Russell."

"Where?"

"I don't know. We're on the run."

"What's going on, Maggie?"

"I'm not sure. Look, I'll call you, okay?"

"I'm headed your way. Keep me posted on your progress."

"Will do."

"Be careful, Maggie."

"I will."

Tori looked at her as she lowered her phone. "Who was that?"

"A friend."

"You've got a lot of those."

"Yeah. He said Gonzalo is bad news." Maggie summed things up while Tori finished packing.

"And this Gonzalo is the guy you found through Skyler?"

Maggie nodded.

Tori checked her gun. "I'm parked just on the other side of the office, third or fourth slot."

Maggie nodded.

"He's probably got a telephoto camera or something, so there's no need trying to slip him a decoy. Just head for the car. Walk, don't run, but make time."

Maggie nodded again.

"Ready, Jack?"

The dog stood and ambled toward Tori.

"Let's go."

She led the way, and Maggie followed closely. Jack trotted along behind them as they walked along the corridor and around the office. Maggie took one glance at the Camaro and saw no movement. Nothing even to indicate the car was occupied. Was Tori just paranoid?

They got into the Saab, and Tori whipped out of her parking spot and turned south on the PCH. They passed the Camaro, still dark. The windows were tinted so they couldn't see anything. Tori continued south, stopping at the light at 6th Street. Maggie kept her eyes in the rearview mirror. Just as the light turned, she saw a car make a U-turn three blocks behind them.

"Uh, Tori . . ."

"I see him."

She turned left on 5th Street. A block inland, she made another left, doubling back to the north. She made a rolling stop at 6th and cursed as they passed 7th. Maggie turned to see a black Camaro coming their way. He turned in right behind them.

"Hang on," Tori said, making a hard right. Maggie had to grab the door handle to keep from flying into Tori's lap. At the next street, Tori veered left, and Maggie was thrown into the door.

"I told you to hang on."

"Yeah."

"Your friend say anything else about Gonzalez?"

"You mean Gonzalo."

"Whoever."

"He had a prior for assault."

"You mentioned that, but thanks for underscoring the point."

"Sorry. No, that's all."

Tori nodded and turned left yet again. Both women glanced in the rearview mirror. The Camaro was still there."

"Yeah, well, ten says that's him behind us," Tori said.

"My guess too."

Tori ran a red light. So did the Camaro. Biting off another curse, she turned north on the PCH.

"You think you can outrun him?"

"We'll see."

*   *   *

10:53 p.m.

REGGIE AND Mouse were maybe fifteen minutes out when Reggie's phone rang. He flipped it open and glanced at the display. It was Ashley, and he thought about not answering it. But that would be foolish.

"Detective."

"Sorry I was out, Reggie, but I got your message. I tracked down the plate."

"Yeah?"

"Belongs to a 2011 Chevy Suburban registered to a Michael Petrovich. We're checking on him right now. Does the name ring a bell?"

"Not until half an hour ago," Reggie said with a sigh.

"Why, what was half an hour ago?"

"I had a friend run the plate."

"Mouse?"

"No. Turned up the same name."

"But you'd never heard of him before? No tie to Jackson?"

"No."

There was a pause from Ashley's end. "What aren't you telling me, Reggie?"

"I'm going to Petrovich's house now."

"Reggie, no."

"Look, I know you need warrants and all that jazz, and we ain't got time for that, Detective. Besides, I can get info you can't."

"Reggie, what are you talking about?"

"I'm talking about doing what I got to do to get J back, man. What he'd do for me."

"That's what I was afraid of. Reggie, please wait. I can get a warrant within the hour."

"It's already been too many hours, Detective. I'm sorry."

"Reggie, don't—"

He hung up on her and turned to Mouse. He rocked slowly in place.

"Look, when we get there . . . This could get messy, Mouse."

"Messy?"

"You should probably wait in the car. When LAPD gets there . . ."

"Yeah?"

"Just wait for them," Reggie said, opening his phone again.

"Who you calling now?"

"Maggie. I want to see if she's found anything."

Reggie had tried her twice but with no luck, and had the same problem again. They'd been out of touch for several hours, and he wondered if she'd found Walker and, if so, she knew anything about Petrovich. Reggie would prefer to know everything before he kicked in the front door. He was about to dial another number when his phone vibrated. Without looking at the number, he flipped it open.

"Yeah?"

"Reggie, it's Olivia."

"What's up?"

"Just checking in. You find anything?"

"Plate belongs to a Michael Petrovich," he said. "That name mean anything to you?"

"Reggie . . ."

"What?"

"Michael Petrovich is a suspected member of a Chechen terror cell."

"What? A Chechen terror cell?"

"Suspected. There's no actionable proof, which is why he's still walking around free in the U.S. If he's involved . . ."

"What does a Chechen terrorist have to do with a dead World War II vet, a hacked off software salesman, and neo-Nazis?"

"I don't know . . ."

"Olivia?"

"What else do you know about Petrovich?"

"Nothing."

"You get a description, address, anything to tell us if this is the right Petrovich?"

"Address in Rolling Hills. Trailhead Court."

"Let me check it out. Where are you?"

Reggie hesitated, then leaned his head back against the seat. "Almost to Rolling Hills."

"What? Reggie, no, you can't."

"They've had J for thirty hours. I don't have time to wait for LAPD or German Intelligence. Whoever this Petrovich cat is, he's got Jack, and I'm going to get him back."

"Reggie, that's crazy. You're one person—"

"Yeah, but I'm fueled by all sorts of mean right now."

"Please. Reggie, I . . . I don't want anything to happen to you," she said, her voice soft. "Please wait. At least, wait for me."

"Where you at?"

"Downtown. I can be there—"

"No. I'm going in."

"Reggie."

He closed his phone on her, biting on his lip.

"You okay?" Mouse asked.

"Yeah." Reggie took a moment to get his bearings, then flipped the phone open again and dialed yet another number.

"Yeah?"

"Russell?"

"Reggie?"

"Yeah. You hear anything from Maggie?"

"She found Walker at the hotel. There was a black Camaro parked out front. They think he's watching them. They're on the move."

"Going where?"

"I don't know. I'm headed their way now."

Reggie took several breaths, thinking.

"Reg?"

"Yeah. I've got a lead on Jackson. He was abducted from the drugstore by some guys in an SUV. We got a plate and tracked it to a guy in Rolling Hills. I'm on my way."

"To question him?"

"To get Jack."

"What about the cops?"

"They know. But their response time is a little slow."

"I've never met Jackson, but the way his friends go to the mattresses for him, he must be quite the guy."

"He is. This Camaro—any idea whose it is?"

"We're thinking it's Gonzalo, the P.I."

"I shouldn't have left Maggie."

"It's all right. I got her. Do what you have to do."

"All right. Call me when you have her."

"Will do. Wait, she's calling now. I got to go."

"Go," Reggie said, closing his phone. He turned to Mouse. "I got another job for you, man."

"What's that?"

"Pray, dude. I think it's all hitting the fan."

*   *   *

11:03 P.M.

DODGING IN and out of traffic, Tori increased her speed to close to fifty, running a pair of red lights that set horns honking. The second time, the Camaro was caught in the scrum, and Tori floored the accelerator.

"You from the area?" she asked.

"Hancock Park."

"I'm lost in Orange County. I'm going to try to get to the freeway."

Maggie nodded and looked back again. "He's free."

Traffic was thick, and Tori had to slow. When she spotted an opening, she zoomed ahead, darted into oncoming traffic before swerving back into her lane. It bought them a little more time, but the Camaro was like glue.

"Switchbacks on side streets don't work. Open road doesn't work. This guy's good. You ever shoot a gun?"

"No."

"You want to try?"

"In traffic? I'll kill somebody."

"Yeah. Bad idea."

They continued north through Sunset Beach. Tori tried again to lose the Camaro on city streets, doubling back, but to no avail. After almost being caught at a stop sign, she returned to the highway and continued north, toward Seal Beach. Maggie made a quick call, updating Russell on the situation.

"Where are you headed?" he asked.

Maggie lowered the phone. "You got a destination?"

"Why?" Tori asked.

"He's going to meet us."

"I was hoping to keep this gathering small, Maggie."

"He can help us. Trust me."

Tori glanced at her, then back in the rearview mirror. "North," was all she said, and Maggie repeated it to Russell.

"Okay, I'm headed east on the 405, just past the 110. Can you keep eluding this guy in the Camaro?"

"We're trying."

"Stay on the PCH. I doubt he'll try anything in traffic. When you get to Highway 19 in Long Beach, take it north. I'll meet you before you get to the 405 and intercept this guy, and you can get on the freeway."

"Intercept him?"

"He's got a Camaro, I've got an Avalanche, Maggie. I'll win a game of chicken."

"Russell. This sounds dangerous."

"Says the woman who threw a propane tank through a door a few hours ago."

Maggie bit her lip as Tori veered into the other lane and around a sedan.

"Maggie?"

"Okay," she said.

"I'll let you go, but put your phone on speaker and leave it on the dash. If something happens, you don't have to call again."

"Okay."

Maggie relayed the instructions to Tori, who was paying more attention to the rearview mirror than anything else. Maggie turned around and looked over her shoulder. The Camaro was right behind them. The highway curved inland and away from civilization, crossing over a marsh and past the Naval Weapons Station. Traffic thinned, and Tori accelerated. But she was no match for the Camaro.

As if powered by rocket boosters, it shot forward and moved onto their rear flank.

"Take the wheel!" Tori shouted.

Maggie obeyed, and Tori reached for her gun with one hand while lowering her window with the other. She leaned out and fired two shots, then ducked her head back in as the Camaro zoomed forward and tapped their bumper.

The Saab swerved violently, and Maggie's hand flew off the wheel. Tori grabbed it and managed to straighten them out, at the same time punching the gas again.

"What's going on?" Russell shouted through Maggie's phone, which had bounced off the windshield and onto the floor.

"He's attacking," Maggie said, grabbing the door handle.

Tori had gained a moment of separation, but the Camaro was back on them in a second. Holding the wheel with her right hand, Tori aimed the gun out the window with her left. She never got the chance to fire.

The Camaro rammed them again. Tori lost control, and the Saab careened off the road, hit an earthen mound, and took to the air. Just missing a telephone pole, it hurtled over a chain link fence and into the marsh.

Maggie felt herself spinning, heard the dog bark, heard a gunshot. Then an airbag exploded into her face, and she slammed against it.

Chapter Twenty-Five

11:09 p.m.

REGGIE PARKED AT the start of the cul-de-sac on Trailhead Court. Petrovich's place was at the very end of the circle, a massive two-story house with an attached three-car garage. A giant oak tree in the front yard shielded much of the house, and more trees, shrubs, and a hedgerow separated the house from the neighbors. Everything looked quiet.

"You sure about this?" Mouse asked.

"No."

"You got a plan?"

"Working on it."

"You sure there's nothing I can do?"

"Actually . . . maybe there is. You up for a little undercover work?"

"M-maybe."

"Nothing dangerous. Just go up to the door and ask for some girl. Make up a name, man. Act like you some dumb kid, and you're supposed to be taking her out."

"At eleven-fifteen?"

"Kids, man. Say you're going to some club."

"Okay, I guess. Why?"

"I need a diversion." Reggie reached into the glove and pulled out a gun.

"Is that for me?"

"Naw, man. Me. I'm going to get out. Drive into the driveway. Ring the bell. Ask for whoever. Don't stay too long, and if they tell you to beat it, beat it."

"Where do I go then?"

"Drive down the block, just around the bend. Park and pray."

"Okay. Good luck, Reggie."

"Thanks, man."

He got out, and Mouse was alone. His heart thudded as he replayed Reggie's phone conversation—something about Chechens and Nazis. What was he getting into? What if they saw through his ruse? What if they took him inside and tortured him? His heart turned into a jackhammer.

Then, from somewhere he didn't recognize, a surge of bravery ran through him. He thought of Jackson and knew what he would do if the roles were reversed. Taking a deep breath, Mouse crawled over to the driver's seat. He didn't even have a driver's license and had never been behind the wheel of anything like Reggie's Hummer. But he figured some dumb kid wouldn't be a great driver anyhow, right?

Mouse turned the ignition, shifted, and stepped on the gas. The Hummer lurched forward, and he hit the brakes, then thought to turn on the lights. He accelerated more slowly this time, entered the cul-de-sac, and turned into the driveway of Petrovich's house. He stepped on the brakes, stopping abruptly, and almost forgot to kill the engine before getting out.

His heart still pounding, sudden bravery or not, Mouse shuffled up to the front steps. The house was quiet, and he wondered if maybe it was empty. Maybe this was even the wrong place. What if he woke up some rich banker with Reggie's scheme?

Mouse took a deep breath before pressing the doorbell. It echoed through the house, and Mouse's heart skipped a beat when he saw a light come on through the window beside the door. A second later, the door opened.

Mouse's mouth slackened. He was looking at a girl. Well, a young woman. Pretty, blond hair, smooth features. She wore a tank top and sweats, probably ready for bed. She was not Michael Petrovich.

"Can I help you?" she asked.

"I'm, uh . . ." Shoot, he'd forgotten to think of a name. "I'm here to see . . . uh . . ." He went with the first name that popped into his head. "Maggie."

The girl frowned, then shook her head. "There's no Maggie here."

"We . . . we were supposed to go out. I'm . . . I'm Kyle."

You idiot, using your real name?

"I'm sorry. You must have the wrong house."

"This is Trailhead Drive, isn't it?"

"This is Trailhead Court."

"Oh. I'm sorry. I'm an idiot."

"No, it's all right."

"Uh, sorry to bother you. Thanks."

Mouse backed away as she closed the door. He practically ran back to the Hummer, backed over the curb, and tore away from the house. When he was around the corner, he pulled to the curb, running up against it. He killed the lights and the motor and let his heart pound.

He hadn't done too badly, except for not figuring out a name ahead of time. But why had a girl opened the door? Surely she wasn't responsible for kidnapping Jackson, was she?

I hope you know what you're doing, Reggie.

*　　　　　*　　　　　*

11:11 p.m.

MAGGIE AWOKE to screaming. At first she thought it was Tori, but as she pushed against the airbag that enveloped her face, she saw that Tori wasn't moving. She realized the screaming was a man's voice. Russell. From her phone. Wherever it was.

"Maggie! Maggie, what's going on?"

Jack was barking and Maggie was still a little dazed. Her phone. It was on speaker.

"Russell. We crashed. Gonzalo ran us off the road."

His reply was muffled, but it sounded like a question.

"By the marsh!" Maggie yelled. The airbag collapsed, and she tried to move. Something still wasn't right. Her chest hurt. And her shoulder. And her legs didn't feel right.

Oh no, I'm paralyzed. God, please no.

Her hair was in her face too. That's when it hit her. She was upside down. Her seatbelt cut against her chest and shoulder, and her legs flopped against the underside of the dash. As calmness washed over her, Maggie realized Russell was still talking, but Jack was barking consistently.

"Quiet, boy."

"What?"

"The dog!" she yelled. "Russell, Tori's unresponsive. Call 9-1-1."

Ignoring his response, Maggie found her seatbelt buckle and pushed the button. At first, it was jammed, but she shook it, jiggled it, and managed to get it free just as she heard a car door slam.

"That was quick," she muttered, trying to upright herself in the upside down car. "Quiet, Jack," she said, brushing the dog's neck. "It's okay."

He continued to bark while she reached for Tori. Her right arm was underneath the airbag, pinned to her chest. Maggie pushed on the deflating airbag and saw blood. On Tori's shirt, on the window, and dripping down Tori's arm from a gash near her wrist. Her eyes were closed, but she appeared to be breathing.

"Tori. Tori, can you hear me?"

Jack's barking grew louder, and Maggie raised her head. That's when she saw the figure coming toward them. Too small to be Russell. He was alone so not a paramedic.

Gonzalo!

He hadn't just run them off the road. He was coming for them.

"Come on, Tori, wake up."

Where was her gun? She'd been getting ready to fire out the window and had probably dropped it.

Gonzalo was less than ten feet away. Maggie had to do something. She reached for her door handle, but it was jammed. Maggie cursed under her breath, giving the door a kick that did nothing. She looked back out Tori's window where the man had stopped, crouching down to look into the car.

The guy was thin, white, gelled black hair, and dark eyes. Not Gonzalo. No, Maggie recognized him from a photo she'd found online. It was Chaz Skyler.

Jack howled.

That's when Maggie saw the gun in Skyler's hands.

Where was the passing traffic? Good Samaritans? Anyone?

He raised the gun, its metal gleaming ominously in the glow of a headlight. For some reason, Skyler paused. And then disappeared.

It happened so fast that Maggie barely saw the figure come flying in from the front of the car. She heard a clunk, and the vehicle rocked slightly. Jack continued to yelp. Maggie scrambled into the backseat to see what was happening, but all she saw was a blur of shapes moving back and forth. Then one stopped moving.

"Maggie!"

She climbed back to the front as Russell's head appeared in Tori's window.

"Maggie, are you okay?"

"I'm fine. I . . . I don't know about Tori. What . . . what just happened?"

"I got here as soon as I could."

"Skyler?"

"I'm afraid I got into another fight."

"You win this one?"

"I did." He felt Tori's pulse. "It's strong. Medics should be here soon. Can you get out?"

"No, my door's stuck."

Russell came around to her side and, with her pushing from the inside, was able to get the door open. Maggie climbed out and wrapped her arms around him.

"It's all right." He nodded toward the road. "They're here."

Maggie turned to see an ambulance and a police car arrive simultaneously. The next ten minutes were chaos as the paramedics freed Tori and carted her to the ambulance while the police apprehended Skyler and took statements from Russell and Maggie. Tori had regained consciousness and didn't appear to be in too bad of shape. She had a possible break in her right arm and some bad cuts and bruises in her left, but nothing life-threatening.

"Which hospital are you taking her to?" Maggie asked as the paramedics prepared to leave.

"Community in Long Beach."

"Take care of Jack," Tori said just before they shut the door.

"I will." Maggie turned.

Jack.

Skyler was standing beside the squad car, handcuffed. Maggie dashed over and grabbed his neck. "Where is Jackson, you piece of garbage!"

She was pulled back by two cops.

"Ma'am, we need you to stand back."

"He knows where Jackson is."

"Who's Jackson?"

Maggie exhaled a few deep breaths. "He's a friend. Skyler kidnapped him."

"We're taking him in for questioning. We'll get to the bottom of it."

"There isn't time. We need—"

Russell pulled on her arm. "I don't think it's him, Maggie."

"What?"

"Reggie called. Jackson was abducted by an SUV. They've got a plate. Reggie's tracking it down now."

"Are you telling me he knows where Jackson is?"

"Maybe."

"Where?"

"Rolling Hills. He didn't give me the address."

"Call him back. Let's go."

"Maggie, I think we—"

"Now, Russell."

He nodded. After checking with the officers, they grabbed Jack and headed for Russell's Avalanche just up the road. While they walked, he tried Reggie's phone but got no answer.

"Rolling Hills isn't that big," Maggie said. "If we have to, we'll drive up and down every street until we see a black Hummer. Come on."

"You sure you're up for it?"

"If it was Jack, nobody'd have to ask him that question. Let's go."

Chapter Twenty-Six

11:12 p.m.

REGGIE CUT THROUGH the bushes leading to the backyard. There were no lights on in Petrovich's house or at the neighbor's, and Reggie was dressed in black. He was pretty sure he wasn't spotted.

A spacious patio fit between two wings of the house. There was an outdoor fireplace, a massive grill, several seating areas, and a huge pool. Almost no actual yard. It all backed against more bushes and trees, giving Petrovich total privacy.

Several windows and sliding glass doors showed nothing but darkness. Reggie paused. If he was wrong, if Petrovich was innocent, he was about to throw away his career—his life. He'd be arrested, charged, imprisoned. He shook away the thoughts. Jackson wouldn't hesitate if Reggie were the one in trouble. Besides, it had been goons in Petrovich's Suburban that had taken Jackson at gunpoint. Petrovich wasn't innocent.

Reggie crept along the side of the house, ducking under windows until he reached sliding glass doors leading in from the patio. He was just in time to see a light go on inside, and then a woman appeared. Reggie could see all the way through the house to the front door, and the woman turned from a hallway and walked to the door. She opened it, talked for less than a minute, and turned back. She was met by a man.

They talked for almost a minute, then she turned for a staircase. The man walked into the living room, and Reggie ducked back out of site.

When he peeked back around, another man had joined the first. They were backlit by the hall light, and Reggie could see they were talking animatedly. Something made Reggie turn his head to his right where he spotted a security camera sweeping the grounds. And quite possibly the corner of the house he had rounded.

He stifled a growl at having missed it. That explained the conference. Guy Two had monitored the alarm, picked him up, and alerted Guy One. Hearing Jackson's voice in his head—"Now or never, Hoss"—Reggie reached out for a pair of brick pavers stacked beside the house. He heaved the first toward a window fifteen to twenty feet away, in another room.

The glass broke, and an alarm sounded. Reggie counted to five, then heaved the other brick through the glass door. He followed it, gun drawn.

"LAPD!" he shouted. "Don't move."

Guy Two was already in the doorway into the hall, and he dashed through it. Guy One held up his hands.

"Where is Douglas?" Reggie asked, hollering to be heard over the alarm.

"I do not know what you are talking about," Guy One said in a slow, even voice. But there was just enough light for Reggie to see the sneer curl his lip.

"You Petrovich?"

The sneer widened.

"One more chance. Where?"

It turned into a full-blown smirk.

Reggie fired his Sig P220, and the bullet tore through Petrovich's shoulder. He fell to the ground with a cry of pain. At the same time, a blur in the doorway caught Reggie's attention, and he saw Guy Two return, brandishing a machine gun. Reggie dove behind the couch as the muzzle flashed and bullets spat into the wall behind him.

He crawled to the far end of the couch, peeking around and squeezing two shots before the machine gun spray turned, and he had to shrink back behind the couch.

The woman appeared at the bottom of the steps. "Mikhail?"

Reggie turned his gun on her. "Walk to me, or I shoot you."

More machine gun bursts sprayed over his head. The alarm continued to clang.

Reggie fired a shot into the doorpost beside her. "Now!"

She timidly took a step, and the machine gun stopped.

"Walk to me!" Reggie said.

The woman took several faltering steps.

"Petrovich!" Reggie shouted. "Tell him to drop his weapon."

The response was a curse, then something in a foreign language.

More shots erupted, and the woman spun around as several slugs ripped through her body. With a cry of pain, she fell to the floor. Reggie was about to pop up and fire when the gunfire turned his way. He ducked down, wondering how long until a slug found its way through the couch.

Click.

Reggie stood, aimed, and fired. It took two shots, the second of which felled Guy Two as he furiously tried to reload while half hiding behind the doorpost. Reggie crawled over to the woman, checking her pulse. She was already gone. He stood and hurried to Petrovich, who writhed in pain. Not far away, Guy Two lay slumped against the wall, bleeding profusely from a wound to the chest. He was a goner. Even so, Reggie kicked the machine gun away.

"Where is Douglas?"

Petrovich snarled.

Reggie shot him in the leg.

"Where!" he screamed, filled with rage.

Petrovich said nothing, snarling in pain. Reggie bent down, his gun to Petrovich's knee. "I have two bullets left. Neither one's gonna kill you."

Petrovich glared at him. "Upstairs."

"Where?"

"Master . . . bedroom."

Reggie reached for Guy Two's gun and slung it over his shoulder. Then he hurried for the stairs.

The alarm bell was still ringing deafeningly, and Reggie climbed the steps both blind and deaf. From the top, a hallway ran straight ahead. It also split behind him, forming two routes around the stairs, before ending in a T with halls running left or right.

Reggie started down the hallway straight ahead. It led to a pair of bedrooms and a bathroom, all empty. He returned, passed the stairs, and took the right branch of the T. Another two rooms. He opened the first and stepped inside.

And was bludgeoned over the head.

Reggie rolled to the side and onto his back, just in time to see a stick of some sort coming his way. He ducked backward and rolled again as the stick sliced through the air. On its return route, it cracked against the bedpost and broke.

Reggie scrambled to his feet. His opponent was a woman, at least technically. She looked like an East German shotputter, guns for arms, thighs like Christmas hams. She dropped the stick and charged. Reggie raised his gun, but before he could fire, she had punched it to the side and pounced.

She drove Reggie back into a closet, splintering the doors. He cracked his head against the rod, a fact that would have concerned him had the woman's hands not been ringing his neck.

He was off balance, and his arms could only flail. He tried to kick but couldn't put anything behind it. She squeezed harder.

Finally, Reggie managed to raise his right hand. He couldn't find an avenue to punch, so he inserted it between hers, using it as a lever to pry her hands off his neck. She lost her balance and fell back with a growl.

Reggie stood up just in time for another charge. He was able to block several punches, but she lashed with a karate kick that just missed its rather low mark. Reggie managed to shove her back, and as she came for another round, he punched first, jabbing her in the nose, causing blood to spurt.

In middle school, Reggie had been bullied, along with half the class, by a kid named Mitch. Then one day, one of Reggie's classmates had had too much. He'd socked Mitch in the nose, and Mitch had fallen to the ground and started crying. Petrovich's lady friend wasn't crying, but tasting her own blood had staggered her. Reggie didn't let up.

He assaulted her with several heavy haymakers, each fueled by thoughts of Jackson and what these people might have done to him. The woman managed a few punches back, but she was no match for Reggie's rage, and his final blow dropped her hard.

Reggie searched through the closet, found a belt, and used it to bind her hands behind her back. Then he retrieved his gun and continued his sweep.

The upstairs was empty, and when Reggie returned to the ground floor, Petrovich hadn't moved, and Guy Two and the young woman were both still very dead. Reggie straddled Petrovich. "Nice try. Your girlfriend now has a massive head trauma. Where is he?"

Petrovich only sneered, and Reggie came a hair's breadth from pulling the trigger and wasting him. But he didn't. Instead, he cracked him with the pistol, knocking him out. Then he found the alarm console on the living room wall and did the same, finally silencing the beeping.

Reggie knew there might be others of Petrovich's crew in the building, but he took the chance. "Jack! Can you hear me? Jack! Give me a clue!"

He listened for a moment, then walked toward the front door. He reached for his phone and quickly thumbed 9-1-1. He knew if the cops showed up and found two dead people and Reggie with a gun, he could be in serious trouble. But these were not innocent homeowners, and getting Jackson help was worth any potential legal issues he might face.

He asked for police and an ambulance, and ended the call as soon as possible. Finding nothing but a closet and a hallway to the kitchen, he turned back toward the room he'd first entered. He stopped at a hallway branching off to the left, opposite the stairway. It led to the garage and, upon further inspection, the basement. Reggie opted for the basement first.

A switch on the wall illuminated the stairs and a door at the bottom. Reggie took the stairs quietly and stopped at the door. He listened but heard nothing. The door was locked, and he stepped back and kicked it just below the doorknob. It snapped and swung back so hard it almost bounced all the way back closed. Reggie pushed it open with one hand, while at the same time dropping to a crouch. The room was dark, void of movement.

"J, you down here?"

Reggie heard nothing but silence in return.

"J! J, man, you here?"

Nothing again, and Reggie began to wonder if he had just made the biggest mistake of his life.

Chapter Twenty-Seven

Five days ago . . .
Tuesday, March 19
4:31 p.m.

PHOEBE HENDERSON SMILED at Jackson with teary blue eyes. The tears may have been a product of relief, embarrassment, or glaucoma. Phoebe was eighty-four, going on 136. Her face was a roadmap of wrinkles, her mouth and eyes sunken into deepening cavities. Her hair was thin and stringy, covered by a cap that she had knit herself years ago. It was blue, pink, green, and orange. She wore a pink and white floral frock and a navy scarf because her neck got cold. When she moved, it was at a speed that would make a turtle chuckle.

But Phoebe, despite her aging flesh and lack of color coordination, was a sweetheart. Her voice was small and high, and she spoke clearly and deliberately and in flowing language as she described her children, her grandchildren, her great-grandchildren, and any other relative she could think of. Unfortunately, she was also suffering from the early stages of Alzheimer's, so her memory wasn't perfect. That, or she had a son and two grandchildren (one male, one female) all named George. But whether she could remember their names or not, it was clear that Phoebe loved her family.

She was also rich. Exceedingly, she told Jackson in a whisper. Not out of fear, he didn't think, but almost as if she was embarrassed for having acquired so much money. And in fact, it had been her late husband Bernard who had earned the money while working for some technology outfit (they must have been tech pioneers, unless theirs had been a May-December romance), and she hated the responsibility of determining where the money would go. Which was why she had contacted Jackson in the first place.

About a week ago, she'd received a phone call from her grandson Trevor, asking for money. He was in a little trouble—nothing illegal—and wondered, could she send him some money? Phoebe was suspicious, especially since she thought Trevor was deployed to Pakistan, but didn't know what to do. Fortunately for her, the guy across the hall had a former pastor he kept in touch with, and that former pastor's grandson was a private investigator. A few strings had been pulled, and Jackson had spent about two days checking up on Trevor. It turned out Phoebe was the intended victim of a hoax, and Jackson was happy to be able to tell her to keep her money.

"So Trevor isn't in any trouble?" she asked.

"No, ma'am. He just returned from Afghanistan. He and his wife Laura have two adorable little girls." He handed her a picture Trevor had e-mailed him. Why Trevor hadn't sent a hard copy to his grandma was a question that had gone unasked.

Phoebe took a moment to dab her eyes with a tissue, then smiled at Jackson. "Thank you, young man. Now tell me how much I owe you."

Jackson's standard fare was $500 per day, plus expenses. But his expenses had been limited to a few phone calls, and although he had worked over the span of two days, he'd put in less than three hours of work to verify that the call had not come from Trevor. He just couldn't bill Phoebe his usual rate, so he prorated it to a very reasonable $75.

"That doesn't seem like nearly enough," Phoebe said.

"It's only fair."

She pointed to an end table beside her bed and asked Jackson to retrieve a music box from inside it. He did and was treated to a tinny rendition of "It's a Small World After All" when she lifted the lid. Phoebe pulled out a stack of $20 bills and counted out ten of them.

"Here. I insist."

"I can't—"

She stopped him with a raised, gnarled hand. "If you argue, I'm just going to give you more."

Jackson smiled and accepted the cash. "Thank you."

"You are more than welcome. I'm just so happy Trevor is okay."

Jackson handed her a business card. "If you ever get another call like this or have any suspicions, you give me a call. Okay?"

Jackson said goodbye and backed out of Phoebe's room at Peaceful Shores Assisted Living Home in Malibu. As he headed for the front entrance, he debated whether he should call Maggie or Sam first. He had nothing planned for the night and figured Maggie had a better chance of not having to work. He was reaching for his phone when the receptionist at the front desk stopped him.

"Are you Jackson Douglas?" she asked.

She was cute—short blond hair that curled out at her shoulders, bright eyes, and a perfect smile. "Yeah, I'm Jackson."

"One of our residents has asked that you stop by his room. He asked for just two minutes of your time."

"I can spare two minutes," Jackson said with a pleasant smile.

The receptionist returned it. "His name's Wilbur Anderson, room 119."

Jackson nodded.

"Can you find your way?"

"I think so," Jackson said, and she almost seemed disappointed. Grinning, he turned around and headed back to the main hallway. Room 119 was on the ocean side of Peaceful Shores, and as Jackson paused at the half-open door, he heard a familiar swing tune. Eyebrows raised, he knocked on the door.

"Come in," a low, gravelly voice responded.

Jackson pushed the door open. An old man sat in an armchair identical to Phoebe's, positioned so he could look out the window at the Pacific. He reached for a remote control on the window sill and clicked off the music.

"Wilbur?" Jackson asked.

He nodded and raised himself from his armchair with apparent ease. He was neither frail nor fat, and his posture was ramrod straight. If he had to guess, Jackson placed Wilbur in his early seventies.

"Wilbur Charles Anderson," the man said, offering his hand. It didn't shake, wasn't covered with age spots, and wasn't shaped like a tree from *The Lord of the Rings*.

"Jackson Douglas."

"Thank you for seeing me."

"Sure thing."

"Can I offer you something to drink?" Wilbur asked.

"No, I'm good. Thanks."

Wilbur nodded as he sat back down. "I reckon you're a busy man, so I'll cut to the chase. Word spread quickly around here about what you were doing for Miss Phoebe, and I thought perhaps you might provide me the same services."

Jackson tried not to wince. The last thing he wanted was to spend the next week finding missing reading glasses and lost canes for all the residents of Peaceful Shores. But Wilbur had asked for two minutes and was only a quarter of the way there. Besides, something about the guy struck Jackson (call it P.I.'s intuition), and he decided to give him a fair chance.

"You need a private investigator?" Jackson asked.

"I need help," Wilbur said. "I'm afraid I can't explain everything in two minutes, so my two-minute pitch is to ask if you'll hear me out. If you don't have time to take on any new clients, maybe you can recommend somebody else. Or if now isn't a good time, maybe tonight or tomorrow." He shook his head. "I don't know who else I can speak to."

It was then that Jackson saw a photograph on the stand beside Wilbur's bed. Nine men, all of them in army uniforms, posing in what appeared to be a window overlooking a majestic mountain and a lush green valley. The faces were too small from Jackson's viewpoint for him to deduce if one of them was Wilbur, but somehow he knew it was the case.

Jackson nodded. "I've got time." He pulled over a spare chair. "What kind of help?"

Wilbur raised a finger to his ear. "If you don't mind, I'd rather we speak elsewhere."

"Are you allowed to leave?"

"There's a path around the grounds. If my slow pace won't bother you, perhaps we could take a walk."

"That would be fine."

Before Jackson could offer a hand to help, Wilbur was back out of the chair. He shuffled over to a closet, where he supplemented his khakis and charcoal button-down shirt with a brown corduroy jacket and a matching trilby hat. Jackson was in shirtsleeves and blue jeans and had been more than comfortable outside earlier.

"Do we need to check in with anyone first?" Jackson asked.

Wilbur held up his arm, showing a bracelet not dissimilar from the ones perps wore around their ankles. Or from a Fitbit. "This tracks our movement. If we get too far away from their sensors, it sends them an alert." He made a downward motion with his slightly raised hand. "We'll be fine."

Jackson let Wilbur lead the way, through an empty cafeteria and lobby and out a back entrance. Peaceful Shores was shaped like a flattened M. The first-story legs of the M contained the facility's amenities—some basic exercise equipment, billiards and ping-pong tables, a shuffleboard court, and lots of tables for playing cards and doing puzzles. The patients' rooms filled the majority of the "arms" of the M and the entire second floor. In between the arms of the M was an open field of grass with a few palm trees interspersed around picnic tables and a gazebo. A concrete path encircled the open space, the entirety of which looked over a small bluff at the Pacific Ocean. A brochure Jackson had thumbed through while waiting for Phoebe to finish up a course of medicine on his first visit boasted of Peaceful Shores' amenities, including three gourmet meals a day, plenty of entertainment options on the grounds, and satellite TVs with DVRs in every room. Jackson wondered if they had a minimum age requirement.

Abundant sunshine made for a pleasant late-afternoon walk as Jackson and Wilbur started to the left down the path. At present, they were the only two people out in the common area, which Jackson assumed meant they had sufficient privacy. But he waited for Wilbur to be ready.

"Ha-aharumgaha."

Jackson looked over to see Wilbur had not been shot in the neck or vomited but had merely cleared his throat. Jackson was used to his grandpa making similar noises, usually when attempting to digest food.

It was another few seconds before Wilbur spoke. "I'm dying."

Jackson stutter-stepped.

Wilbur was matter-of-fact. "You need to know that first of all."

Jackson nodded.

"I have a brain tumor. It's benign, but it keeps growing, and one of these days, it's going to cut off the supply of blood to my brain, and that will be it. I've been to a number of doctors, and they say there's nothing they can do. No treatment, no surgery. I'm going to die. And I've made peace with that. My soul is right with God, so I'm not afraid of death."

Jackson nodded again as they shuffled along.

"I have no family," Wilbur continued. "My wife passed away years ago, and we never had any children. No brothers, no sisters. It's just me."

"I'm sorry."

Wilbur shook his head and waved a hand. "Don't be. I'm not. I've enjoyed a good life and a good family. I'm just telling so that you understand what comes next."

"Okay."

"I went to the doctor Friday, and he told me I have a week to live. Two at the absolute most. I don't doubt it, because every time I go, they tell me I have less time than they previously thought. Again, my fear isn't of death. In fact, I wish I could die right now. But if the Good Lord wanted me gone, He'd take me."

Jackson nodded again, wondering where Wilbur's story was going. This was not what he had expected when the old man had asked him to take a walk.

"I said I wanted to hire you," Wilbur continued. "I need someone to protect me until I die."

"Protect you from what?"

"That is a rather complicated story. And before I tell it, I need to know if you're up for the task."

Jackson walked beside Wilbur for a few paces. Other than the upcoming NCCA Men's Basketball tournament—"March Madness"—

Jackson had nothing on his plate for the . . . rest of his life. And although he had no idea why Wilbur needed protection or from whom he needed it, something about the man resonated with Jackson, almost like he was talking to his own grandfather. So he nodded. "Yeah. I'm up for it."

Wilbur nodded. Then he gestured toward a bench beside the path, overlooking a small beach below the bluff and the ocean beyond. They sat down, and Wilbur crossed his left leg over his right and folded his hands in his lap. "Bear with me, Jackson. This story's a little long."

"I've got nothing but time."

Wilbur nodded again. "First an amusing little backdrop: I enlisted in the United States Army in May of 1944. On Memorial Day, I shipped out to Camp Blanding, Florida, for seventeen weeks of basic training. On October 13th, I returned home for thirteen days of furlough before being sent overseas. On November 13th, I was the thirteenth person to board a ship making its thirteenth voyage to Italy. Guess how long our voyage to Italy took?"

"Thirteen days?"

Wilbur's lips parted in a very thin smile. "Yep. I spent the better part of two years in Italy, Austria, and Germany. I was very fortunate that my unit was not involved in some of the heavier fighting. But we did see our share of skirmishes."

Wilbur paused for a moment, smoothing a wrinkle in his pants. "One in particular occurred in a tiny little German village in the mountains just north of the Austrian border, shortly before the Germans surrendered in May of '45. We were surprised to find an unusually high level of resistance for such a small village in the middle of nowhere. There were no known compounds or airfields or factories anywhere nearby. We didn't know what to think. But after we had secured the village, we discovered a German bunker built into the mountain. Our orders at the time were to secure all military installations, so we advanced on the bunker. We were again surprised at the high level of resistance, but we managed to take the bunker."

Wilbur paused for another bench-rattling throat clearing. "When we got inside, we realized what this bunker was—a missile silo."

"A missile silo?"

Wilbur nodded. "Occupied by several Nazi officers and triple the number of troops it should have taken to defend such a place. They put up a very spirited defense, but we kept coming and outnumbered them. I was a staff sergeant, and my squad was sent to secure the control room. When we arrived, we found there were actually two different rooms on either side of the silo. I split our squad, four of them going to one room, and myself and the other four going to the other. We arrived to find a Nazi officer and two soldiers feverishly preparing to launch a missile. We exchanged fire, killing all three of them. The other half of our squad was successful as well, and no missiles were launched."

"Sounds exciting" would have been a major understatement and possibly an insult, so Jackson just nodded.

Wilbur continued. "We quickly looked around to make sure there was no imminent threat. That was when we noticed the numbers."

As Wilbur kept talking, Jackson had to chase from his head images of a time-traveling Scotsman and a bald-headed mystic in an experimental underground station on an island in the middle of nowhere.

"It was some sort of launch mechanism, and a Nazi officer was entering a combination on a series of dials."

"A launch code?"

Wilbur nodded. "I quickly scrambled the dials, but those eight numbers were emblazoned in my memory. Especially after we had fully secured and locked down the bunker and learned that the missiles had been pointed at London and Washington D.C."

"The Germans had ICBMs?"

Wilbur nodded. "Experimental V-5 missiles, far more advanced than anything either side had at the time. And they were carrying a nuclear payload."

Jackson brushed his hand across his mouth and chin. He looked around, seeing only an old woman seated at a picnic table in the shade, well out of hearing distance. He met Wilbur's intense green eyes. "You're telling me the Germans had nuclear capability before we did?"

"Yes." He cleared his throat, this time more quietly. "My unit was temporarily assigned to guard the bunker after we realized what it was. We were there when the Allied EOD team arrived to identify the payload as a very crude atomic bomb, not too different than what we eventually used on Hiroshima and Nagasaki."

"And they were aimed at London and D.C.?"

"Yes. Apparently, it was a last-ditch effort by the Nazis, whether to try to win the war or to cause as much pain and death as possible in defeat, I don't know. But we were told that had we been two minutes later, the missile intended for Washington would have been fired. The other missile was less than five minutes from being launched."

All Jackson could manage was a quiet, "Wow."

"The EOD team determined the weapons weren't stable enough to move or be dismantled. They feared any efforts might accidentally trigger a launch, or cause a meltdown. So they simply locked everything down."

Jackson raised his eyebrows.

"Unfortunately, they didn't have the good sense, or perhaps the wherewithal, to bury them with concrete. So they only locked the silos and covered them with a thin layer of earth. My unit was retasked, and we never returned to the area. I was discharged in the summer of '46 and have been a civilian ever since." He looked at Jackson. "But to this day, I can still see those eight numbers, try as I have to forget them."

Jackson sat back. "So if I have this straight, you're telling me that there are two World War II-era Nazi missiles buried in the mountains of southern Germany with active nuclear payloads, and you have the launch code necessary to fire them?"

Wilbur nodded slowly. "That about sums it up."

Chapter Twenty-Eight

4:56 p.m.

JACKSON PONDERED HIS first question to Wilbur for almost a minute, letting the breeze carry sounds of gulls across the grounds. "Have you told anyone?" he finally asked.

"I reported to my superiors having seen the code and having scrambled it," Wilbur answered. "I also mentioned it to someone from the EOD team as well once I learned that the missiles contained nuclear payloads. I thought perhaps they would need the code to disable them, but no one ever asked for it. Beyond that, several members of my old unit saw the same things I saw, but I have not told anyone else. Not even my wife." He lowered his voice. "Virginia had a weak stomach when it came to matters like this. Her sister lived in Washington, and if she knew how close she had come to . . . well . . ."

Jackson stood and paced, then returned to stand in front of Wilbur. "Why do you need protection?"

"I know nothing about missile launch systems or codes, and I have no idea what happens to a nuclear payload after almost seventy years—particularly with such primitive nuclear technology. Perhaps the only danger is that the bombs would explode and contaminate the surrounding countryside. But it is also possible that those nuclear payloads are still potent, those missiles still functional, and the launch systems and guidance systems still effective. If the wrong person or group were to gain access to them . . ."

Jackson nodded. He sat back down. "And you're afraid someone is going to come after you to get that code?"

Wilbur nodded.

"Why now? Why after almost seventy years."

"After the war, Germany was separated into two countries."

"East Germany and West Germany."

"Yes. The bunker was in the American Zone until the Federal Republic of Germany was founded. I assume their government, and thus the current German government, is aware of the silo's existence, as is our current government."

"And you think that knowledge could have funneled down to someone who would abuse it?"

"That is possible. I consider myself a patriotic American, Jackson, but I am not naïve enough to believe our government doesn't have its share of sinister people inside of it. The same is true of the German government, then and now. But to answer your question, no, that is not my concern."

Jackson shook his head. "One of your old unit?"

"In a manner of speaking. I trust each of those men implicitly, as I had to in order to survive back in the war. But several years ago, Private Ervin Wilkerson, a member of the squad I led into the control room, wrote a book about our experiences in Europe called *We Saved the World*. Perhaps you have heard of it?"

"Doesn't ring a bell."

"Wilkerson's book related stories from dozens of soldiers, from those who stormed Normandy and Omaha Beaches to the men who fought in the Ardennes Forest and Iwo Jima and Midway. The day we took the bunker in the Wetterstein Mountains was one of the accounts in the book, and he perhaps overstated the significance of our efforts. But that's beside the point. What is important is that he described our actions in great detail, including our shootout in the control room."

"And the code," Jackson said.

Wilbur nodded. "Unfortunately, he wasn't clear on one thing. He made it sound as if we all saw the code."

"That's good, isn't it? Takes pressure off of you?"

Wilbur slowly shook his head. "Wilkerson died about a year ago from lung cancer. He had a filthy habit of smoking. And Strasbourg died in Korea. That leaves Waters, Klein, and myself of the five in Control Room A. Waters and Klein have both died within the last week of heart attacks."

"You're suspicious?"

"We kept in touch. Neither of them had a heart condition. I find it awfully coincidental."

Jackson looked around again. The old woman had gone back inside. A nurse was pushing a different old woman along the path in a wheelchair, but they were still a ways away from Jackson and Wilbur.

"What exactly did Wilkerson say about the code?"

"He quoted something I told him, about the numbers being 'etched in my mind.' It sounded as if they were his own words, which I don't quibble over. He was making the story more personal. The problem is, the way he wrote it also suggested that we all had these numbers memorized."

"And you think someone is killing you one by one?"

Wilbur nodded.

"Probably after 'interrogating' them first," Jackson said.

Wilbur nodded again. "I do not fear death, Jackson, as I told you before. I do not even fear the torture—not much. What I fear is not being able to withstand it and surrendering the code to terrorists or fanatics . . . neo-Nazis intent on reviving the Third Reich or al-Qaeda seeking to kill thousands more Americans. That is why I seek your protection."

Jackson nodded. "Why me?"

"I don't know anyone else. When Miss Phoebe hired you, I had my friend Reuben look you up. He understands this internet business better than I do. He told me about you, and I thought you were worth speaking to."

"Why not the police, or the government?"

"I contacted the police. They said there was not a 'credible threat' and suggested I hire a private party. As for the government, well . . . I seriously doubt I would be at the top of their list. And even if I was, I'd be long dead before they could cut through all of the red tape. Jackson, I need protection right here and now."

The nurse and the lady in the wheelchair were approaching, and Wilbur turned slightly, crossing his legs the other way. "Afternoon, Miss Annabelle."

"Good afternoon," the woman in the wheelchair croaked.

"Hello, Nancy."

"Hello, Wilbur," the nurse replied.

Wilbur waited until they were out of earshot. "I know what you're probably thinking, that this is all the fear and paranoia of a very old man. And that may indeed be the case. I can't say for sure after all these years, but I don't think any of the other men in my squad actually saw the code before I scrambled it. I'm the only one left who knows it. Once I'm dead, the missiles are rendered inert." He shrugged. "Perhaps they are already. But I don't dare take the chance."

"Are you sure the code is necessary to activate the missiles?"

"It was part of the launch mechanism, not just a lock on the mechanism. I'm no expert, but I don't believe those missiles could be fired without it. Not without some rather major modifications."

"But someone could theoretically remove the payloads."

"Yes. But if the payload is separated from the missile and the guidance system, it alleviates at least the immediate threat of such a weapon being launched at the United States. It is certainly still a threat, but far less of one than if attached to a honed, live missile."

Jackson sat back again. He had to admit, it was all pretty far-fetched. Terrorists sneaking into Germany, unearthing an old missile silo, and firing World War II-era weapons at Washington D.C. or London, all without the German military—or the U.S. military, for that matter—finding out about it? It was somewhat improbable, if not impossible. More like the plot of an episode of *MacGyver* than a legitimate, twenty-first-century threat. After all, if the modern TV shows were right, nuclear material was as readily accessible as fertilizer and diesel fuel, meaning Wilbur's really old rocket wasn't essential for al-Qaeda. But as a turnkey solution for some knockoff terrorist organization or up-and-coming anarchists with a beef with the U.S. or the Brits . . . And the deaths of Waters and Klein were at the very least suspicious.

And he had nothing better to do.

"We have a couple of hurdles, Wilbur."

"Such as?"

"If I'm going to protect you, I don't know that I can do it here. We'd have to get you out of Peaceful Shores. Is that possible?"

"Aside from Peaceful Shores staff and immediate family, the only person authorized to take me off premises is my physician."

"I don't suppose I could impersonate him."

Wilbur shook his head. "Her name is Melinda."

"And they know you don't have any family?"

He nodded.

"So we'd have to sneak you out."

"Yes."

"Won't that be a problem with your bracelet? They'll know you're on the move."

"Hmm."

"Can I see it?"

Wilbur extended his arm.

"Is this just padding?" Jackson asked.

"It chafes my wrist," Wilbur replied. "This is a special model they have for those of us with sensitive skin."

Jackson gently slid the bracelet toward Wilbur's hand, eyeballing the size of the actual bracelet. "If we could get the padding off . . . I think it might fit over your hand."

"Lucky I don't have arthritis," Wilbur said with a grin.

Jackson fiddled with the padding for a moment. "Okay, I think we can negotiate that. Second hurdle: are you on any medications or do you require any treatments?"

"I have a life expectancy of seven to ten days," Wilbur said with a laugh. "What medication could I need? I sometimes take Tylenol for aches and pains, but that is all."

"Third hurdle," Jackson said. "Nurse Nancy and Miss Annabelle know you had a visitor. The pretty girl at the front desk knows my name. So does Reuben. If you're right and someone does come looking for you, they also have my name."

Wilbur looked down. "I'm sorry. I didn't mean to drag you into this. I didn't even think—"

"That's not what I mean, Wilbur. I mean, I can't just take you to my place to watch TV. We'll need to go off the grid."

"If you're worried about expenses, I have money."

"It's not that. It's . . . and I don't mean to be insensitive here, Wilbur, but what happens when you die?"

"The arrangements have all been made for my funeral. I can write a note explaining everything, to be opened only by the coroner in event of my death."

Wilbur's solution didn't satisfy Jackson, but it was something that could be worked on later. Just so he didn't end up in jail for the murder of Wilbur, Waters, and Klein.

"Okay," Jackson said. "The next question is when. As soon as possible, I assume?"

Wilbur nodded.

"Sunset's around seven," Jackson said. "When are visiting hours over?"

"Nine. By ten, the building is locked down for the night unless there's an emergency. All of the overnight staff arrive by then and don't leave until at least six."

"Then I'll come after ten."

"How?"

"Can you leave your window open?"

"Only opens a foot. Not enough for one of us to get out."

"I can get in through a foot," Jackson said. "Just make sure it's open."

"What if they come before then? Klein died three days ago. Waters was two days before that."

"If you're right, and Waters and Klein's deaths were covered up murders, it means they were done stealthily. Which means I don't think anyone's going to storm in here and take you by force. That would attract attention. Lock yourself in your room. No nurses, no visitors, no dinner. Don't touch or do anything until I come back."

"They'll suspect if I don't come to dinner."

Jackson slouched slightly. "And if you claim you're sick, they'll want to check in on you."

Wilbur nodded.

"How is dinner served?"

"Buffet style. Staff gets food for those who can't."

"I take it you can get your own?"

"Yes, sir."

"Just don't leave it unattended. Don't let anyone touch it. You should be fine."

Wilbur nodded. "A nurse usually checks in around seven or eight. Takes vitals, that sort of thing."

"I don't suppose we can avoid that either," Jackson said. "Unless . . ."

"Your brain's spinning, I can see it."

"Are you allowed visitors at dinner?"

Wilbur nodded.

"I can stay until after dinner and the nurse's checkup. Then I'll leave before visiting hours end at nine and come back later."

"That sounds like a plan. But I warn you, the food's not as wonderful as the brochures indicate."

"It never is, Wilbur."

They went over a few more details, and then Wilbur suggested they head in before his legs got too stiff. He was, after all, pushing ninety years of age.

"You've aged well."

"I lived clean."

Jackson grinned.

"There is one other thing we need to discuss," Wilbur said. "Your fee. I said before I have money, and I do. If I'm trusting you with my life, I can trust you with my money too. I'll pay ahead for however long you deem necessary. We'll just have to arrange a stop at a bank."

"That won't be necessary," Jackson said.

"What?"

"I'm not charging you."

"Why not? If you pity me or think—"

"Wilbur, you fought in World War II. I agree with Wilkerson—you guys did save the world. Without your sacrifice—without what you guys did . . . As far as I'm concerned, you've already paid me."

Wilbur studied Jackson for a moment, and when he concluded he was serious, a lump seemed to appear in his throat. Finally, he swallowed it and offered Jackson his hand for the second time that day. "It warms my heart to hear someone from your generation say something like that. Thank you very much."

"No," Jackson said. "Thank you."

Chapter Twenty-Nine

AS JACKSON DROVE back toward home, he reflected on everything Wilbur had told him. Somehow listening to hours of war stories over dinner and in Wilbur's room made the threat Wilbur felt seem much more imminent. Even if he was almost ninety and even if he did have a brain tumor, there was nothing about the man to suggest that he was crazy or paranoid. Wilbur was playing with a full deck of cards, and the fact that he was worried was enough to convince Jackson there was something to this.

But what? Who would be after such ancient technology? Then again, how ancient was it? Hadn't the U.S. stolen German engineers and scientists after the war? Maybe Hitler's Nazi's had been cutting edge. Maybe their guidance systems and V-5 missiles and coded launch systems were still viable today . . . at least viable enough to be dangerous if they fell into the wrong hands.

So it brought him back to the question of who. Rogues in the German or U.S. government or military were the first suspects, but since Private Ervin Wilkerson's book had been published, anyone literate was suddenly in the mix. And what was better for a terrorist than a nuclear weapon that didn't require separate transportation and guidance systems. It was enough to make Jackson shiver, because if there was one Axis Powers abandoned military silo with weapons aimed at the U.S. that the history books and documentary programs had never brought to light, how many more might there be?

Jackson was also troubled by the thought of Wilbur—as well as Waters and Klein—being tortured. No one—except for maybe al-Qaeda operatives at Gitmo—deserved that, much less decorated war veterans.

Jackson had always appreciated history, and he recognized the sacrifice made by all in the military, but he had an especially soft place for World War II and its veterans. They were called the Greatest Generation for a reason. If this all turned out to be Wilbur's paranoia, then so be it. But Jackson, like his new client, wasn't taking any chances.

It was a balmy, breezy night in Southern California, reminding Jackson of his earlier plans to call Maggie or Sam to see if either of them felt like hanging out. As he walked from his driveway to the front door, he thought about checking in with them before he went off the grid. Then he thought better of it. If anyone did come looking for Wilbur, they could likely connect him to Jackson. The last thing Jackson wanted was to leave a phone trail leading to his friends. He switched off his phone, then disconnected the battery and the SIM card. He was pretty sure even Special Agent McGee couldn't track him now.

Reaching for his keys with one hand, Jackson opened his screen door with the other. Then he stopped. Sitting on the sill was a very small bouquet of flowers. He had no idea what kind. Tucked into them was a folded up piece of paper, and Jackson tucked the flowers under his arm as he opened it. The words Glennon Insurance were stamped in the bottom corner. Scrawled in the middle was a simple phrase.

Ivan's here ~Allie

Jackson read it three times, looking for any other meaning than the one that first came to him. He concluded he would need to make a phone call before long. But Wilbur took precedence, so he pitched the flowers and the note in the trash and headed upstairs.

Jackson dug out his laptop, and while he packed, he priced rental cars and did some rudimentary research. He didn't expect to find much, and he didn't. He only confirmed that Ken Waters from Salt Lake City and Albert Klein from Dallas had died of apparent heart attacks in the last five days. He didn't even know if they were the right Waters and Klein.

While completing a car rental reservation, Jackson jammed enough clothes into his duffel bag to last a week. Wilbur had insisted on at least paying for expenses, and if he were still alive in a week, that would include some quarters for laundry. Jackson thought long and hard about packing a gun. He decided against it. If it came to the point of having to defend Wilbur with a firefight, things would have had already gone severely off the rails. Jackson also debated taking his computer, but he figured that if he connected to the internet, there was someone somewhere who could find his location through an IP address or something. And there was no sense going ninety-nine percent off the grid.

A little before nine, Jackson left the house. His first stop was an all-night convenience store that sold prepaid cell phones, one-liters of Mountain Dew, and snacks. He bought a phone with a thousand minutes and enough snacks to last till morning, all while wearing an old Nike baseball cap pulled low over his eyes. Leaving the store, he ditched the cap in the trash.

Next, he headed for the LoCal Rent A Car office in Santa Monica, where he traded in his Granada for a charcoal gray Toyota Yaris. With his bag in the trunk, he started west shortly before ten p.m. As he cruised along the Pacific Coast Highway, he tried out his new burn phone, trying a very old phone number and hoping.

"This is Tori Walker. I'm unavailable at the moment, so please leave me a message, and I'll get back to you shortly."

"Hey, Walker. I got your very cryptic little note and the lovely bouquet. Give me a call. Three-one-zero, nine . . . Wait, hold on. Sorry. That's no good. Uh . . . just call me back at whatever this is. Sorry."

He clicked the phone off, then thought better of it, and turned it back on. He thumbed his way to the vibrate setting while managing not to run off the road. Fifteen minutes later, he was nearing Peaceful Shores Assisted Living Home and turned his concentration to the task at hand.

The M-shaped building was on a somewhat isolated piece of property between the coast and the highway. There was a condominium complex about a hundred yards north of the building, separated by a row of bushes and a few groves of palm trees. Jackson parked in the lot of the nearest condo and made sure no one was looking as he got out. He wore dark jeans and a black long-sleeved T-shirt, making him hard to spot without identifying him as an intruder if he was spotted.

Taking another look around, Jackson darted into the bushes. They were a little prickly, and he wondered how Wilbur would mind them on the way back. Better than a needle and heart-attack-rendering truth serum.

Hiding behind a palm tree, Jackson scouted the Peaceful Shores building. A few of the resident lights on the two-story facility were still on, but most of the rooms were dark. He crept along the row of bushes, keeping low and out of sight from any curious folks in the condos. He spent five minutes scanning the grounds, making sure no one was out for a late stroll. Wilbur said the building was locked by ten, and it was closing in on ten-thirty. Realizing the coast was as clear as could be, Jackson took off on a steady run across the open space between the bushes and the near elbow of the M. He covered the ground in near-Olympic time and stopped to catch his breath.

If his mad dash had alerted anyone or set off an alarm, there was nothing to suggest it. So Jackson dropped to his knees and crept under several first-floor windows, counting off until he was under Wilbur's room. His back to the brick wall of the building, he again eyed the grass between him and the ocean. Then he raised his head.

Wilbur's window was closed.

Jackson dropped down and looked the length of the building in both directions, counting and recounting the windows. This was room 119. Wilbur's room. He sighed.

Jackson himself had opened the window before leaving. Had a nurse come in and closed it? Had they seen the suitcase packed and hidden in the bathtub? Had Wilbur's fears come true and some neo-Nazi group gotten to him? Or had the old guy gotten cold?

Jackson raised himself up again and peered into the window. It was too dark to see anything inside, especially with a half-moon reflecting off the glass. He'd come this far, so Jackson rapped on the frame of the window. He waited almost a minute, and then a light flipped on. For whatever reason, Jackson decided to hide, and flattened himself against the wall halfway between Wilbur's window and the next one down.

Another minute passed, and Jackson was about to knock on the window again when he heard a faint clunk and then the squeak of the window being raised. He stayed put, waiting. He heard voices, Wilbur's and a woman's, but he couldn't make them out. After a minute, they died away, and then Jackson heard another sound.

"Pssst."

He inched toward the window. "Wilbur?"

"It's safe now."

Jackson moved in front of the window. Wilbur was bent down, pushing with no luck on the window, which was only open six inches. "I can't raise this thing any higher. Too cottonpickin' old."

Jackson smiled. "You or the window?"

"Both," Wilbur said. It turned into a harrumph. "Just after you left, another nurse stopped in. Apparently, the left hand doesn't know what the right hand is doing."

"And she shut the window?"

Wilbur nodded. "Thought I'd catch a draft. I had to call another nurse to open it."

"Okay," Jackson said. "Just give me a minute to get this screen off."

"I've got nothing but time."

Jackson had brought a screwdriver and pliers and, using the two tools, he was able to remove the screen. Turning it on its side, he passed it through the six-inch opening to Wilbur. Then he pushed the window open as far as it would go, twelve inches.

"You aren't going to make it."

"You struck me as a lot more positive this afternoon," Jackson said as he peeled off his outer shirt. He handed it to Wilbur as well. Then he hoisted himself up and stuck his arms and head through the window. His shoulders and torso made it without a problem, but his belt buckle got stuck. Bracing himself on Wilbur's chair with one hand, he used the other to finagle the buckle until it slid free. From there, it was easy, although a little awkward until he could bend his knees on the inside.

"That was graceful," Wilbur said, offering Jackson's shirt back to him.

Jackson smiled and took the shirt. "Everything else ready to go?"

"The suitcase is still in the tub. I just have to change."

"We should put the screen on first," Jackson said.

"Oh, that reminds me, Irene's coming back in about fifteen minutes."

"Coming back?"

"To close the window. That's all I could get her to open it for."

"Then we'd better double-time it with the screen," Jackson said. "You get back in bed and pretend to be asleep. When she comes back, I'll hide in the bathroom."

Wilbur nodded, and Jackson busied himself replacing the screen from the inside. It was not easy, but he got it to snap into place. After lowering the window to its six-inch opening, he made sure Wilbur was squared away in bed and that there was no evidence of his presence. He then hid in the bathtub.

Irene was late. She didn't return until after eleven, and fortunately, did nothing more than close the window. When Jackson heard the door close behind her, he crept out of the bathroom. Wilbur was already sitting up. Jackson went over the plan with him again, making sure Wilbur was on mission, while at the same time stuffing several pillows under Wilbur's bedding. If a nurse investigated, the lack of a head would probably ring some alarm bells. But if they did a peek-in-the-door bed check, it might fool them.

Using the flat-head screwdriver he'd brought, it took Jackson five minutes to pry the padding off Wilbur's medical bracelet. He managed to do so without gouging Wilbur with the screwdriver. It took another two minutes to finagle the bracelet over his knuckles, not without scraping them pretty good. But he managed not to draw blood, and Wilbur was plenty tough and didn't so much as grimace.

"You ready?" Jackson asked, tucking the bracelet into his bed.

Wilbur took a look around. "I'm not coming back here," he said. Then he nodded. "Yeah, I'm ready."

"Okay. Stay close."

Jackson opened the door and looked up and down the hallway. It was clear. So he picked up the suitcase holding Wilbur's belongings and started down the corridor. The halls were quiet, dimly lit, perfect for an escape. All doors were locked for the night, according to Wilbur, and armed with alarms. Knowing they would have to find an alternate way out, Jackson had done some scouting during the afternoon and had a plan.

The entrance to Peaceful Shores was in the middle of the M, at the bottom. The cafeteria was on the opposite side, inside the M, overlooking the common area where Jackson and Wilbur had talked that afternoon. The kitchen was in the north wing, and the administrative offices were in the south. The nurse's station was behind the front desk and was manned 24/7. That was a problem. Although the view from behind the desk was partially blocked by a staircase and an elevator, if the nurse on duty stood, she would have a view of the hallway and the cafeteria. That meant Jackson either needed a distraction or luck. Or both.

"Okay, hold up here," he said as he and Wilbur ducked into an alcove. It was a stub branching off the main hallway, leading to a janitor's closet and an unmarked door. Jackson reached for his cell phone, the burner he'd bought on the way, and dialed the main number at Peaceful Shores. It brought him to a menu, and he pressed 4 to be connected to the nurse's station.

"Peaceful Shores Assisted Living, this is Irene, how can I help you?"

"This is Jerry Goldman," Jackson whispered. "I just got off the phone with my Uncle Reuben. He said he came down with the stomach flu after dinner and really wasn't feeling well. But he's kind of stubborn and doesn't ask for help, so I'm just wondering if you could check in on him for me. He didn't sound too good."

"Of course, Mr. Goldman. I'll look in on him right away."

"Thank you so much."

Jackson closed the phone and winked at Wilbur. Reuben was stubborn and did have a nephew named Jerry. And if he knew he was helping Wilbur, he would happily have gone along with the ruse and with some poking and prodding by a nurse. At least according to Wilbur.

Jackson peeked around the corner until he saw Irene come around the desk and start down the hall in the other direction. He held out a hand to stall Wilbur until he saw her enter Reuben's room.

"Okay, come on."

As fast as Wilbur could shuffle, the duo hurried down the hallway and into the cafeteria. Except for some recessed lighting along the walls, the room was dark. Which was why they didn't spot the woman sitting in an armchair behind the elevator. She didn't see them either, at least not at first, because she suddenly jumped when they passed in front of her. At her spastic twitch, Wilbur turned casually, indicating his heart was strong as ever. Jackson's almost stopped.

"Miss Millie, what are you doing here?" Wilbur asked.

"I'm reading."

"You don't have a book."

"How's that?"

"You haven't got a book."

"Oh?"

Wilbur shook his head.

"Hmm. I must have forgotten it tonight. Who's this?"

"My grandson, Lionel."

"He's rather handsome," she said, patting the back of her fluffy hair. "But isn't it after visiting hours?"

"He'll be leaving shortly."

She looked down. "He has a suitcase."

"Yes, he was visiting for a little while."

Jackson touched Wilbur's elbow and made eye contact.

"Uh, Miss Millie, do they know you're out of your room?"

"Of course they do. They know I come here to read every night." She looked down. "Although you'd think they'd have noticed I don't have a book."

"Or a light," Wilbur said.

"How's that?"

"No light, either."

"Maybe I should call the nurse."

"I think maybe you ought to go back to your room," Wilbur said. "It is rather late."

"How's that?"

"Rather late," he repeated a little louder. Reuben was old, so Jackson hoped he'd have symptoms of some kind to occupy Irene for a while.

"I suppose," Millie said. "I've got nothing to read anyhow. Perhaps your grandson could help me up?"

Jackson reached down and lifted Millie's frail arm, assisting her out of the chair. She reeked, a combination of mothballs and mint, both smells so strong he wasn't sure how the other odor had a chance to compete.

"Would you care to walk me to my room?" Millie asked.

"I'm afraid not, ma'am. Wilbur and I were going to see about a snack."

"Hmm." She wagged a bony finger. "Your generation could use some lessons in chivalry," she said, then trudged around the elevator in a pace that made Wilbur look like Usain Bolt. He and Jackson waited until Millie was out of sight.

"That was close," Wilbur said.

"Yeah. Let's . . ." Jackson stopped.

"What?"

"Shh."

Miss Millie's voice carried back to them. "I just saw Wilbur wandering the halls with his grandson. Can you believe that? At this hour?"

"Wilbur doesn't have a grandson, Millie," Irene said. "And I just checked on him not half an hour ago. He's sound asleep in his room."

"Oh, drat, I must have been dreaming. I forgot my book tonight."

"Let me help you back to your room, Millie."

"You're a dear."

"Come on," Jackson said, leading Wilbur around behind the serving counter. He set down Wilbur's suitcase, and they both crouched behind the counter, out of Irene's sight when she returned from tucking in Miss Millie.

"A double close one," Wilbur said.

"Sure was, Gramps." He reached for his lock picks. "Lionel?"

"First name into my head."

"Hmm."

"You do a lot of lock picking?"

"Enough," Jackson said. A minute later, the kitchen door was unlocked. Checking to make sure Irene wasn't looking, Jackson pushed it open so Wilbur could slip through. Then he took another look back at the nurse's station and entered himself, closing the door behind him.

Two windows on the south side of the room let in enough moonlight that Jackson could see without the penlight he'd brought along, and while Wilbur waited by the door, Jackson approached the far window. He unlocked it and opened it with only a minor squeak. Unlike the windows in residents' rooms, these opened wide and were only two feet off the ground.

Jackson popped out the screen, then found a stepstool for Wilbur. He motioned for Wilbur to join him. "I'll go first," he said. "Then you use the stool and sit on the window sill. I'll catch you and carry you through the window."

"There's a certain lack of dignity in old age," Wilbur said.

"Nothing of the sort. Just one man helping out another."

Wilbur nodded.

Jackson climbed through the window and had Wilbur hand him the suitcase and the screen. After scanning the grounds one more time, Jackson motioned for Wilbur to climb into the window. It took a little doing, but Wilbur's joints were pretty flexible. Bracing himself with his hands on the open window, he leaned back and into Jackson's arms. The old guy was heavy, but not so heavy that Jackson couldn't hold him. He set Wilbur down gently, each of them breathing a little heavily.

"You good?" Jackson asked.

"Yeah."

"Okay." He closed the window and placed the screen back in place. "Okay, let's go."

They walked slowly, ducking under windows, and made the end of the building without problems. Now they faced one hundred yards of mostly open grass before the bushes between Peaceful Shores' property and the condominiums.

"See that palm tree," Jackson said, "the one that's crooked on the bottom?"

"I see it."

"When you're ready, start walking toward it. It's about a hundred yards, so go at your pace. I'll be behind you, keeping an eye out for any signs that we've been detected."

"And if we are? I make like Tim Conway?"

Jackson grinned. "Something like that."

"Okay. Here goes."

Jackson waited until Wilbur was a third of the way across the field, then followed, continuing to look over his shoulders. It was an agonizingly slow walk, but they reached the shadows of the palms and cover of the bushes without any sign of detection.

Wilbur was breathing hard but said he was fine.

"Okay. My car is on the other side of the bushes. Just stay with me."

"Whatever you say."

Jackson led the way this time, pushing through the bushes and making sure they didn't swing back and slap Wilbur in the face. The condo parking lot was quiet, and Jackson manually unlocked the car, Wilbur's door first, then his own. He helped Wilbur with his seatbelt, then started the car.

"We did it," Wilbur said with a grin.

"How long since you've been out?"

"Aside from visits to the doctor, two and a half years."

"We've got a bit of a ride," Jackson said. "Are you comfortable?"

"A little cold."

Jackson adjusted the heat, then accelerated out of the parking lot and onto the Pacific Coast Highway. Peaceful Shores Assisted Living Home was quiet as they drove past, and Jackson had to conclude that Wilbur was right. They had done it.

Chapter Thirty

11:54 p.m.

JACKSON AND WILBUR stopped at an all-night McDonald's in Santa Monica before continuing through Los Angeles on the 405. At some point between a pair of McChicken sandwiches, Wilbur asked Jackson where they were going.

"Huntington Beach."

"Why Huntington Beach?"

"Plenty of motels we can hide out in with views of the ocean. We're still in L.A. so it will be easy to blend in, but we're far enough away from home that it won't be obvious to look for us there."

"You have a place in mind?"

"Not really. You?"

"No. It's strange, you know, picking the place where you're going to die."

Jackson concentrated on the car in front of him.

"I'm not complaining," Wilbur said. "I'm ready to go, like I told you. It's just strange."

The silence lasted until Wilbur asked for his third McChicken. Sneaking around made him hungry, and besides, he hadn't eaten anything but cafeteria food for years. Anything different was welcome, he said.

"So where was that picture on your end table taken?" Jackson asked.

"The Berghof," Wilbur answered. "Near Berchtesgaden, in far southeastern Germany. Adolf Hitler's vacation home, and one of his most used headquarters during the war." He took a bite of his sandwich, chewed, and swallowed with a gulp. "It was bombed by the British in April of '45, then set on fire by the retreating *Schutzstaffel*. We arrived in

May of '45. That mountain in the background is the Watzmann, the third highest in Germany. Beautiful, just beautiful."

"My great-grandfather served in World War II," Jackson said.

"Now you are making me feel old."

"He wrote that the scenery was absolutely breathtaking . . . when it wasn't obscured by smoke from shells and gunfire."

"Very true," Wilbur said. "Your great-grandfather. Did he return home?"

"He did," Jackson said. "He was awarded the Purple Heart and the Silver Star. A hero."

"Did you know him?"

Jackson shook his head. "No. I just know of him. His letters."

Wilbur nodded and took another bite of his sandwich. He chased it with a slurp of his soda.

"My favorite site was Salzburg," Wilbur said. "Or Vienna. They were both beautiful. I wish I could describe to you the magnificence of the Alps. And everywhere you look, there's so much history . . . America, it's only been here a few hundred years."

"Which seems like forever to mere mortals."

They continued south, the freeways mostly empty at the late hour. Wilbur regaled Jackson with stories from his time in Europe during World War II. The more he talked, the more Jackson appreciated the man beside him. Gone were any qualms he'd had about breaking Wilbur out of Peaceful Shores. He knew in his heart he'd done the right thing.

A little before one a.m., they arrived in Huntington Beach, and Jackson drove up and down several streets, looking for the perfect hotel. He had viewed several satellite images of the area, zooming to street level to check out a few options. He already had it narrowed down to a handful of possibilities, and the brief tour confirmed his choice.

Just south of the Huntington Beach Municipal Pier, off the PCH, was a single-level motel with ocean views in all rooms and parking behind the hotel, unseen from the street. A flickering neon sign tabbed it The Pierless Motel and advertised "acancies," free HBO, and an outdoor pool. The price listed was $29.99 per night. Jackson had plenty of cash.

He parked in back and told Wilbur to wait while he checked it out. The clerk was a loser with dreads, a long beard, and red eyes. The lobby smelled of weed, and Jackson had second thoughts. But he had the loser show him a room anyhow. It had two queen beds, was reasonably clean, and the Pierless did have the best parking options of any motels in the area. The room also had a working deadbolt and locks on the windows. Considering the parking, Jackson took it.

He paid $250 in cash and dug out eighteen cents for a week's worth of room and tax. Then he went to get Wilbur. They walked under a carport and down to room 1C.

"It's not the Ritz," Jackson said as he locked the door behind them, "but it's off the grid."

"I slept on an Army cot for two years, Jackson. This is fine."

Ten minutes later, they were both asleep.

*   *   *

Wednesday, March 20
6:21 p.m.

OFF AND on thunderstorms were currently on as Jackson pulled into the parking lot of the Pierless Motel. It was a pun that really made no sense, unless the Huntington Beach Municipal Pier was to suddenly break off and fall into the ocean. Then, maybe. But the linens had been clean, and he and Wilbur had both gotten a good night's sleep. And Wilbur had awakened, which wasn't a given anymore.

Jackson parked behind the building and hurried to the cover of the carport. He carried two boxes of takeout from a nearby diner, a burger for him and chicken fried steak for Wilbur. It was his favorite meal, one he hadn't had in a very long time, and Jackson figured the guy deserved to be treated, even if it did mean going out in public again.

Jackson doubted he had much to worry about. He had watched the news that noon, and there had been no mention of a disappearance from a retirement home in Malibu. Oh, the police were probably involved, but there wasn't a citywide dragnet out for Wilbur or Jackson yet.

But that could come, which was why Jackson wanted to limit his exposure. To that end, he and Wilbur had gone out that morning to get several thousand dollars from Wilbur's savings account. Wilbur had plenty of money and no one to bequeath it to. So whatever was left of his estate would go to various charities. Whatever Jackson didn't need for expenses, he promised to donate to one of them.

After visiting the bank, Jackson had dropped Wilbur off and then gone to Walmart, where he'd purchased a suite-size refrigerator and a miniature microwave, along with a week's worth of groceries. He had smuggled them into room 1C at the Pierless Motel, providing he and Wilbur a safe house, of sorts. But come dinnertime, he hadn't been able to help himself, deciding he and Wilbur needed a decent meal.

Wilbur was watching a rerun of *Are You Smarter Than a 5th Grader* when Jackson let himself in. He locked and bolted the door, and the duo sat down to dinner, Wilbur in the room's lone chair and Jackson on his bed. They both concluded they had the elementary school crowd outwitted.

"So how much did you tell the police, Wilbur?" Jackson asked during a commercial break.

"Less than I told you. Just enough to determine they had no interest in what I was saying."

"And you haven't told anyone else?"

"Not since 1945."

Jackson nodded and reached for some fries.

"You think they miss me yet?" Wilbur asked.

"Oh, I think it's fairly certain. You ever had anyone wander away from the facility?"

"Miss Millie, the bookworm from last night? She made it to the road once."

"By now they've probably put two and two together and know I was involved."

"They don't know your name though."

"The girl at the front desk does. You had her ask me to stop by your room."

"Hmm," Wilbur said, reaching for a napkin and dabbing some gravy from the corner of his mouth. "You think they'll finger you?"

"It depends. I have a reasonable reputation, and there's no proof I was there after eight o'clock. I kept my face hidden at the bank. Depends how doggedly they investigate."

"A missing old man isn't going to be high on their list of priorities."

"Likely not."

Wilbur cut into his steak and took another bite. "This sure is delicious. I don't know how to thank you."

"There is one other thing we haven't covered yet," Jackson said. "But it's a little touchy."

"My health."

Jackson nodded.

"What do you want to know?"

"You said you had about a week to live. Are we going to have any warning?"

"The doctor said I would experience headaches, which I do. They may become more frequent and more intense, and I may feel more fatigued. But there could also be very little indication until . . . I go."

"I hate to bring this up, but when that happens . . . I'm going—"

Wilbur waved. "You'll have a dead body on your hands. Here." He reached into his pocket. "I drafted this while you were out. It's a signed note releasing you from all wrongdoing in my ultimate death."

Jackson took the note from Wilbur and scanned it. The penmanship was a little shaky, but it outlined his medical condition and his desire, for personal reasons, to die privately. Jackson had been contracted to ensure that privacy. There were a few more details, and then Wilbur's signature.

"I'm sure it wouldn't be legally binding," he said when Jackson looked up, "but it's the best I can do. Unless that phone of yours takes video?"

"This cheap thing," Jackson said. "No way."

"You having another thought?"

Jackson's poker face needed work. "I'm sure I could buy a cheap camcorder." He grinned. "I doubt they're called camcorders anymore. Anyhow, it's a legit business expense. Then we could get video, but . . ."

"What?"

"I don't know how we prove it wasn't shot under duress."

"You mean they'll think you kidnapped an old man, forced him to confess that it was his idea, and then killed him of natural causes?"

"When you put it like that . . ."

"Put it on my tab," Wilbur said. "We can even shoot it with the news in the background, so they know it isn't years old or fudged after the fact."

"You mean they'll think I propped you up after you died and forced you to talk?"

Wilbur stuck his knife at Jackson, but with a twinkle in his eye. Then he lowered the knife and cut into his steak. He took another bite and closed his eyes. "This really is marvelous."

Jackson concluded once and for all he didn't really care about the consequences down the line. Wilbur's security—both actual and mental—was what mattered. And looking at Wilbur enjoying his chicken fried steak, he would never have guessed he was hiding from neo-Nazis while waiting for a brain tumor to end his life.

*　　　　　*　　　　　*

Friday, March 22
4:25 p.m.

JACKSON AND Wilbur watched *Jeopardy!* while debating what to eat for dinner. Their second and third days in hiding had been long ones, watching game shows, the news, and parts of a couple war movies that Wilbur found inaccurate to the point of being insulting. The only highlights—aside from not having LAPD or the *Gestapo* show up at their door or having Wilbur keel over—were the stories he told of his time in the service. Like when one of his fellow soldiers had come after him with a knife while in a drunken stupor. Or when the convoy he'd been leading had been stopped by Russian soldiers who forced him at gunpoint to transport them a few miles up the road.

While Jackson enjoyed the stories, they also made him sad. Wilbur shouldn't be living out his final days in a slummy hotel with him. He should be receiving Presidential Medals of Freedom or teaching future generations about the sacrifice his had made to protect freedom around the world. But "should" and "shouldn't" didn't mean a whole lot in life. So Jackson did what he could to make Wilbur feel secure while showing him the respect he deserved. Somehow tuna sandwiches or microwaved pot pies didn't fit that bill.

Jackson's burn phone rang just as the contestants were mulling the Final Jeopardy! answer. He and Wilbur looked at each other. The phone shouldn't be ringing.

Jackson slid across the bed and reached to the dresser where he'd left his phone. The display showed a familiar number. Still, Jackson exercised caution.

"Hello?"

"Douglas?"

"Walker?"

"Somebody broke into my apartment," she said, breathing heavily. "They were there when I got home."

"Are you okay?"

"I am now. I kicked one in the groin, and Jack took a chunk out of the other's arm."

"Jack? Who's Jack?"

"My dog."

"What happened to Bo?"

"He died."

"So you named your dog after me?"

"Can we focus here?"

"Yeah. You're okay, right?"

"I'm not hurt. But we misjudged him."

"Skyler?"

"Who else?"

"You have proof it's him?"

"I saw him the other day, Douglas. And he saw me. He knows."

"What were these guys doing at your place? And where have you been? I called you three days ago."

"Out of town, working, avoiding. My cell didn't have service, and then the battery died, and I just got your message when I got back to civilization. I was going to call you when I got home, but that plan changed. Jack, I don't—not you, be quiet."

"What?"

"Jack the dog." She sighed. "I don't know what to do."

Jackson thought for a moment. "Um, where are you now?"

"The 405, headed north past LAX."

"You have a destination?"

"Bakersfield? Modesto? Oregon?"

"I've never seen you this spooked, Walker."

"You didn't see the guys at my apartment, Douglas."

"Can you about-face? I'm in Huntington Beach," he said, sending Wilbur what he hoped was a reassuring nod.

"Why are you in Huntington Beach?"

"A long story."

No answer.

"Walker?"

"Yeah, I'm here. Why should I come to you?"

"So I can talk you down from driving to Oregon, for one thing. You called me originally, remember? Left me that cute note and flowers."

"Yeah. Sorry, I'm just a little on edge."

"It's understandable."

She sighed. "Where in Huntington Beach?"

"There's a Surfside Diner on the PCH at about 6th or 7th Street. Meet me there at . . . five-thirty?"

"All right. You look the same as five years ago?"

"Marginally more handsome, perhaps. You?"

"My hair's straighter."

"I'll see you at five-thirty."

Jackson closed his phone and looked at Wilbur. It was obvious he wanted to ask, but dignity kept him from prying.

"She's an old friend in trouble," Jackson said.

"Bad trouble?"

"Sounds it. But don't worry, Wilbur. You're my first priority. I won't endanger you to help her."

"Do what you need to do, Jackson. A friend should always help a friend."

Jackson nodded. "If you can wait a little while, I'll bring you back another chicken fried steak."

"Only a fool'd turn down that deal."

Chapter Thirty-One

5:32 p.m.

"I LIKE YOUR hair, Walker."

Tori stared at him with vivid, green-brown eyes, just like he remembered. "The first thing you say to me after five years is, 'I like your hair'?"

"Just trying to lighten the mood."

She stared for a moment longer, then sat back. "Sorry. I'm wound tight."

"Don't worry about it. You want to order before we get down to business?"

"I'm not very hungry."

"I should have picked someplace Mexican."

"You remembered," she said, a smile breaking onto her face. It was a pretty smile, framed by chin-length auburn hair. Five years ago, it had been thatched, unkempt in a stylish sort of way. Now it was straight, a bob or something of the sort, and Jackson did like it. Not quite as fun and feisty, but professional and feminine.

"I did," he said. "But the burgers here are great, and they have about four billion to choose from. And nothing is going to happen to you here. Relax. Eat. Pray. Love."

Tori shook her head. "You're still a dork, I see."

Jackson just grinned and opened his menu. In reality, the Surfside Diner had eight burgers, and Jackson opted for a different one than he'd selected the night before. When the waitress was gone, he rested his arms on the table.

"So last I know you were working for a P.I. firm in Vegas."

"And to think, I missed you when you stopped by."

"Your partner was more than helpful."

"I wish I could have been there."

"We'd have made quite a team."

She huffed. "I'd have talked you out of your crazy plan."

"If only. So what brings you back here?"

"Got tired of the glitz. And the people. Ugh." She flicked hair from her forehead. "I moved to L.A. because going 'home' home just seemed weird. And I opened my own P.I. business."

"Good for you."

"Sort of. It's been a challenge making ends meet. I just recently contracted with several insurance companies, doing some of their investigative work. Not what I had planned on, but it pays the bills. And I still get a few of my own cases."

"Where you at in L.A.?"

"Manhattan Beach. But most of the firms I work with are in The Valley." She took a sip of her soda. "And I see you're making big waves as your own man too."

"I'd settle for quiet seas for a while."

Tori nodded.

"Okay, so tell me what's going on," Jackson said.

Tori took another sip of her soda, then pushed it aside. "Monday morning I had an appointment at Turner Insurance in Burbank, updating them on a couple of accounts. As I introduced myself at the front desk, who's coming down the hallway with another agent but Chaz Skyler? He looked right at me and didn't say a word, didn't veer off his course. But I know he saw me, Douglas. And I know he heard me say my name. He knows I'm not Allie Dawkins."

Jackson nodded. "Go on."

"I didn't know what to do. We took him for a hundred and twenty-five thousand dollars. I had to assume that once he found us, he'd come after us."

"So you led him to my doorstep. Thanks, Walker."

Tori pursed her lips. "I was going to call you, but I thought I might be panicking. And I had a busy afternoon. But the more I thought about it, the more I started to think, what were the odds that Skyler just happened to show up at the same insurance company I contract with?"

"You think he was onto you already?"

"I think it's possible."

Jackson shook his head. "He wouldn't do his own dirty work. He'd send in a P.I. with a smartphone to snap your picture."

"Maybe. Unless it was personal. Unless he wanted to send a message."

"I suppose that's possible."

"Anyhow, I finally did decide to call you, but the number I found online wasn't in service."

"Yeah, I switched my number when I went into business. You should have looked me up. I'm in the phonebook."

"Nobody uses phonebooks anymore," she said with a shake of her head. "And I wasn't thinking clearly. Especially after Tuesday night."

"What was Tuesday night?"

"I was in court most of the day, but when I got home, there was a car watching my place. That's when I decided to get away for a few days."

"How do you know it was watching your place?"

"Because nobody in my neighborhood drives a Buick Enclave. I had some loose ends to tie up in Quartzsite, so I figured now was as good of a time as any. I left town that night but first tried calling you again. When that didn't work, because you had a new number, I sent you the flowers. I don't know what I was thinking, Jackson," she said with a sheepish smile. "I was nervous, and I guess . . . I figured if Skyler somehow intercepted the message . . . I don't know."

"What time was that?"

"I don't know, six-ish?"

"I tried calling you . . . about nine. You were off the grid already?"

"So to speak," she said, looking down.

"What's so to speak mean?"

She sighed. "I had a date, which didn't go so—"

"You had a date?"

"What, is that hard to believe or something?"

"No, of course not. I just . . . No, it's not."

"I know it's odd to squeeze a date into all this mess, but I thought I really liked this guy, and we'd been swapping schedules for weeks to make something work, and . . . Anyhow, I had my phone muted until ten or so and then didn't think to check messages before I left. By the time I did, I had no service, and then the battery died."

Jackson frowned. "Why didn't your date go well?"

She sat up. "I didn't say it didn't."

"You were going to."

She huffed. "The date was fine. I just wasn't really in the mood after a full day of court and with the whole Skyler thing."

"And yet it lasted until ten?"

"What are you, my dad?"

Jackson shook his head. "Nope."

"Just amusing yourself?"

"Yep."

"Well, I'm glad my misfortunes are so entertaining."

"So the date was a misfortune?"

"Will you cut it out?"

He grinned.

"If I didn't know better, I'd think you were jealous."

"What can I say, Walker, I've missed you."

Tori shook her head. "I should have just gone on to Bakersfield."

"Okay, no more jokes," Jackson said.

She flashed a conciliatory half-smile.

"Can I help it if you have pokeable ribs?" he asked as the waitress arrived with their dinners. They took a few minutes to sample their food. Jackson's burger was even better than the night before, and it appeared Tori's appetite had returned by the way she attacked her chicken sandwich.

Jackson washed down a few bites of his burger with a gulp of soda. "So what's Glennon Insurance?" he asked.

"One of the companies I work for. I have the notepads everywhere."

"Florist didn't provide a notecard?"

"I bought the flowers at a corner drugstore and paid some kid twenty bucks to deliver them, okay? I was in a hurry."

Jackson held up his hands. They ate a little more in silence.

"So, why did you call me tonight?" he asked.

"Uh . . . I was scared."

"I know. I mean, what do you want me to do?"

"I don't know. I didn't really think it through. Like I said, I panicked."

"Did you call the police?"

"No."

"Why n—"

"Because we stole a hundred and twenty-five big ones from Skyler," she said, leaning forward and lowering her voice. "What do I tell them?"

"Some guys broke into your apartment."

"Yeah. And they'll ask, 'Any idea why, ma'am?' 'Well, maybe because my friend and I stole a bunch of money from their boss.'"

"You don't know the two are related. Maybe it's another case. Maybe it was random."

Tori stared at him.

Jackson sat back. "I'll look into it. See if I can figure out who the guys were, tie them to Skyler, and then figure out a plan to bust him."

"Thank you."

He winced.

"What?"

"Well, it's just that I'm working another case right now, a protection detail. And we may have . . . bent a few rules, plus there may be some pretty big heavies after us, so I kind of have to lay low."

"Big heavies? Like who?"

"Nazis."

Tori looked at him over her sandwich. "Nazis?"

"Probably not actual Nazis. But it's complicated."

She shook her head. "I can find someone else. I just thought—"

"No, I'll help you out. I've got skin in the game too, Walker. It's just that it might take me a little while. In the meantime, you should probably lay low. You got any vacation time coming?"

"I'm my own boss, Douglas. I can go on vacation whenever I want."

"There you go. I hear Cabo's nice this time of year."

"Well, first, my budget affords me something more along the lines of Santa Barbara, and second, I have cases."

"Big ones?"

"Very little ones. But I can't just leave them for a week. After three days in Quartzsite, I'm even more behind. I can't afford to run anymore."

"Three days in Quartzsite?"

"It's a long story. Don't get me started."

He held up his hand, then shrugged as he reached for his soda. "Well, you should at least lay low for a while." He took a slurp. "Can you check into a motel under some alias?"

"Yeah."

"Good. I'd buy a burn phone and call me with the number. Stay off the internet if you can—You know the deal."

She nodded.

"What are you driving?"

"The Saab."

"You still have the Saab?"

Tori nodded.

"Well, it's not quite a Ferrari, but a red Saab hatchback kind of sticks out."

"What about you? The Granada still running?"

"It is, but I rented a little Toyota. Inconspicuous."

"We could switch," Tori said.

"And lead Skyler to me?"

"He's looking for a woman in a red Saab. If he even knows what I drive. And if there's any chance your Toyota's traceable, when it leads to me, it will be a dead end."

Jackson swallowed a bite of his burger. "One problem. I can't drive your Saab."

"What?"

"Stick."

"You can't drive stick?"

He shook his head.

"Why not?"

"Because I wasn't raised on a farm in the '70s, Walker. The same reason I don't listen to cassette tapes. Technology has improved."

"This from the guy who drives a car that Henry Ford personally inspected."

"I see you haven't lost your charming wit."

Tori tipped her head and smirked.

"It was a nice idea," Jackson said. "But I'll stick with my Toyota."

"And I'll call you when I have a new phone and check into a hotel."

"Sounds like a plan."

Tori leaned forward, elbows on the table. "You think I'm overreacting?"

"I'm hiding a World War II vet from Nazis. No, I don't think you're overreacting."

"And you're sure you have time for this?"

"I'm sure, Walker.

The waitress appeared, asking if they wanted dessert. Just a chicken fried steak and extra mashed potatoes, to go, Jackson said. He picked up the tab, then walked Tori to her car. A golden retriever sat in the back, head out the open window. When he saw Jackson, he raised his head a little, licking his lips.

"This my namesake?"

"This is Jack," Tori said.

"I think I'm insulted."

"It was a compliment, Douglas. My last dog was named for Bo Jackson."

He shrugged.

She handed him her apartment key. "Thanks . . . for putting up with Frazzled Tori and helping me out."

"Don't thank me yet."

"I'll call you?"

"Be careful."

"You too. I'd hate for you to end up in the hands of Nazis."

Chapter Thirty-Two

Saturday, March 23
12:14 p.m.

TORI'S APARTMENT IN Manhattan Beach was part of a complex containing sixteen units, eight upper and eight lower. Her key in hand, Jackson took the stairs to the second story as if he owned the place. If anyone asked, he was a boyfriend. Nobody asked.

The apartment was a mess. Papers thrown everywhere, photo frames knocked over, a lamp on the floor. It looked ransacked, and yet . . . it didn't. Jackson couldn't put his finger on why, but something about the mess seemed staged. As if two guys had tossed the place so when Tori showed up, they could grab her and make it look like she'd walked in on a home invasion.

But who invaded apartments in Manhattan Beach? During daylight? Certainly not random burglars. The intruders had wanted something, either what Tori had, or Tori herself.

Jackson spent half an hour sorting through the mess, trying to find any clues. He found a few drops of blood, probably from when Tori's dog had taken a bite out of one of the attacker's arms. Otherwise, the mess made it hard to reconstruct exactly what had happened. Not that he doubted Tori.

Jackson stood in the center of her living room. If Skyler had sent the goons, what was his game? Kill her? Kidnap her? Then what? Demand ransom? It didn't fit. Unless Skyler was behaving irrationally. That didn't match his bio, but getting swindled could cause a guy to act out. Seeing her at the insurance company could have rekindled a quest for revenge, and he'd snapped.

But Tori was a P.I., and that meant there were other people who had a beef with her. Maybe nobody that stood out, but they could have been behind the attack too. The only way to know for sure was to link the attackers to Skyler, and Jackson couldn't do that without some idea who they were.

After concluding the apartment didn't hold any valid clues that he could glean, Jackson spent the next half hour knocking on neighbor's doors. He was Tori's boyfriend and had seen some unsavory characters hanging around the day before. He was worried—there were kids in these apartments. Had anyone else seen anything? He got nothing. Apparently, folks had been watching TV or getting an early start on dinner and had missed the attempted abduction or whatever it was.

Having crapped out, Jackson made a call as he headed back to Huntington Beach. Wilbur was napping, but Jackson didn't like leaving him alone for long. He was, after all, his primary responsibility.

"Dick Davis."

"Hey, Dick. It's Jackson Douglas."

"Well hey, probie," Dick said. A former Marine, he called all people lower than him on the totem pole probie—Jackson had no idea why. Back in the day, when Jackson and Tori had worked as assistants at MTR Investigative Services in San Diego, Dick had been one of the associates. A throwback to the '70s, Dick was a stereotypical private eye. He smoked, referred to women as broads, and even sported a fedora now and again. He was old and crusty, but a good operative.

"To what do I owe the pleasure?" Dick asked.

"I need a favor, if you can swing it."

"Try me."

"I need a bio on Chaz Skyler."

"Skyler. Ain't he the guy you and what's-her-name . . . Welker—the guy you and Welker took back in the day?"

"Walker, and yeah."

"So what's the deal?"

"She spotted him the other day," Jackson said. "And somebody broke into her apartment. We can't tie him to it, but she's suspicious. Frankly, so am I. And I've got another case that's forcing me to keep a low profile and stay here in L.A. I thought you might be able to poke around a little down there and see what ol' Mr. Skyler has been up to."

"I can poke around," Dick said.

"I appreciate it, Dick."

"Call you at this number?"

"Yeah. Thanks."

"Keep your head down," Dick said just before the click.

Jackson turned off his phone and merged with traffic on the 405. It was a glorious day in Southern California, and Jackson spent a few minutes lamenting going back to the Pierless Motel to wait. But he imagined Wilbur and hundreds of thousands of other young men had lamented leaving their loved ones behind to walk into a German *blitzkrieg*. But they had done it. This was the least Jackson could do to repay an entire generation, let alone Wilbur.

*   *   *

4:58 p.m.

JACKSON PUSHED through the front door of Scotty's and went blind. Outside, the sun had been sinking but still bright, its rays skipping off the surface of the Pacific. If there were lights inside the lounge other than the candles that flickered on the tables, Jackson couldn't spot them. Everything was black, except for the gray smoke that hung in the air like a blanket.

Slowly the shapes of booths and support columns and the bar in the distance began to take shape. Jackson's eyes rested on a soft blue neon sign above the bar, spelling Scotty's. The Y had been transformed into a martini glass. How original.

Very much missing the sun, Jackson nodded at a vulture of a hostess and headed for a corner booth where a pretty but nervous brunette waited for him. She slid over as he arrived.

"Nice place, Walker."

"I wanted someplace secluded."

"So you picked the 1970s. What was wrong with the Surfside Diner?"

"Nothing, but I hate to turn into a regular if someone's looking for me."

Jackson nodded.

"Besides, this is close to your hotel. Isn't that good?"

"Yeah. I'm just afraid Angel's eavesdropping from the next booth over."

"Very cute."

A waitress sauntered over, her blond hair mostly spilling out of the clip that had once held it up. Her name tag identified her as Missy. Perfect. She handed them menus and asked if she could get them a drink.

"Just water," Jackson said.

"Make it two."

Missy nodded and left. Jackson opened his menu. Tori didn't. Instead, she leaned forward. "What'd you find?"

"For one thing, you need a housekeeper."

"You're making a bunch of jokes while I worry to death?"

Jackson lowered his menu. "You're awfully edgy. What'd you do all day?"

"Watched a lot of *Raymond* reruns on cable. Apologized to Jack for keeping him cooped up."

"I thought you had cases."

"Not much I can do when I'm sequestered. I did a little legwork this morning and made a few calls, but that's about it. So you didn't find anything at my place?"

"No. Just that it was tossed, which doesn't make a lot of sense if it was Skyler."

"You still have doubts?"

Jackson shook his head as Missy returned with two glasses of water. Jackson ordered chicken tenders and fries, and having not yet opened her menu, Tori again made it two. Missy gave her an odd look before shuffling off.

Jackson leaned forward. "I called Dick this afternoon and asked him to check Skyler out. He called me back just a few minutes ago."

"What'd he find?"

"A few interesting tidbits. For one, Skyler spent three months in rehab in the fall of '08."

"Rehab?"

"Heroin."

Tori traced the rim of her water glass with her finger. She looked up. "Did we . . . ?"

"Drive him to it?" Jackson raised his glass. "Yeah, I think that's a safe bet."

"Do you think . . . we made a mistake?"

Jackson shook his head. "No. I've been thinking about that most of the afternoon. Skyler ripped off a bunch of churches, and we made it right again. We may have operated outside the law, but no, I don't think it was a mistake."

Tori sat back. "What else did Dick say?"

"Skyler got out a week before Christmas '08 and landed a job with an L.A. software company in January. A place called CyberSoft. He's been with them ever since."

"So he lives here?"

"North Hollywood."

"Next door to Burbank."

Jackson nodded.

"Anything else?"

"From Dick, no. I also drove out to Turner Insurance, snooping around, trying to see if I could figure out who Skyler was and what he was doing there, that sort of a thing."

"And?"

"Got nowhere."

"What'd you do, try to flirt with the receptionist?"

"No, she was old. So I played the charming young man card. No dice."

Tori sighed and took a drink. "So where does that leave us?"

Jackson sighed. "Right now, nowhere."

"Super."

"The way I see it, we've got three options. One, we confront Skyler. Two, I shadow him and see if I can get a lead. But I can't do that until I'm done with my current case. Three . . . we let the police handle it."

"You forgot four, live in fear forever."

"Well, that too is an option."

"What do you think?"

"I think call the police. Tell them your place was broken into. Let them sort it out."

"And if it leads back to Skyler, we could go down for fraud."

"Yes, but then so does he."

"So we all share a jail cell together?" Tori shook her head.

"It won't come to that. He won't cut off his nose at the risk of spiting his face."

"I'm not sure you're using that idiom right."

Jackson frowned. "Yeah, me either. But the point is, he won't incriminate us because, in order to do so, he'd have to incriminate himself."

"How comforting. What's your second choice?"

"Find some better stuff on cable."

Tori sighed.

"Seriously, Walker, if you can, wait. I don't think it'll be long before my case is over. Then I can investigate Skyler more thoroughly and either tie him to the break-in or clear him."

Tori bit her lip but reluctantly nodded. "You know in the movies, the vigilante Robin Hoods never have to deal with reprisal."

"Of course not. They need material for the sequel."

*   *   *

6:02 p.m.

JACKSON SPENT the better part of his dinner with Tori trying to assuage her fears. But he couldn't really blame her. It wasn't as if she could go home as if nothing had happened, but she couldn't hang out at a hotel in Huntington Beach forever either. They had discussed an additional option—her investigating Skyler and the break-in herself. She was, after all, a private investigator. But her fortes were the insurance and confidence games, not home invasions. And if Skyler was up to something devious, Jackson didn't want her in harm's way by herself. He persuaded her to wait until the weekend was over. If Wilbur didn't survive, grim as it was, Jackson would be free to help her. If Wilbur was still alive, they would figure out what to do then.

After agreeing to meet for dinner Sunday night, they split up. Both had come on foot, and Tori headed north to her hotel while Jackson turned east to a drugstore recommended by Missy. Wilbur had complained of headaches throughout the afternoon, and if a World War II vet was complaining about a headache, it had to be bad.

The drugstore was a local job, not one of the bigger chains, and it doubled as a tourist trinket merchandiser. Jackson pushed past the spinning racks of postcards and the row of coffee mugs, shot glasses, and photo frames. He found the pain relief pills and looked for the strongest over-the-counter meds available. It wasn't like Wilbur had to worry about long-term side effects.

He found a bottle of Excedrin and grabbed a two-liter of cream soda for himself.

"Interesting combo," the Asian guy behind the counter remarked.

"Mmm, Combos. You got any of those?"

"Yeah, over there," the clerk said with a nod.

Jackson went over to select a package of pizza-flavored Combos, in the process losing his place in line. He waited behind a heavyset woman buying powdered donuts and was tempted to get some for himself. He passed and paid for his Excedrin, cream soda, and Combos. The Pierless Motel was a few blocks down and a few blocks over from the drugstore, and Jackson hoped the plastic bag the Asian guy had given him would hold his two-liter bottle of cream soda the whole way. He also hoped Wilbur was still alive.

It was another beautiful SoCal evening, and Jackson took a few moments to stare off at Rancho Palos Verdes beyond the Port of Long Beach, admiring the scenery as the sun drenched the Pacific and rocky coastline in golden hues. He was once again overcome with gratefulness for people like Wilbur who had helped ensure he could enjoy such views in freedom—something too many in his generation, himself often included, took for granted.

When Jackson turned his head back toward the sidewalk, a black SUV had stopped in front of him. Both doors on the passenger side opened, and two men jumped out. One held a gun.

"Get in," he said, terse but calm. "Now."

Jackson hesitated, dropping the bag.

"Now," the man said again, this time with an edge.

Jackson glanced to his right, toward the street, an action that caused the other guy to grab his arm and usher him into the SUV. A third man took hold of him from inside, pulling him into a captain's chair behind the driver's seat. As the doors closed behind the other two men, the third man pulled out a black hood and roughly fit it over Jackson's head.

Blind, Jackson felt the SUV take off. He heard rustling around him, but none of the men spoke. Had Skyler hired them? Or were they after Wilbur?

He didn't get a chance to think it over. As the SUV careened onto the street, Jackson was thrown against the door. He felt a prick in his right arm, and before his brain finished processing the pinch, he blacked out.

Chapter Thirty-Three

JACKSON'S EYES OPENED, but he couldn't see anything. He assumed it was because the hood was still over his head until a supernova of light flashed in his eyes. It was a single bulb, about six thousand watts by the look of things, and it seemed aimed right at him.

Jackson could feel that his wrists were bound, but he struggled against them to see just how securely. Very. Behind his back and the back of what felt like a metal folding chair. He tried moving his legs but found them also restrained, each one taped to one of the legs of the chair. At least he assumed they were taped, because it felt like duct tape that bound his wrists.

A shape moved in front of the light, and a man's face appeared to Jackson's left. It was round, chiseled, with a hawk nose and short, spiked blond hair. When the man spoke, it was quick and clipped, almost bored.

"Where is Wilbur Anderson?"

In an instant, Jackson realized all of Wilbur's fears were true. Someone thought the missiles—or at least their payload—were still viable and that someone wanted them badly enough to hunt down a dying old man. That meant Ken Waters and Albert Klein hadn't died of heart attacks; they had been murdered. And Jackson was all that stood between Wilbur and a similar fate.

"I am not a patient man."

Jackson looked up at the man, his eyes dark cavities untouched by the bulb behind him.

"You're not a very smart man, either."

"Why is that?"

283

"Because I have no idea where Wilbur Anderson is."

Freakishly fast, the man shot his left hand up and backhanded Jackson in the cheek. His hand might as well have been a brick, and Jackson dreaded the thought of this man hitting him with a closed fist.

"I am not interested in games either. Do not play dumb."

"Why, afraid you won't be able to keep up?"

Jackson braced himself for the blow this time, but it still stung.

"Where is Wilbur Anderson?"

"I don't know."

The words were barely out of his mouth before he was struck again, this time on the other cheek. Jackson was starting to feel a little like Chris Tucker in *Rush Hour*, but there was only one guy.

"Where is Wilbur Anderson?" the man asked again, still calmly, still almost bored.

"If you'd quit smacking me I might be able to get a full sentence out," Jackson said. "I don't know, anymore."

"You are lying."

"Makes a guy wonder why you go through all the hassle of kidnapping me then."

"You will tell us the truth."

"Us?"

The man's face displayed emotion for the first time in the form of a very thin smile. Jackson started to wonder why, but only had half a second to do so before he was drilled in the jaw with a punch that nearly knocked him off the chair. Flexing his jaw and tasting blood, he looked to his right, where the punch had emanated.

He saw more blond hair, this time longer, coming to the shoulders of a woman with a face of stone. Technically, it might have been good-looking, but it was too carved to be attractive. The woman wore a sleeveless shirt that revealed a pair of pythons attached to her shoulders. Her fingers were covered by grappling gloves, which suggested to Jackson she was going to hit him a lot and didn't want to bruise or break her knuckles.

He sighed. "Great. I get the Nazi version of *Mr. and Mrs. Smith.*" He looked up. "I take it you are Naz—"

Mrs. Smith punched him again, a blow he never saw coming, and this time his jaw actually cracked as his chair slid a few inches on the floor.

"Where is Wilbur Anderson?" Mr. Smith asked.

Jackson spat. "She keeps hitting me in the jaw, and I'm going to have to blink it to you in Morse code."

"Then you had better talk."

"Two days ago, he was at my house. I bought him an open train ticket and drove him to the station. He could be anywhere."

Mr. Smith grinned a full-faced grin this time. Mrs. Smith's blow came to the solar plexus and left Jackson struggling for air. Mr. Smith grabbed his hair and jerked his head back. "One more chance. Where is Wilbur Anderson?"

"On a train."

Mr. Smith shook his head, then turned and nodded to Mrs. Smith. She stepped directly in front of Jackson and delivered a rapid series of punches to his face, chest, and stomach, working him over thoroughly. It lasted no more than half a minute, and she didn't even break a sweat. Jackson felt as if he'd gone fifteen rounds with Muhammad Ali. Or in this case, Laila Ali.

Mr. Smith knelt in front of him while he snorted and swallowed blood, simultaneously trying to catch his breath.

"It is seven minutes past nine o'clock. In fifty-three minutes, we will return. We will not ask so gently."

He turned, the light went out, and Jackson listened as Mr. and Mrs. Smith's footsteps died away. His head was ringing, but it sounded like they were walking on concrete, and he knew he heard a door slam shut. It sounded like a wood door, likely an interior door. If he had to guess, he was in a basement. But where, and when—nine p.m. Saturday night still? Nine a.m. Sunday morning?

And better question, what was he going to do in fifty-three minutes?

*   *   *

Sunday, March 24
12:57 a.m.

IT WAS absurdly embarrassing, but it took Jackson a while to think to pray. He wasn't sure, but it had to be about time for Mrs. Smith to return for another hourly beating. She had ratcheted it up each time, the most recent of her pummelings lasting for about a minute. Her concluding salvo had knocked Jackson off his chair and slackened the tape around his wrists. He'd hoped when they left him alone he might be able to get free, but Mr. Smith had jerked him back to an upright position and re-taped both his wrists and ankles.

Mrs. Smith had yet to speak, and Mr. Smith had only asked Jackson the same question: "Where is Wilbur Anderson?" Once before the beating, once after. When Jackson gave him nothing, Mr. Smith declared that they would be back in an hour. So far, they were like clockwork.

Jackson had tried to survive the poundings by using the brief opportunity while the light was on to gauge his surroundings. He had spotted concrete blocks on the wall to his left and a metal pole to his right—a support column. He was definitely in a basement, but he had no idea where.

He also had no idea who it was who had him, other than people who were interested in finding Wilbur. The man had no accent, and the woman had yet to speak. They could have been Germans, could have been Americans, could have been Russians. Was it just the two of them? No, there had been three or four in the SUV that kidnapped him. So was it just three or four, or were they part of a larger cell? He knew nothing.

So he prayed. First, for Wilbur's ultimate safety. Second, for his mental state since Jackson was well overdue from his dinner date with Tori. Third, that he would have strength to hold out and not divulge Wilbur's location. And fourth, that he would get out of this mess.

The door opened, and Jackson tensed. He could still taste blood on his lip from the last barrage. He figured he could buy time with a dummy location, but it wouldn't be convincing if he gave in too easily, especially after being a smart aleck thus far. And while the beatings hurt, Jackson knew he could hold out a while longer. And he still hoped to come up with a better plan, one that maybe would get him out of this mess while at the same time protecting Wilbur.

The light flicked on and was immediately eclipsed by Mr. Smith. "Where is Wilbur Anderson?"

"Where's your lady friend? Beauty rest? 'Cause she could use—"

Jackson was socked in the back of the head, causing his neck to snap. "Ow."

"Where is Wilbur Anderson?"

Jackson looked around, trying to gain more of his surroundings. He didn't get much chance, because Mrs. Smith came around to the side and decked him, knocking him over. His entire head vibrated, and he thought maybe he was going to get away with one punch. Instead, Mrs. Smith dropped to her knees and pummeled him in the chest and stomach. It felt like it lasted longer than before, and when she quit, Jackson couldn't breathe.

Mr. Smith roughly lifted him up, checked his bonds, then knelt in front of Jackson. Every single one of his ribs hurt, and he had the worst stomachache of his life. Yet. It was the third time he'd lost his breath, and Mr. Smith gave him a moment to catch it before asking again, "Where is Wilbur Anderson?"

"I've got to admit . . . she impresses me. I didn't think . . . didn't think she had a ground and pound game."

The light went off, and Jackson exhaled. He'd survived another beating.

His chair leg was kicked out, and he fell backward. His head hit the floor with a thunk, and for the next few minutes—or perhaps longer—Jackson was in and out of consciousness. When things finally cleared, he didn't know how much longer he had to wait for the next assault. He'd suffered through five beatings, one per hour, starting at nine. That meant it was sometime between one and two a.m. Assuming they had started at nine p.m.

He tried wiggling free, but the tape was tight, and movement hurt too much. So he prayed some more, thought some more, and tried to gauge his supply of resistance.

They returned sooner than he expected, repeating the routine. "Where is Wilbur Anderson?" the man asked in the same tone as always. Perfectly patient, perfectly calm, even though he had admitted before he was not patient.

Jackson looked over at Mrs. Smith, then lowered his head. "Keane."

"Keane?"

"The band. *Somewhere Only We Know.*"

Mr. Smith circled around behind Jackson while Mrs. Smith took her place in front of him. But she didn't strike. Jackson heard a knife open, and then heard and felt the tape holding his ankles to the chair being cut.

"You've decided to let me go? How nice. Should I call a cab?"

Mr. Smith slit the tape on his wrists, and as soon as they were free, tipped Jackson out of his chair. He fell to the ground, and before he could respond, Mrs. Smith drilled him in the side of the head with a roundhouse kick.

Jackson rolled back, stunned, but also aware that he had a fighting chance—literally. He tried to get up, but Mrs. Smith pounced, unleashing another torrent of fists to his head and chest. Jackson tried to deflect them, but it was pointless. So he lunged forward, into the onslaught, driving her up and back. She kept punching, he kept pushing, and ultimately tipped her back. She landed with a thud, and Jackson scrambled to his knees to get in better position to throw the punches that would free him.

He never got the chance. From nowhere, Mrs. Smith blasted him with a kick to the side of the head. Stunned, he fell back, sagging on his knees. She jumped to her feet and took her time standing before him. In slow motion, she drew back her fist and walloped him in the side of the head.

Jackson was out before he hit the floor.

Chapter Thirty-Four

6:00 a.m.

A SPLASH OF water in the face woke Jackson.

Woke might have been a little strong, because it implied actual sleep. He'd only been dozing for the last few hour-long breaks. Something about knowing another beating was coming made it impossible to get real sleep. That and the pain. He had a headache, maybe a concussion, and the light that shone in his eyes every hour was starting to hurt. But worse than his head was his entire upper body. Now that the punches had time to settle in, a dull ache was growing by the minute.

Mrs. Smith had returned two—maybe three—more times since she had cut him loose and mopped the floor with him. Each time was the same. While he was tied to the chair, she pummeled him for thirty seconds to a minute. Once it was exclusively head shots that left him dazed. Once it was punches to the chest that bruised his ribs. Another time, she punched him in the stomach and side, going for the kidneys. He shuddered to think where she might strike next.

Each time, Mr. Smith was with her, asking the same question. It never varied, and Jackson wondered if their strategy was to get an answer or just beat him to death. They certainly hadn't watched recent seasons of *24*, because their torture techniques were somewhat low-tech. Nevertheless, painful. So far, Jackson was holding out, but he didn't know how much longer it would last.

He blinked a few times, getting the water out of his eyes. When they cleared, Mr. Smith stood in front of him. "Where is Wilbur Anderson?"

Jackson sighed in response.

With a nod, Mr. Smith stepped to the side, and a man dressed in black stepped forward. Not enough black. The tank top was tight and revealed arms that could have been legs. He had an ugly sneer on his face, which at the same time, looked blank.

"I guess that makes you Vince Vaughn," Jackson said. "I was hoping for Jennifer Morrison."

With speed Jackson couldn't even imagine, "Vince" struck him in the jaw. His head reeled back, threatening to snap off his neck.

"Where is Wilbur Anderson?" Mr. Smith asked.

Jackson chuckled. "Peas."

"What?"

"She made peas."

Vince struck again, and this time Jackson couldn't help but moan.

"Where is Wilbur Anderson?"

"You losing track of time? It hasn't been an hour sin—"

His jaw cracked with the next punch.

"Where is Wilbur Anderson?"

Jackson spat blood, a great shot that hit Vince just under the eye. He didn't flinch. Instead, he slowly brushed it off with the back of his hand. A second later, the other hand cracked Jackson in the eye.

"Where is Wilbur Anderson?"

Silence.

Punch.

"Where is Wilbur Anderson?"

Silence.

Punch.

"Where is Wilbur Anderson?"

Silence.

Punch.

"Where is Wilbur Anderson?"

Jackson coughed, then spat again, this time on the floor. He braced himself for another punch, but it didn't come. Instead, the light went out.

Jackson spat again. "See you in an hour then?"

He was answered by a door slamming, and he nearly cried.

*   *   *

10:00 a.m.

THE LIGHT flashed on. It was accompanied by a rumble of thunder. Jackson lowered his head, deflecting his eyes from the beam. It was similar to the beam that had shone in his eyes for hours, but different. This one was brighter. Purer.

Jackson was no longer in the basement. He vaguely remembered hourly beatings, most at the hands of the brutish blond woman. Occasionally she was replaced by the man in black. Jackson's jaw rang. His head pounded. His entire upper body was a mass of bruises. He hadn't eaten that he could remember, and his mouth was parched.

But now it was raining. It must have been, because he heard thunder. And he was wet. And cold.

So where was he? It was still dark. Or dark again. The light was so bright that everything else was black, and Jackson couldn't identify any of his surroundings.

A form appeared, blurry at first. Then it moved in front of the light and took shape. A woman. She had long, dark hair and wore a flowing, ankle-length gown. White or light blue. She sauntered toward him, one slow step at a time. As the features of her face began to emerge from the blur, Jackson realized her gray-blue eyes were locked on him. Her stride had purpose. Jackson's eyes widened as he recognized her face.

"Maggie?"

The corners of her mouth turned up, dimples appearing in her cheeks. She raised her hands and reached for Jackson, curling her fingers to gently trace his cheeks with the back of her hand.

"Oh, Jackson. What have they done to you?"

"You . . . you should see the . . ."

He tried to lift his arms to embrace her, but they wouldn't move. He couldn't even feel them.

"Ssshh." She gently pressed a finger to his lip. Her head shook slightly, curls of brown hair fluttering across her shoulders. "Jackson, you can end this. Just tell them what they want to know."

He raised his eyes to meet hers. "Maggie . . . I can't." He shook his head. "I can't."

Her smile widened. Too wide. It began to resemble the Grinch.

The smile turned to a soft chuckle . . . a laugh. Then she threw her head back and guffawed. The sound began to change. It got deeper, louder. It cackled.

She lowered her head, and when she did, she had transformed. Her eyes were the color of mahogany, her skin dark. She was bigger—taller and broader. Gone was the gown, replaced by a button-down shirt and jeans. And her hair was suddenly short, accompanied by a . . . beard?

"Reggie?"

"J, J, J. You are makin' a mess of things, man." He shrugged. "Tell these people what they want, J."

"I can't."

Reggie shook his head. "Suit yourself, dawg."

He raised a fist, looked at the ring on his finger, and jammed it into Jackson's stomach, just under the ribs. Jackson's body tried to collapse but was held in place. He became aware of his arms, bound behind his back around a thin tree.

Jackson raised his head. "Reggie. What are—"

He was punched in the stomach again.

"What?"

The man just cackled as he hit Jackson in the chest, stomach, chest, stomach again. The blows continued for several minutes, then stopped suddenly. Jackson slumped forward, his arms holding him semi-upright. Then everything went dark.

Jackson passed in and out of consciousness. He had no idea how much time passed, but he stirred awake, suddenly lucid. Even though it was dark, he knew he was still in the basement, bound to a pole. And neither Maggie nor Reggie had really been there.

The light flicked on again. Jackson heard footsteps and felt his shoulders pulled back. His arms were jerked backward and he was trussed even tighter to the pole.

For the first time, Mr. Smith didn't ask about Wilbur. He just stared blankly. Another man stood beside him. He wore a button-down shirt and khaki pants, and his expression made Mr. Smith's jovial by comparison.

"You just received a mild psychotropic," the man said, emphasizing the word "mild."

"W-water."

"A side effect is thirst. Tell us where Mr. Anderson is and you can have a drink."

"N-no. He's on the water."

The man turned over his shoulder as Mr. Smith stepped forward.

"Where is he?"

Jackson managed a grin. "There, that's what I missed."

"Where?"

"I put him on a cruise to the Riviera."

Mr. Smith only stared.

"I'm serious. It's two weeks. He figures he'll be dead by then. I figure it makes him almost untouchable."

Mr. Smith thought for a few seconds. "What is the name of the ship?"

"*Carnival* something-or-rather. I don't know, I'm having a little trouble with my memory. It's almost like I've been drugged or something."

"I could have Katya return to jog your memory."

"No, I think it's coming. *Carnival . . . Sensation.*"

"When did it sail?"

"A day or two ago. When is it?"

"If you are lying," Mr. Smith said, "the next dose will not be mild."

Chapter Thirty-Five

12:48 p.m.

MR. SMITH RETURNED.

He was not smiling.

"The *Carnival Sensation* leaves from the Port of Tampa at four p.m. today."

Jackson swallowed. He had known they would check out his lie and eventually find it was just that. And he had known they would probably beat the crap out of him when they returned. But he had hoped to buy Wilbur some more time. And maybe figure out a way to escape. He'd failed on the latter, but he also hadn't been beaten in a while.

That was about to change.

Vince was back, and he held a stick in his hand. A bamboo reed, maybe. Jackson's imagination ran wild.

"I will ask you one more time," Mr. Smith said. "Where is Wilbur Anderson?"

"Only?"

"Only? Only what?"

"Only one more time? Because if so, it's been a real pleasure."

Mr. Smith licked his lips and stepped back. Vince raised the stick, flexing his fingers around it like a Major League slugger. Then he swung.

The stick snapped into Jackson's side, just under the bottom rib, and he howled in pain.

Next Vince rapped it across Jackson's stomach.

He spun it around, swung left-handed, and hit Jackson on the other side.

Then he smacked him in the chest.

Each blow stung on already tender flesh, and though he tried his best to keep silent, Jackson couldn't help groaning.

Vince circled around him, toying with him. Jackson prayed for strength not to give up Wilbur. He also racked his brain for a thought on how to escape. Trussed to a pole getting caned wasn't going to do it. He had to find a way to get them to untie him. But how?

Vince repeated the series of blows, and Jackson's cries of pain grew quieter. On the last blow, he managed to stifle his scream, but his eyes were watering from the strain.

Mr. Smith approached him. "Where is Wilbur Anderson?"

Jackson panted. "He's dead."

Vince jammed the end of the stick into Jackson's ribs with a new amount of force. Jackson heard a crack, and a sharp pain surged through his body. He groaned and clenched his teeth, his eyes looking to kill Mr. Smith.

"Where. Is. Wilbur. Anderson?"

Jackson clinched his teeth again, found a tiny amount of saliva, and shot it forward into Mr. Smith's face.

"Have it your way."

Vince swung the stick again, hitting Jackson squarely in the rib that he had just cracked.

The pain nearly caused Jackson to vomit, but he passed out first.

*　　　　　*　　　　　*

4:03 p.m.

SHE APPEARED out of the mist.

Blond hair flowed in front of and behind her shoulders, which were bare. She wore a light blue tank top and black pants. She carried something, but Jackson's eyes wouldn't clear enough or focus on the object. To be fair, the left one hardly opened anymore.

She was thin, at least compared to Mrs. Smith/Katya. She didn't look like a fighter. But neither had the guy with the mild psychotropic.

She set down whatever it was she was carrying. A toolbox, or maybe a bait box. She opened the lid, lifted a couple of items out, and stood and approached Jackson. His muscles tried to tense but didn't have the strength.

She paused directly in front of him, looking him in the eye. Singular. She was young and pretty. Jackson's gaze flitted down to the objects in her hands. A water bottle and a towel?

"My name is Mara," she said in a voice softer than melted butter.

Jackson swallowed. He tried to look around. He was still in the basement. He looked at Mara. His vision blurred in and out, but when it was clear, it honed in on high cheekbones, a smooth complexion, and the bluest of eyes.

It hit him that there was more light in the basement than before. It wasn't the blinding light in front of him, but a light that radiated throughout the room. It was whiter, softer. Everything was soft, including Mara's touch when she gently brushed his cheek.

At first, he recoiled, but then he realized she wasn't striking him. "Wh-who . . . What are . . . what are you doing?"

Mara unscrewed the lid off the water bottle, covered the opening with the towel, and turned the bottle upside down. She righted it and removed the towel. "I'll be gentle," she said, her voice again like velvet.

She dabbed at his cheeks, each touch reminding him of all the blows he'd suffered at Katya and Vince's hands. His head ached steadily, a pain muted by that in the rest of his body. His nose, if not broken, was severely disjointed. Blood had run into his mouth, joined more blood there, and formed rivers down his chin. At least two teeth were loose, and his lip was split in multiple places.

Mara was indeed gentle, wiping the blood from around his mouth. She moved up to his forehead, and he winced as she found a cut above his nearly shut eye.

"I'm sorry."

"Who are you?" he croaked.

She didn't answer, instead bending down and exchanging the towel and water bottle for a clean bottle. She opened the lid and raised it to

Jackson's mouth. He was standing, his hands behind him, handcuffed around a pole. With every beating, as his body was jarred back and forth, the cuffs tore against his skin, cutting and chafing.

Mara stood as tall as she could, raising the bottle so Jackson could drink. He got a few quick sips, the first food or drink he'd been allowed since being captured. He could barely swallow and almost choked, causing Mara to lower the bottle.

"M-more."

She raised it again, and Jackson gulped, half of the water spilling down his chin. Not until the bottle was half empty did Mara remove it. Jackson swallowed the last of the water in his mouth and sucked in air, causing sharp pain in his chest. Vince had wailed away with the bamboo, undoubtedly cracking multiple ribs. Every breath stabbed. Still, the questions continued from Mr. Smith.

"Where is Wilbur Anderson?"

"Where is Wilbur Anderson?"

"Where is Wilbur Anderson?"

Once, he had almost given in. But he thought about the troops wading ashore at Normandy, watching their friends fall left and right at the hands of Nazi gunners. He thought about rows and rows of white crosses in quiet fields across Europe, marking the graves of thousands who had died to defeat evil and defend freedom. He thought about Wilbur Anderson and his unit, risking their lives in a firefight in the Wetterstein Mountains. He thought about Ken Waters and Albert Klein and their "heart attacks." Somehow, he managed to suffer in silence. That had been a few hours ago.

Mara broke several crackers into pieces and fed Jackson one at a time. After two or three, she gave him more water.

Who was she? Had they sent her? Had she sneaked in?

"Wh-what time is it?"

"Four o'clock."

"S-Sunday?"

Mara nodded. She gave him the last of the water. She set down the empty container and, without a word, began feeling Jackson's head. She moved slowly, tenderly, her hands as gentle as a butterfly. Next came Jackson's arms, then his chest and torso. At several spots along the way, the least touch caused pain to surge through him, but Mara never pushed.

She quit at his waist and stood. She moved within inches of Jackson's face. He smelled perfume. Mara placed her hands on either side of his jaw. Her eyes were filled with concern.

"They will kill you, Jackson."

He didn't answer.

"I have seen their work. They are ruthless."

"Y-you're telling me?"

Without squeezing, she applied the least pressure with her hands. "You must tell them what they want. It is the only way to end this torture."

Still soft, her voice now carried urgency. And with it, maybe the least trace of an accent.

Katya. Mara. Blondes.

Russians?

It was classic. Beat the tar out of him, then send in the pretty girl to appeal to his senses. Or in other words, bad Ruskie, good Ruskie.

"Just tell them what they want to know," she said, almost pleading. "Or they will not stop until you are dead."

Jackson blinked. "C-can I ask you s-something?"

"Yes."

He took a few painful deep breaths. "Do you believe in miracles?"

Mara's face frowned ever so slightly.

"U . . . S . . . A."

"You are making a bad decision.

"U.S.A. U.S.A."

"Please," Mara said.

"Go tell your b-boss . . . to pound sand."

Mara's lips pursed. She backed away. "You will be sorry."

The lights went out.

*   *   *

9:52 p.m.

THE LIGHTS flashed on, and Jackson opened his eyes. It felt like longer than an hour since Mara had left, and he wondered if this was it. She had warned him that he would be sorry.

From behind, his hands were uncuffed, then roughly shoved upward. His ribs felt like they were poking through his skin, and he had to muffle a cry of pain. The cuffs were slapped back on, and as Jackson tried to lower his arms, they met resistance. They were not only cuffed around the pole but over something that held them up.

Mr. Smith appeared in front of Jackson. Vince and Katya stood beside him.

"Wilbur Anderson is dead."

Jackson met his eyes. They didn't appear to be lying. He exhaled. "Did you kill him?"

"No."

Jackson exhaled again. Then he smiled.

"This is good news to you?"

"It means you failed, comrade."

"No. We still have one source remaining."

Jackson shook his head. "You Russians are as stupid as in the movies. Why would Wilbur tell me anything? The whole point was to protect him till he died so that what he knew died with him. If he's dead, you're out of luck."

"We will see."

Mr. Smith stood back, and Katya punched Jackson in the stomach. The blow knocked the wind out of him, and his struggle to get it back hurt doubly with his injured ribs. Then Vince punched him in the side, right on the sorest of his ribs and Jackson couldn't contain a cry.

They took turns pummeling him, one blow after another after another after another. As much as he tried to resist, Jackson was reduced to tears by the pain. His ribs had to be powder.

Finally, they stopped.

"Tell us everything Wilbur told you and we will stop."

Jackson panted for breath. Suddenly, he remembered his third-grade history.

"I . . . I only regret . . . that I have bu . . . but one life to lose for my country."

Mr. Smith shook his head, and the beating resumed. Jackson made it less than half a minute before the pain was so extreme that he lost consciousness.

Chapter Thirty-Six

Sunday, March 24
11:39 p.m.

"WHY ISN'T HE answering?" Maggie asked

Russell didn't reply but gripped the wheel tightly, swerving in and out of traffic, racing west toward Rolling Hills at fifteen miles over the speed limit. Twice already he had prayed out loud, and both times Maggie had checked to make sure his eyes were open.

"What did he say exactly?" Maggie asked.

"I already told you," Russell said, pausing to pass a truck that laid on the horn afterward. "Jackson had been abducted from the drugstore by an SUV. Reggie had a plate and had tracked it to Rolling Hills and was going there to do what had to be done."

"Cops?"

"Maybe."

Maggie called again. Still no answer, and she growled in disgust.

"Try Leroy."

"He'll be asleep. Mouse." She quickly dialed his number, and he answered almost immediately.

"Yeah!"

"Mouse, it's Maggie."

"Y-you're safe?"

"Yeah, I'm fine. Any word on Jackson?"

"I . . . I d-don't know. Reggie—"

"Slow down, Mouse."

He took a breath. "Reggie went into a house. He had me knock on the door, and he went in the back. That was like thirty minutes ago, and I'm still waiting. And I think I heard gunshots."

"Where are you, Mouse?"

"R-R-Roll-Rolling Hills."

"What street?"

"Trailhead C-Court."

Maggie repeated it to Russell, then switched her phone to speaker so she could find the location on the internet. "Call 9-1-1, Mouse. Tell them where you are and that you heard gunshots."

"Okay."

"We're ten minutes out. Maybe fifteen."

Maggie closed her phone and reported to Russell, interspersing driving directions to Trailhead Court.

"You got a plan when we arrive?" he asked.

Maggie shook her head.

"Maybe I should pray again."

"You just drive. I'll pray."

"Whatever you say."

Maggie closed her eyes. *God . . . I don't even know what to ask. Just please let Jackson be okay.*

*　　　　*　　　　*

11:54 p.m.

REGGIE WAS about to call out again when he heard a moan. Faint, but discernable.

"Jack, that you?"

The moan was louder.

Reggie felt along the wall but didn't find a switch. The room was pitch black and filled with who knew what.

"Hang on, J, I'm coming!"

Reggie hurried back up the stairs. There was a closet off the hallway, and it only took a few seconds for Reggie to find a flashlight. He tested it and took the steps two at a time. Gun ready, he clicked the light on, revealing nothing but empty space in the basement. Except along the far wall where several portable lights were rigged. They were aimed at one of the metal support poles and at the body stretched out against it, his hands cuffed over a bolt extending out of the pole.

"J!" Reggie hollered, hurrying over.

Jackson rolled his head and made eye contact. Barely. One eye was completely shut. The other was puffy. Jackson's face was cut and bruised, blood—some dried, some fresh—dripping from his nose and mouth. His shirt was soaked with sweat and didn't look right. Reggie realized it was because Jackson's ribs no longer had the form they were supposed to. Reggie had seen a lot in his time, and still he wanted to wretch.

Reggie cut through the handcuffs with a hacksaw and reclined Jackson on the floor. He moaned in pain at each movement, and Reggie feared he'd done even more damage. But he couldn't stand having Jackson stretched out against the pole any longer.

"J, man, what happened?"

Footsteps sounded on the staircase, and Reggie raised his gun and flashlight.

"Whoa, it's me."

"Olivia?" Reggie lowered the gun. "What are you doing here?"

"I came to help. Is he . . ."

"Dead?" Jackson croaked from the floor. "Not quite." He coughed, then cried.

"What happened?"

"They tortured him."

"They who? Who are they?"

"I don't know."

"Rush . . ." Jackson coughed. "Russians."

"That reminds me, I left one of them upstairs," Reggie said. "I'm going to check on her. Stay with him?"

"Of course," Olivia said.

"Be right back, J."

Jackson moaned in response, and Reggie hurried up the stairs. He'd called 9-1-1 almost ten minutes ago. Where was the ambulance? He took the steps two at a time to the second story, then slowed as he approached the master bedroom. Gun raised, he peeked around the corner.

The woman was struggling against the belt Reggie had bound her with but wasn't free. She cursed him in a foreign tongue as he checked the tightness of the belt. Then he pistol-whipped her to shut her up and to make sure she remained unconscious until the cops arrived.

With her taken care of, Reggie hurried back down to the basement.

"He's in bad shape," Olivia said. "Talking nonsense."

"You shouldn't be talking, J," Reggie said. "Just hang in there."

"Wil . . . Wilbur?"

Reggie sighed. "He died, man."

"How?"

Reggie shook his head. "They don't know yet."

"Did . . . did they get to him?"

"I don't know, man. I don't think so."

Jackson closed his eyes.

"Reggie, there's something you need to know," Olivia said.

"What's that?" he asked as he pulled out his phone to check the time again. He'd give the cops and medics two more minutes and then he was calling 9-1-1 again.

"I wasn't entirely forthcoming with you."

He looked at her. "What do you mean?"

"It's complicated, but we knew about Wilbur."

"Knew what? We who?"

"The BfV. The German government. That's why I'm here, to find Wilbur."

"What's the German government want with an old man from Malibu?"

"We think he knew the location and launch code of an armed nuclear weapon in the German Mountains."

Reggie looked at her incredulously, but more moaning from Jackson distracted him. "Hang on, J." He reached for his phone to dial again but stopped when he heard a distant keening.

"What is it?" Olivia asked.

"I think I hear sirens. You mind checking? Tell 'em it's clear and send the paramedics down here ASAP."

"Sure."

She stood and headed for the stairs, and Reggie knelt beside his friend. He drew his phone, ready to dial if Olivia reported a false alarm. He heard footsteps and thought she was returning until a voice boomed from the top of the stairs. "Sheriff's Department!"

"Down here," Reggie said. He put his gun on the floor and kicked it away from him. "I'm the one who called," he said just before a powerful flashlight flooded him.

"You Cameron?" the voice asked.

"That's right."

"Hands on your head."

"Yes, sir."

Reggie waited while two uniformed officers approached, retrieved his gun, and frisked him. "He needs an ambulance," Reggie said.

"So do several upstairs."

"They're the ones that did this to him."

"We'll get to the bottom of everything. Right now, we need you to come with us."

"I'm not leaving him."

"I wasn't asking."

Reggie met the officer's gaze. The other officer tensed.

"Okay," Reggie said. "Just please make sure he gets attention right away."

"Medics are on their way in."

"I'm going to handcuff you," the officer said.

"That necessary?"

"Until we sort out what went down, yes."

Reggie licked his lips. "All right."

"Give me your hands. I'll put them on in front."

Reggie nodded, accepted the cuffs, and let the officer lead him upstairs and out the front door where Mouse was waiting. He had been joined by several officers. A pair of ambulances were just arriving, backing up a third that was parked at the end of the driveway. Olivia was nowhere to be seen.

"What's going on?" Mouse asked.

"Just precautionary," Reggie said as the officer opened the back door of one of the cars.

"Watch your head, please."

Reggie sat down, the officer closed the door, and Mouse stared blankly.

That's when it all hit Reggie. He'd killed a dude. Maybe two.

Justified, sure. He had no doubts that he'd done the "right" thing. But it certainly made for a sticky situation.

*   *   *

Monday, March 25
12:02 a.m.

"NEXT RIGHT," Maggie said, looking up from her phone to the road ahead of them. What she saw took her breath away. Two ambulances, lights flashing, raced toward them, then made a sharp left turn.

"That's Trailhead," Russell said somberly.

"God, no . . ."

"If what I hear about Jackson's true, they might be for the other guys."

"Or Reggie."

Russell followed the ambulances to the end of the court. He parked haphazardly in front of a house that was already swarming with police officers and a third ambulance. Reggie's Hummer was parked on the other side of the cul-de-sac. Lights were on in all the surrounding houses, and several robe-clad people had emerged onto their front porches and walks.

Maggie unbuckled her seatbelt.

"Wait," Russell said. "We don't know what's going on."

She ignored him, throwing open the door as soon as Russell stopped. She raced up the sidewalk toward the driveway, her eyes taking in more details. Two paramedics running into the house. Officers securing the scene with police tape. Mouse standing around looking lost. Everything bathed in red and blue lights.

"Maggie!" Russell shouted from behind, but she pushed on.

"Hold it, ma'am," an officer said, reaching out an arm to stop her.

"I'm with him," she said, pointing at Mouse.

He noticed but only stared.

"I can't let you—"

She shoved him off and ran, at the same time spying Reggie in the back of a sheriff's car. What had happened?

"Mouse!"

"Maggie."

"Ma'am . . ."

"Maggie!"

She looked back at the officer and Russell. Back to Mouse.

"What happened?"

"Jack . . . He's inside."

At that moment, the front door opened and two paramedics came out, wheeling a stretcher. Maggie again pushed past the officer and approached the medics. Jackson was on the stretcher, a breathing mask over his face and an IV in his arm. The mask couldn't hide the carnage.

"Jackson."

"Ma'am, we need you to step back," one of the medics said as they hurried past. This time the officer grabbed hold of her arm.

"Please step back," he said.

"Is he all right?" she asked.

The paramedics said nothing.

"Ma'am, please, come with me. This is a crime scene."

"What happened?"

"Maggie, just give them some room," Russell said.

"Did you see him? I need to know—"

"Maggie."

She turned toward the voice. Deep. Calm. Reggie. She half ran away from, half dragged the officer over to the police car. It was away from the house, so he obliged.

"Reggie. Is he okay?"

"He's hurt bad," Reggie said. "But he's still wisecracking."

Maggie didn't know whether to laugh or cry, so she did both.

"What about . . ." She pulled herself together. "What about you?"

"I caused a little mayhem rescuing him," Reggie said.

With a sharp blast of the sirens, the first ambulance pulled away from the curb.

"Ma'am, we really need you to move outside the perimeter," the officer said.

"Come on, Maggie," Russell said, guiding her arm.

"Where is he?"

All heads whipped to the loud, feminine shout. A short blond woman was walking toward a pair of officers. She pushed through them and approached the car. "Get him out of there."

"Ma'am?" the officer asked.

The woman whipped out a badge. "Detective Larson, LAPD. Why is this man in the backseat of a squad car like a criminal?"

"He was involved in several shootings inside," the officer said.

"He's working with me. I'll take responsibility for his actions. You can release him to my custody."

The officer nodded. Protocol or not, Maggie didn't know, but she wouldn't have crossed the diminutive detective either. The officer opened the door and uncuffed Reggie. No sooner was he free than Ashley wrapped him in as big of a hug as she was capable.

"Is Jackson okay?"

"I think so," Reggie said. "But they did a number on him."

"Where'd they take him?"

"I don't know."

"Officer?"

"I'll find out." He stepped back and spoke into his radio. Another pair of medics came out of the house, also wheeling a stretcher. A third medic attended to a man as they walked, a gunshot victim by the looks of things.

"All the way up to Santa Monica-UCLA Medical," the officer replied. "Mr. Douglas's request."

"If you want to follow me," Ashley said, already turning for her car, "I can give you a police escort. We'll beat them there."

Chapter Thirty-Seven

12:23 a.m.

AS SOON AS Sam saw the time, she knew the phone call that had awakened her was either really good news or really bad news. Sitting up in bed, she blinked the grogginess from her eyes and reached for her phone. "Hello?"

"Sam, it's Reggie. We found him."

"Oh, thank the Lord. Is he okay?"

"He's been beaten pretty badly. They're taking him to UCLA Med."

"In Santa Monica?"

"Yeah."

"When? Now?"

"We just left Rolling Hills."

"I'm on my way."

"I'm stopping to pick up Leroy. Look for the police convoy."

"Okay. Thank you, Reggie."

Sam swung her legs out of bed and hurried to grab some clothes, all the while praying and thanking God for mercy and asking for some grace. Jackson was alive but hurt, and it killed her to think of him in pain. First being shot on New Year's Eve. Now this. He needed a different line of work.

In five minutes, Sam was dressed and ready to leave. She took a minute to calm down and make sure she had everything she needed. With another short prayer, she headed down and out to her car.

The night had grown cool, and Sam wished she'd dressed in more than a long-sleeved T-shirt. Hospitals were cold anyhow. But she didn't take the time to worry about it. Instead, she got into her Fusion and drove as fast as the law would allow, arriving at the hospital in a matter of minutes. She parked in the visitor lot and hurried in the Emergency entrance. This was like déjà vu.

"Sam, what are you doing here?" Aurora asked at the desk. "You work tonight?"

"No. I'm here to see a friend. Should have just arrived in an ambulance from Rolling Hills."

"Let me check."

Sam tapped her fingers on the desk while she waited.

"Nothing here. Might still be on the way. Let me check with dispatch."

Sam waited again. Behind her, the ER doors whooshed open. A very fast stride sounded, and a short woman stopped beside Sam.

Aurora lowered the phone. "They're actually pulling in now," she said to Sam, then turned to the woman beside her. "Can I he—"

"Detective Larson. I'm here to see Jackson Douglas. Bus should have just brought him in."

Sam looked at the woman. "You're here to see Jackson?"

"Yes. You Sam?"

"Yeah. How—"

"Reggie told me. He's on his way."

"You can both have a seat," Aurora said. "I'll let you know as soon as you can see him or I hear anything."

"Thank you," Sam said. She and Detective Larson headed toward the waiting area, a cluster of chairs around coffee tables stocked with old magazines. A black man with an Angels baseball cap sat in one corner. Two other people stood with their backs to Sam, looking out the window. They turned as Sam and Detective Larson approached.

"Russell?" Sam asked.

"Sam. Hi."

"You know each other?" the woman with Russell asked. She was familiar. Very familiar.

"Yeah," Russell said. "Sam's a regular. Front left, three or four rows back."

Sam smiled. "That's right."

"Front left?" Detective Larson asked.

"Church," Russell said.

Church. The familiar woman, the same one Sam had seen the day before in the church foyer. The one who had looked familiar then. Because she was Russell's girlfriend, maybe? But why were they here? Concern over a part-time parishioner? And how had they even found out?

"The lady at the desk said he'll be here soon," Larson said. "I told you we'd beat him here."

"Beat him?" Sam asked. "From where?"

"Rolling Hills."

"You were with him?"

"Just after the fact," Larson said. "I don't know where Reggie and Mouse are."

"They went to get Jackson's grandpa," Sam answered.

"Where does he live?"

"Marina del Rey."

Russell sat down. "We might as well get comfortable. We could be here a while. I doubt they'll let us in to see him as soon as they arrive."

Sam took a seat. Russell and the other woman sat adjacent to her. Larson paced.

"You two know each other?" Russell asked.

"I don't think so," Sam said. "You look familiar."

"I'm Maggie. I think we met at Jackson's."

"After he'd been shot," Sam said, the realization hitting with a haze of confusion.

Maggie nodded.

They both smiled cordially.

Behind Sam, Larson was on the phone, getting animated. Sam picked up a magazine but couldn't concentrate. She replaced it after a minute.

"Either of you ladies want something to drink?" Russell asked.

"No."

"No."

He nodded and got up.

"What exactly happened?" Sam asked.

"We're not really sure," Maggie said. "We got there just as they were wheeling Jackson out."

"Was he . . . responsive?"

"Reggie said he was making wisecracks."

Sam smiled. "I guess that's a good sign."

Maggie nodded.

Sam sat back. It was stupid, what with Jackson fighting for his life in ER, but she wondered exactly how Maggie and Jackson knew each other. And how well. She had been at his house when Sam had stopped by to change his bandage a few days after he'd been shot. Girlfriend? Sam didn't think so, because Jackson wouldn't act the way he did around Sam if he had a girlfriend. Would he? Was she a friend in the same way Sam was? Just friends, but with the tug of something more than that underneath? Again, Sam didn't think so. Jackson wouldn't do that.

Judging by the look in Maggie's gray-blue eyes, she was wondering similar things about Sam. It really was ridiculous at such a time, and Sam told herself to forget about it.

Russell returned with a cup of coffee that he blew over, sipped, and made a face at. He glanced at Maggie as she rubbed the back of her neck. "Are you sure you're okay? Maybe you should have them check you out."

"I'm fine."

"You did flip over in a car today."

Sam's eyes widened. "What?"

"It was nothing," Maggie said. "Some lunatic tried to run us off the road." She looked at Russell. "Jack."

"He's fine."

Sam frowned.

"The dog," Russell said. "He's in the truck."

"We should check on Tori."

"Tori Walker?" Sam asked. "Was she in the car?"

Maggie nodded.

"Is she okay?"

Russell nodded this time.

"Is this all part of what happened to Jackson?"

"We don't know," he answered.

The ER doors whooshed open again, and Reggie, Mouse, and Leroy walked in. Sam, Maggie, and Russell all stood, but Larson beat them all to Reggie.

"No word yet."

Reggie sighed. Then he nodded at Sam, Maggie, and Russell. So did Leroy. So everyone knew Maggie except Sam? What was she missing?

The door leading from the waiting area to the ER opened, and a woman in scrubs emerged. Sam recognized her as Diana, a newer nurse she didn't know very well.

"Which of you are here for Jackson Douglas?"

"All of us," Larson said.

"That's his grandfather," Reggie said with a nod at Leroy.

Diana nodded too. "We're prepping him for surgery right now. By far the worst of his injuries are a lacerated kidney and a punctured lung. He's also got a lot of broken ribs, multiple external injuries, and very possibly a concussion. But he does seem to be coherent, and all of his vitals are good, given the circumstances."

The group sighed collectively.

"The prognosis is good?" Leroy asked.

Diana nodded. "We think so. It's going to be a couple of hours, though, so make yourselves comfortable."

*　　　　　*　　　　　*

2:47 a.m.

LEROY SAT vigilantly in his chair, waiting, praying, thinking.

Reggie had gone to get food for everyone, and he now sat against the wall, his eyes closed. Leroy doubted he was sleeping. His shoulders looked heavy, as if they bore a great burden. Or more accurately, had just released it.

Mouse sat beside him, rocking in place. He'd been rocking for two hours, saying little, looking very edgy. From what Jackson said, that wasn't unusual for Mouse.

Sam and Maggie had made occasional conversation that had seemed stilted. Leroy grinned to himself as he thought of the panic that would ensue if Jackson knew they were both here at the same time.

Russell had flipped through every magazine in the place. He was currently reading an old *Sports Illustrated* while Maggie reclined against his shoulder, asleep or close to it.

And Ashley paced a hole in the floor, making and taking a few calls, but mostly just pacing.

There had been no update on Jackson. He'd been in surgery for a little over two hours, if Leroy was any judge of time.

The group had talked a little while eating, recapping various events. The best Leroy could tell, Jackson had been kidnapped by Russians. There was no apparent tie to them and Wilbur or to them and Tori and her accident. Or from her and it back to Jackson. The details were still coming in.

Speaking of Tori, she had been released from the hospital and was catching a ride to Santa Monica to see Jackson. The more the merrier.

The ER door opened, and a man in scrubs walked out. All eyes, even those closed, immediately turned his way.

"Mr. Douglas?"

Leroy stood. The others clustered behind him.

"Jackson is out of surgery. Everything went well, and we're moving him to recovery now."

"Thank the Lord."

"He's going to be here for a few days while we make sure his kidney and lung are performing up to par. We've done what we can with his ribs, but often times, there isn't a lot to do. They need to heal on their own. Given the extent of his injuries, he'll be out of commission for quite a while."

"What about his grill?" Reggie asked. "He going to be able to look in the mirror again?"

The doctor actually grinned. "He may not want to for several days. He does have a couple of hairline skull fractures, but they should—*should*—heal on their own with plenty of rest, and there doesn't appear to be any permanent damage."

"When can we see him?" Sam asked.

"It'll be a little while before he's settled in his new room, and then we'll start with family and see how he feels. He'll need rest, so any visits will have to be short. I'll send Diana out to let you know when he's ready."

"Thanks, Doc," Leroy said.

The doctor nodded and retreated.

Leroy mumbled under his breath, "Tougher than old hayin' strings."

Chapter Thirty-Eight

9:43 a.m.

JACKSON AWOKE SLOWLY, as if coming out of a fog. His eyes rested on his grandfather, seated in a chair beside the bed, reading a newspaper. He snapped it shut and looked Jackson's way. "Hey, kiddo. How you feeling?"

"Ugh. Terrible. Thanks for reminding me."

"You're alive at least."

"The jury's still out." Jackson swallowed, hard given the dryness of his mouth. "I assume I'm hopped up on drugs?"

Leroy nodded at one of the tubes flowing into Jackson. "Morphine drip."

"So this is what being murdered alive feels like when medicated. Awesome." He sighed. "You been here all night?"

"We took shifts. Reggie had to go answer more questions for the police, take Mouse home. He was in bad shape."

"Reggie?"

"Mouse. Pacing, rocking."

"That's normal."

"Mumbling something about getting married."

"Mouse?"

Leroy shrugged.

"Put him on my call sheet. Connie too."

"Reggie said he was going to swing by and let her know you're okay."

"Good. Well, she should be around shortly with several casseroles then." He sighed. "Reggie in much trouble with L.A.'s finest?"

"I don't think much."

"Who else is here?"

"You mean of the female persuasion?"

"Did I see Sam, Maggie, and Ashley all here at the same time?"

Leroy grinned. "You sure did, kiddo. Walker too."

Jackson groaned.

"I told you this would catch up with you."

"Like that Western dream episode on *MacGyver*. Tell me I had pants on."

"Covers. Good as."

"For the purpose. Have they said anything about feeding me?"

"You hungry?"

"I think some skinny blonde brought me Jell-O, but I haven't eaten since I don't know when."

"I'll get the nurse."

"And tell her I have to pee, too."

"Got news for you on that one, bud. You've been peeing all night."

"Catheter?"

"Would I be sitting in here else?"

"Great. Not only do Sam, Maggie, Ashley, and Walker all come see me at once, but they see my pee in a bag too."

Leroy waved. "Don't worry about it. Considering what your face looks like, it's the least of your concerns."

Jackson sighed.

"I'll get the nurse."

It took her ten minutes to check all the vitals, then the doctor had to come and offer his own opinion. Close to half an hour after Jackson awoke, he was finally served some hospital breakfast. Hot broth. Yum.

While Jackson ate, Leroy worked a crossword puzzle, asking Jackson for answers. Jackson was too busy eating to think, and Leroy seemed content just to mumble his questions aloud. He gave up just as Reggie knocked and entered the room.

"Hey, J, how you feeling?"

"About as well as I look."

Reggie turned to Leroy. "My sympathies on your loss."

"Funny man." Jackson tried to sit up and it nearly killed him. He winced. "You in the clear?"

"Yeah," Reggie answered. "Thanks in large part to Detective Larson."

"Pretty soon I think she's going to be done owing me."

"I think pretty soon is here, man." Reggie said and sat down.

"You got any scoop?"

"Not much. I just talked to her. They're still trying to figure it all out."

"What about Walker?"

"She's fine. She said she'd stop by again later today."

"Great. Maybe Sam and Maggie can arrange to be here then too. Why didn't you intervene, man?"

"What, tell them not to get here at the same time or they might run into your other girlfriend?"

Jackson sighed.

"Play with fire . . ." Leroy said.

"Yeah, yeah. Who was the stiff?"

"The stiff?"

"Good looking guy with Maggie?"

"Russell something."

"What's his involvement?"

"I don't know, man. He just showed up with Maggie. I didn't ask no questions, man."

Jackson sighed again.

"They give you any update on a prognosis?" Reggie asked. "When you might get out? If you'll ever be able to pee on your own again? Recommend a plastic surgeon?"

"You guys are a barrel of laughs, you know that?"

Reggie grinned. "I'm just glad we're laughing, man. You had us worried."

Leroy nodded his assent.

"Yeah, well, I had my worries too."

"Knock, knock."

Jackson leaned over to see Ashley appear in the doorway. She looked both beautiful and exhausted at the same time.

"Hey," he said.

She walked over and kissed him on the forehead.

"What was that for?"

Ashley stood back. "How much do you know about the people that captured you?"

"They were all finalists on *The Ultimate Fighter*?"

"More like members of a Chechen terrorist cell."

"Looking to acquire a nuke?"

She frowned. "It's been rumored. Why?"

Jackson shook his head. "Just a guess."

"Um-hmm. Anyhow, we found a computer in the downstairs bedroom. A treasure trove. The FBI, Homeland Security, NSA, and CIA are all fighting over it now. It could bring down the entire cell."

"One computer?"

"It had names and names, bank info, the works. This guy Petrovich was the head of the snake."

"Petrovich?"

"You didn't know his name?"

"We never got around to exchanging pleasantries."

"Well, I'll give you a full debriefing once you've had a chance to rest and once I know more. But in the meantime, just know you're a hero again."

"Super."

She patted his knee somewhere under the blanket. "Get some rest. I'll check in on you tomorrow."

"Thanks, Ash."

She smiled and left, and Reggie leaned forward. "Hero, huh. Without me, you're still chained to that pole in the basement."

"Don't worry. I'll let you borrow my congressional medal once in a while."

"Once his girlfriends stop swooning over it," Leroy said.

"You should have seen the looks Sam and Maggie were giving each other," Reggie said. "Confusion, a little jealousy, but mostly confusion. Like both of them sensed who the other was but couldn't bring themselves to believe it."

Jackson dropped his head onto the pillow. "Can you get the nurse, please? I'd like a sedative."

*   *   *

1:19 p.m.

AFTER STOPPING at Cameron's to make sure the joint was still running (and to grab some lunch), Reggie returned to the hospital. He was to the automatic front doors when he saw movement to his left and looked just before Olivia called his name.

He frowned. "Olivia."

"Hi."

He shook his head. "Where have you been? I sent you to see if the medics were coming, and you disappeared."

"It's complicated."

"Yeah, you said that last night."

"How is he?" she asked, tipping her head to the side, causing curls to fall around her forehead. She wore an orange tank top, faded jeans, two-toned canvas shoes. Despite his confusion and frustration, Reggie couldn't deny she looked good—The casual foreign agent look was in.

He nodded. "He's all right. No permanent damage the docs don't think."

"Good." She hesitated. "Can I see him?"

Reggie narrowed his eyes.

Olivia looked around. "What I said last night about finding Wilbur was true. According to a book written by one of Wilbur's squad members, his unit found a missile silo buried in the Wetterstein Mountains. It contained operational V-5 missiles with nuclear payloads aimed at Washington D.C. and London."

"Okay."

"Wilbur's squad took out the German company guarding the missiles just before they could be launched, and they scrambled the codes so the missiles couldn't be fired. But Wilbur and the men in his squad saw the codes."

320

"And no one else did? They didn't tell anyone?"

She shook her head. "No. Wilbur was the last member of his squad still alive, and thus the last person, theoretically, who had the ability to launch or deactivate the missiles."

"After all these years?"

She nodded. "They've just been sitting there, locked underground, but in an easily accessible silo, ready to be fired by anyone who knows the code."

"And you think Wilbur passed that knowledge on to Jackson before he died?"

"Possibly. I'd like to talk to him and see if he knows anything."

"Why didn't you tell me this?"

"Because the number of people who know the truth is microscopic. It was classified information that I shouldn't be telling you now."

"Then why are you?"

"Because I care about you, Reggie, and I feel terrible."

"You should feel good, O. You run a convincing con."

"It wasn't a con, Reggie," she said, approaching him.

"*Wolfskinder*, a plot to kill Jackson's family, kill him? That wasn't a con?"

Olivia looked down for a moment, then back up. "That part was, yes. That was a lie. But everything else—who I am, who I work for—that was all real."

"Your sources, constantly running from tying up loose ends to greasing wheels?"

"All true. I couldn't tell you about the nukes for obvious reasons. Everything else was true . . . including . . . how I feel about you." She touched his arm, but Reggie turned and took several steps. He looked back at her.

"Did you break into J's house, before coming to see me?"

Barely perceptibly, she nodded. "At the home where Wilbur was living, they gave me Jackson's name. When I didn't find him at home and couldn't reach him, I let myself in and looked around."

"And cut yourself on the counter?"

She nodded. "When I couldn't find him or any clue to his whereabouts, I moved on to his best friend. I thought you might know where he was, but if not, I thought we could work together to find him."

"So not everything else was real."

"Reggie . . . please. I'm sorry."

"Let me ask you one more thing. If you'd have found J before all this, what story would you have given him?"

She looked down again.

"Would you have come clean about Wilbur, or would you have given him some story about German terrorists taking out his parents?"

Olivia licked her lips.

He nodded. "Jackson's inside," he said, and entered the hospital without looking to see if she followed.

*   *   *

1:24 p.m.

"LAST TIME you brought candy," Jackson said, winking at Sam. It wasn't much of a wink because his eye wasn't working all that well yet.

"I'm more worried about the next time," Sam said. "Your grandpa says you're indestructible," she said with a glance toward the couch where he was half asleep, "but one of these days . . ."

"Sam, if Russian terrorists can't kill me . . ."

She closed her eyes, and when she opened them, they revealed exhaustion. Jackson opened his hand, and she placed hers in his. "Are you okay?" he asked.

Sam swallowed hard. "It's been a rough week, let's say that."

"Why?"

"Knock, knock," someone sing-songed.

Jackson lifted his eyes to the doorway, where Tori Walker stood holding a bouquet of flowers in one hand, her other arm in a sling. "Is this a bad time?" she asked.

"No, it's fine," Sam said, withdrawing her hand from Jackson's. She stood.

"Sam, right?"

She nodded.

"I really didn't mean to intrude," Tori said.

"It's fine. I should be going."

"You don't have to," Jackson said.

"I promised Stephanie I'd stop in to see her this afternoon."

"Give them my regards."

"I will."

Sam smiled at Tori and headed out of the room.

Tori grimaced. "Did I interrupt?" she asked.

"Too soon to tell. Those for me?" he asked, nodding at the flowers as she stopped beside his bed.

"Yeah, well, they didn't have any chalupas in the gift shop."

"You really don't have to keep buying me flowers."

"I owe you big time. If you hadn't been working for me too, those thugs might never have found you."

"Mights and maybes," Jackson said. "Besides, friends don't owe friends, Walker."

"Not what the cop tells me."

"Ashley?"

"I have to say, Jack, you're certainly doing well with the ladies."

"I cut a sympathetic figure."

"He means pathetic," Reggie said as he entered the room. "How's the arm, Walker?"

"Dislocated shoulder. Now relocated. This is precautionary. And this," she said touching a bandage on her forehead, "is a flesh wound."

"Aren't they all," he said, taking a seat beside Leroy, who stirred and harrumphed.

"How are you feeling?" Tori asked Jackson.

"Marginally better than I look."

"That bad, huh?"

"So what's the word on Skyler?"

"Attempted murder, so he's not getting out anytime soon."

"He just snap, or what?"

She shrugged. "Apparently."

"Our dirty little secret coming to light?"

Another shrug. "Not as of yet."

"Well, that's something."

Someone knocked on the door—an actual knock this time—and Jackson looked around Tori to see a thin, attractive woman with curly black hair. Tori looked too, then turned back with a raised eyebrow at Jackson.

"Mr. Douglas," she said. "I'm Agent Olivia Williams, with the German *Bundesamt für Verfassungsschutz* or BfV. Could I have a few minutes?"

"I'll catch you later, Jack," Tori said.

"You can stay."

She set the flowers down. "I'm in town now. We'll catch up."

"Sure," Jackson said. "I'm in the book. Give me a call."

Agent Williams asked for the room, and Reggie and Leroy both cleared out, albeit hesitantly on Reggie's part. After a slightly more detailed introduction, Olivia spent half an hour basically corroborating Wilbur's story, filling in a few things he hadn't known—such as the likelihood, based on the probable design of the V-5, of needing the launch code to deactivate the weapons. Jackson filled in a few things too, such as the fact that Wilbur had taken great pains to make sure no one knew the launch code. He also suggested the German government bury the missiles in about a million cubic yards of concrete. Eventually, Olivia realized he knew nothing relevant that she didn't already know. She thanked him for her time before exiting the room.

"I feel like I'm auditing beauty pageant contestants," Jackson said when Leroy reentered.

"Don't you wish."

"Where's Reggie?"

"Chatting up Agent Williams."

"Oh? What's their story?"

"Not entirely sure, bud."

Reggie returned a minute later, and Jackson stared him all the way to the couch where he again sat down beside Leroy. "Well?" Jackson finally asked.

"Long story, J."

"I'm not going anywhere. I can't go anywhere, in fact."

Reggie exhaled. "She lied."

"About what?"

"Originally, pretty much everything. Used me to try to get you, told me a bunch of crap about how some German terrorist group was after you."

"She's an intelligence agent, Reg. It's an instinct."

"Yeah, well, it's not a real good foundation for a relationship."

"For a rel . . . a relationship?"

Reggie looked at him.

"You mean that foxy German chick with the exotic accent was into you and you're letting her go because she blurred the truth in an investigation?"

"Not that simple, J."

"Shoot, make like she's a wingback on a jet sweep and chase her down."

"Not that simple. She didn't just fake her profile pic, man. She made up stories about you, your folks, broke into your place and lied about it." He shook his head. "And she would have fed you the same line if it'd have helped her find Wilbur. Not something I can overlook. Telling me a pack of lies is one thing. But messing with you like that . . ."

Jackson lay his head back. "A relationship? Man, you go off the grid for a week, and your wingman starts playing Sonny Crockett."

"Don't you mean Tubbs?"

"Why?"

"Cuz' he was the brother."

"Sonny was the skirt-chaser, wasn't he?"

"I don't know. I'm not a boomer, man. I don't watch '80s TV religiously." He looked to Leroy. "When's he due for more meds?"

"Not soon enough," Leroy mumbled.

Jackson raised his head. "Seriously, Reg. You and her could have been an item?"

He nodded.

"And you're sacrificing that because of me?"

"That and I ain't got time for a relationship with a beautiful, globe-trotting woman from the Caribbean." He looked at Jackson and managed to keep a straight face. "At least not if I got to keep pulling your butt out of a sling all the time."

Chapter Thirty-Nine

JACKSON SAT ON the deck, watching a brilliant Easter Sunday fade over the Pacific. The breeze was cool but not cold, lifting strands of his shaggy hair across his forehead. He didn't bother to replace them, largely because any raising of his arms over his head still hurt like a knife was cutting him. He had spent a week—the first two days in the hospital—doing little but laying around, letting his ribs heal, his facial swelling go down, and his head clear.

His kidney and lung were both on the mend, according to the doctor. He was peeing on his own without problems, although he was still supposed to keep an eye out for blood or pain or restricted flow or a bunch of other things they talked about on commercials during golf telecasts. The doc had also advised him against too much brain stimulus as he recovered from a concussion. Little TV, no video games, not a ton of reading. Jackson didn't have any memory or cognitive function issues, but the repeated blows to the head had done their damage, and he was happy to oblige.

Jackson's only real activity of the week had been to attend Wilbur's funeral on Thursday. The cause of death had been ruled to be his tumor, to Jackson's relief. Petrovich and his gang hadn't found him. The cops had had a few questions about the circumstances of Wilbur's disappearance and death, but Jackson's answers—along with Ashley's lawyerly, motherly defense—had appeased them.

The funeral had been short and simple, minimally attended since Wilbur had no family. He had received military honors, complete with a three-volley salute, honor guard, and "Taps." For some reason, in the absence of family, Jackson had been chosen to receive the flag presented as a symbol of appreciation for Wilbur's honorable and faithful service. With a tear in his eye, he had listened to the soldier's quiet words, and the flag now resided in a framed case in his living room. If only they knew what Wilbur had really done.

To that end, Jackson had not heard from any government agents—foreign or domestic—since talking to Reggie's friend Olivia with the German *Baklava für Fashion Shoes* or whatver it as called. According to Wilbur, both the U.S. and German governments were already aware of the V-5 missiles in the silo in southern Germany. Olivia had confirmed it. Jackson was sure between the two governments, they could find the missiles and bury them or render them inert or somehow disarm them before any other terrorist groups found them. Jackson didn't know any additional details, as Wilbur had intended for the secret to die with him. Jackson was happy to let the knowledge pass as well.

The sliding glass door behind him opened with a click, and Jackson turned his head.

"I let myself in," Maggie said.

"You mean out."

She nodded. She wore jeans and a brown polo, her hair down. Jackson wasn't sure, but he thought he detected a slight bounce in her step.

"Have a seat," he said, reaching for the glass of iced tea on the table. "There's more in the fridge if you want some."

Still standing, she nodded again and retreated back into the house. A minute later, she sat down beside him, a glass of tea in her hand.

"So how are you doing?" she asked.

"Not well enough to be a gentleman and get you your tea."

"So same old, same old?"

"Cute."

"You look better."

"The doctor assures me I'll be as handsome as ever."

"Quite a guarantee."

"If you came over here to bust my chops, somebody beat you to it."

"Sorry." She took a drink. "Seriously, how are you?"

"Sore, sleepy, bored. I can't do much but sit around."

"So more of the same old, same old?"

"Please, my ribs, stop the humor."

Maggie grinned as she took another drink.

Jackson turned his head toward the ocean. Maggie had something on her mind, he could tell. So he waited.

"What's the latest on the people that had you?" she asked after a minute of silence.

"Ashley said my captors were part of a Chechen terrorist organization that, according to various intelligence reports, has been seeking to acquire a nuclear or dirty bomb for several years."

"And they thought this guy Wilbur knew where one was?"

"Something like that."

"And that's why they took you, to get to him?"

Jackson nodded.

"So is this organization out of commission now?"

"Pretty much. Petrovich was the bigwig, and he's in custody. Two more of his people are dead and another four in custody with him. Ashley said the FBI had made three more arrests Monday and Tuesday as Petrovich's underlings tried to flee the country. Plus they have a ton of intel on the cell. She made it sound like it was all but destroyed."

"Good. I'd hate to think of them coming after you again."

"I'm investing in some cyanide capsules just in case."

"And there never was a connection with Tori and Skyler?"

"No. A coincidence, if you'll believe it."

"Have you heard from Tori?"

"As a matter of fact, she was here yesterday. She said to thank you for taking care of Jack. I think she meant the dog."

"She's doing okay?"

"She's fine."

"Did she tell you everything that happened Sunday night?"

"Except for the parts where she was blacked out, yeah."

"Any word on what's happened to Skyler?"

Jackson nodded. "The cops are holding him for reckless endangerment and attempted murder or something of the sort. And apparently he also borrowed his P.I.'s Camaro without permission, so the P.I.'s pressing charges. Add some grand theft auto."

"That should take care of him for a while."

Jackson nodded.

Maggie had another drink.

"You want to stay for the late-night talk shows too?" Jackson asked.

"Huh?"

"You just got the news. What's the deal, the *Times* not covering my kidnapping?"

Maggie looked down. "I'm not working for the *Times* anymore."

"What?"

"They fired me."

Jackson sat up and immediately winced. "What happened?"

"I got too religious."

"Really?"

Maggie nodded.

"So what are you going to do?"

"You won't believe it, but Fox just called me."

"Fox as in Jack Bauer, lousy football coverage, Bill O'Reilly—that Fox?"

"More the latter, but yeah. They're interested in interviewing me for a role as an online columnist and contributor."

"Wow, that's great."

"Now I just need to find a place to live."

"You're leaving L.A.?"

"No. Just my apartment."

"How come?"

"I got kicked out."

"What? How come?"

Maggie shrugged. "Don't know. Walter fired me a week ago Wednesday, and when I got home, I had an eviction notice in the mail."

"Wow, quite a day."

"Yeah. And then my best friend wasn't answering his phone, so I didn't know where to turn . . ."

"Sorry. Wilbur and I were watching *Wheel* at a dive hotel all week. That is until the Petrovich clan decided to use me as a Babushka."

"That doesn't even make sense."

"Yeah, well, you'll forgive me. Repeated blows to the head and all that."

Maggie winced. "Jack . . . how bad was it?"

"Bad. I thought they were going to kill me. The last few hours were especially brutal. I started egging them on, hoping they'd finish me off quickly."

Maggie looked sick.

"Fortunately the big fella showed up when he did. I was running out of one-liners and Russians to make fun of."

"You know, you didn't make it real easy for us to find you."

"That was kind of the plan, you know. When Wilbur came to me, I thought his concerns might be a little unrealistic. But in case they were legit, I didn't want anyone to be able to track me down or tie my friends to me. If I'd have known I'd end up going fifteen rounds with Drago with my hands behind my back, I might have left a few bread crumbs."

Maggie drained her tea.

"You want a refill?" she asked.

"Uh, no. Peeing's still not the everyday task it used to be," Jackson said. "But go ahead."

She headed inside, emerging a moment later with a full glass. She sat down, took a drink, then traced the rim of her glass with her finger.

"Um, Jack . . . there's something else I need to tell you."

He looked over. "Shoot."

"I don't know how else to say it but to say it . . ."

"So say it."

"I'm seeing someone."

"Seeing? As in, dating?"

She nodded.

He nodded back.

She swallowed. "Russell James."

"What's he, a stagecoach robber?"

"Russell James, Rick James' son."

"You're dating 'Super Freak's' son?"

"Pastor Rick James, dummy. From church."

"Oh. That Russell. The guy from the hospital."

Maggie nodded.

Jackson took a drink.

"I didn't know what to do Wednesday night, and I ended up at church. He was there, we talked, I told him about work and my apartment and you and . . . he was somebody to talk to. He ended up working with us to find you, and, I don't know. Things just sort of happened," she said, looking up from her glass.

"Maggie, you don't have to explain things to me."

"I know, I know. It's just . . . I mean, we never had any sort of a defined relationship, but we both know there was something there. I . . ."

"Like you said, Maggie, we never defined anything. I had my chance."

She shook her head. "No, you didn't. You had standards I didn't meet, and then when I did—"

"I said we should wait. I had my chance. Although, a week is kind of quick."

"I know."

"I mean, you said you're seeing him. How many times can you see somebody in a week?"

Maggie tried to hide a grin.

"Oh good grief, you're in puppy love."

"I am not."

"It's kind of cute on you, not that it's my place to notice anymore."

"Jack."

"Maggie."

She sighed. "Can you not make this any harder?"

"Yeah, it's rough going out with six-three, good-looking hunks, isn't it?"

"Jack."

"Maggie," he intoned.

She shook her head as she rolled her eyes.

It was his turn to sigh. And to get serious. "You were saying?"

"I just sort of feel like I owe you something."

"You don't owe me anything, Maggie."

"I owe you my soul, Jackson. Without you, I don't know where I'd be."

"Well, you'd have no chance with a pastor's kid, that's for sure."

She grinned.

"It's okay, Maggie. Seriously. I appreciate you telling me, but you don't owe me an explanation, and you don't have to feel bad about it. If there's something there, then you should go for it."

"You mean that?"

"I mean it."

"We'll still be friends?" she asked. "I know that's hokey and dorky and clichéd, but . . . promise me we'll still be friends."

Jackson nodded. "Of course we'll be friends, Maggie."

"Good," she said with a smile.

Jackson took a long pull on his tea, his eyes turning to the distant sun-splashed ocean.

Still be friends?

Yeah, sure, that would work out.

Acknowledgments

I'M ONCE AGAIN indebted to the usual cast and crew for their assistance. My wife, Sierra, listened to countless ideas and answered untold questions, and put up with the life of a writer. My parents, Doug and Jean Birr, as well as my sister Tiffani and brother-in-law Mark all provided assistance with proofing, critiquing, and listening to assorted thoughts and plot possibilities. Chris Hembel also added her analytical eye to the manuscript, which I deeply appreciate.

I mentioned them in the Author's Note at the beginning of the book, but I would be remiss if I didn't also pause here to thank the men and women who have served and who serve in our armed forces. There are countries around the world where publishing a fictitious tale such as this wouldn't be allowed or wouldn't be possible. Thanks to their efforts and sacrifice, the U.S.A. isn't one of them.

Experience has taught me mistakes and errors will remain. They are mine.

Read the backstory to Jackson and Tori's relationship in

Short Sail
A Douglas Files Short

One good con deserves another.

Jackson Douglas and Tori Walker are little more than paper pushers when their detective firm stumbles upon a scam artist. Since the company lacks the motivation to pursue him, the would-be private investigators decide to take matters into their own hands. During trips to the beach and over dinner at her apartment, they hatch a plan to con a conman not once but twice.

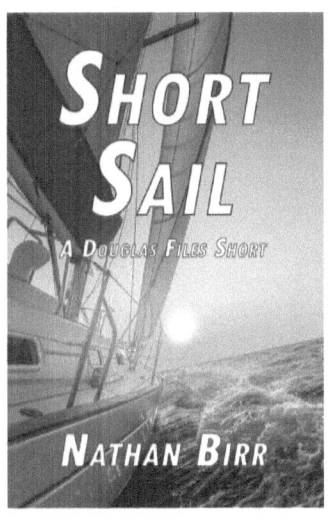

Can Douglas and Walker pull off their complicated confidence game on short notice, with limited funds and minimal resources? Will their chemistry work for them or cause a distraction? What happens if the scammer spots the scam? And is righting a wrong really worth the risk—a risk that could put them on the wrong side of the law, or worse?

Short Sail is a fast-paced but lighthearted adventure that will leave you craving more of Jackson Douglas.

Get it today at www.nathanbirr.com!